Praise for *FOREVER*
Book One in *THE FOREVER SERIES*

I loved this book! Once I got into the book, I couldn't put it down. There are tons of twists and turns in this book, and it's a must read.

Lisa, Abby & Lisa's Book Blog

Be ready for an emotional roller coaster in *Forever*. Be ready for twists and turns you weren't expecting to happen. I will admit, tears were falling at the end.

Sassy Girl Book Reviews

Wow! This book is emotional. Filled with angst, pain, lies, deception, and more that will grip you until the end. Can Walker and Reese get a HEA? Have a tissue or two handy while reading this book. You will need it.

Tanya, Book Obsessed Momma

Outstanding Story - This is probably one of the hardest books to write a review for. I loved this book so much that there really isn't any great word to describe how great this book is. Terrific. Awesome...the best book ever. Mary writes her books so it feels like you are standing right next to the character, and you are seeing everything and feeling every emotion that they are going through. I promise you will fall in love with this book and it will live with you...Forever.

Tiffany, Once Upon A Twilight blog

SECOND CHANCE

at

FOREVER

BOOK TWO IN THE FOREVER SERIES

MARY A. WASOWSKI

Printed in the United States of America
First Edition: June 2014
Library of Congress Cataloging-in-Publication Data

http://authormaryawasowski.com/

Wasowski, Mary A.
    Second Chance at Forever (*Book Two in The Forever Series*) / 1st ed
    ISBN-13: 978-0989623858

    1.   Second Chance at Forever—Fiction.   2.   Fiction—Romance
    3.   Fiction—Contemporary Romance

DEDICATION

"Nothing in life is to be FEARED, it is only to be *understood*. Now is the time to UNDERSTAND more, so that we may fear less."
—MADAME MARIE CURIE

I'VE ALWAYS LOVED this quote. I have it written down on several notebooks, folders, and papers I saved throughout the years. The first time I wrote this quote down, I was in high school. I still have that folder from my freshman year. It's old and tattered, but I can't seem to part with it. It holds my writing from my younger years when I was trying to find a place to fit into this big wide world.

I think fear is one of the most natural emotions a person can feel. It makes us human. It makes us real. It also teaches us to take risks, and with each bold move we make, maybe the next one will be a little easier to overcome.

This book is lovingly dedicated to my family and friends. With your love, support, and encouragement, I fear less and gain confidence with every book I write. I am a believer that dreams come true, but also believe you need a little help along the way.

If I've missed a phone call with you, or even a few, I'm sorry. If I'm overdue for a visit, I'll see you soon.

And if I forget to tell you that I love you, the next time that I say it, I'll say it twice.

For my readers: Another quote I love. This one is for you…

"The idea is to write it so that people hear it and it slides through the brain and goes straight to the heart."

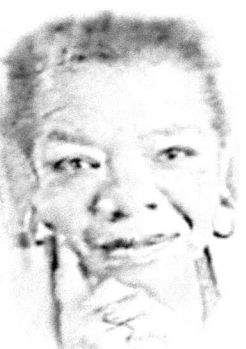

—MAYA ANGELOU

A NOTE FROM THE AUTHOR

THANK YOU, READERS, for taking time to purchase *Second Chance at Forever*. Writing for Walker and Reese has taken me on many twists and turns. They were quite the challenge. Believe me, I had my moments where I was mad at Walker and wanted to shake Reese. In the end, I truly hope you enjoy where I have taken their love story. It's not over yet, not by a long shot. We will see them again in *Our Forever Promise,* where their story concludes, but may continue for others. Stay tuned. You never know what I have planned.

The best gift you can give an author is to leave a review. It doesn't have to be many words, a simple sentence if you can. Feedback is so important, and it is vital to my future as a writer. I love and welcome each and every comment and message I receive, but I would also love to see them on the sites you purchased this title on.

Thank you so much! And enjoy Walker and Reese.

With love,

Mary

PROLOGUE

Walker

"MR. REED, EXCUSE ME, sir, for the intrusion, but you have a visitor here to see you."

I looked up from my computer screen with agitation directed at my temporary assistant filling in for Jenny while she was out sick today. She looked like a scared rabbit, as she should be. I always without fail expected my requests understood and met with no misinterpretations.

"Catherine, I believe I gave you strict instructions not to disturb me this morning." *God knows this day was hard enough already.*

"Yes sir, I understand, but not even for your father?" She replied with a hint of sarcasm in her voice. I once again looked up from my computer with a warning look that had her checking her attitude at my door.

Dammit! What the hell is he doing here? And without calling first. Of all days to get a visit from my father. It was Jackson's birthday, and sadly the anniversary of his mother's death. I had a love/hate relationship with this day. I lost my wife, my best friend, and the mother of my child—my only child. What should have been the greatest day of our lives went dark when she was taken from me, and from *our son.* I was extremely busy today of all days, and then I got an unexpected visit from Phillip Reed himself. I stopped glaring at my assistant and tried to calm my already rising blood pressure. "Catherine, you may show him in."

"I was beginning to think that I would be barred from seeing you. Knowing you, Walker, I might have thought I was on a proscribed list. I don't appreciate having to stand out in the hallway and be expected to wait to be granted access to you," he said as he strode in with his always cool demeanor. Not getting up from behind my desk to greet him as he expected me to, I simply just looked up at him.

"That's what you get when you interrupt one's work day. Hello, father, and what are you doing here in California?"

"Can't a father drop in on his only son and say hello?"

"Not when you live in New York. So what do I owe the honor of this impromptu visit?"

He walked over to my bar and helped himself to my favorite malted scotch. "Walker, I was up in San Francisco taking care of some personal business and wanted to stop by on my way home to visit with Jackson. After all, it is his eighteenth birthday. Would you mind if I take him out for the day?"

"Father, you don't need my permission to see Jackson, and I am well aware of what today is. If you want to see your grandson, then you know where to find him. He has a lighter class schedule today and should be home from school in about an hour. I do have plans with him this evening, so your time with your grandson will be short." *I'll be damned if I was going to rearrange my plans with my son to accommodate my father. He should have made better arrangements if he wanted to celebrate Jackson's birthday with him.*

"Son, I know how hard this day is for you, and I don't want to make it worse for you by being here." He looked almost remorseful, but I knew better. Phillip Reed didn't give a rat's ass about my feelings, and he sure as hell didn't know what I was feeling especially when it came to that day.

"Walker, while I wait for Jackson, how about we have a chat? I have some matters that I would like to discuss with you. I noticed that a bid proposal was submitted for Johns Hopkins Hospital again. Why is that? Didn't we already do an expansion project for them?"

And here he is...my father. A few empty words of condolences, and then it's business as usual. Counting to ten to remain calm, I fixed myself a much needed drink and knocked it back before I answered him.

"You know we did, father, and why do you care what comes across *my* desk anyway?" I wanted to make it clear to him whose office he was in.

"I was just wondering, son. We usually don't take on projects of this nature."

"You're right. We normally don't."

"Why then?"

"What is this, Twenty Questions? You know why we built that building. An opportunity presented itself to me, and it was my way to honor Elizabeth."

"Oh yes, by putting her name on a building."

"Careful, father. I don't know what you're trying to pull out of me, or deflect me from the real reason to why you're here, but my patience is wearing thin."

"Why so defensive, son? I am merely asking a question, and here you are, flying off the handle."

"Father, it's not a manner of being defensive. This is me knowing you all too well that this is not a social call. You asking questions to something you already know leads me to believe that you're here for something else."

"Walker, I have no hidden agenda."

"No agenda? Oh please! The wheels in your head are always spinning in a thousand directions. You breathe, eat, and sleep hidden agendas, but okay—I'll bite. When the hospital initially approached me with their bid proposal, I was skeptical at first. My team carefully went through the proposal, and once I learned what the building was intended for, I immediately approved it. So yes, father, my late wife's name sits proudly on a building that *I* designed in memory for her. I hear the neurosurgeon that this wing is intended for is making great strides in stroke research. He is supposed to be the best in the country, and the hospital is doing everything in their power to keep him happy. Johns Hopkins has asked me to consider designing an extension wing to what they have now, a bigger space for his research. I haven't had any opportunity to peruse the proposal yet, okay? Now that you've been updated, are we done with the Q and A part of this discussion?"

"It's a shame that you never made the ribbon cutting ceremony. I was all too happy to step in for you and support Jackson."

Son of a bitch! He didn't just go there. His mentioning of Jackson's name hit the one trigger that I possessed.

"You're unbelievable, father! You of all people know why I missed it. I can't believe for rhyme or reason why you would remind me of that. I was in Europe at the time, and you know why I was there. I would have never missed that dedication ceremony if I didn't have to clean up yet another mess you left me before officially retiring. Oh, and let's make one thing very clear…You will never fill my shoes when it comes to my son!"

"Walker, I wasn't trying to."

"Good. It will be a cold day in hell before I ever let anyone come between me and my son, least of all you. Now that I have answered your questions, give me the same courtesy and answer one of mine. Why are you here?"

"I believe I answered that question already. I wanted to see Jackson, and just because I don't participate in the day to day doesn't mean I'm not privy to what is going on around here."

"Father, that's where you're wrong. I run this company! And I alone. You, Phillip Reed, are retired. You needn't worry about what comes across *my* desk. This includes past, present, and future projects that Reed Global will be involved with. Are we done here? Because I know I am." My father was silent while rubbing his fingers along his chin. I continued, "Now, if you don't have anything else to say, please show yourself out."

No words? I glanced back over to him, and he looked as if he was contemplating his next chess move. Not wanting to wait and growing tired of this, I continued to talk. "Father, I need to leave for my meeting."

My dismissal of my father may have been cold, but it paled in comparison to how he treated me over the years. I usually go a few rounds of friendly war-like banter with my father, but today was not the day for the usual tongue lashing we seemed to give one another.

I never handled the anniversary of this day very well, but I always held back for my son's sake. I had a nightmare the night before. I usually can keep them buried deep down, but as the anniversary of Elizabeth's death approached, they always returned. I shot up out of my bed that morning with cold beads of sweat covering my head and body. It was still dark outside with no signs of the early morning dawn. I quickly dressed and phoned my trainer. I needed to rid my lingering nightmare out of my mind, and the best way I knew how was to punch the bag until my knuckles bled.

I went three rounds with my trainer until he knocked me on my ass. I ran six miles on the treadmill, and then I must have done one hundred sit-ups. My muscles were on fire. After my hot steam and shower, I felt a little better but guilty that I ran out on my son before wishing him a happy birthday. I phoned him on my way to the office, and of course he was understanding. He always understood how I felt about this day and gave me the time I needed to work my way through it. It was unfair to him. His birthday should be celebrated with no pains from the past. I promised him we would celebrate when I arrive home. Jackson simply agreed with what I had arranged and wished me a good day. Now my father was unexpectedly standing in my office, and I wanted him gone. I blinked back into the now and stopped myself from revisiting my nightmare and deal with the matter at hand...Phillip Reed. My father was silent as he turned to leave my office and stopped abruptly at the door. He shocked me with what he said next.

"Are you happy, Walker?"

What the hell? "What kind of question is that?" I asked him.

"It's an honest one, Walker, and I would like an answer."

"Define happy, father? I run this company, and I have my son. Anything beyond that doesn't matter."

"You don't get to pick and choose what matters, son. It doesn't work that way. Everything matters. You're more than just the man who sits here all day in this big office. I was that man, dammit! And I don't want you to become me. I'm sorry, Walker. I never meant to have things work out the way they did."

Pinching the bridge of my nose, I felt a headache coming on. I listened to my father drone on and on, and I didn't have the slightest inkling on what in the hell he was talking about. I walked over to my father to look in his eyes. I couldn't believe what I was hearing. Pain radiated through my jaw muscles as I clenched my teeth.

"Father, I am exactly who you wanted me to be. You say you're sorry? For what, may I ask? I can't do this dance with you anymore; it's just too late. I have done everything you ever asked and wanted me to do, and yet you stand here and ask me if I'm happy. You want the truth? No, I'm not! Because this is not the life I wanted…but I got it…so I live it. The one thing I wanted and have always wanted, I can't have. I focus on what I do have, and that's Jackson. My son is my only priority. Now I know that's not something you're familiar with, but in my world it's everything. On her deathbed, I promised Elizabeth that I would always put our son first. She gave her life for our boy, and I vowed never to let him down."

I had rage emerging from the deep depths of my soul. I thought I had laid my demons to rest when it came to my father, but somehow they always seemed to resurface at my most vulnerable time. Today would be one of those days.

"Who made you this way, Walker? I'm looking into your eyes, and I see no light behind them. They are dark and cold. For a man that has everything, you would think you would be happier," he said as he gestured his hand around my office.

The old man has got to be losing his mind. I laughed to myself.

Trying to remain in control was never easy while dealing with Phillip Reed. I took a deep breath before answering him.

"You made me this way, father. Please don't stand here and try to say otherwise. I am my father's son, the mogul you groomed me to be." At that moment, my mind went directly to Reese. She was what I wanted, who I always wanted, but I lost her for reasons I still to this day did not know and understand. Today of all days, my loyalties should only be with Elizabeth. It would be a dishonor to her to name my former lover in this conversation.

"I would prefer that you leave, but you staying gives me no choice than to have this conversation with you. You say I have everything? Well, if that were true, then Elizabeth would be here right now, but instead I had to put her in the fucking ground. In the ground, father! Two days after our son was born. How is that everything? No amount of money and power can ever bring her back to me and Jackson. My eyes are dark today because even after all of these years that have passed, I still miss her. She was taken in the cruelest way possible, and my son had to grow up without his mother. She never even held him!" I shouted at the top of my lungs.

He stared at me as I took in my ragged breaths. He was the last person I wanted to share my feelings with. I had buried them deep for so long, it was taking every ounce of control not to be enraged at my father. I was sure half my staff had heard me by now. I threw my hands in the air and looked to him, trying to figure out what he was hiding behind his eyes.

"What is it, father? Are you looking for absolution or something? My eyes were wide open when I took over this company from you. It was my legacy, remember? So to question my choices now after all these years would simply be futile at this point."

He finally responded. "I am so sorry, Walker, so very sorry. I have made many mistakes with you, son. You can't even begin to understand why I've done what I've done. Walker, I need to…"

In all my life, I had never seen my father behave in that manner. *Phillip Reed: apologetic?* He paused right when we were about to reach the crux of what the real issue was.

"What, father? Will you just tell me what you're sorry for? What are you trying to tell me? I don't know what you're expecting to find here, but if it's peace of mind you're seeking, then I can't give that to you; only you can. I had to live with my choices, father. I expect you to do the same with yours."

I ran my fingers through my hair in complete frustration. I hated when my father spoke in circles. A timid knock once again interrupted me. "Come in!" I shouted.

"Excuse me, sir."

"What is it now, Catherine?"

"Mr. Monroe has arrived. He's waiting for you in conference room B."

"Tell him I'll be along shortly. And Catherine, the intercom does work. Learn how to use it before you interrupt me again."

"Yes, sir. I'm sorry, sir." Catherine quickly turned and closed the door behind her.

I turned back to my father, who at the moment was just staring at me silently. "Are we done here?" I asked once more.

"I guess we are. I'll be on my way, Walker. Sorry to disturb your...day. I'll phone Jackson and spend some time with him before I leave for home. Your mother misses you. It would be nice if you made some time to visit with her soon."

As I turned to go back to my desk, my father did something that I never expected him to do. He grabbed me by my arm and pulled me into a hug. A quick pat on my back and he whispered, "Goodbye, Walker." Then he turned away and walked out the door.

"Goodbye, father." Two simple and small words were all I could manage to say. I stood there, stunned into silence by his rare display of affection.

That would be the last time I ever laid my eyes on Phillip Reed. Three days had passed when I received a call that he was dead from a heart attack.

I never understood his reason for visiting me that day. I was angry when he tried to talk to me. That day was always hard for me, and when he unexpectedly showed up, it only angered me more.

To understand Phillip Reed took many years of skill that I just didn't have the time or patience for. I instead looked over to my son, who was grieving for his grandfather. Jackson loved him very much. No matter what my feelings were for my father, he was Jackson's grandfather. I was thankful that Jackson was able to see him one last time. We had flown to New York for his service, and Jackson insisted on staying at the house with my mother.

I hated this house and all it represented, but I did it for Jackson. I played my role well. I was the prodigal son who had returned home to mourn his parent and support the grieving. I shook many hands and listened to stories of how my father conquered the business world and how at times he had to be ruthless. *Oh, don't I know that?* "Try being his son," I wanted to say, but I held my tongue. My parents' closest friends, the Townsends, paid their respects. I expected no less from Elizabeth's parents. Jackson was thrilled to see them, and their presence alone made it easier for Jackson to grieve for Phillip.

After our last guest left our home, I found myself in my father's office. I walked around the room where I could still feel his presence all around me. I ran my fingers along the surface of his mahogany desk. Not one dust particle to be found on it; his office was always set in a meticulous manner. I poured myself a scotch and was face to face with my father again, but this time it was his portrait staring back at me.

No matter where I stood in the room, I could feel my father's eyes following me. My hands clenched around the glass I was holding. If I held it any tighter, it would have shattered. I emptied my glass and said my private goodbye to the mighty man himself. I felt a chill run down my spine as I exited his office, but somehow I didn't feel any closure when I did.

MARY A. WASOWSKI

CHAPTER ONE

Back here again...

ONE MONTH LATER, traveling to New York City was not what I had envisioned for my son's spring break. I planned on taking Jackson to Europe, but my son had other plans. It was extremely rare for me to compromise on any decision I made, especially when it came to my son. His heart was set on attending New York University in the fall. The university was hosting a meet and greet for new students and their families during the same time I planned our trip. I only conceded because he was still grieving over the loss of his grandfather. We were only here a short time ago for his grandfather's funeral, and to be back so soon didn't sit well with me. But it was for him, I kept reminding myself.

Jackson had been talking about attending NYU Film School ever since I had taken him at ten years old for his first viewing at the Tribeca Film Festival. He was entranced by it all and had been making short films ever since. I had wished for him to attend school in California, but his heart was set on New York. If he stayed behind in California, I could keep a better eye on him and not be insanely panicked by not being a constant presence in his day to day life. UCLA had one of the finest programs for Jackson and it would meet all of his needs, but we had exhausted that argument enough. I finally conceded and allowed him to apply to NYU, his dream school.

I attended NYU for my business and finance degree. For the most part, it held good memories for me until my senior year when my life, as I knew it, fell apart. I was madly in love with Reese Mitchell. Reese was a transplant from Atlanta. She began her senior year at NYU. She was beautiful and easily noticeable in a crowd. She was close to five feet ten inches in height with long, slender legs and the most beautiful smile that lit up a room when she entered it.

I thought my heart was going to stop beating when I first met Reese. We met in the library, of all places. I had seen her around campus a few times, but I never approached her. I thought I was smooth by casually sitting at her table, but she never looked up at me. She had her nose buried deep in her psychology book while wearing large black frame glasses. I had to meet her, but I was awkward at best. Reese totally ignored me, a first for me.

I never had a problem talking to girls, but this beauty had my insides all twisted. I could feel my lips moving, but heard no sound. When she finally broke away from her book, she wore a puzzled expression on her face, and I could have sworn I heard her laugh at me. I never said a word to her until we met again, this time at a local coffee station on campus where I almost plowed into her. She was startled and dropped the books she was carrying. I leaned forward to help her as our eyes locked on to each other. I could feel electric pulses running through my body. She didn't look away, but her caramel brown eyes burned right through me. After helping her with her books, I walked over to a nearby table and placed them down. I was hoping she would acknowledge my presence and finally speak. I was willing her to talk so I could hear her voice. When our connection finally broke, she introduced herself.

Extending her hand out to me, she said, "Hi, I'm Reese Mitchell. Um...thank you for your help." She smiled up at me.

"It's no bother at all. I'm Walker Reed." Her skin was soft to the touch. It took all my restraint not to pull her into me and kiss her right in front of the other students around us.

She looked right at me with a confident stance. "I know who you are. I've seen you at the library. And I believe you were in my psychology class, but I only saw you there once." Another smile swept her beautiful face.

"You certainly have a detailed memory, Reese. Yes, I was in psychology, but I would have never dropped that class had I known you were in it. How foolish of me." Her cheeks flushed the brightest shade of pink as I smiled at her. I couldn't help but stare at her. She was beautiful, and I was getting lost in her eyes.

"Well, Walker, pleasure to meet you. As much as I would like to continue this friendly banter between us, I need to get home. May I have my books back please?" Southern manners at its finest. How could a few words from her mouth have excited me so much?

"I will give you your books back, but on one condition. Please join me for dinner on Friday night."

"That sounds lovely, but Friday is not good for me."

"What about Saturday? We don't have to eat dinner, any meal time would suffice."

"I may be working on Saturday as well, I'm sorry. My week-ends this month are booked with appointments."

"What has you so busy that you can't squeeze in a meal with a friend?"

"Now, Walker, I just met you; I hardly consider you a friend."

"Let me change that, Reese, and by the time we are finished with our date, I will be so much more to you than a friend."

"You seem pretty sure of yourself."

"I am, Reese...believe me. When I want something, I usually get it. I will work around your schedule and anything you have on your calendar."

"Okay. Friday night I have a job in Central Park, you can pick me up at seven. We can go to dinner after I wrap for the night."

"I'm confused, Reese. What do you do for a living?"

"I'm a model. I'm shooting a layout for Fashion Week. My best friend is one of the many designers that will be participating in the event."

Sweet Jesus! She's a model. I smiled as I felt my pants shift with my growing erection. "That sounds amazing. I will see you on Friday at seven."

Reese gave me the sexiest smile I had ever seen as she walked away. This girl lit a fire through my soul. Reese's southern accent alone was the sexiest sound I had ever heard, and I knew I would never be the same after that. I planned on making Reese Mitchell mine in every way, beginning Friday night on our date.

My ringing phone brought me back into the present. It was a tedious, but necessary, work call.

Dammit! After all of these years, I could remember Reese as if it were yesterday. I branded every detail of our first encounter to memory, and it still made me feel alive when I revisited that day. I didn't know if it was my father's unexpected visit the previous month, or him dying, but once again, I resurrected all my feelings when it came to her. Reese Mitchell, the one who owned my body, heart, and soul. The one who broke me first and left me shattered before Elizabeth finally completed my circle of pain by leaving me and Jackson. *Damn you both for ripping my fucking heart out, and for invading my daily thoughts.* I rubbed my temples, and wanted to just wish the past month away. Hell, I wanted to do more than that, but I had some more calls to make before departing for New York, so it was business as usual for me.

I was just finishing up with my last call when my son, Jackson, barreled in through my office with Jenny trailing behind him. Making hand gestures, Jackson grew impatient. He was so eager to leave, but he knew I was never a person to be rushed. Raising my eyebrows up at him, he took a step back and waited without the use of theatrics to hurry me along. I watched Jenny scold him with her eyes, and he patiently took a seat while I finished up with my call. Bless that woman. She was one of the few people in my life that kept me grounded and kept this office running smoothly. Catherine had appeared to finally rise up to meet the demands of what I expected in my assistants. She only covered for Jenny that one day while she had fallen ill, and she dealt with my wrath as I endured my unexpected interruption from my father. Catherine seemed to have grown a thicker skin since then, showing me her competence. That was a good thing, because I had no patience for the weak at heart. I run my company at a high level of control and discipline, and I expected no less from the people I employed.

"Have the plans been finalized for the Reinhart building yet? That's fantastic news. I want them messengered over by three o'clock....My plane arrives in New York around the five o'clock hour, and you can reach me after that. We can pick up this conversation tomorrow, but now I have other matters that need my attention."

Removing my Bluetooth from my ear, I looked up to Jackson, who was pacing the floor of my office. I ignored him and called Jenny to come in to my office.

"Yes, sir?"

"Jackson, please excuse me. I need a moment with Jenny." Throwing his hands into the air, clearly frustrated, he exited my office.

"I'm sorry you had to witness that. My son is impatient and rude," I said to Jenny as she shook her head.

"Sir, may I speak freely?" I looked over to Jenny, and for the first time today, I actually smiled. She was one of the precious few who had a free pass. I trusted her implicitly.

"Yes, Jenny, what is it?"

"Mr. Reed, please be patient with Jackson. This trip means so much to him, and he is still grieving. He may not show you all the time, but he is. We have talked quite a bit, and he misses you and wants nothing but to please you. He wants you to be proud of him and support his decision to go to school in New York."

I sighed and slumped back into my chair.

"You just don't understand. I need him here with me, and it is killing me to come to terms with his decisions and his fierce independence."

"He sounds a lot like someone I know," Jenny responded.

I winked at her, as she smiled back at me.

"He will be fine, and so will you. You spend every waking minute here in this office. Your son is going off to college, maybe it's time for you to take a long overdue break and live a little. Not for the company, not for your son, but for you. I can't even remember the last time you actually enjoyed yourself socially."

"My entire life is this company and Jackson. I have no time for anything else. I'll let you know when I'm ready to spread my wings."

"I hope you do, sir, because I have a stack of social engagements waiting for you to RSVP to."

"I guess that will have to wait until we both return from our trips. You need to go and begin your vacation, Jenny."

"I'll just finish up with a few things, and I will be on my way. Everything is taken care of for you in New York. Have fun, will you?"

I scoff at my assistant. "What's fun?"

She was right about one thing...I did work way too much. I said goodbye to Jenny and had Jackson come back in. I took one look at him, and he was all fired up.

"Dad, we are going to miss our flight. You promised me no work on this trip."

I rose from behind my desk and strode over to my son. "Come to think of it, you promised me something too, but you don't see me overreacting because I'm not getting my way. Jackson, we will not miss our flight, we are taking the company jet. They run on my timetable. Secondly, this visit to New York is all about you. But please don't shame me, because I have a company to run."

"Dad, I know you're disappointed that we didn't go to Europe, but it's not going anywhere, we can arrange another vacation. Please understand how important this New York trip is for me."

"Oh, believe me, son, I know how important this trip is for you. Not a day goes by that you don't remind me. Let me ask you a question: Where does your girlfriend factor in on your decision to attend school in New York? Getting involved in a relationship right now is the last thing I want for you. Your priority is school and nothing more, are we clear on this?"

"Dad, I know what my responsibilities are. You remind me every day. I can have both in my life. I would like to think that you know me better than that. I would never base my decision that will ultimately change my future because of a girl, and Riley is pretty amazing, dad. Her coming into my life when she did was just icing on the cake. The unknown forced her way in and right through my heart like Robin Hood's arrow. I care for her more than you know."

Jackson's words reminded me of a similar conversation I had with my father once. This was exactly what I thought when I met Reese.

"Dad, I can't believe we are having this conversation again! Please, dad, you have to trust me."

"Jackson, I do trust you, more than you know, but you need to give me some time to adjust to this newfound independence you have now been accustomed to. It doesn't sit well with me. I knew this day would come when you wanted to strike out on your own, but to be honest with you, I'm not happy with my only son living on the other side of the country. I'm trying, son, I really am, but cut me some slack. I will bend on this for now, but Jackson, make no mistake when I say you're my priority and your well-being means everything to me. If I see you not living up to your fullest potential, then you will return home to California."

"Dad, what are you so afraid of? I'm eighteen years old and can be trusted to make my own decisions. Have I ever given you reason to doubt me?"

To look at my son with his mother's eyes staring back at me, simply cut me to my core. He so reminded me of her. How could I even begin to explain to him my deepest fears and insecurities?

Life was unpredictable with no guarantees. Having to lose his mother to something I couldn't control still haunted me. Jackson was cheated from loving and knowing his mother. He had to celebrate every milestone without her. I missed Elizabeth for our son. She would be so proud of the young man he had become. I prayed I did everything right by him. I couldn't take this stress between us, and I looked to Elizabeth for strength. He had so much of her spirit running through him.

Without another word, I grabbed my son and held him while tightening my arms around his shoulders. I needed to have things right between us. He didn't back away, just hugged me back with a silent understanding between us.

Flying on my company plane made my life easier at times. I had a built-in office and everything I needed to work and still run my company. At the time, I had three major projects going on at the same time. I had been working twelve to fourteen hour days for months now. I missed my son. We hadn't spent a lot of time together, and with his grandfather dying, it just separated us even more.

Phillip Reed was a selfish bastard. He was arrogant in his personal and business life. He softened a bit when Jackson was born. He loved his grandson more than he ever loved me. My father's death had been hard on Jackson, but with this trip to New York, his spirits were brightened. I wanted to see him smile and would do everything in my power to have that smile remain.

I should have planned to visit with my mother while I was in town, but driving out to the Hamptons was not what I cared to do. I needed to go through my father's papers; his lawyer had been urging me to do so. I finished up my pressing matters and decided to focus on Jackson for the rest of this trip.

I changed out of my suit and into jeans and a t-shirt. My son was always reminding me to loosen up a bit. *Have I changed that much that I don't know what fun is anymore?* Maybe Jackson and Jenny were right. I did need to relax and live a little. *Yeah right, Reed! Doubtful.* I sat with Jackson, as he looked up at me from his laptop. He wouldn't be following in my footsteps, as the Reed men before me, but he sure did look like one, especially when he was

8

concentrating on whatever he was working on.

"I spoke to Riley. She and her mom will join us at the restaurant for seven. Where do we have reservations?"

"I had my assistant reserve a private dining room in Brasserie Les Halles."

Jackson looked disappointed. "Dad, can't we eat somewhere more down to earth? We are not dining with your business associates."

"Jackson, Brasserie is one of my favorite restaurants I like to visit while I'm in the city. The food is delicious. What's the issue?"

"Dad, I just don't want to come off as this pretentious rich kid from California who only eats at five star restaurants. I want to impress Riley and her mom, but not look like a jerk."

"Sorry to disappoint you, son, but you *are* some rich kid from California, and also the kindest and down to earth person I know. Brasserie is the restaurant, end of discussion. Your girl may surprise you and appreciate what I have chosen. If she cares for you, as you say she does, then why does it matter where we eat? It should be your company that she values most. Now, what can you tell me about her parents?"

"Dad, there's something you need to know before we meet Riley and her mom."

"What is it?"

"I haven't been completely honest with her on who I really am."

"How so? What doesn't she know?" I shuffled in my seat with apprehension. The thought of my son lying for any reason raised alarms with me. "What is it? Obviously whatever you have to say to me is weighing heavily on your mind. Don't make me ask you again."

"I'm sorry, dad, but this is hard for me to say. I can't ever remember a time when I was angry with you, but when you couldn't make mother's hospital dedication and I had to go with grandfather, I just felt lost. I didn't want to be there without you, and I resented you choosing work over me. I was so proud of the building that was built in her honor, and I knew what you donated would help many people, but I was still hurt and feeling alone. After the dedication, I found myself staring at the portrait of my mother that was chosen for the lobby, and this beautiful girl was suddenly standing beside me. It was Riley. She took my breath away while making me forget why I was sad and angry with you."

"Okay, I'm trying to follow, but I'm confused. So how did you lie?"

"I lied by not telling her who I was, and why I was really there. She was there for her father, and I was there for my mother. We had gone for a walk around the grounds, and then when she asked me my name, the first name that came to mind was Townsend, not Reed. I didn't think I would ever see her again, and I just wasn't ready to explain my reasons for being at Johns Hopkins. When she asked me, I told her that I was visiting a sick friend. When I was in New York last summer, I never knew that our paths would cross again until I saw her at the film festival. To meet up with Riley again after a year later seemed like fate, and I all I wanted to do was get to know her better. We had too many coincidences between us. The building that houses mother's picture is the same building that is meant for Riley's father and his research."

Still trying to get a handle on all that Jackson was telling me, I fought the urge not to overreact at his revelations. "What does her father do exactly? He's a doctor? What field does he practice in?"

"He's a neurosurgeon. He's pretty famous at his hospital. Riley always downplays it, but I think she is pretty proud of what he does for his patients. You know, rock star of medicine."

That's the second time in a month I have heard the mention of Johns Hopkins Hospital. Now I find out that Reed Global built a building for this doctor who happens to be the father of the girl my son loves. My building...that proudly displays Elizabeth's name. I only made one trip out to Maryland when I signed off on the project. My right hand man Donovan was completely in charge of it. I don't believe I even met the doctor. I was completely wrapped up in the design aspect of it, which took all my time and focus. That one and only trip was about getting me to sign on the dotted line. The board of directors was so busy schmoozing me that some of the faces are now a blur. I tried not to think about the coincidence, but my father did mention it while he visited with me. Shrugging it off for the time being, I continued my conversation with my son.

"Jackson, I'm so sorry that I hurt you by not attending the dedication. I would have never missed that if the circumstances had been different. It pains me to hear this, son, especially knowing you kept this from me all this time."

"Dad, please forgive me, I need you to know that it was a knee jerk reaction, and it means nothing. I just didn't want one more person feeling sorry for me. Every time I get close to someone, they always ask about my family. And when they learn about mom, all I see is sadness and another person feeling sorry for me because I had to grow up without a mother."

"I am a Reed through and through dad, so please believe how proud I am to carry your name. But for once I just wanted to be known for me. If I had to explain to Riley about mom, then I feel she would have reacted like every other girl I ever met. I now realize I have to tell her the truth, but first I had to tell you, and say how sorry I am for denying you. Dad, I know what our name represents to you. I swear I am not ashamed of it. Can you understand why I did what I did?"

Remembering Jenny's words to be patient with my son, I held myself back from reacting to his news. I let out my breaths and simply nodded at his question before continuing our talk.

"I now understand why you were so apprehensive about our get together with Riley and her mother. Jackson, you must know that if you have any real chance with Riley, you need to always have honesty with one another. You should prepare yourself for a strong reaction from Riley. You've kept something very important from her, and in any friendship or relationship it comes down to trust. Without trust you have nothing. How will you explain the false name?"

11

"Exactly how I explained it to you, and I pray she understands. She knows a lot about me already, dad. The missing piece to the puzzle is my real name. But she is amazing, and I hope she understands my reasons for lying to her."

"Anything else I need to know before I meet them?"

Rolling his eyes at me, he quickly turned his head, knowing that would make me angry. "Dad, without meeting her parents, it's kind of hard telling you about them. I only know what Riley has told me. One thing I know for sure is that I am crazy about her. I am without a doubt convinced meeting her at mom's dedication was meant to be. I truly believe it was mom sending me a sign from heaven. Now she's my girl, and I care about her. Doing the long distance relationship has been tough, but in a few months we will be in the same city, same college. How can you say that's not fate?"

I saw Jackson give a quick nod, something he always did when he thought of his mother. It made my heart ache for his loss, but maybe it was his small way of keeping Elizabeth close.

"Are we okay, dad?" Jackson looked over to me with a very guarded expression.

"Of course we are, son…we always are."

I hugged my son with all that I had. I felt his tension slowly leave his body, as he wiped away a fallen tear. Once again my son had completely beguiled me. He expected me to be angry with him after learning his lie by omission, but he was wrong. Jackson had been my greatest gift in this life, and I vowed never to be the way my father treated me. It would only hurt my son, and I would never risk that.

I left Jackson to be on his own for a while, as I processed all he had told me. I found solace in my office and took some calming breaths. I opened my wallet and took out a worn picture that I carried with me in secret all of these years. That familiar ache was always present, but it also gave me comfort. After listening to his heartfelt words about Riley, what could I say after that? My son was me, but with almost two decades between us. It was like when I fell in love for the first time. The time I fell in love with Reese Mitchell.

As soon as we landed, Jackson turned on his phone to call his girl. I just took it all in as we stepped off the plane. My heart began to beat faster. I always felt anxiety when I was in New York. As controlled as I appeared to be, this city held no good memories for me anymore. It would be a long week for me to endure. You would think after all of these years, I would have lain to rest the ghosts of my past, but no…they still haunted me. They seemed to all come crashing down at me at the same time every time I was in New York.

My driver, Stephen, met us at the gate.

"Welcome to New York, sir. How was your flight?"

"Hello, Stephen, long as usual. Has everything been arranged back at the apartment?"

"Yes, sir. The apartment has been fully stocked with everything you and Jackson will need while you're here in New York. I will drive you, and I have Richard driving Jackson anywhere he wishes to go."

"Excellent. Has everything been sent over to the Four Seasons Hotel?"

"Yes, sir. Jenny took care of all the arrangements before leaving on her vacation." *Thank god for Jenny. I would be lost without her, but even the most perfect assistant needs a vacation once in a while.*

"Dad, I already arranged a welcome package to Riley's hotel. What else did you have Jenny send over?"

"Jackson, you need to relax, son. I arranged for flowers and a basket of treats to be waiting for them upon their arrival. I thought it would be a friendly gesture to welcome Riley and her mother to New York. Now they'll have two packages, I guess. This is the first time you're meeting her mother, and good manners always win out. Jackson, I am sorry about missing your mother's dedication. You have to know how displeased I was having to depend on your grandfather to step in for me. I would have rather had Grandpa Henry escort you, but Phillip insisted. Not being there for you will always be a regret for me, and now that I know how much it hurt you, it will be a long time before I can forgive myself."

"Dad, this is one of the reasons why I never shared my feelings with you about this. You take on so much and always put me first above anything else. The first time you couldn't, I didn't take it very well, but instead of talking to you about it, I hid it from you. I shouldn't have done that. You have always been honest with me, so I owed you the same in return."

"Jackson, telling me then wouldn't have changed how I feel. I can't stand the thought of hurting you…ever. The one true thing in my life is you, my son. Your opinion means everything to me, and I will never disappoint you again."

"You could never disappoint me, dad. You're amazing in everything you do. I know mom was shining down on all of us. You worked so hard to see your vision come alive in that building. Dad, I am so proud of you and honored to be your son. I love you, and mom would have loved it too."

"Thank you, Jackson. I needed to hear that."

"I'm happy I told you the truth, dad. I promise I will never keep anything from you again. I'm going to have Richard drive me over to Riley's hotel, so we can go grab some coffee. Wish me luck?"

Giving him a friendly slap on his back, I said, "Everything will be fine, son. You're incredible, and you already know Riley thinks so. When you tell her the truth, give her time to process it, and let her work it out on her own. I think Riley will understand. Hell, if I could, then she could." My son laughed at me. I guess we needed that to lighten the storm we just survived. "Once you kiss and make up with your girl, it will only be a matter of time before her mother loves the Reed charm too."

"Let's hope so. I'll be back soon."

I couldn't help but be jealous of Jackson. He was so happy and in love. I hadn't had feelings like that for many years now. I still couldn't find someone to share my life with, but I still only desired one woman who still remained bonded through the deepest depths of my soul.

I thought my world had shattered the day I discovered the note left for me by Reese. She explained why we couldn't be together, and I should move on without her. I clutched the note to my chest and wrapped myself around a bottle of scotch until I couldn't feel anything.

She left me, and all I was left with was a note. I didn't know what I had done to make her decide to do that. I searched for her all over the city, leaving no stone unturned. Her apartment had been emptied, leaving no trace of Reese. I banged on the doors of the few friends she had known, but they were all shocked as much as I was.

The only person I knew who would have known something was Freddy, as he was her roommate when she first arrived in New York. They were very close, and he had to know something. Arriving at his apartment left me with another dead end. He had left town days before, and no one knew when he would return. Freddy's uncle had been there cleaning the already abandoned apartment. He was my last hope, and I was at a loss.

I left numerous messages on her voicemail until her inbox was full. She never returned any of my phone calls. *Why, Reese? Where are you?* I was angry and hurt by her betrayal. My actions only proved to my old man that he was right about her and I should forget I ever knew Reese Mitchell. I tried my best to keep Reese isolated from my family. My mother was always kind, but Phillip was another story. He had a plan for me that didn't include Reese. I argued constantly with him and told him to mind his own business. Now after Reese left me, it gave him the opportunity to say, "I told you so, Walker." Oh, how that killed me.

The months that followed, I found myself lost. I was just merely existing, and my full life that I had was reduced to an empty shell. I retreated from everything that mattered. I was nursing my broken heart the only way I knew how…alone. This should have been a happy time for me; I was about to graduate and begin working with my father. Reese had planned on joining me in California; she was going to continue with graduate school and model part-time.

My last night I spent with Reese was amazing. We had dinner delivered and made love through the night in front of the fireplace. I knew every inch of her body, and she knew mine. We worshiped each other as I made her mine over and over again. I could never get enough of Reese, especially when we made love. Reese willingly gave herself to me in every way possible. We made promises to each other that night and planned our future. I believed with my whole heart that she loved me and that we would be together forever.

The next morning while she was still asleep, my phone rang. I answered it quickly, not wanting to wake her. It was my father's assistant asking me to come down to the office. An emergency had arisen, and my immediate attention was needed. I was hesitant at first but was assured that it shouldn't take long. How wrong she was. If I hadn't left Reese that morning, then she wouldn't have left me.

My biggest regret was leaving her, as well as the events that followed. I had other plans that were occupying my mind, but if I could hurry and finish up with whatever was happening at the office, then I could return home to Reese. I leaned in and kissed Reese on her forehead and whispered "I love you" close to her ear. I had left my beauty sleeping soundly. When I finally did return home, she was gone. The lights were off. The darkened room was cold. Something felt not right. I searched and called out for Reese, and only silence greeted me back.

"Where are you?" I whispered, as panic rose in my chest. I entered my bedroom to find her letter left for me. The sight of the letter instantly sickened me. Bile was rising up into my throat as I reached for it. *What the hell happened?* I began pacing the bedroom as if she would materialize at any moment.

My eyes traveled the room looking for her once more, now seeing that her things were gone, and confirming what I had known the minute I stepped inside my apartment. Reese had left me.

I held her note with my shaky hand. It read…

My Dearest Walker,

This is the hardest letter I have ever had to write. I can't even begin to explain the reasons behind it, and I know you will never understand. I pray one day you will forgive me for the hurt I'm about to cause you. I'm sorry. I'm sorry I was a coward and didn't find the courage I needed to be honest with you last night. Instead, I led you to believe that we have a future together. I'm sorry, Walker, but we don't.

We are not suitable for each other, we never were. You have your new life waiting for you in California, one that will not include me. I have decided to pursue modeling full-time and will be leaving New York, today. With Freddy gone now, I have no reason to stay. I will never forget what we have shared and will keep you with me in my heart forever. I love you, Walker. Please forgive me for the choices I have made here today, it was my only choice. You need to move on without me, it is for the best.

Reese

Her words left me emptied and broken. Why did she think that leaving me was better? Her goodbye letter shattered me and splintered my heart into thousands of pieces. I was left to question every detail of our relationship from the moment I laid eyes on my beautiful girl. Why did she leave me? And in the manner she did? Reese vanished without a trace. No matter who I hired to find her, it was always a dead end. She was a ghost that just vanished. Her actions proved to me that she didn't want me to find her.

Before meeting Reese, my entire future was planned out for me, and then she turned it upside down and changed the course of my life with just her smile. I loved that girl with every fiber in my being, and I never doubted her feelings for me. I begged her to trust me and not run, but in the end, that's exactly what she did. If it weren't for my best friend Elizabeth pulling me out of my self-induced circle of suffering, I think I would have sunken even lower into the depths of my despair. I drank too much, and I cut out my friends and family. All I wanted was Reese, and it was clear to everyone but me that she wasn't returning home to me, where she belonged.

Elizabeth was my lifeline during that time. Growing up together, she knew me better than anyone else. Elizabeth loved me, and never missed a beat telling me so. I always cared for her, but never returned her affections that she so desperately wanted. I knew my rejection and parading endless girls around Elizabeth had hurt her. I guess I was a bit of a man whore back then. I was a Reed, and my name carried clout around town. My entire perspective changed the day my eyes met Reese's in the library. Reese had stopped me in my tracks, and the days of bedding nameless faces were over for me.

I only had eyes for Reese Mitchell. My entire life shifted off course, and I had never been happier. I remembered everything about her and how in the end, she was the one person that hurt me the most. Then there was Elizabeth, my friend, my savior.

While mourning my lost relationship with Reese, Elizabeth put me back together again. At times when I was cold and heartless, Elizabeth set me straight, and in the end, I let my defenses down. One weekend in the Hamptons was the game changer for Elizabeth and me.

Glancing down at my watch, I was brought back into the present. It had been a while since my son left. I was about to call him when I heard him call out to me first.

"Dad!"

"Hey, there you are, and you're smiling. I guess all is well with you and Riley?"

"She's amazing, dad. Richard drove us to the coffee house that I had taken her to when we met again last year. She was so happy to see me. All I wanted to do was hold her, and pray she would understand and forgive me. I guess she sensed my tension and asked me what was wrong. Dad, she actually thought I was breaking up with her. I quickly explained to her that was not the case, and just blurted out my real name. She was taken aback at first, and then I explained everything, and she told me that there was nothing to forgive. I knew what I was hearing, but still had a difficult time believing it until she wrapped her arms around my neck. She pulled me down to kiss her, and I was in, head over heels. She's amazing, dad."

"Yes, son, you've said that. I'm happy you worked it out. It will make our evening go a lot smoother knowing all the secrets are out in the open. Did she say how she will explain it to her mother?"

"Riley wasn't too worried about it, so I'm not either."

"Like I said earlier, women have a hard time resisting the Reed charm. Her mother will love you."

"Well if anyone can charm a woman, it's you, dad. I learned all my skills from you."

I now let out a much needed laugh and looked back over to Jackson.

"You better believe it, son."

CHAPTER TWO

Reese

...seventeen years later

"OH, NANA, RILEY has raided my closet again, leaving not one accessory or article of clothing untouched!"

Oh, how I loved my daughter, but my closet should be off limits to her. She had a fully stocked walk-in closet of her own, but always tended to shop out of mine. That's what I get for having a daughter, but I loved her so much that I just laughed and smiled. Nana laughed over the phone too.

"I can remember those times when you used to do the same thing, my dear Reese. You used to walk around in my shoes, and oh, poor Bubba, how you dressed up that dog."

"He loved it, and you know it," I remarked, as we both reminisced about Bubba.

Bubba never left my side and always protected me during the thunderstorms that still get to me even now. I missed him very much. He lived a long time, sixteen years to be exact. I would never forget the first time coming home for a visit and instantly feeling lost when Bubba didn't come charging for me. They never did get another pet. Nana and Granddaddy missed him so much.

"Oh, Nana, I didn't want this phone call to make us sad, and now it has."

"Oh, sweet girl, don't you go worrying about poor old Bubba, he's running around the beautiful skies of heaven, probably causing a ruckus too. What I really want to know is when you're getting yourself back home to Pottersville for a visit? It's been way too long, and your Granddaddy has been asking for you, and I want to see my Riley girl too!"

"So you can spoil her some more? Believe me, Nana, that daughter of mine has many of us wrapped around her finger."

"Well that's fine by me, she's my only great grandchild, and I love her to the moon and back."

Oh that one hurt. It still hurts every time I think of my baby boy that wasn't strong enough to be born. What hurts the most is that I never even told Nana about him...Walker's and my child. I made so many mistakes back then.

"Reese...Are you still there?"

"I'm sorry, Nana, yes I'm here. My mind drifted away for a bit. Anyway, I promise to visit soon, and with Riley."

"What about that husband of yours? Will he bless us with his presence?" Clearly she wasn't a fan of Samuel.

Granddaddy always treated my Nana like a queen. Nana knew my marriage to Samuel was not an easy one to be in. We seemed to keep it going for appearance sakes and for our daughter, but Nana knew I wanted out. With Riley going off to school, this was my time to leave once and for all. I did try once, a long time ago, but he convinced me to stay, and he would be better. It was okay for a while, and then he left me alone again while he focused on his work. This had been our life for many years now, and I was just playing my part.

"Nana, I have to go now, but I promise to call you soon."

"Reese, may I say something first?"

"As if I could stop you." I smiled as I listened.

"Reese, I hope you know I would never encourage one to divorce and abandon their marriage, but you know this marriage has not brought you the happiness that you should have had with..." She stopped before mentioning his name.

"Nana, what are you trying to say?"

21

"Oh hell! I'm trying to say that you need to find what makes you happy. A husband can't just make a guest appearance once in a while. He needs to be in it—all in it—forever. If you know deep down in your heart that Samuel is not that man, then you need to stiffen that backbone of yours and finally set yourself free."

I knew the hidden message Nana was trying to get me to understand, but she never mentioned his name. My true love who I had been separated from all of these years.

"I love you, Nana, so very much. I promise to see you soon."

"I love you too, my sweet granddaughter."

Our call ended, but my sadness remained. She was the only one who could see right through me, and yet I kept her and Granddaddy in the dark all of these years, never explaining why I left Walker. What would be the point after all of those years anyway? They were happily retired and enjoying their golden years together. Thank god they were both in good health. We still owned Mitchell's Café and Book Depot. Of course it was run by a younger staff that could handle the day to day operations, but Nana still liked to make her presence known. She also still baked her famous apple pies that the town loved. I sacrificed my own happiness for the two people who never let me down, and they still have what I fought for them to keep. Somehow knowing that made the bitter pill of my past a little easier to swallow.

I was hopeful that the trip to New York would ultimately change my life. I'd been in contact with Marsha, my agent back in New York when I modeled and signed on with Elite. She was still in the game but on a smaller scale. Her daughter and son ran her office, while she travelled and kept her feet wet in the fashion scene. She was one of many friends from my past who I just simply walked away from when I said goodbye to my old life.

What the hell what I was thinking back then? And Freddy…my poor Freddy. He must have hated me for abandoning our friendship the way I did. Our last goodbye was in the hospital after I miscarried my baby. I promised I would stay in touch, but I broke that promise and never looked back. Marsha once told me how heartbroken Freddy was with the loss of what we had personally and professionally. While I was encouraged by Samuel to leave it all behind, including my modeling work, Freddy was one of the wounded I had hurt. I convinced myself that leaving Walker to save my family was the right thing to do, but I never had to leave my friends. But I did. It was one of the hardest decisions I ever had to make, and I regretted losing touch with everyone after all of these years.

The trip to New York could possibly reunite me with my best friend. Marsha had phoned me a few weeks back and told me that Freddy was doing a fundraiser fashion show in Central Park. I was beyond excited when I heard the news. Central Park held many amazing memories for me and Freddy. It was our favorite place, but also I would never forget my handsome stranger at the base of the catwalk as I walked toward him. My memory took me back to my first date with Walker Reed. He was unbelievably sexy, dressed all in black. His eyes never left me as I strutted down the catwalk. His eyes hungered with carnal desire for me. God! I wanted him so much, but he made me wait. I couldn't even begin to go to those places in my mind anymore. Walker was part of my past, but so easily present every time I entertained a happy thought of him.

I couldn't contain my love and joy for Freddy once I heard what he named the upcoming fundraiser event. He founded a charity after volunteering in orphanages throughout Israel and called it "Peaches Promises." Marsha explained that he took a pilgrimage trip and just fell in love with the children. He toured the war torn cities of his parents' beloved country. Doing well in his career, with no worry for money, he decided to give something back. This made his parents so immensely proud of him. The foundation had recently celebrated its tenth anniversary, and Freddy had created a children's clothing line with half of the profits going back into his charity. My heart was bursting with love for my friend. I missed him so much. To be in New York again was meant for Riley, but now with Marsha's help, she was paving my way back to Freddy. I just prayed he would talk to me. Looking at my watch, I knew I needed to get going soon, but I still had my closet to clean up first.

As I surveyed the mess, a box toppled over and its contents spilled out. I picked up my tattered journal, and my eyes found his. Walker's picture was staring back at me. I only kept this one picture of him. Fleeing the life I had shared with him didn't leave me with time to take more mementos with me. Most of our pictures together were at his apartment prominently displayed all around his living and bedroom. I carried this picture of Walker in my wallet for many years until I finally removed it and placed it in my journal. It would forever be sealed and wrapped up in the words that I wrote when I left him. If I could turn back time and go back to that day, I wouldn't have done what I was being forced to do.

I often wondered what would have happened if I stood up to Walker's father, Phillip. It's not that I didn't try, but he was too powerful for me to go up against. And with that last threat he delivered to me, I was convinced that he would destroy me and everyone I loved. He bullied and threw me out of his son's life. I was in love with Walker and carrying his baby.

I planned on telling him at breakfast, but never got the chance. He distracted me the night before with his desire to fuck me on every surface of his apartment. Walker, always the attentive lover, never stopped touching or loving me with his body. He easily could make me forget my own name when I was around him. But that was all over and lost. What was to be my forever just slipped through my fingers and was gone.

A knock at the door snapped me out of my reminiscing and brought me back inside my messy closet.

"Mom, may I come in?" Riley asked for entrance. I wiped away my falling tears before answering the door. I looked in the mirror before answering her; my face was flushed and clearly she would notice. I composed myself and called out to her.

"Come in, honey."

"Mom, can I borrow...what's wrong? Have you been crying?"

Her worried eyes found mine.

What could I say to Riley? *Yes, I've been crying over my old lover and still mourn the loss of my broken relationship?* "Everything is fine, honey. I'm crying because I am going to miss you so much when you move to New York."

"Mom, I'm not leaving until August. We have the summer to have fun and spend lots of time together."

"Thank you, Riley, but you can't devote your entire summer to me because you're going away for college. You have your friends, and this is your time to have fun. You're only young once, so be carefree and happy."

I gave my daughter the same advice my best friend Freddy gave to me when I met Walker. I wasn't too sure about him after our awkward first encounter at the library. I pretended not to notice him, but I did. *How can I not?* He was breathtakingly good looking, and it was obvious he was interested. I remember going home that night and telling Freddy all about it. He urged me to go for it and take a chance on the handsome stranger. Our time together was short, but Walker changed my life.

Riley was waving her hands in front of me to get my attention. "Mom, where did you go just now?"

"Oh, I'm sorry, I was just thinking about Freddy Mac. I miss my friend." It has been way too long since we have talked or even seen each other, but hopefully that will be changing soon.

"Freddy Mac? The same Freddy Mac who I'm wearing right now? Oh my god, mom! How do you know Freddy Mac? And why am I finding this out now?"

I had to hold my ears as my daughter shrieked on the top of her lungs. Oh lord, I really just opened my mouth and inserted foot. My past was in the past, and I was very discreet about it. I guess now that I had my slip of the tongue, I would tell Riley about him…the short version.

"Calm down, Riley. Yes, one and the same. Freddy was my friend from Atlanta many years ago. He moved to New York, and we kept in touch. When I decided to transfer to NYU, he offered me his spare room. We were incredibly close."

"I can't believe I am finding this out now. Tell me more, mom! What is he like? When was the last time you talked to him?"

"It's been quite a while, Riley. I lost touch with Freddy after I left New York." To say that to my daughter just saddened me even more. I didn't just leave Walker, I left Freddy, Marsha, and my entire life I was trying to build.

"Wow, mom! Can you tell me more about him? I'm sure if you shared an apartment, then you must have some great stories about him?"

"Okay! You win. I will tell you something that he swore me to secrecy about, but you must never tell another soul what I'm about to tell you." Squealing with delight and crossing her heart, Riley promised. I couldn't help but smile at my daughter, but also talking about Freddy made me happy. "One night Freddy finally cracked under my powers of persuasion and revealed to me his real name."

"What? Freddy Mac is not his real name?" Riley asked with curiosity.

"Not exactly, he had shortened it after arriving in New York. We had been playing poker, and if I won, then my prize would be the knowledge of knowing his full real name. I knew I wasn't going to lose; my Granddaddy taught me well. When I revealed my hand to him, he almost fell over. I said, 'Okay, Freddy, aces over eights, I win. Now tell me what the birth certificate says.'"

Laughing and smiling now, I remembered his exact words. "You really are a vixen, Reese," he responded.

"Stop stalling and tell me," I pressed him.

"Okay, but on our friendship you must promise never to tell anyone. When I become a famous designer, I only want to be known as Freddy Mac, not Frederick Xavier Mackelstein, originally from the Bronx, but moved to Atlanta for his father's job. Can you imagine a New York Jewish boy living in the suburbs of Atlanta?"

"I never laughed so hard in all of my life. I knew we would be best friends forever after that."

"If that's true, mom, then why haven't you kept in touch with each other?"

I wiped away a tear that fell. *God, how I missed my best friend!* "Another long story and one that we don't have time for. Ask me again someday."

More tears were falling now, and I let them. I didn't want to give Riley the wrong idea about my friendship with Freddy. It had been years since we had spoken. I had to prepare myself that I may not get the happy reunion with Freddy that I was hoping for.

"That was a great story, and believe me I want to hear more. If only Freddy could see you now. You're still hot, and any guy would be drooling all over himself after meeting you."

"Riley Taylor Briggs, you're incorrigible. 'Hot' would not be a phrase that I use to describe myself, but thank you anyway for the compliment."

"Mom, you act as if you're old. You barely just turned forty. Why do you think half my friends are guys?"

"I don't even want to know that answer. Oh, I'm going to miss you, my daughter. You're very good for my ego."

"Don't worry, we will see each other, and what better place to visit than New York City? I don't doubt you will be busy once I leave, and you still have daddy to keep you company."

The mention of Samuel depressed me, and my happy moment was gone. My husband was married to his work, not to me. He gave his full attention to his patients and his new hospital wing built just for him. In our marriage, I was alone and had been for quite some time. I had been contemplating leaving him. My talk with Nana only proved to me what I knew for a long time now…It was time to leave my marriage.

I wanted to wait until Riley moved out and went off to school. I wanted to take some time to talk to her about it, but remembering Walker and Freddy put that conversation on the back burner. I was about to say something and then we heard the front door open and close. I couldn't believe that Samuel actually made it home in time to see me and Riley off.

Riley screeched "Daddy's home" and ran down the stairs to greet her father. She nearly knocked him over; she was beyond excited to see him. As close as a mother and daughter can be, Riley was a daddy's girl, and so proud of it. They were thick as thieves. I was almost jealous at times, but at least he was paying attention to someone in this family.

I watched Riley from the balcony with her arms wrapped around her father's neck. Her hero had returned home.

"Daddy, I am so happy you're home. Mom and I were just about to call for the car. Are you sure you can't come with us?"

"Riley, sweetheart, settle down and come up for air. You know I would if I could, but you know I have two difficult surgeries planned. I already explained this to you. I hope you have an amazing time, and when you return home, you can tell me all about it."

Riley's happy face had just fallen. Was he blind? How could my husband be so observant to the needs of his patients, but not see what was right in front of him? He clearly saddened and disappointed our daughter with his rejection. This trip to New York had been planned for months; he could have arranged it on his schedule. But his work always came first.

"Okay, honey, you and mom have a great trip."

He kissed our daughter on her forehead and turned away from her. Riley released a lone tear drop down her cheek. I immediately rushed to her side and held her in my arms.

"Riley, please don't cry. You know your father and how important his work is to him."

"Mom, that's the problem. When are we going to be just as important? I love him so much, but let's face it, he's never here anymore. And now that I'm leaving, you will truly be alone. I'm sorry mom. I never considered what it would be like for you when choosing my school."

"Riley, please sit with me for a minute. I don't ever want you to second guess your decision to go away to school. NYU is your choice, and it always has been. You're incredibly talented, and NYU will be lucky to have you. I wish I had the wisdom of your great grandmother, but she is one of a kind. I want to tell you so many things, but sometimes it's hard for me to find my words. I love you, Riley. You have been my entire world from the moment I found out I was pregnant with you. You have grown into this amazing and accomplished young woman. Don't ever be afraid of going after what you want, and be happy with the decisions you make for yourself."

Lunging herself into my arms, she wrapped her arms around my neck and went in for a huge hug. "Thank you, mom. I needed to hear that. Are you okay? You look so sad."

"I'm fine, sweetheart. Don't worry about me. I'm going to take a few minutes to speak with your father, and then we can leave for the airport."

"Okay, mom, I'll be outside waiting for the car, and I'm going to call Jackson."

I could feel my anger rising up within me. How could Samuel be so selfish? We had already been arguing last week over him not wanting to go with us, but now this? It was time to get some things off my chest. I always knocked when Samuel's office door was closed, but not today. I loudly entered through the door, slamming it behind me.

Samuel looked up from his desk and raised his voice at me. "What the hell, Reese?"

"Damn you for hurting our daughter. Can't you see how you have disappointed her today?"

"Reese, I don't have time to argue with you about a silly trip to New York."

"It's not silly, Samuel. This trip is very important for Riley and to her future as an attending student." He smiled mockingly as I stood there furious with him.

"If you ask me, our daughter is more excited on seeing the boy who has all of her attention these days, rather than her college choice. Can we talk about this later? I only came home because I forgot a patient file."

"You mean to tell me that you only came home because you forgot your file? She and I actually thought you made a special trip home just to say goodbye. But I guess work really is your priority, like always. You really are an asshole."

I couldn't believe I just said that. I rarely raised my voice at Samuel, but I think that was my limit. I could never stand to see my daughter upset for any reason, and I knew not having her father join us on this trip was breaking her heart.

"Now listen here, Reese. Don't you ever speak to me like that. You're out of line. I spoke to Riley last night and explained to her why I couldn't make the trip. She understood, so why are you busting my balls?"

"Only last night you explained to her? This trip has been planned for... You know what? I can't do this anymore, Samuel. Our marriage is not working, and we are both miserable."

This got his attention. I went to leave his office, and Samuel was at my side in a second. Slamming the door and pinning me up against it, he glared at me. His strong arms caged me in.

"You can't do what anymore, Reese? Be my wife?" Stroking my face with his fingers he let out a sigh. "Let's end this conversation right now before one of us says something that we can't take back. And by the way, I'm not miserable."

"I want a divorce." I barely got my voice above a whisper, but he released my arms and his expression turned cold. He leaned up against the door trying to catch his breath.

"Reese, you're my wife, and you will not leave me. Do you understand?"

"Samuel, you can't make me stay where I'm not happy. I gave up who I was when I married you. I left my friends. I gave up my career and followed yours. It's time I get some of that back. Why do you care anyway? You're never here for me anymore. You make a guest appearance once in a while, but never stay. Riley is leaving for college in a few months; I have no reason to continue on this way. Please let me go, and let's end this farce of a marriage."

"How can you say that? A farce of a marriage? As if the last eighteen years have meant nothing to you. I will never let you go, Reese. I love you, and I know you may not love me like…but…I can make it up to you."

"What were you going to say, Samuel? I don't love you like… what?"

"It's not important, Reese. We are not getting a divorce, end of discussion. When you return from New York, we will plan a vacation and take some time to sort things out."

"A vacation is not going to fix what has been broken with us, it's too late. Don't you see, Samuel? We need to let go of 'us' before 'us' gets bad to the point that we will be irreversibly broken. This has been a long time coming, you must know this in your heart. We have grown apart and have been living two very separate lives. I want more, Samuel, and what we have here is not enough for me to stay. Samuel, I'm not trying to hurt you, but this conversation is long overdue. I want a divorce, and nothing you say will ever change my mind."

"Please don't do this, Reese. We can go away. It can be a start, a new beginning for the two of us. I'm so sorry that I haven't been the most attentive husband, but I've tried to be. Haven't I given you a great life?" He gestured around the room. "You have everything you could ever want or need."

There was no greater distance between us than right there in that room. We were just staring at each other when Samuel finally spoke again. "Come here, Reese."

Hesitating at first until his eyes slowly pulled me in like a magnet, I walked over to him, and as I got closer, he pulled me into his chest.

"Reese, what can I do to prove how much I love you?" he whispered into my ear.

"Let me go," I whispered back.

He took in a ragged breath and held me tightly to him as he declared his love for me. Or maybe it was a declaration of his ownership of me. "I have never broken my promise to you since the day I proposed to you, Reese. I have loved you from the moment you woke up in that hospital room and you looked up at me with your beautiful eyes. Give me a chance to be that man again? Let me show you, Reese, how much I love you and can keep my promises."

I tried to free myself from his hold. He was trying, but he didn't hold my heart, and I couldn't stay in this marriage for one more day. All those years I carved out this idealistic life for myself and built the walls around myself like a protected fortress. This was not the life I wanted, but I lived it. My greatest gift was my daughter, Riley, that was it.

Waiting for my answer, Samuel never took his eyes off of me. He began to unbutton my blouse, as my tears fell silently. He always got turned on every time we fought. Sometimes it was an amusing foreplay tactic, but other times it was just so inappropriate or frightening. Like this time. He had me trapped, and I wanted to scream at the top of my lungs for my freedom. Looking into his hurt eyes, I saw him clearly. He was a good man, always had been, but he deserved more than I was willing to give him. Our relationship had been barely existing over the last few years. Didn't he know this? I tried to reach for his hands and talk to him once more.

"Sex is not going to magically repair the holes that are in our marriage. I can't do this anymore, Samuel. Please let me go."

He clenched his jaw and bore his eyes into mine. "You're right, my love, it's not always the answer, but at this moment it's going to make me feel a lot better."

I tried to walk away, but he pulled me back into him. He turned me around and placed me on his desk. Holding my hands above my head with one of his, he began pressing his hard length into me. I was quiet and still. Samuel never hurt me, but when he showed this dominant side to him, sometimes it frightened me.

"Samuel, please, Riley is waiting for me. We can talk about this when I get home."

"No, Reese, we won't. Now stop fighting me, and let me love you." I wanted him to stop, but he held on to me with a tight grasp. He could be so delicate when he had a scalpel in his hand, but also so incredibly strong. His grip tightened on my wrists. In one swift move, he pulled my skirt up and ripped my panties away from my body. He entered me with force, showing me that he was again in control. There was a time when I enjoyed this type of rough sex and the pleasure I got from it, but it wasn't with Samuel. I closed my eyes and thought of Walker. *Curse me for ever leaving him.*

With one last thrust, Samuel climaxed inside of me. Releasing my hands, he cupped my face, and now his anger had been sated. "I love you, Reese, please don't leave me. I promise you that we can make our marriage work. Losing you is not an option, Reese, and it will never be. You'll go to New York, have fun with our daughter, and then you will come back to me, and this conversation will be forgotten, okay?"

He lifted me up and held me to his chest while breathing in my scent. Tears began to fall down my cheeks. Samuel kissed them away and released me. I stood there for a minute to compose myself and take in what just happened between us. How could Samuel ever believe that what he just did to me will fix anything between us? If anything, it's sex that complicated our situation even more. I asked him for a divorce, but I just was spread out all over his desk not five minutes ago. If that's what he felt he needed to do to make himself feel good, then fine. He only took my body. It's what was in my heart that was now leading me down the right path, and my journey ended today with Samuel. He was so smug, as he completely ignored me while he went back to work at his desk. No matter, I had nothing else to say to him.

As I made my way to his office door, I glanced back at him and whispered, "Goodbye Samuel."

My marriage was over, at least for me. He couldn't make me stay, no matter how much he tried to control me with his words or sex. This was not what I wanted; hell, it was never what I wanted. I climbed the stairs back to our room to change into fresh clothes, hoping Riley wouldn't notice. My face was flushed and blotchy. I fixed my hair and make-up quickly, hoping to cover up my goodbye fuck with Samuel, because that's exactly what it was. I made sure to pack the precious pieces of jewelry and memories that I held onto all of these years, including my journal.

I didn't know what was waiting for me once I stepped out of this house, but I would take my chances with what Nana called my stiffened back bone. It was time to find me again, and that's exactly what I intended to do. The car service arrived fifteen minutes later to take Riley and me to the airport. Samuel's office door was closed, clearly telling me that we had nothing else to say to each other.

I met Riley outside, and she told me that Samuel actually just left. By the way my daughter was looking at me, she knew something was wrong. I played it off, and we headed for the airport. I held on tightly to a certain picture that was now in my pocket. I shouldn't have picked this time to drop the divorce bomb on Samuel, but I was angry with him. I would always care about Samuel, but never love him in the way he deserved to be loved and cared for.

He saved me the night I miscarried my baby. He had been working the emergency room to help out when I was brought in. I remember waking up in recovery and my hand was being held by a stranger. I was startled by an unfamiliar touch and jerked my body.

"Shhh, it's okay. Hello, I'm Dr. Briggs. I attended to you while you were being treated in the emergency room."

Calming myself after realizing where I was, I groggily said, "Hi, I'm Reese Mitchell." The realization hit me like a punch to my stomach, and I knew why I was there. My best friend, Freddy, had convinced me to return to New York to find Walker to explain why I left him. I never got the chance to do so after becoming violently sick, and then I started to spot. I was just beginning my second trimester of pregnancy. My head was spinning, and I was alone in my hotel room when I fell to the floor. I managed to get to the phone and call 911, and that was the last thing I remembered until waking up there with Samuel.

"Reese, you're here at New York Presbyterian Hospital. You were unconscious when the ambulance arrived. I examined you and did an ultrasound. Your placenta ruptured, causing you to lose your baby. I'm very sorry for your loss. There was no way we could save the pregnancy. We had to perform a D and C to remove the fetus, so you will have to stay here another day for observation. Can I call someone for you?"

"That won't be necessary. I don't have any family here in the city."

"What about your husband, or a boyfriend, perhaps?"

"I don't possess either one of those at the moment, but I will be alright, doctor. Can you please hand me my bag? I need to make some calls. Can I ask you a question, Dr. Briggs?"

"Yes, you can ask me anything, Ms. Mitchell."

"Dr. Briggs, why were you holding my hand?"

"I was holding your hand because you looked very peaceful as you slept, and I knew once you woke up, you wouldn't be. Again, I am very sorry for your loss. I don't usually work down here in the emergency room, but I'm happy I was here for you."

"Dr. Briggs, what was the sex of my baby? A boy or a girl?"

With head hung low, he whispered, "A boy. The pathology report said it was a boy."

Tears flooded my eyes to the point where I couldn't see. *I lost Walker's son...my baby boy.* My last connection with Walker was now gone, and I had nothing left. My tears were beginning to flow uncontrollably. I wanted to just die at that moment along with my son. Dr. Briggs held my hand again and asked if he could do anything for me. I pulled away from him.

"Thank you for answering my questions. If you're not an emergency room physician, what do you do here at the hospital?"

"I'm a neurosurgeon, but rest assured, I was fully qualified to treat you. If you need anything, Ms. Mitchell, just hit the button for your nurse, and she will page me right away."

After Dr. Briggs left my room, I placed my hand over my stomach. Remembering my last appointment with my doctor, I had heard the baby's heartbeat. The sound echoed throughout the room. It was the most amazing sound I ever heard in my life. I wanted to record it and play it over and over again, and now Walker's child was gone. I had lost my last connection with the only man I would ever love. Why did this happen to me, and to us? Phillip Reed was to blame for that. His fucking bodyguard grabbed me so tightly, holding me back from getting to Walker. *Please, God...take me to my son! I don't want to be without my baby! Please, God, take me to him!*

I must have been crying in my sleep. I could feel wetness on my cheeks, as I struggled to open my eyes. I couldn't move my hands, and when I was finally alert, I realized my hands were bound and secured to the bed rails.

"What's going on? Why am I being restrained?" I called out to the nurse, and she quickly entered my room.

"Calm down, Ms. Mitchell, the restraints are there to protect you, not hurt you."

"Protect me? Why?" I was crying again and very scared.

"Let me call your doctor, and he will explain it all to you." I know she was only doing her job. It's not as if she wasn't kind, but I wanted to scream and demand for her to release me. I just lost my baby, and now this? I didn't understand why this was happening. My chest was beginning to hurt, and I couldn't breathe. The beeping on the machines in the room was getting louder, and I was gasping for air. There was a scurry of activity in my room. All I could see was an oxygen mask covering my nose and mouth, and I could hear loud voices above me. My eyes began to close, and darkness consumed me. I saw no light around me. Just darkness. And then I heard a voice. A chilling voice that I would never forget.

"I warned you, Ms. Mitchell. I warned you." It was Phillip Reed, Walker's evil father.

I SCREAMED BACK with all my strength. "You did this! You killed my baby with your hate. Why couldn't you have let me be happy with Walker? WHY??????????"

I woke up with such a force, my head sprang back into my pillow. I was still restrained, but I now heard a calming voice beside me.

"Shhh, Ms. Mitchell, try to take some calming breaths." Dr. Briggs was stroking my cheeks and tucked my hair behind my ears. "I'm going to have my nurse take your blood pressure and vitals, and then I'll be back to speak with you. Please, Ms. Mitchell, continue taking calming breaths, and I'll be back in a few minutes." I didn't understand what was happening to me, and then the same nurse entered my room to examine me.

"Welcome back, Ms. Mitchell."

"Please call me Reese. What's happening to me, and why do you have my hands restrained?"

Dr. Briggs will be back in a minute, and he will answer all of your questions." She politely smiled and then left my room. *Dr. Briggs? What happened to Phillip?* My head was so fuzzy, and I was very confused to what was happening. Just then, Dr. Briggs walked back into my room, and he looked sad and troubled.

"How are you feeling, Ms. Mitchell?" He asked with a worried tone to his voice, how strange coming from a doctor, no less. He was a stranger to me, but yet I felt comfortable around him.

"Please call me Reese, and I'm not sure what's going on."

"If you answer my question first, Reese, I'll answer yours."

"I'm okay." I lied. His one eyebrow rose with doubt. *He doesn't believe me, and why should he when I don't myself. How can I be okay after losing my baby?*

"How's your pain level? Any discomfort at all?" he asked me as he checked my eyes with his light.

"I'm not in pain…physical pain, that is, but I am a little sore. My head is fuzzy, and I'm thirsty, maybe even a bit hungry."

"Thirsty and hungry are good signs. I'll have some soup brought in for you right away."

"Will you feed me as well? You know with my hands being tied to the bed."

I didn't want to be rude to the kind doctor, but after all, I was still restrained and didn't know why. He looked at me and once again stroked my cheek with his soft hands.

"If you promise to remain calm and try not to hurt yourself, then I will release you from your restraints."

At that moment, I didn't think I could feel any worse. All of my painful childhood memories about my depressed mother flashed back at me. Still restrained, I looked into his concerned eyes, and I began to cry.

"Dr. Briggs, I would never try to hurt myself…It's just not possible. You must be mistaken."

"I'm sorry Reese, but you did try to harm yourself. After I left your room, I along with my nurse heard you scream. By the time we reached your room, you were screaming and crying. You ripped out your I.V. You nearly fell to the floor trying to get out of bed. I had no choice but to sedate and restrain you. You slept for nearly six hours, and when you finally woke up, you began having an anxiety attack that mirrored a heart attack. Your heart rate accelerated, along with your blood pressure. Your breathing was unstable, and I needed to calm you before you went into cardiac arrest. Honestly, Ms. Mitchell, you scared me. I don't ever remember a time when I was ever scared like that until I witnessed what happened with you."

"You don't even know me, Dr. Briggs, but I can assure you that whatever you were seeing was my reaction to losing my baby. I would never try to hurt myself; this I know for a fact."

He removed my restraints, and his nurse assisted me with a shower. I was still very sore, but nothing I couldn't handle. I refused the pain medicine. Having to feel this physical hurt right now was nothing compared to what my heart and mind were going through. I wanted to feel everything. This was my punishment for leaving Walker.

Dr. Briggs explained everything from the beginning. How I was screaming that I wanted to die, to pulling out my I.V. I can now see the bruising up my arms. I was shocked that I had slept all those hours, but my kind nurse that I now knew as Francesca explained that with the heavy medication I was on, this was normal. I had been dehydrated, and with the loss of blood, my body was very weak.

My meltdown didn't help my condition, and after I finished my meal, I was forced to endure an hour long conversation with a psychotherapist. I was exhausted, but I knew I had to make some calls. The psychotherapist was convinced that I wasn't a danger to myself or anyone else for that matter. What I was feeling was normal. *Oh I hate that word. I just lost my baby. I lost the love of my life. Having to endure what I've been through over these months, I think I was entitled to scream a bit. This was my fault, and my fault alone. I should have taken better care of myself. If I had, my baby would still be here.* I stopped myself, because I didn't want to begin feeling sorry.

I finally phoned my agent and Freddy. Marsha was out of her mind with worry and didn't know where I was. It took me forever to calm her and explain what happened. She told me that my disappearance was about to make the evening news. I was horrified by that revelation and afraid that Walker would see me. Thank goodness she was being her usual melodramatic self, because that didn't happen.

Freddy hurried over to the hospital right away. He was crying as he hugged me. He was taking all the blame onto his shoulders, because he was the one that begged me to come back. This was simply not true. I don't know why I lost my son, but I knew I had to move on and put the pieces of my broken heart back together. Freddy stayed with me for a couple of more hours and then he had to board a flight to Milan. I hugged my friend, and we said our goodbyes through our tears.

Little did I know this would be the last time I would see Freddy. After my disastrous encounter with Walker's father and his body guard, I phoned Marsha to book me something in New York. His father had eyes everywhere, and he was determined to keep me from his son. I used my job to get back here, and once I did that, I was determined to find Walker. I finally explained everything to Freddy, and he said he wanted to hire a hit man to take out Phillip Reed. I needed my best friend when I was ready to face Walker. Freddy was in Europe, and for me to ask him to come back went beyond the bonds of friendship.

I chickened out, and then Freddy convinced me to come home. No one could predict what was going to happen to me. I don't know if it was the universe telling me that having Walker's child was not meant to be, but I never believed that. I should have told him about the baby from the beginning and stand up to his father. I never gave Walker a chance. I had it all planned out. I would find Walker and tell him everything. I would crawl on glass if I had to, just for him to listen and take me back.

I was hoping Walker would forgive me for ever leaving him, and prayed he would take me in his arms and tell me my nightmare was over, but that didn't happen. Losing my child and suffering this immense loss was too hard to bear, but this misery was on me. To blame Phillip Reed was easy, but ultimately I blamed myself. If I had trusted Walker to help me, he would have protected me and not let his father hurt me or my family.

I didn't do any of that. I committed the one act I swore I would never do, I became...*her.* My mother was weak, and I am my mother's daughter. I succumbed under all of Phillip's threats, and all I was left with were the consequences of my actions.

I was gathering my things when my hand holder of a doctor walked in.

"Good morning, Ms. Mitchell. How are you feeling today?"

It had been several days since my meltdown, and now I was being released. I was beyond ready to leave this place.

"I'm better, Dr. Briggs. Thank you for asking."

"I just signed off on your discharge papers, and left all your post op paperwork with your nurse. You will have to take it easy for the next week or so."

"Thank you, I will manage just fine."

"I don't doubt that at all, Ms. Mitchell." He winked at me with a sparkle in his eyes. I smiled back at him.

"You can call me, Reese. Ms. Mitchell sounds so formal and it makes me feel like I am back in school."

"Fair enough. Now that we are on a first name basis, will you please call me Samuel? I was about to sign out for the day. Would it be too forward of me to ask you out for coffee?"

"I guess under normal circumstances it wouldn't be considered forward, but this is not normal. I was your patient up to a few minutes ago, and you know why I was here."

"Reese, don't over think things. It's just coffee. Please let me escort you back to your hotel, and we can dine there."

Over think too much? Oh man, I am the queen of over thinking, and to hear those words again just breaks my heart. Walker was forever telling me that.

"Thank you, Samuel. I would love to have coffee with you."

Samuel walked with me through the hospital valet area to retrieve his car all the while keeping his hand on the small of my back. He was forward with his mannerisms, but after what I had been through, this was a welcomed comfort.

He drove us back to my hotel, where Marsha was waiting for me. She had me booked on an early morning flight back to California. Samuel was eyeing her up and down, not too sure what to make of her. I don't think he knew that I was a model.

"Oh, thank god, Reese! I was going out of my mind with worry. I phoned the hospital, and they told me you were released. I didn't know what happened to you. Freddy is back in Milan, no one tells me a thing. I'm supposed to be your friend, for cripes sake, and now you're here."

Grabbing my hands, and eyeing me up and down, she forcefully pulled me into her. I was considerably taller, so I almost toppled her. Samuel remained quiet while Marsha's mouth was going a mile a minute.

"Marsha, please calm down. I'm alright, can we take it down a few notches?"

"I'm sorry, Reese, but oy vey! The last time I heard from you was days ago, and then when I finally do, you're in the hospital? How do you expect me to react?"

"I'm sorry too, Marsha. I never meant to worry you, but I've been through a lot. I can't explain it all right now. Can you please bring my things up to my room, and I will meet up with you later?" I turned to Samuel and smiled for the first time in days. "I promised the good doctor here a cup of coffee."

I could tell that Marsha wanted to say something after sizing up Samuel, but she held her tongue. A miracle on her part. I watched her clip clop all the way to the elevator. I couldn't help but laugh under my breath.

"Your friend is quite the character. What exactly do you do, Reese, that requires you to have an agent?"

"I'm a model, Samuel."

"Wow, I feel stupid. The only magazines I tend to read are medical journals. I'm sorry I didn't recognize you."

"Don't be sorry, Samuel. I am not nearly as famous as you may think I am. I only began modeling full-time a few months ago."

"Forgive me for asking, but how could you model and be pregnant at the same time?"

I tried not to cry because of the harsh reality hitting me that I was no longer pregnant. Dr. Briggs looked so unsure at the moment, and probably regretted asking me his question. I wasn't angry with him. He had a shy innocence about him; his awkwardness was adorable, on top of being very handsome.

"To answer your question, I guess I was lucky not to be showing that much yet. Not all my modeling jobs consisted of full body shots."

"I'm sorry and feel very stupid. I shouldn't have overstepped with my questions."

I assured him that he wasn't prying and that I was not insulted by his questions. We sat down in the lounge of the hotel and ordered a late breakfast. I was in need of a glass of wine, but settled for coffee instead. Samuel was charming and asked me everything about my life. He told me about medical school, his upbringing, and his plans for the future. I had a different vision on how my life was going to be, but after losing the baby, I was only sure of one thing. Reconciling with Walker was never going to happen now.

From what I had read and seen in the papers, Walker has clearly moved on with the daughter who reigns from one of the Hamptons elite families. I'm sure his father was gleaming with delight. I didn't care what was reported on his lifestyle and all that was being played out in the papers. I believed that once Walker learned the truth behind my reason of leaving him, he would leave Elizabeth and come back to me.

Samuel and I had been talking for most of the morning. It felt good to talk to someone and share my feelings. But I was getting tired and my body was still recovering from all that I went through. "Thank you, Dr. Briggs, oh sorry, I meant Samuel. I need to meet with Marsha, who is waiting on me. But thank you again for breakfast and the talk."

By the time I had reached my room, I was exhausted. True to form, Marsha was waiting inside for me. She began rattling off question after question, and I was just too tired to answer her. Anything we needed to discuss could be done tomorrow on our flight back to California.

Marsha startled me the next morning by barging into my suite. "Rise and shine, Peaches! We have a flight to catch."

"What time is it?"

"Time for you to get up and get ready. You slept close to sixteen hours."

"I did *what?* I can't believe that I slept that long."

"You have to be starving. I had room service bring you dinner, but you never answered your door. That must have been some breakfast with that handsome doctor of yours."

"Stop it, Marsha. He was just being kind."

"Oh please! I think I saw a little naughty than kindness in his eyes. Did you not see how he couldn't take his eyes off of you?"

"I'm going to take a shower now. When I get out, I expect you not to be here. The flight will be long enough to endure with all of your incessant questioning."

"Have it your way, Peaches. I know lust when I see it."

"Goodbye, Marsha."

I was finishing getting dressed when I heard knocking at my door.

"Marsha! I said I would meet you downstairs," I said as I flung the door open. Samuel was standing there with two cups of coffee. He was the last person I expected to see.

"Hi, what are you doing here?" I asked him.

"Didn't you know coffee delivery was one of our services that we provide?"

I smiled and invited him in.

"Thank you, Samuel. It was very thoughtful of you."

"You're welcome. It was my pleasure. Can I ask you something?"

"Of course," I responded.

"Reese, do you have to go back to California?"

"Yes, I do. I have to get all my shoots rescheduled. I'm going to take the good doctor's advice, and take some time off." *Physically I would heal. Mending my broken heart would be another issue.*

"What would you say if I asked you to not get on the plane today? I would love for you to stay here with me in New York."

What? "Samuel, you don't even know me. How can you ask such a question like that?"

"I know everything I need to know about you, Reese. You're

amazing, and I feel drawn to you for some reason. If you stay, we can get to know one another better."

"I'm sorry, Samuel, but I can't. My work over the next few months will keep me very busy. I will mostly be traveling, and I don't think that is how you want to start off anything with me. I'm sure you have more important things to take care of than to date me."

"You, at the moment, are all that I want."

"I'm flattered, really. But I can't, Samuel."

I didn't have time to respond to him. Samuel pulled me into his chest and kissed me. I let him, and for the first time since I left Walker, I realized this was what I needed. I wanted to feel a physical connection again, and being held in Samuel's arms allowed me to do so. I returned his kiss, until he broke our connection and placed his forehead against mine. *What am I doing?*

"Go to California. Here, take my card. It has all my numbers on it. Finish up with what you need to do, and we will talk soon. I'm on my way to Maryland. I have been offered a position at Johns Hopkins. Maybe once I get settled, you can visit. We can take all the time in the world to get to know one another. I want to, Reese, believe me. There is something about you that makes me want to know you better. I'm probably the most predictable man you will ever meet, but with you, I'm willing to change that. I would be a fool if I didn't try to court you and show you all that we can be. This is me taking a chance. Will you, Reese? I promise you won't regret it."

"I'll think about it."

CHAPTER THREE

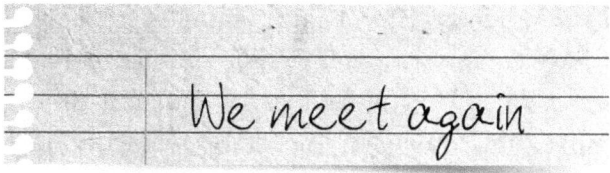

...where past and present collide

WE HAD SOME time before we were to meet Riley and her mother for dinner. I did some work in my study while Jackson settled into his room. The minute our plane touched down in New York, his phone was ringing off the hook. He tweeted to his friends where to meet up later in the evening. Jackson was very excited for his friends to meet Riley. He wanted to go into the Village tonight and show Riley around the city. I didn't have any objections, but I didn't know her mother and how strict she was with her only daughter. Jackson was always accompanied by our driver who doubled as his personal bodyguard. I rarely worried when he was under the watchful eye of Richard, who was never too far behind.

I closed the lid to my laptop and looked around my office. This apartment held the best memories of my time spent here with Reese, and the most painful ones. I never would have predicted after leaving her asleep in our bed that it would be the last time I would lay my eyes on her. And the last time my mouth would ever kiss her lips. I kissed her goodbye, and added to memory her beautiful scent. It was a scent that I craved on a daily basis, I could never get enough of her. My family owned this building, and this was my private home that I shared my time with Reese in. After she left me, I could never bring myself to completely abandon it. After leaving New York for California to begin what I believed would be my new life, I packed up my personal things and said goodbye to not only New York, but to Reese.

Over the years, I used this penthouse when I was in town for work. It never brought me joy after Reese, or Elizabeth, for that matter. After Elizabeth died, I had the entire penthouse redecorated, all except my bedroom.

My bedroom was the last place I shared with Reese, and I wasn't ready to let it go, maybe not ever. Walking over to the safe, I opened it and looked at its contents. I had stowed away some of her pictures, along with her first professional magazine cover. She looked absolutely breathtaking. This lovely girl who I was to share my life with was smiling back at me, and then she was gone. I traced her face with my fingers, trying to remember what she felt like under the warmth of my hands against her skin. She completely submitted to me when we were making love or fucking hard up against a door or a wall. She was mine. Reese was my woman.

Damn me for not trying harder to find her. But then Elizabeth telling me that she was pregnant with my child was the game changer for me. Reese was gone, and Elizabeth was with me and pregnant with Jackson. In that moment, I put away all of my hurt and pain, and I knew I needed to step up and try to be the man Elizabeth deserved. I owed her that much.

I was about to close the safe when my eyes found the old, tattered ring box. I couldn't handle opening it, so I shut the safe door and closed the painting over it. Why was I torturing myself with the painful reminders of my past? That damn ring! Her grandmother repeatedly returned it to me. I lost count of how many times I attempted to send it to her. That Lila Mitchell was almost as stubborn as her granddaughter. God, I miss that woman. It was years since I even allowed myself to remember her. I wasn't sure if Nana was even alive.

I fixed myself a drink and clutched the back of my neck. *I have to let this go, I just have to, but how do I do this? This is what happens to me every time I am in this fucking city.* My private line was ringing, and I cringed on who would be calling me. As I expected, it was my mother. I had been dodging her calls for a week now. She must have phoned my office and was told where I was, unless Jackson told her. He loved his grandparents very much, despite how I felt about them. After losing Elizabeth, I was left alone to raise our son. I don't know what I would have done if Jackson died along with his mother.

His birth was touch and go for a while there. His cord was tangled around his neck and the doctors were unsure if he was deprived of oxygen. My wife was on the operating table. She was declared brain dead after suffering a massive stroke. Elizabeth was never going to recover, would never know our child. Life was incredibly unfair and cruel. I held her hand as I listened to her breaths being controlled by a machine. While the doctors worked on our son, I leaned into my wife's ear.

"I am so sorry this happened to you, and to us. I never thought I would be doing this without you. How can I do this? I will never be able to thank you for this incredible gift you have given me...our son. I promise you that I will be the best father I can be and always tell our son about you. You were my lifeline when I was drowning. Thank you for loving me, Elizabeth."

I said my goodbyes to my wife and friend. She deserved so much better than half of a man who loved someone else. I kissed her forehead and was startled by the sound of a newborn crying. Our son made it and was screaming at the top of his lungs. I never heard a more beautiful sound in all of my life. The nurse brought him over to me.

My hands were shaking. I was afraid to touch him. The nurse led me out of the room so the doctors could now finish up with Elizabeth.

I sat down in a rocking chair and was given my son. Jackson looked just like me when I was a baby. His hair was dark, and he had my nose. He stopped crying, and he wrapped his finger around mine. No turning back now; I was hooked. My son captured my heart with one touch. His eyes were so bright, they matched his mother's. *I would have to tell him one day about her. How would I explain why she's not here to raise him? It was my job to be mother and father to him, but how?*

Jackson was examined by a team of doctors. I spared no expense when it came to my son. He was perfectly healthy and could go home in a couple of days. After our son was settled into the nursery, I was approached by a transplant team. Elizabeth's organs needed to be harvested, and time was of the essence. I needed to make a decision on what to do. She never told me she was an organ donor, and although she suffered a stroke, her organs were still viable but would eventually shut down.

I signed the transplant papers but wanted to bring Jackson to his mother first. I placed him in his mother's arms. I knew she was gone, but the machines kept her heart still beating, and I wanted our son to feel her. With Elizabeth attached to machines, I couldn't take a picture of them, so I just mentally stored the image in my memory. I would relive this moment with Jackson when he was ready to hear it. I held my son as I watched Elizabeth be taken away by the team of doctors. That day, she would be responsible for saving lives, while hers was lost.

Walking over to my desk, I picked up my wedding photo. Elizabeth looked stunning. Her face was glowing. I questioned God every single day why my Elizabeth was taken from me and from our son. I would have given my life to switch places with her. Jackson needed his mother, but fate served us an incredible blow and took her from all who loved her. I only had a few pictures of her in this home, and of course, Jackson had many in his room. I truly had no time to grieve for my wife. I had a son to raise alone and a company to run. My life completely changed the minute I saw Elizabeth die in front of me. I knew I had to be strong for my son. I made promises to Elizabeth, telling her how much I would miss her and how I would always be the best father I could be to Jackson.

Holding her picture against my heart, I leaned back in my chair and just let my tears flow. This was not an emotion that I was used to or ever allowed myself to feel. I had held back for so many years now for Jackson's benefit. I didn't even know how long I was sitting there without noticing that Jackson had entered my office.

"Dad, are you okay? I tried knocking a few times, but I got worried when you didn't answer."

I quickly wiped my face, and placed the picture back on the desk. Jackson stared at me with worry written all over his face. This was not how I wanted his vacation to begin.

"I'm fine, son. Sorry, I didn't hear you come in."

"Grandmother has been calling. She phoned the desk downstairs, and now has been calling my cell. She's worried about you and says you're avoiding her calls." I sighed and made my way over to my son.

"Jackson, please don't worry about your grandmother. Once again, she is being melodramatic and is only seeking attention. I am not avoiding her calls." I lied.

"I just have a lot on my mind right now, and being here is not helping. I'm sorry."

"Dad, I'm sorry to have dragged you here. I know you only said yes to make me happy. We should have gone to Europe instead."

"Jackson, please don't feel bad because you're in a place that you love. This is an exciting time for you. I want you to enjoy every last bit of it and not worry about your old man, okay?"

"You were crying, dad. I don't even think I can count on one hand how many times I saw you cry. Maybe zero."

"You're right about that, son. This is something I rarely do, but most of the tears were happy ones." I lied.

"Remembering your mother makes me feel all kinds of emotions, and even after all of these years, I still feel her presence. How can I not? I see her in you every day. You have her beautiful eyes."

"You say that to me all the time. Even grandma and grandpa say it."

"It's true, Jackson. The minute I held you in my arms and looked into your eyes, I felt as if I was looking into your mother's eyes, and she was living on through you. Now, let's put this to rest and get ready for dinner."

"What about Grandmother? Will you call her?"

"I will, but tomorrow. Now…let's go meet that girl of yours."

We arrived at the restaurant promptly at seven o'clock. Jackson looked suave for his girl. He wasn't overdressed, but looked good enough to get her attention. The maître d' escorted us to the private dining room that I had reserved for our party. I barely sat down when Jackson spotted Riley walking in. He looked like his heart had just stopped beating. I knew exactly how he felt, because I had experienced that look a long time ago with Reese. She ran into his arms, and he scooped her up into a hug. After witnessing a very public display of affection, I expelled a grunt to let them know they weren't alone.

"Dad, I would like you to meet Riley Briggs. Riley, this is my father, Walker Reed."

I was about to extend my hand and welcome her to New York when her familiar resemblance stopped me in my tracks. I almost felt my heart stop beating when I took in her appearance. She looked like a younger version of Reese.

"Dad, are you okay?" I felt an elbow jab into my ribs, as I came out of my daze. Jackson leaned into my ear and whispered, "Dad, you're staring at my girlfriend. Snap out of it."

I extended my hand to Riley and apologized for my behavior. "My apologies, Riley. You seem to remind me of someone I used to know."

"No worries. It's a pleasure to meet you, Mr. Reed. Jackson has told me so much about you. You could pass for brothers instead of father and son."

I laughed at her compliments, such a beautiful young lady who had sunshine radiating off of her. God, she reminded me of Reese, but I quickly shrugged it off.

"Please, let's all have a seat and order some drinks," I said.

Jackson, always a gentleman, pulled out her chair and gestured his girl to sit. He also placed a linen napkin across her lap. That was the Reed charm at its finest. I needed to calm myself before meeting her mother. Her mother must have been beautiful as well. Jackson must have been embarrassed by my actions. I was sure he would let me know about it later.

"Is your mother joining us, Riley?" I asked.

"Yes sir, she is. Mom had to meet up with a friend before joining us here. She sent me ahead with the car. She sends her apologies for running late, only explaining that she needed to take care of something that couldn't wait."

"I understand, no need to apologize. We can now have some time to get to know one another. Tell me about your family? What does your father do?" After having an earlier conversation with Jackson about Riley, I felt it was only fair to get to know the girl in person who had snared my son's heart.

"Dad, we've only been here for ten minutes. Can you ease up a bit?"

Riley responded, "Jackson, it's fine. That's what this dinner is all about." My son had mouthed the word "Sorry" to his girl. *Oh, he didn't stand a chance against this beauty.* "As you know, we live in Maryland, right outside of Baltimore. My father is a neurosurgeon at Johns Hopkins Hospital. He is also the director of Neurology and the Neurosurgery Aneurysm Center."

"Wait a minute." I had to stop her right there, "Is your father Samuel Briggs?"

"Yes sir, do you know him?"

"In a way, I do, although we never met in person. Three years ago my company was commissioned to build the new wing that now houses the new Aneurysm Center at Johns Hopkins. I had planned

52

on meeting with the surgeon that this building was being built for, but I never had the opportunity. As you now know, the building is named after Jackson's late mother, Elizabeth. I was out of the country during the ribbon cutting ceremony, but my father had taken Jackson to commemorate the day. Jackson told me that was the same day he met you. Thank you for showing him such kindness."

"I'll never forget that day, Mr. Reed. My father was in all his glory with the unveiling of his new wing. He was incredibly proud of his research and the great strides he and his team were working toward. I went to support him in his moment, but I really didn't get a lot of time with him. He was too busy."

"I'm sorry to hear that, Riley. Your father sounds almost heroic. I'd love to shake his hand one day," I said to my son's girl.

"It's okay, Mr. Reed. I can't be bitter about it when the highlight of my day was meeting Jackson."

I can't get over how much this girl resembles Reese. She even blushes like her. I quickly turned to Jackson to shake this déjà vu feeling I was experiencing.

"Jackson, what else can you remember about the dedication? What was your Grandfather doing?"

"I remember Grandfather shaking a lot of hands and posing for photographs." I rolled my eyes. *Yeah that sounds like him, never missing an opportunity to work the crowd.* "After the dedication, I was just hanging out in the background until Grandfather was ready to go. The best part of the day was watching the unveiling of mother's portrait. Dad, I wish you could have seen the reaction on everyone's faces when the curtain was pulled off the painting. When the crowd cleared, I just found myself staring at it, and that's when I met Riley. I hope her father's research can save many lives."

Jackson's face saddened with the mention of his mom, but I also didn't miss him squeezing Riley's hand and glancing up at the ceiling. Another thank you to his mother in heaven. He never got the opportunity to know how extraordinary she was, but he always seemed to find a way to acknowledge her presence. He seemed to be once again comforted by Riley, who was still holding his hand.

"I'm sorry about your mom, Jackson. I visit my father quite often at his hospital, and to see your mother's picture when I'm there makes me feel a bit closer to you. You have her eyes."

My son wiped the lone tear that fell down his cheek. Riley hugged him, and my heart hurt for him. I figured I should lighten the mood. I clapped my hands together and brought Jackson back into the present.

"Well, if I can be sure of anything, I know all of us being here tonight just proves what a small world we live in. My son is dating the daughter of the surgeon I built a building for."

Jackson's cheeks turned three shades of red. "Dad, can you be any more embarrassing?"

"Of course I can, son, but why don't we spread it out during the course of our evening?"

Riley, now smiling, left Jackson with no choice but to laugh. The ice had been broken, and we were all enjoying each other's company. I was wondering what was keeping her mother when Riley received a call. Her mother had just arrived and will join us in a few minutes.

Just then my phone buzzed in my pocket. "I'm sorry, son. I have to take this call. Jacques will escort your mother to our table, Riley, and I will return as soon as I can."

"No worries, Mr. Reed, she was late first."

"You're too kind, and thank you for understanding." *Oh what a sweet girl! Let's hope her mother is just as charming.*

As I exited our private dining room, I met Andre, who escorted me to another room where I could take my call in private. "Donovan, I thought I had given you strict instructions not to disturb me with anything that wasn't pressing."

"I'm sorry, Walker, but it couldn't be helped. Our German counterparts are up in arms with the plan delays."

"How can that be? I just spoke with Tom earlier today, and he said everything was a go and that the plans have been finalized for the Reinhart Building. Now you tell me they're not? I want answers, Donovan, and I want them now!" I realize I was raising my voice a bit louder than I wanted to, but this was unacceptable. And I will not accept this level of incompetence from my staff.

"Walker, I have the master files back at the office. I've already spoken to and calmed Sebastian and Viktor. They were upset at first, but I can assure you that I worked it out. Tom is waiting on me now, and I will personally make sure the building plans are in Sebastian and Viktor's hands by tomorrow morning."

"They better be, Donovan, because if they're not, then it will be your ass that I will hold accountable. E-mail me with the answers I want to hear. This is my time with Jackson, and if it's not time sensitive, then do not call me again. Work it out!"

"Yes sir." I ended my call and clenched my jaw. This was all I needed. This project had been in the works for over two years now. Hours and hours spent on brokering this deal to both our advantages, and I asked a simple task to have the finalized plans messengered over, and that's too hard to handle? I calmed myself, and shut my phone off, preventing anymore interruptions.

I tried to make my way back over to my table while being stopped by Andre. "Mr. Reed, I take it everything has met your expectations so far?"

"Yes, Andre, everything is fine. This is why Brasserie is my favorite restaurant."

Now making the poor sap grin from ear to ear, he escorted me back to my private dining room. I stopped him and made my way back on my own.

As I reached the threshold of the room, I began to feel a familiar magnetic pull. A feeling I hadn't felt in many years. I shook it off. *Stop torturing yourself, man! You're just getting déjà vu because your son's girl looks like your girl!*

Then the feeling became stronger when I heard her voice. The sweet southern twang that could bring me to my knees just above a whisper. *No fucking way! Can it be? Could it?* I scanned the room to catch a glimpse of what I couldn't believe to be true, when my eyes found hers. I actually felt physical pain shooting through my heart. How was this possible? Reese Mitchell cannot be sitting at a table talking and laughing with my son. This was why I felt an instant connection to Riley when meeting her. She was Reese's daughter! I waited all these years to see her again, and yet my feet were planted to the floor. The love of my life was five feet in front of me. I was willing myself to try to step forward when Jackson surprised me.

"Dad, there you are. Riley's mother is waiting to meet you. Come on." He begins to reach for me. I take several steps back.

"Jackson, I need a minute to catch my breath." Clearly taken aback with what I just said, my son's excited expression had fallen to apprehension.

"Are you okay? Are you sick dad?" *Not sick, more like shocked, like when you see a ghost! I want to tell him. She may as well be a ghost, considering how she disappeared without a trace.*

"I'm fine, son. I just finished with a very intense business call, and my blood pressure has risen a bit. I need a few minutes to compose myself."

"Dad, you're three shades of white. Should I get you some water?"

"I'm fine. Please extend my apologies, and I'll be along in a minute."

I send Jackson back inside, and once again try to get myself in check. The last thing I want to do is lose it in front of my son, but this was all too surreal for me. I never thought I would be face to face with my past tonight. I had to admit, she'd been on my mind quite a bit lately, but to see her now was unbelievable. She was still so breathtakingly beautiful. With one last breath, I made my way inside. My son quickly rose to introduce me to Riley's mother.

"Dad, I would like you to meet Riley's mother, Reese. Mrs. Briggs, this is my father, Walker Reed."

Our eyes locked on to one another, and neither one of us said a word. Our kids were looking at us as if we had lost our minds. Reese was silent with glazed over eyes. *Yes, my love, it's me in the flesh. The man who vowed to love you forever, and you tore his heart out by leaving him without ever saying a word.*

I was the first to break our connection and extended my hand out to hers. I slowly pulled her hand to my lips, but made sure I placed an ever so gentle kiss to the inside of Reese's wrist. Always an erogenous zone she could never resist. Bang!! I felt her tremble as if her body recognized my touch.

Seeing her again catapulted me back to the last night I spent with my love. I hadn't looked into her gorgeous brown eyes since that last night together. I had to blink a few times to believe what I was actually seeing was real. I wanted to do something, *I don't know? Take her in my arms? Kiss her madly? I didn't have a clue*, but all I heard in that moment of having my past walk back into my life was the sound of my pounding heart.

"Dad, what's with you tonight? Are you okay?" He asked again.

I tried my best to play it off for Jackson's benefit, and knocked myself back into the present. Riley looked confused, and Reese stood there in silence. I never discussed my private life with Jackson, at least not about Reese. I wasn't sure if this was the right time to reveal it to him. Watching Reese's reaction to me, she wasn't ready either.

"It's a pleasure to meet you, Reese. Please forgive me for my absence when you first arrived. I shall shut my phone off for the rest of our evening, and we can get to know one another better." I wink at her, causing Reese to visibly show me a physical reaction to my suggestion.

Oh hell yes, baby. If I didn't have an audience right now, I'd have you spread out under me, and demanding to know why you left me. Still holding my hand, Reese continued to tremble beneath my touch. She simply said hello, and we took our seats. In under an hour, my life had shifted into another realm. How was this happening? We had been apart from each other for nearly eighteen years and now she's sitting calmly across the table from me. It took every bit of self-control I had in my body not to just take her right here and now. When I kissed her wrist, I could feel her body respond as if it was returning home to me.

I needed a drink—a strong one—to calm my nerves. I signaled over to the waiter and ordered drinks for myself and Reese. She only wanted sparkling water. I ordered a double scotch on the rocks, earning a raised eyebrow look from Reese. What the hell? It was bad enough she pretended not to know me, but to judge me as well on my drink choice? Our eyes were locked on one another, and she dropped her eyes down to the menu. The kids were engaged in their own conversation while Reese and I continued to stare at each other until the drinks arrived.

I cleared my throat and finally was able to speak after draining my glass. I quickly ordered another one.

"May I call you Reese?

"Yes, of course." She politely replied.

Incredibly beautiful, as if time stood still, she was beyond calm. After all of these years, her voice was still the sweetest sound I have ever heard. Her accent alone makes me hard, it always did. I loved her voice, especially when we made love and she was screaming my name. *Oh my god, I have to get some control, or I'm going to lose it.* She made me feel like a teenage boy. I took a breath to calm myself, and I turned to my beautiful angel sitting across from me. *Yes I said it...**my angel**. I never stopped loving her, and I can't even begin to process how she is even here after all of this time. But just you try walking away this time...**Hell No!***

"Before you arrived, I was having a very enlightening conversation with your daughter." *I was about to have some fun with Reese, and I wanted to see how I could make her squirm with my questions.* "Did you know that it was my company that was responsible for your husband's new research wing at Johns Hopkins? Isn't it amazing how life works? Strangers from all over the country can know each other without realizing they are connected by something or someone else?"

I watched Reese shift a bit in her seat. You could tell she was trying to not to be affected by me, but her body told me different, it always did. We never needed words between us. Our bodies spoke for us, and hers was telling me a lot right now.

"Anyway, I only had the opportunity once to travel to Maryland, pity I didn't make more trips. You look so familiar to me; haven't we met before? I don't believe I would have forgotten you if we had." *Mission accomplished...* Reese had turned three shades of red and clearly was uncomfortable, but she held her own.

"Well, Walker, you didn't forget a missed encounter, because we haven't met until tonight. I'm not involved with the hospital in that manner," Reese responded.

"What do you involve yourself in? Do you work? Oh, let me guess, you must have been a model in your younger days. You're quite beautiful, if you don't mind me saying so," I smirked at Reese without ever breaking eye contact with her.

"I actually do mind, Mr. Reed, and I believe my *husband* would as well."

That went to Reese, and right through my fucking heart. I guess I deserved that hit. My son kicked me under the table. I ignored him and his way of getting my attention. I didn't care about anything else at the moment but Reese.

"As a matter of fact, I did some modeling while I was in college. It helped pay for my tuition, and it was something I enjoyed doing."

"Did you ever just wake up one day with the realization that you wanted to drop everything and pursue it full-time?"

"Modeling was never my first choice as a career, but it was a way for me to see the world."

See the world...my ass! You left me to see the world? Didn't you know you were my world? I never stopped telling you that.

"So how long did this modeling career last for you? Where would I have seen your work?"

"I was primarily a runway model for designers. I did some magazine layouts, but I stopped after I met my husband."

Now that hit me hard, as if she just punched me in my stomach. *Husband? Dammit Reese, I should have been your husband. None of this is making any sense.*

"What about college? Where did you attend school?" I asked.

"For my first three years I attended Georgia State University. I transferred to NYU for my senior year."

"I attended NYU, but I don't seem to remember you," I snidely remarked.

"I left school before I was to graduate. I received my degree several months later."

"Forgive me for asking, but why would you leave school if you only had a few months left? Was there a reason why you had to do that?" I was trying my hardest to break her down, but she remained calm and steady. She took my questions as bullets that bounced off her bulletproof vest. I was the one who was exhausted after questioning her, but I wanted answers, dammit.

Before Reese could answer me, Jackson interrupted her. "Dad, how about we change the subject? Riley and I are getting a serious case of whiplash with the back and forth match you two have going on. Mrs. Briggs, I apologize for my dad's behavior."

I couldn't believe what I just heard: my son apologizing for me? This was a first.

"Jackson, do I need to remind you who the adult is at this table?"

"No, sir, but I think you're making Mrs. Briggs and Riley uncomfortable with all your questions. I'm sorry, dad, if I overstepped."

I was angry at my son for calling me out in front of Reese, if he only knew what she had put me through. I was at a loss for words now, and Reese was just sitting there not saying a word while I took the fall.

Now looking back to Reese and Riley, I say, "You have to excuse me, I was simply wanting to know you better. Sorry if my questions were a bit much."

Riley was the first to speak up. "Mr. Reed, I actually enjoyed it. My parents hardly talk to one another, so this was fun to watch."

My ears pricked up a bit as I raised an eyebrow. *Very interesting to hear that...*

Reese finally spoke again. "Riley, that's not true, and please don't speak of your father in that way."

"I'm sorry, mom, but it's the truth."

Hearing Riley say that about her parents spoke volumes on what kind of marriage Reese was involved in. Clearly by looking at her, she wasn't happy with the mention of her husband. After things calmed, we managed to get through dinner with minimal conversation. The kids were once again in their own private bubble chatting away, while Reese and I were just numb. She hardly looked up at me, and when she did, her eyes were glazed over.

I couldn't bear to see her cry, but dammit, she owed me an explanation on why she left. *Come hell or high water, she will talk to me.*

Jackson asked Reese a question. "Mrs. Briggs, if it's alright with you, would you mind if I take Riley out and show her around the city tonight? I have our driver to accompany us. Richard will make sure to get her back to your hotel."

"Please, mom, can I go?"

"Yes, you may go, Riley. Please keep your phone on, and don't be too late."

Riley jumped up and down and hugged her mother. Jackson gave me a look telling me that we would talk later. I didn't doubt that we would. Jackson couldn't possibly understand why I behaved the way I did tonight. I lost my mind at the sight of Reese. She was still so beautiful, and I couldn't help but want her.

After dinner, we walked our children out and watched as they drove away. Reese turned away from me and attempted to hail a cab. What the hell was she doing? I would be damned if I was going to let her leave me now, especially without answering any of my questions as to why she left me so many years ago.

"Where the hell do you think you're going?"

"I would think that would be obvious, Walker. I'm going back to my hotel."

"The hell you are, woman. Our evening is just getting started, and you're not going anywhere. You left me once, and I will be damned if I will let you go again without the long overdue explanation you owe me."

Reese was seething with anger, I couldn't tell if she wanted to slap me or scream. She turned away from me again and began sprinting in her stiletto heels. I reached her within seconds, and now I was done playing this cat and mouse game. I hoisted her body up over my shoulders and signaled to Stephen to pull over.

"Put me down, Walker! You can't just manhandle me in the middle of the street."

"I can, and I will, Reese. If you remember anything about me at all, you should know I never walk away from a challenge, unlike someone I know."

I slid Reese down my body and placed her into the back of the limo. She felt so good. Her smell was so intoxicating. My erection was already rising under my pants. She was so close to my proximity, my body craved her.

She was ignoring me, and her silence was pissing me off. I tried to calm myself and regain my control, but seeing her sitting before me was everything I had wanted since the last night we spent together. How she is here with me now is nothing more than fate returning her back to her rightful place.

I shifted in my seat, while Reese continued to look out the window, ignoring me. Now that I had her here, I needed to get her to communicate with me, but how? She looked angry, but yet she was the one who left me.

"Reese, will you look at me please?"

I tried to soften my voice. She refused; no one ignores me. I took a deep breath and placed my hands on her shoulders to turn her to face me. She had her head down, and then I cupped her beautiful face into my hands. I stared into her eyes of caramel brown; any man could get lost in them for days. I wondered if her husband knew how lucky he was to have her. Without thinking another thought, I stroked my thumb over her bottom lip, and her body easily responded to my touch. We felt each other's trembles, as we reconnected.

I was back to the last night we spent together. I saw the fire in Reese's eyes, the carnal hunger we both had felt with each other. All I had to do now was kiss her. She was now biting her bottom lip: *Green light...go!* I pulled her into me and slammed my lips onto hers, never giving her a chance to pull away. She would decimate me if she did. I hung on for as long as I could until our connection finally broke.

Her lips were now puffy and swollen, a beautiful sight. I wanted to take Reese right there in the limo. My hands were traveling up her thigh and under her revealing skirt. Reese let out sexy moans of pleasure, as I continued to touch her and got reacquainted with her body. Her hand finally found mine and stopped me. "Walker, please stop. I can't do this." She straightened herself up and turned away from me again.

"I'm sorry, Reese. I shouldn't have done that to you. All logic and reason gets lost when I'm around you; how is that even possible after all these years apart? Can we go somewhere to talk? I need answers, Reese, and you're the only one that can give them to me."

"I'm not the only one, Walker," Reese replied, still breathing heavily.

"What is that supposed to mean? What are you not telling me?"

"Walker, you can ask your father why I left you. After all, he was the sole reason behind it."

My head began to spin with this revelation. What did my father do to her? I always felt he could be the reason, but I never had enough to implicate him in anything. I needed to know now more than ever; she was not leaving this car until I knew.

"What about my father, Reese? What does Phillip have to do

with you leaving me all those years ago?"

"You need to ask him, Walker. I can't tell you."

"Reese, my father can't tell me either because the arrogant bastard died a month ago. Whatever he did to you, I must know…now!"

"Gee, I'm sorry for your loss, Walker. I won't sit here and pretend that I will mourn his death. He ruined my life and our life together."

"Reese, what did he do?" I was so angry that it felt like I clenched my jaw with every word I mouthed to Reese. "I will not ask you again. Please talk to me and tell me what he did."

Reese was fighting her resolve to talk to me. She looked like she wanted to scream it and tell me the truth, but something was holding her back. What did my father have on her? He loved his blackmail and threats. He was a man of his word. If Phillip Reed wanted to hurt you, he could easily do so. He had resources at his disposal with just one phone call. He must have had something on Reese and forced her to leave me. It was the only logical answer. She was crying now, and her lips were trembling. I wanted to take her in my arms and comfort her.

I could never bear to see her in pain. No man who loves his woman ever wants to see her cry. I felt as if a knife was being plunged into my chest. I couldn't take it anymore, and I wrapped my arms around her body. Reese continued to cry into my chest, as I gently stroked her back up and down. If she didn't start communicating with me, my body was going to do all the talking.

CHAPTER FOUR

Talk to me...

WHAT AM I supposed to say to Walker? Sorry about your father dying, but he was a selfish bastard who destroyed me by forcing me out of your life. My cheek was still pressed into Walker's chest. He was waiting for me to explain, but giving me the time I needed. This was the man I had always loved. As angry as Walker could get, he would never hurt me, and he would always show how much he loved me. In my wildest dreams, I never could have imagined that my entire world would shift tonight when I walked into that restaurant.

I was the coward who ran from him, like an escaping fugitive. I never considered what my leaving really did to him. He must have been out of his mind when he came back to his apartment to find me gone. I had one hour to get out of town, according to Phillip's instructions. He was cold, determined to erase me from Walker's life.

I looked up and took in Walker's chiseled features. Time had been kind, and Walker was still devilishly handsome. I cleared my throat and tried to erase the dirty thoughts I was now having as I continued to look at him. My life with Samuel was not even a thought in my head at the moment. I wanted to rip off Walker's shirt and trail my tongue up and down his chest. Walker was giving me all the signs that I could take back what was mine...he wouldn't stop me.

If a bucket of cold water were present, I would douse myself and cool off. No matter what signals my traitorous body was showing him, I was still a married woman. I couldn't betray my marriage. Finally coming to my senses, I removed myself from his arms. And already felt the loss of our connection.

"Walker, I'm sorry. I don't know what came over me. I shouldn't have kissed you or even let you touch me the way you did. I crossed a line here tonight."

"I don't see it that way at all, Reese. Turning around to see you standing in front of me after all our years apart only proved one thing."

"Which was what, Walker?"

"My feelings for you have not changed, Reese. I almost passed out when I met Riley. She's you, eighteen years ago. Jackson had to elbow me in my ribs to snap me out of my gazing at your daughter. She must think I'm completely nuts."

"I wouldn't worry about Riley. She only has eyes for your son, and she probably didn't even notice."

"Well, Jackson did, and I'm sure he will let me know how he felt about it when I see him again. What are the chances that our children will be attending the same school we attended, and have now fallen in love?"

"That thought has been crossing my mind as well. Let's just hope the apple doesn't fall too far from the tree. Hopefully he's nothing like his grandfather."

Now Walker's calm demeanor changed. I had insulted him just now, what the hell was I doing? It was his father who I was angry with, not him.

"What does that mean, Reese? You don't even know Jackson. He is the best thing I have in my life."

"I'm sorry. I didn't mean to say that about your son. Jackson seems wonderful, and Riley cares for him a great deal."

"Then why the snide remark about him? Will you now tell me

what my father did to you, and to us?"

"It's complicated, and a very long story. I don't even know where to begin."

"Lucky for you, I have all the time in the world and have waited long enough to hear your reason why you left me."

"I hate how you keep saying 'how I left you.' Walker, don't you know that I not only left you, I left us? I mourned the loss of our relationship every day since I walked out of your apartment, or shall I say…was forced to leave."

"Reese, you don't have to be afraid any more. I am here with you right now, please talk to me. You talk about mourning us; you have no idea what I have been through. I should hate you for leaving me, but instead I sit here forgetting all the pain I suffered. And I all I want to do is just bury myself deep inside you and fuck you until you scream my name. How sick is that? I'm back there again, Reese, our last night together at my apartment. I remember every detail about that night. I can even tell you what you were wearing when you arrived, until I removed you from your clothing."

REESE SMILED AT me. She didn't forget how I pulled her in and took her right up against the door. It had been many days since we had seen each other. Our schedules were busy with school, our work commitments, and I was traveling back and forth to California. I couldn't help myself when my eyes met hers. I was on fire with desire for my woman. We made love throughout my apartment, never making it to the actual bed.

"Walker, how can I begin to tell you how sorry I am for leaving you? I should have been stronger, and not let your father bully me. I remember feeling you kissing me in the early morning. I believe I even heard you say that you would be back soon. I must have drifted back to sleep, and then I heard knocking at the door. I thought you forgot your key. I wrapped myself with a sheet and ran to the door to greet you. To my shock, your father was on the other side with his lawyer, scowling back at me. Without asking if you were home, they walked right in, as if they knew I was alone. Your father ordered me to dress and meet him in the living room. I was praying you would return, so I wouldn't have to talk with him. Your father didn't give me a choice, so I dressed and sat down."

Reese continued, "He declined coffee. He wanted to get to the point for his reason for being there. I sat down and listened. His lawyer, Jacobson, retrieved two manila folders from his brief case. He handed them over to your father, and Phillip showed me what they contained. I was horrified at what I was looking at. Walker, the folder contained the very pictures that I never wanted you to know about. They were the same nude modeling pictures that your father had threatened me with on New Year's Eve so many years ago. I thought I would never have to think about them again after you confronted your father. He obviously knew they could still hurt me, and believe me when I say that they did, in ways that I can never explain."

"Reese, I told you that I didn't care about those photos. I told you repeatedly how I knew and loved the real girl, not the one in those photos. You and those other girls were victimized, and preyed upon by that sleaze of a photographer. Please tell me, baby, that you didn't run because of those photos? You had to know that I would have never let my father hurt you that way. Reese, please talk to me?"

TO LOOK AT Walker, after all these years hurt my heart more now than the hurt I felt the day I left him. He looked so broken at that moment, and he sat there asking me to relive the most painful time in all of my life, but this was his story too.

"Walker, there is so much more you don't know." He took my trembling hands and folded them into his, willing me to talk to him.

"Enlighten me, Reese, I must know everything," he said.

"Walker, when you confronted your father and declared our love for one another in front of him and all of his friends, I thought our fight with him was over, but I was so wrong. Your father hated me, and he stopped at nothing to remove me from your life. I have no explanation to why he did what he did to me, and to us, but I was a fool to believe that he would just stop."

I WAS REELING from what Reese was telling me, but I needed to allow her to continue with her story. She looked so drained now. She asked for some water and needed to take a few breaths to compose herself before continuing.

"After perusing the file, I ripped up the pictures and slammed the file down onto the table. Your father laughed at my reaction, telling me that he had many copies. He threatened to show you the photos and expose me to the world. He would begin with you, and then stuff every mailbox of all my professors at NYU. He didn't care that I had already told you about it, he said that the pictures would speak volumes about me, and the whore behind them. He told me that you would be disgusted and would never be able to move past it. I never believed that, Walker, and again I tried to argue with your father that you loved me and wanted to marry me. I even showed him my locket, and he just didn't care. Walker, your father was ruthless. I believe that was the word you used when telling me about him, but he was so much more. He was cold, heartless, and what he showed me next completely destroyed me."

"What was it? My god you were twenty one years old! You didn't have time for a past, let alone do anything that would have made you leave me. What the hell did he have on you, Reese?"

"Mr. Jacobson handed me a check for one hundred thousand dollars and told me to take it to start a new life."

"Stop the car!" I screamed at Stephen. I leaped out from the back of the limo and emptied the contents of my dinner all over the sidewalk. I was retching and couldn't catch my breath. Oh my god, my father paid off Reese to leave me. He fucking ruined my life. Reese put her hands on my shoulder, but I pulled away from her. I never felt so betrayed in all of my life. I loved this woman standing in front of me for most of my adult life. How could she do this to me?

"Did you take the money, Reese? Please tell me that you didn't."

"I didn't take it, Walker. I would have never done that. Walker, please understand there is so much more to tell you."

I calmed down and stepped back into the car. Reese joined me and continued with her story.

"Walker, after I refused his money, your father told me something that I hadn't had the chance to tell you. I had planned the night before, but you distracted me. I was going to tell you when you returned to the apartment, but never got the chance."

"What, Reese? What is it that you're not saying?"

"I was pregnant, Walker, and carrying your child. Your father somehow knew this and told me that if I even dare try to have your bastard child, he would ruin me and make me suffer for trapping you. He told me that I was only a means to an end for you. After you had your fill of me, you would leave me and marry Elizabeth. He convinced me that this was your plan, and I was easily disposable. I wasn't thinking clearly, Walker, so for a second I believed him, and he knew he had me. Then his lawyer handed me the other envelope. They both sat there waiting to take pleasure in seeing my reaction."

"What the hell did it contain, Reese?"

"Your father had the deed to my grandparent's properties in Georgia. He said he had the power to own them all, and once he did, he would level the properties to the ground. If you believe anything, Walker, please believe that I tried to fight back. I begged your father on my hands and knees to not hurt my family and let me stay with you. I cried, clawing my way through his thick coat of armor, but he wouldn't listen to me, Walker. He told me that I was the one responsible for this, and it was my fault. If I didn't want to hurt my family, then my only choice was to leave you. He had it all arranged. All I had to do was walk out the door, and out of your life. He promised not to hurt my grandparents, and he would take care of you. Please say something, Walker."

I felt tired and defeated from all of these shocking revelations. I was trying to process everything. I asked, "What happened to the baby, Reese? Do I have another child out in the world that doesn't know I exist? Is Riley my daughter?"

"No, she's not, and no, you don't, Walker. Your father left me devastated and ripped open to my core. I had no choice but to leave you. I went to my apartment and packed a bag. I was on the next flight to Los Angeles, and I never looked back."

"Yes, I know that, Reese. I was there, remember? Answer my fucking question. What happened to the baby, Reese? Did you have an abortion? Did you give the baby up for adoption? What the fuck happened?"

"I would never hurt our baby, Walker. I loved him from the minute I found out that I was pregnant."

71

"You loved him so much, but yet you didn't tell me. How could you keep this from me? And my father knew this entire time, but I was kept in the dark about my baby? Wait a minute. You said...*him*."

My head was fucking spinning right now. I had a son, my first son, and I never knew he existed. I turned back to Reese and begged her to go on with her story.

"I need to know everything, Reese. Please tell me what happened next."

"I can't, Walker. Please, it's too painful, and I'm exhausted."

"Exhausted? Really? How about all the nights that I went without sleep after you left? You leaving nearly destroyed me. You had to know that it would."

"Of course I knew! I begged your father not to do this to us, but he wouldn't listen. When I left you that note, I had no time to really even think about my words, and that bastard of a lawyer actually checked what I had written to you. Your father read it too, and he almost laughed at me. But he gave his nod of approval, and then his lawyer handed it back to me. I was praying you would read between the lines and figure out that I would never have done this on my own. But you never came for me, and every day that passed, I was more lost than ever."

"It was the same for me, Reese. The unknown was the hardest to come to terms with. I did search for you. I hired private detectives, but all the leads came up empty. It was as if you just disappeared off the grid, never to be heard from again. Now after all this time wondering what the hell happened to you...you materialize right in front of me. Please tell me the rest, I need to know everything."

She continued, "When I left New York, I had no idea where to go. I couldn't go back home to Georgia. I was too ashamed, and I knew if I told Nana and Granddaddy, they would have wanted to go up against your father, and I just couldn't risk that. If anything were to happen to them and their land, I would have never forgiven myself."

"You had to know that Pottersville would be my first place to search for you. I took the first flight out, Reese, and when I got there, Lila was heartbroken. She said that you called her and told her to tell me not to look for you. Why? How could you ask her something like that? It broke her heart."

"That was another choice that I had no control of, Walker. Your father watched my every move. He knew you would search for me and he thought I would go home, but I went to California instead. I spent the next three months in a small one bedroom apartment. I owned nothing but the clothes on my back and the picture I took from your nightstand. It was my saving grace every time I looked at it. Every single day and night, I prayed on it for you to find me. I never wanted to leave you, Walker, not in a million years. I'm so sorry."

"Reese, I'm having a difficult time wrapping my head around this. How could you be in California and not seek me out? You knew that's where I was moving. We were in the same city, and our paths never crossed? What the hell? Why didn't you try to contact me? You mean to tell me that my father had you on what, twenty four/seven surveillance? Come on, Reese, if his goal was to eradicate you from my life, then why track your every move? You were gone already."

"Yes, I was, and he wanted me to stay gone. I was still a liability Walker, don't you get it? I was pregnant with your child, and although he forced me out and held my grandparents over my head, he knew I was still going to try to reach you. All I wanted was to tell you the truth, but every time I tried, he stopped me. Right before I flew back to New York, I saw you on the grounds of Reed Global. You were walking the path to the entrance with your father. I saw you stop and look around. Did you feel me there Walker?"

"Oh my god. Yes! The gravitational pull I was feeling was strong, and I instantly felt you. Why didn't I see you then?"

"Before I could call out to you, I was grabbed from behind. He covered my mouth and held me until your father joined us."

"Who was it, Reese?"

"Your father's bodyguard, Ralston."

"Motherfucker! Did he hurt you?"

"Not physically, but mentally the two of them kicked me over and over again, until I was completely shattered, kind of like what I'm feeling now."

"I'm so sorry, baby, I'm so sorry. I know this hurts you to relive this, but I need to know everything. Please go on."

"I tried to stand up to your father, and I told him that I told my family everything, and we were willing to fight him. I threatened him with empty promises thinking it might work, but all it did was anger him more, and then I collapsed. I was on my knees again, begging him to please stop this crusade of hating me and let me go to you. I wanted to tell you so badly about our baby and beg you to forgive me, but again, Phillip wouldn't listen. He said you moved on without me, and I was to take my bastard child and go away and never ever to return again. What could I do, Walker? He won, and I let him."

Reese continued, "Shortly after my confrontation with your father, I managed to return to New York, and it was Freddy who convinced me to try to find and talk to you. I was willing to do anything to see you. I was going to beg for forgiveness and ask you to take me back. If we found our way back to each other, then I would have told you everything about what your father did to me. My agent, Marsha, if you remember her, booked me into the hotel under a false name. I was going to rest a bit before calling you. I wasn't feeling well on the plane, and I just got sicker once I checked in to my room. It was early morning, and I tried to eat some breakfast, and while going through the papers, there you were on Page Six of the newspaper. You were hand in hand with Elizabeth, looking so happy, and she clearly looked like the happiest woman in the world. She finally got her man, but it didn't matter. I had your child, and nothing was going to stop me this time."

She went on, "I thought I was strong enough to leave to find you, but after seeing what I saw, the pain in my stomach intensified, and it literally brought me to my knees. Something was horribly wrong, and I was afraid I was losing the baby. I called for help, and when I woke up, I was in a New York City hospital. I'm so sorry, Walker. The baby didn't make it. I was just beginning my second trimester of pregnancy and was told that our baby may have had abnormalities that contributed to the miscarriage, but I never believed that."

"So I'm clear on all of this, Reese. My father blackmailed you with something from your past. He knew you were pregnant with my child and purposely kept it from me. He fabricated lies on top of lies to make you leave me, and then when you finally decide to return to me, you lose our baby. Is that all of it? Or do you want to rip my heart out even more? …And a Page Six picture, Reese? A stupid fucking publicity photo made you so physically sick that you lost our baby over it?"

"Walker, don't you dare turn this around on me! It wasn't just seeing the picture. How about me finding out I'm pregnant, and I'm scared to death and all alone. I barely had time to process what was happening, and then your father and his lawyer and bodyguard bullied me out of your life, and then put me through more months of stress and heartache. That's what contributed to losing our son, Walker. I never stood a chance against your father, and he knew it all along. You were just as much his puppet as I was. Only the difference is that he played you behind the scenes, without you ever knowing anything."

I had always known my father to be a bastard, but I never knew what he was truly capable of, until hearing Reese's story. It was my story, too, and I was just another pawn in his chess game of controlling my life. As much as it pained me to hear this, I couldn't lash out at her. This was not her fault.

"Reese, can I please hold you?" I asked.

She didn't hesitate this time and threw herself into my arms. I needed to feel her body against mine. *My sad, broken girl. Hell, I was broken too!* Whispering into my chest, Reese was crying, and I could barely hear her struggling voice.

"I'm so sorry, Walker. You can blame your father for all of this, and for a long time I did, but the blame also falls onto me. I should have been stronger and not be afraid. If I stayed and waited for you, I could have told you everything, but I ran like a coward and risked my health. If I could go back in time to change the course I was foolishly led on, I would do it, but it's too late for us now."

"The hell it is, Reese. Don't you see that this was meant to be? Even after all of these years, we are here and we can begin again. I love you, and I never stopped wanting you."

"Walker, how can you say that? You married Elizabeth, and you had a child with her. A son who is now falling in love with my daughter? How can you possibly see us together after everything I have told you? What about Elizabeth? Where does she fit into you wanting to be with me?"

"Elizabeth suffered a stroke while in labor with our son. She was placed on a machine while our son was delivered by a caesarian. She never regained consciousness and was ruled brain dead. As her husband, I had to make the decision to respect her wishes and remove her from life support. I brought my son home two days later, and we buried his mother. The building that I built for your husband to perform miracles in that is my shrine to her. The building is dedicated in her honor, and it's what brought our kids together."

"I'm so sorry, Walker. I never knew that she died, I feel three shades of foolish for not knowing that."

"How could you know, Reese? I was living out in California and about to begin my new role as a widower and father. I was twenty two years old. I thought I would have Elizabeth with me to help raise Jackson, and then the unthinkable happened. My father handed me over the business, and it was mine to run. Sadly, I confess, it's all I know. I have raised Jackson on my own and became the mogul my father always wanted me to be."

"Walker, I know I don't have the right to ask, but what made you stop looking for me?"

"You have every right Reese, but the truth is, after you called me and I begged you to come back to me, I was just done. I lost all hope on ever finding you. Freddy cut me off, and anyone that knew us had no clue to your whereabouts. Like I said, Reese, you just disappeared."

"Um…Walker, I never called you."

"Yes, you did, Reese. I received several calls from you, but you never answered me back, you just stayed on the line and listened to me pour my heart out, until it shattered even more."

"I swear that wasn't me. It had to be your father trying to throw you off. If you were so close to finding me, and then you got a mystery call allegedly from me, then he had to know you may eventually reach your breaking point and give up. Clearly, you did. I'm sorry, I don't mean to say it with such vehemence in my tone, but it hurts like hell, maybe even more so now."

"Reese, I never believed that you left me on your own. I didn't want to, something always felt wrong about it, but I never could prove my father's involvement in it. He always admitted to not liking you, and he never tried to hide it. So that was his way of manipulating me out in the open. Yes, I married Elizabeth, but Reese, you were always in my heart. After you left, it was Elizabeth who saved me. I drank myself into anything that would numb my pain, and then she was there to pick up the pieces of my life. I don't know how I would have survived if it wasn't for Elizabeth. I know this hurts you to hear that, but it's the truth and why hide anything now."

"Walker, do you think she knew what your father was up to?"

"I can't believe she willingly had anything to do with our breakup. You didn't know Elizabeth like I did. We grew up together, and she was not like the rest of the rich, high society girls that were in our circle. She was kind, and very beautiful inside and out. She helped me return to the land of the living and saved me from self-destructing. Elizabeth knew who my heart belonged to. I never kept my feelings from her, but she didn't care and loved me anyway. I never deserved her, but she always told me that I did and we could start our own happiness on our terms. After I graduated, we became lovers, and I guess you can call it dating. I wasn't ever with anyone else. Our families were thrilled, and I was on my way to taking over the throne at Reed Global."

"We married shortly after Elizabeth discovered she was pregnant with Jackson. As much as I loved you, Reese, I married her, because I was about to become a father. I stepped up and tried my best to be a husband for her. We lived happily until she died."

Reese and I had been in this car for hours now. We still had so much to talk about, but I knew we each needed to get back to our kids. My cell phone beeped a while ago, and it was Jackson telling me that he was on his way home. I was still holding Reese, as she had her arms wrapped around my waist. I gently kissed the top of her head and inhaled her beautiful scent. She always smelled like exotic berries mixed with vanilla. I always laughed at her crazy mixtures of products. She used to combine several scents to get the perfect one for her hair. I playfully teased her about her career choices. She should have been a chemist instead of a model or teacher.

I could have stayed in that car forever with her, but our time together was coming to an end, at least for now.

"Jackson and Riley are on their way back from the Village. Check your phone. I'm sure Riley texted you as well."

"Can we stay like this for a few more minutes?" she whispered to me.

"You can stay…forever." She looked up at me and let her tears fall, but she pulled away before I could wipe them off her cheeks.

"Forever." If only…

Hearing Walker repeat the same words to me now like he did back then gave me a glimmer of hope. The fantasy was always better than the reality. I could easily get caught up in believing we could be together again, but how? I was married to Samuel. I had built an entire life around my husband, our daughter, his career, and left no room for me.

I wouldn't allow myself to dream of a future with Walker, it was too late for us. I had to stop this and get out of this car before I allowed myself to fantasize a future with him. Once and for all, I would close the door to the life I was supposed to have with Walker Reed.

But how could I? Walker sat beside me, anticipating my next move, smelling great. I was still afraid to show him how much I loved him.

My mind was revisiting me asking Samuel for a divorce. He didn't take it well, and he showed me what he thought of my request.

The proximity of Walker and me was overwhelming. I needed to get out of the car. He stared at me in silence. God, what must he be thinking right now?

I checked my phone, and sure enough Riley let me know she was on her way back to our hotel. They had a fabulous time with all of their new friends and Jackson's friends from his years spent in New York. My daughter was falling in love with Walker's son. How would I ever begin to explain my connection to his father? I couldn't keep this from my daughter or my husband. Who knew how Samuel would react to knowing that the man that built his precious hospital wing was also the love of my life and the man who still held my heart. Samuel already showed me that he was not willing to let me go. The faint bruises on my arms proved that.

CHAPTER FIVE

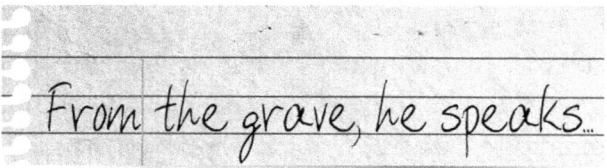

From the grave, he speaks...

WE WENT BACK to Reese's hotel. I didn't want her to step out of this car, and my life, again. I needed more time with Reese, but our kids were waiting on us. Up until I walked in to that restaurant tonight, I never thought I would ever see Reese again. How could I ever return to anything I ever considered normal in my life? How can I resume the life I had been living without Reese in it? It's impossible.

"Walker, I have to go inside now. Riley should be back in our suite by now. I don't even know what I will say to her."

"Reese, I don't keep secrets from my son. Jackson will ask me how I spent my evening and question my behavior at dinner. It's not that I didn't want to share our history with him, but my life with you all those years ago was private, and it was mine. He never knew his mother, and why tell him the reasons I was with her? I may have no choice now. Will you tell Riley?"

"I may have to do the same, Walker. Riley is a very inquisitive young woman, and we are very close. The real issue is how do I explain you to Samuel?"

"Did you ever tell him about me?"

"Yes, I did. I told him everything about us and how in love we were."

"Did he also know about my father and his orchestrated plan to remove you from my life?"

"Yes. I had no reason to keep anything from Samuel. After losing the baby, I truly had lost everything that mattered. I was starting over, and with Samuel. He too knew who my heart belonged to, but didn't care." She was about to say something else, but she was interrupted by her cell phone beeping.

"Walker, it's Riley. She's upstairs waiting for me. I really need to go."

"Reese, please wait. Will you meet me tomorrow? I have to make a trip out to the Hamptons, but when I return, I would like to see you. Please say you will think about it?" My heart raced, waiting on Reese to answer me.

"Okay. Call me when you get back into town." That was all she said, and then she was out of the limo and walking through the hotel doors.

I felt sick again in the wake of her absence. I couldn't bear to let her go after finding out why she left me all those years ago. I was a smart man who believed that if you crossed the street without looking, you may get struck by a car. Seeing Reese tonight was simply fate. It was our destiny to be together. I had to make her see that she belonged with me and that we could have the life that we were cheated out of having. Our future was taken from us, and it was time we took back what was always meant to be.

"Stephen, take me back to the penthouse."

"Yes, sir, right away."

The first thing I needed to do was call Miles Jacobson. He would regret ever making the decision to help my father hurt me and Reese. I dialed his number, and he answered on the second ring.

"Good evening, Walker, what a pleasant surprise hearing from you."

"I need to see you first thing in the morning at my family home in the Hamptons. Call my mother and arrange to have our meeting there. I need to go through my father's papers and anything else you may have. Am I making myself clear to you, Miles?"

"Of course, Walker. I can be there by nine."

I ended my call with Miles, just barely holding back my anger. I usually get right to the point when discussing all matters of business, but this was personal. Stephen silently listened to the tone of my voice. He was not only my personal driver; he was also my go-to man when I needed something done. He was fully equipped with many skills that had proven to be useful to me. I needed him to take care of several tasks before I met with my mother and Jacobson. I walked in through our foyer to see Jackson waiting for me. I'm sure he wanted to talk to me about what happened at dinner.

"Hey, dad, where have you been?" My son actually looked concerned, but this was odd of him to question me. "I texted you a few times, but you never replied back."

"Were you worried about me son? I'm a big boy and can take care of myself."

"Yes, dad, I was. After your weird behavior tonight at the restaurant, and then not responding to my texts, I was worried about you. You're my father, and my only parent."

Looking back at Jackson, I already regretted being curt with him. I knew he was telling me the truth.

He worriedly whispered, "You don't have to tell me if you don't want to, I just want to make sure you're okay."

"I'm fine, son, but can you give me some time? I'm exhausted from traveling today, and I need to get some sleep. Your grandmother needs to see me, so I will be leaving first thing in the morning to drive out to the house."

"Dad, can't grandmother drive into the city to see us? I was really counting on you attending the parent's luncheon with me."

"I already made arrangements with Riley's mother. She will attend the luncheon with you both, and I will join you all later for dinner."

"Dad, I have plans tomorrow night with Riley, remember? We

have tickets to the theater and then on to dinner with friends."

"Jackson, please understand I would never break plans with you if it wasn't important. I need to see my mother tomorrow. I may miss the luncheon, but I will make the alumni meet and greet. I give you my word, I will be there." I hated this position my dead father had placed me in. Now I have disappointed my son when he needed my support.

"I understand, dad. Please give my best to grandmother from me." Jackson turned away from me and walked upstairs to his room. He touched on the subject about dinner, but never asked me anything else about it. I was wondering if Riley was questioning Reese.

There was no way I could keep my connection with Reese a secret from Jackson. I would get the information I needed first, then sit Jackson down and explain it all to him. He had a very kind soul; he got his goodness from his mother. I could only pray that I would not tarnish her memory in Jackson's eyes. He never knew his mother, only knowing her through pictures and home videos. He had a solid relationship with her parents, and they were close. They kept their daughter's memory alive for Jackson's benefit, and that was always something I admired about Elizabeth's parents.

The Townsends were good people. Elizabeth's father made his fortune through real estate. He owned many properties throughout New York City. He and his wife now lived in Arizona. He was retired and spent his days on the golf course. Jackson spent two weeks on their ranch last summer. Elizabeth would be happy knowing our son remained close to her family. The thought that she may have taken part in this ruse to hurt Reese sickens me. I couldn't go there, not Elizabeth; she wouldn't hurt me for all the gold in the world. If I could be certain of anything, this I knew.

I left the city early with Jackson still asleep in his room. My mind was still reeling from all that I had learned in the past twenty four hours. Betrayal was all around me. Trusted people in my life had hurt and destroyed my relationship with the one person I cherished most. I ached for Reese. I craved her touch and could still feel her lips on mine. I wanted her back. Hell, we should have never been separated at all. They tore us apart. I was about to face one of the men who was responsible for our pain. And fuck up his life the way he fucked with Reese's. I was wondering how Reese was feeling this morning. I hardly slept, and when I finally managed a few hours of sleep, Reese took over my dreams. I could still smell her intoxicating scent. She was still the most beautiful woman I ever met. As I held her in my arms last night, it felt like nothing had changed between us.

The reality was that Reese was married and our children were dating each other. Was she happy with her husband? She didn't say much about him. If Reese was living the picture perfect life with Samuel, she would have never stayed with me as long as she did last night. Thinking about Samuel reminded me to check in with Stephen. I needed to clear my head before seeing my mother. I had several cars that I stored in my parking bays to use when I was in New York.

My Audi R8 was the perfect car to let off some steam. The weather was gorgeous, not a cloud in the sky. I took it to over a hundred miles per hour once I got on the open road. I didn't care if I got pulled over, but luckily for me this didn't happen. I arrived at my parents' estate before my scheduled time with Jacobson. The drive did me some good, and I was ready to crush Jacobson. And if my mother had anything to do with this, then she would suffer my wrath as well.

My phone buzzed as I exited my car. It was Jackson.

"Good morning son, how are you?"

"Hey dad, are you at grandmothers yet?"

"Yes, I just arrived. Do you need anything before I go in? I plan to shut off my phone for a while."

"I just wanted to check in with you before I head over to the campus. Richard is driving me to pick up Riley."

I couldn't help but ask Jackson how Riley and her mom were doing. He said Riley was very excited to tour the campus, but Reese wouldn't be joining them after all. She had made plans to see a friend in the city. *I wonder who?* At least Jackson was talking to me this morning. Based on his demeanor last night, I wasn't sure if he was angry with me. I still may not know.

"Mother, are you here?" I called out for her. Usually I am met at the door by staff, but maybe she had dismissed them for the morning. "Mother," I called out again, and then I heard voices coming from the library.

I heard my mother's voice. "Miles, why is Walker driving out here?" I listened as quietly as I could without alerting them of my presence. "My son has been avoiding my calls since Phillip died. Thank goodness Jackson keeps in touch with me, or I wouldn't know anything about my son."

"Olivia, Walker coming up to the house today is not a social call. He and I have business to take care of regarding some things Phillip left for him."

"I don't understand, Miles. The will has been read and all is in order with Phillip's estate. What could Walker possibly be seeking?"

"It's not what Walker wants, it's what was left for him personally by his father. I don't even know what the box contains, but I can assure you it has nothing to do with Phillip's original will."

"What are you not telling me, Miles? You were always a dubious character, especially when it came to protecting Phillip. What did you do to my son?"

I burst into the library. "That's what I would like to know as well, mother. You do know why I'm here, Miles, don't you?"

Before he could realize what was happening, my right hook met Miles' jaw, knocking him on his ass. My mother gasped in shock.

"Walker! Have you lost your mind? Why did you hit Miles? Are you okay?" My mother knelt down to help Miles get up from the floor.

"Yes I'm fine, Olivia. Don't be angry with Walker, that punch was long overdue." I watched as Miles pulled a handkerchief from his pocket to wipe the blood away from his lip. I didn't usually go around punching people, but he did have it coming and deserved much more than a punch to the face. "Olivia, will you please excuse Walker and me for a little while? I need to discuss a few things with your son."

"That won't be necessary, Miles." I said. "What I have to say involves the both of you, and don't you ever dismiss my mother again in her own home. Am I clear?"

"Walker, I meant no disrespect for Olivia. I just figured you would want to speak to me in private."

"Sit down, Miles. Let's end this guessing game and get right to the point, shall we?" Miles nodded his response to me and joined my mother on the sofa.

"Reese Mitchell, remember her, Miles?" His only response was to nod at me. I wanted to punch him again.

"Miles, you've known me my entire life. You were my father's friend, and at a time, were like an uncle to me. How could you go along with my father's plan to destroy my life?"

The man before me was not the same man that I had respected all these years. I could see his guilt radiating off of him. Miles was quickly coming to the realization that he had no choice but to come clean and tell me the truth.

"I loved that girl with everything I had, Miles. I had planned on asking Reese to marry me and join me in California, where we planned on beginning a new life together. You conspired with my father to blackmail my girl and convince her that she was nothing to me. You knew she was pregnant with my child. How the hell did you know this, and in good conscience, keep this from me? Were you and my father having her followed?"

I had no control left. I lunged at Miles, and pulled him off the couch with my hands around his neck. "Tell me you son of a bitch, why did you do it?"

"Walker, have you lost your mind? Get off of him, now!" My mother was screaming at me to let him go.

I finally did and Miles fell to his knees while gasping for air. I flipped over the glass table, shattering it into hundreds of pieces. I thought I was going to have a heart attack, my heart was beating so fast. I had never in all of my life lost control, and to physically assault someone was completely out of character for me. I stood there in silence watching Miles struggle to breathe. Once recovered from my second assault, Miles was re-joined by mother sitting by his side on the sofa. All alarms went off in my head when I saw him cover her hand with his own. *What the fuck? My father is dead for merely a month, and his best friend moves on to his wife? My mother? He doesn't have a snowball's chance in hell if he thinks I will ever allow this to happen.*

"Olivia, please leave us. I need to speak to your son." He stared my mother down, and against her better judgment, she exited the library, but not before giving Miles a small smile.

"Walker, if you let me explain, I will tell you everything."

"Miles, you had your chance to come clean to me. I trusted you, and I loved you probably more than my own father. How could you betray me like this?" I fixed myself a double scotch and sat down. I turned to the wall to see my father's portrait hanging in all of its glory. I wanted to tear it down and shred it. I could feel his eyes staring back at me. This room was filled with his ghost.

"When you began dating Ms. Mitchell, your father had asked me to do a background check on her. I, of course, didn't say no to his request. Your girlfriend didn't have anything come up in the background check. We saw no red flags at the time. After her parents had died, she was raised by her grandparents. She attended college in Georgia for a few years before transferring to NYU. I was about to deliver my report to your father when my investigator found additional information. He found the naked modeling photos and the whereabouts of the photographer who originally took them. I tried to explain to your father how she, along with the other models, were victimized by this photographer, but he wouldn't listen. Phillip wanted to expose Ms. Mitchell as someone who wasn't worthy of the Reed name. He did have her followed, and that's how we knew she was pregnant. I thought after learning this news, he would have changed his mind about her, but he remained firm in his decision. That morning we waited for you to leave, and then we confronted Ms. Mitchell with what we knew."

"What if I had never left that morning? What would you have done next? Call out 'I object,' as I recited my vows to her at our wedding?" I poured myself another drink. This was too painful to hear. "Miles, where did Elizabeth fit into my father's grand scheme?"

"Walker, if you believe anything, please believe this: Elizabeth did not have anything to do with this. Your parents were friends with her family, and your father always fancied Elizabeth. He would say how she was your perfect match."

"The hell she was, Miles. My match was Reese. Elizabeth was only a friend. I never had feelings for her, and the fucked up part of all of this is that she knew and accepted me anyway."

"The story was fabricated by Phillip. I swear to you, she didn't know. After Ms. Mitchell left town, Elizabeth was just at the right place, at the right time. Your father was thrilled that you were spending time together with each other."

"Wake the fuck up, Miles. You know why I was with Elizabeth? It's because I was using her to fill the black hole that Reese left me with. I was drowning myself in scotch, then fucking her to feel something other than pain. Each time I spent with Elizabeth ripped my heart out even more. Don't stand here and try to make it sound like it was a blossoming romance. I only stayed with Elizabeth after finding out she was pregnant. Finally getting my shit together, we married, and then she fucking died, leaving me alone to raise Jackson. I hope you're happy on how it all worked out."

I took the decanter that contained my father's favorite scotch, and heaved it at his portrait. I never wanted to taste scotch again. "Did my mother know about this? You might as well tell me all of it."

"No, she didn't, Walker. Your father never discussed these matters with Olivia. Your mother at the time was quite shocked after your break-up with Ms. Mitchell."

"Miles, we didn't break-up! You and my father broke us. Aren't you going to even ask about the baby? Or do you know that my child is dead?"

"I know, Walker. I kept surveillance on Ms. Mitchell and was alerted of her arrival when she came back to New York. Your father didn't want Ms. Mitchell seeking you out, so we had her watched. Unfortunately, we found out that she was rushed to the hospital and later lost the baby."

"Wow, you certainly are dedicated to your work, Miles. You could have told me then, Miles. I would have never moved forward with Elizabeth had I known about this. Just how many sins do you have on your conscience in the name of Phillip Reed?"

"Too many to count, son. I am very sorry for all that I did to you. I will never be able to repent for what I have done to you and to Ms. Mitchell. I can't tell you what was going through your father's mind at the time; he would never listen to reason. Here is what I wanted to give you from your father. I don't know what this box contains, but I was under strict instructions to make sure this was delivered to you."

"Miles, what if my father hadn't died? Would I still be receiving this mystery box?"

"I don't know, Walker. He never once amended his will until last year after he suffered his first heart attack. Shortly after he recovered; he called me and asked me to revise his will.

He handed me the box with the instructions attached to it. Walker, I have told you everything. I am so sorry. I will be leaving now."

"Miles, I have one more thing to say before you go. You. Are. Fired. You're no longer employed with Reed Global, and your office has been cleaned out with your personal effects sent to your residence. Don't ever come near my family again! This includes my mother."

Without any parting words, Miles Jacobson turned away from me and left our home. My mother came in shortly after to check on me.

"Oh Walker, I'm so sorry. I didn't know what your father did to you. I should have been a better mother to you and not let Phillip do the things he did. Can you ever forgive me? You and Jackson are all that I have left. Please don't punish me because of your father. Forgive me? Please, Walker, I will not lose you."

"Mother, there is nothing to forgive. I would never keep Jackson from you. He is his own man, and he loves you very much. This is between my father and me. He did this, and now I have to pick up the pieces of the life that I thought I had lost. Mother, I intend to get Reese back in all areas of my life."

"Walker, you can't be serious, son? She probably has a family by now and has happily moved on."

"That's where you're wrong, mother. She is married, but far from happy. Her daughter happens to be your grandson's girlfriend. How about that for karma? I bet the old bastard is rolling over in his grave with that bit of news."

With my father's deep dark secrets now revealed, it was too much for my mother to bear. She retired to her room to lay down. I believed Olivia Reed when she said she knew nothing of her husband's machinations.

My mother was the queen society girl herself. She was involved with her charity work, posed for the perfect photo op, and of course looked pretty on my father's arm.

He was a bastard, this I knew. He loved my mother and never strayed. By not revealing his duplicitous side, he was protecting her.

I sat in my father's chair and ran my fingers over the cherry wood box. My father's initials were engraved on the top. This boxed was locked, and sitting in my hand was the key to my past. I looked up to my father's now defaced portrait. Even with the smears of scotch running down the portrait, the old bastard was still laughing at me. What did he know that I didn't? It was time to open the box and find out.

I slowly turned the key and the only content inside was a sealed envelope with our family's crest burned into it. Not an hour ago, I swore off scotch, but now I thirsted for one more shot before reading this. It was a handwritten letter addressed to me by my father.

Dear Walker,

I don't want to sound like an old cliché, but if you're reading this letter, then I am dead. I took the coward's way out and chose to write my failures down in this letter instead of talking to my son.

Where do I begin? I will start with: I'm sorry I wasn't the father that you needed me to be. I'm sorry I was the arrogant bastard that you proudly named me, when you should have simply called me father. I am very proud of the man you turned out to be and the father you are to Jackson. Believe me, son. I take no credit in this accomplishment. You did everything on your own.

You have met every expectation that I have ever set before you. No father could have been more proud of a son than I was of you. I'm just sorry I didn't tell you as often as I should have. I do thank you for allowing me to be in Jackson's life. That boy of yours is an amazing individual. He is filled with kindness and compassion. Every time I looked into his eyes I saw Elizabeth shining through. What a tragedy for him to not have known her. Will you please share something with Jackson for me? I know I don't have any right to ask, but if you would bestow my last wish for my grandson, I would rest in peace. If you take the key that opened this box, you will find another lock inside. Turn the key to the right, and its drawer will open. Inside you will find my father's watch. I want Jackson to have it.

Your boy meant a great deal to me, and I will always cherish my time spent with him. Please watch over your mother for me. Olivia Walker Reed was my life. I know you always believed that I had ice that ran through my heart, but not when it came to loving your mother. Loving a woman like your mother, you would have thought I could be more understanding when it came to my son's life. I wasn't,

Walker, and I completely destroyed your happiness with Reese Mitchell. I haven't uttered her name since the day I forced her out of your life.

I'm sorry son for what I did to you both, and the pain I caused you, and the hurt you must be feeling right now. I had the power to tell you over and over again, but never did. That girl loved you more than her own life, and I destroyed her. At the time, I didn't feel she was right for you, and I labeled her as a gold digger. When I discovered she was pregnant with your child; I had convinced myself that she was exactly who I thought her to be. I was wrong, son, and she paid the price for my mistakes.

Do you remember that day in your office when I unexpectedly came to visit? Of course you do. Your instincts were correct as always, and you had a right to be suspicious of me. I left something for you while I was at your home. Go to your study and retrieve the title Redemption...Sins of the Father. You will find the missing link that you will need to right the wrongs that I have done to you. Along with that, you will find what you will need to seek revenge on the ones who helped me put all of this in motion. Walker, you're a smart man. I hope you don't think I acted alone? I may have hurt your lovely Reese Mitchell, but there was a greater power even mightier than me. Read the papers, and they will lead you in the right direction. Why did I leave the book? Why, after all of these years, am I confessing now? Read the papers, and you will have your answers. I'm sure your head is spinning with my favorite scotch coursing through your system right about now. I'm so very sorry, Walker. You will never know how much.

As I reflect on how much I wronged you and Ms. Mitchell, I still couldn't be honest with you and tell you the truth. I was relieved when you found Elizabeth. I know you're probably wondering if she was also conspiring against you. I swear on your mother's life that she was innocent and not involved. She simply loved you for many years and accepted anything you were willing to give her. Again, I am truly sorry for your loss.

I hope one day you can forgive me and find happiness again.
You're a good man, Walker. A better man than I ever was.
Sincerely yours,
Phillip Alexander Reed

Reading my father's farewell letter did not give me closure, if anything, it resurrected old wounds and opened up new ones. Pain was not something I was immune to. First to lose Reese, and then to watch Elizabeth slip away from me, was incredibly hurtful to endure. Why, after all these years, he chose now to look for absolution for his sins. Now I understood more than ever why he visited me that day at my office. I never gave him the chance to tell me, and thank god I didn't. To hear it from Reese's point of view was a mind fuck at catastrophic proportions. So if my father would have confessed, I probably could have killed him with my bare hands.

Phillip Reed stopped at nothing to achieve what he had wanted, and in the end I made it easy for him. Reese's leaving shattered my heart, and I gave up way too easily. I should have searched the world for her until I found my other half of my heart, but I succumbed to my weakness and drowned in my own shit. Repeatedly Reese blamed herself for what happened, even shifting the blame from my father to her. It was I who let him navigate and charter the course for my life. I thought I was the one in charge of my destiny, not him. It was an illusion that I created, and I believed what I was telling everyone else.

The realization of it all was slamming me right into my gut. Nearly eighteen years later, I was still broken, but not for long. Reuniting with Reese was my game changer. She broke the chains that had bounded me to this life of just existing and going through the motions. By walking back into my life, it all changed, and now I was on a different path…leading right back to my woman.

I still don't forgive you, father.

The old man was right about one thing. I would seek my revenge on every last single breathing soul that hurt us. This I promised on the rotting corpse of my father, Phillip Reed. They would pay for the pain and loss they caused us, every fucking one of them.

Reese Mitchell was meant to be my wife, and I would not give her up without a fight, husband or not.

CHAPTER SIX

No words needed...

THOUGHTS OF WALKER dominated my dreams all through the night. I could still smell his cologne on my body. My bottom lip was still swollen from his kiss. *What am I doing? I'm married to Samuel and can't be fantasizing about my former lover. But Walker was so much more than that. Walker was my...forever.*

When we were together, every time I had closed my eyes, I could see our future together and all it could be. Walker and I talked for many hours about our plans and how we would marry, work in our chosen careers, and eventually start our family. The day his father showed up at his apartment, my dreams became a distant memory, my reality a nightmare.

What would it be like to make love with Walker again? He held me so close to his chest last night. I could have easily let my walls crumble around me and do him right there.

What the hell? I have to stop this...and now. I had my chance with Walker, and it was me who walked away. I have had to live with and accept the choices I made all those years ago. To see him now after all of this time apart, brought it all back.

I want him back. I've always wanted him. Stop it, Reese! This was not getting me anywhere, and looking at the clock, I can't believe I was still in bed. Enough daydreaming for one day. I had to get ready for this luncheon and show Riley all of my favorite places on campus where Walker and I used to go. I mean the places, *I* used to go. *I think I should take a cold shower to knock some sense into me.*

I felt a bit better after my artic shower; nothing like dousing yourself with cold water to extinguish the flames of your fantasy. *It's exactly that...a fantasy.* Was I fooling myself all those years ago with Walker? We were so different, but he never cared about our social circles, he just wanted me. As I sat at the vanity table, I looked at my sad reflection staring back at me. My mind began to wander again, getting lost in the memories of my past.

*I am a foolish woman. I never deserved him, because I truly didn't trust his love, I see that now. All he ever wanted from me was to believe in what we had, and although I told him that I did believe, maybe somewhere deep inside, I didn't. I thought I was so tough, but I was weak, just like **her**, my sad mother who didn't have the strength to fight. I did this to us. I let his father control me and destroy what we had and any chance of building our future together. This is on me. Stupid woman!*

I quietly sobbed for a brief minute, and when I opened my eyes, I saw that the table mirror was shattered into pieces. *Oh my god! What am I doing? How will I explain this to my daughter?* I needed air. I had to get out of there and clear my head.

I called out to Riley from my bedroom, but heard no response. I looked for Riley, only to find a note that she had left for me.

Hey Mom,

Left early to meet Jackson for coffee. You were sleeping, and I didn't want to wake you. My day will be pretty busy with all of the departments I plan to visit. Take your time getting here. Check in with you later.

Love, Riley

So much for spending quality time with your mom, Riley. She was quite the sneak, leaving me a note and sneaking out to meet her boyfriend. I sighed. I was jealous of my own daughter. She was in love with a wonderful boy, and I was here alone in my hotel room. My husband was a workaholic who paid no mind to me at all, and when he did, I was thrown over a desk for a passionless and meaningless fuck.

I felt a sudden headache beginning to form, and I massaged my temples. Grabbing my coat and purse, I made my way to the door, when I heard something. *Is it **him**? Walker? He's here? But why?* I dropped my things on the couch, and before opening the door, I quietly listened.

"Reese, are you there? Please open the door…I need you." He sounded so sad and defeated. My heart hurt just listening to his voice. He knocked again, and then again. I took a step back from the door, and let out rapid breaths. I'd been there before with Walker, and I was no fool to know what would happen next, but I just didn't care anymore. I gave up believing on fate when we were separated. So why question fate now? *He's here now. My love is here, no more questions.*

I opened the door to see Walker standing before me. My eyes scanned over his body. He looked breathtaking in his three piece black Armani suit. I could feel my heart beating faster as he stared back at me with the same carnal desire. No words were needed between us, our bodies communicated for us. Walker stepped in to my hotel room and pulled me into his chest. He kicked the door, closing it behind him, and he crashed his lips onto mine.

Walker's touch awakened feelings that had been suppressed deep in my soul since the day I had left him. My body craved Walker like a drug. I was on fire with every touch he placed on my body. I parted my lips, allowing his tongue to plunder my mouth. He sucked and pulled on my bottom lip until it swelled.

Walker lifted me into his arms and carried me into my bedroom. He locked the door behind him to keep the rest of the world out, and we were in our own private bubble. All of our years apart, and my body still responded so easily to his.

He slid me down his hard muscled chest until my feet touched the floor. My legs felt weak and unsteady after our kiss. He turned and sat in the chair that faced me. Walker asked me to remove my clothing and to do it slowly; I willingly complied. I wanted him…I hungered for him…I would do anything for him.

I remembered how this game of ours was played. Walker loved to watch me undress, as he issued his commands one by one. First, I unzipped my black pencil skirt. I slowly pulled the zipper down, and let it fall to my feet.

Walker knelt down in front of me; asking me to step out of my fallen skirt. Gracefully, I managed to do so. He ran his hands up the insides of my legs, feeling the silk stockings that I was wearing. Silk stockings were always his weakness. When we made love for the first time, my stockings remained. I could see that his preference hadn't changed. Walker leaned backwards onto his heels and whispered, "Continue."

I began to undo my white frilly blouse; it was low cut with only three buttons. I opened one side at a time, noticing Walker running his tongue over his lips. When my blouse was completely open, I let it drop to the floor to join my skirt.

I gave Walker quite the floor show. I twirled my body around and placed my hands on my hips, seeking his approval. Wearing my new La Perla silk thong and matching bra, I was silently thanking Riley for dragging me on a shopping trip to Neiman Marcus.

To my surprise, I began stroking my hands up and down my silk covered thighs until they reached my sex. I always enjoyed teasing Walker. It got me off, and I knew he was turned on by it. Walker asked me to touch myself; he didn't need to ask me twice.

My hands glided on the outside rim of my now soaked-through panties. I arched my back and moaned out my pleasure. Walker leaped up and scooped me into his arms. He shrugged out of his suit jacket, as I tore at his shirt. With trembling fingers, I reached for his belt and undid his pants.

He looked deep into my eyes, as if he were telling me what to do next; I knew exactly what he wanted. My hands found his waist again, and I slowly slid his pants down. Standing before me was a beautiful, naked Walker.

Walker's stomach was lined with perfect sculpted abdominal muscles while the rest of his body was lean and toned. He had tribal art running down the insides of his ribs with an inscription written through it. Walker never had a tattoo while we were together, so this intrigued me.

I stepped back to admire him. To be a wise ass, Walker gave me a twirl and placed his hands on his hips. I smiled and stepped forward again, this time dropping to my knees in front of him. I took him into my mouth and began circling my tongue around his tip. He tasted delicious. Walker aggressively placed his hands on the sides of my head and guided my mouth over his long, hard length. He was a savage, and I was the prey. I took him in deeper and deeper, until his hands gripped my hair causing a touch of pain, but so pleasurable.

"Reese, stop it now. If you don't want me to come in your mouth, release me...now!"

The hell with that! He didn't want to come into my mouth, but I wanted him to. I needed him to mark me again. I clamped my lips around him, and at that moment, he let go and hot liquid oozed down my throat.

Walker's body shook from the aftershocks of his orgasm. He pulled me up from my shoulders to once again crash his lips onto mine. He leaned into my ear and whispered, "Your turn, baby." Quickly reaching down to lift me into his arms, he kissed me again. "I love how I taste in your mouth. Have you missed it?"

"What?" I just looked at him with my glazed over eyes. He placed me in the middle of the bed and rolled his tongue over his lips, hungry with carnal desire for me.

"Have you missed me, Reese? How my hands feel when I run them up and down your delectable body? Have you missed my fingers entering your pussy, hitting every spot that gets you to scream my name?"

He entered me with two fingers, and at that moment my hips bucked forward and just wanted more. "Say it, Reese! Say how much you've missed this. Say how much you've missed me. Say it, dammit! Scream it if you have to, but say it!"

"Yes, Walker, yes to all of it. Please, Walker, I need you inside of me. I want you Walker. I've always wanted you. It's been so long...please fuck me."

"Fuck you, I shall."

I'd never felt freer than at this climatic moment with Walker, he could spin my body around with one touch. My body needed this...It needed him...We needed this.

"Keep the stilettos on and your eyes open. I want you to watch me make you come."

Oh holy hell! Walker opened my legs as wide as he could. He ran his teeth along my panties and ripped them off of my body. He skimmed his tongue over my clit until he parted my folds with his lips.

I knew I wouldn't be able to hold on for long, clutching the sheets as Walker worked me over with his tantalizing tongue. Only Walker could make me come undone, sending me teetering on the edge of the precipice until my body exploded with multiple orgasms. Electric pulses ignited through me. The current intensified as Walker went deeper inside of me. He stopped and commanded me to let go, and my orgasm exploded onto him. My body was trembling from my climax.

Walker stretched my hands over my head, as he continued to lap his tongue over me. I was ready to make love to him. Walker owned my body and soul since the day we met. I was ready to return to him, and be his. We could taste ourselves as we kissed each other.

Walker climbed on top of me and plunged himself inside of me. I winced from pleasure as he buried himself deeper. Walker waited for me to get used to him again. His dick was huge and could rip me in two. I took him all in, and our movements were matched, thrust for thrust. My body remembered his, every last inch of him. Walker was amorous and had the same amount of intensity he always showed me when we made love years ago. Anywhere from hard fucking to sweet love making, he always knew how to make our bodies fall into a rhythm with each other.

Walker consumed me and stripped me bare of all of my demons that held me back since we parted. Our bodies quivered as we climaxed together. My legs were still wrapped around his waist, as Walker began to take calming breaths and pelt my forehead with gentle kisses. Our bodies were still connected. He always stayed in me for a few minutes after we came together. I was in no rush to let him go. He looked into my eyes, and I was catapulted back to our last night together, when we forever sealed the promises we had made to each other.

I was home...again.

Tears were beginning to fall down my cheeks. After everything his father had put us through, to be here right now with Walker is something I never imagined would ever be possible again. He has returned back into the gentle lover I remember, holding my face, wiping away my tears. Staring back at me with his blazing eyes, I'm already consumed with him, and I never want to let go of this feeling.

"Reese, I love you. I always have, and I always will. You have to know that this changes everything in both our lives. I can't send you back to him. You…Are…Mine. Reese, you were always my… forever."

He rolled me over and pulled me onto his chest of corded muscles. Our naked bodies were tangled together under the covers. He was holding me tightly as he kissed the top of my head.

He wanted my answer. I wanted out of my marriage, that much is clear, but I had failed in the past, never making it out the door. I was determined this time to leave my marriage once and for all, but I still had to deal with Samuel, as if he would ever allow me to leave freely. I already tried explaining to Samuel how I felt…He didn't take it well.

"Walker, we need to talk." I tried to wrestle out from his hold, but his strong arms pulled me back down. He answered me with his lips. Walker was making it clear to me that he didn't want to discuss anything at the moment, and we made love again until I was screaming his name and we were well sated. We finally collapsed against each other and drifted off into a deep sleep.

When I awakened, I sat up to see a sleeping Walker stretched out before me. The sheet was barely covering his naked waist. His lips were parted and forming the perfect O shape. I smiled, grateful that my Walker was not a loud snorer, like Samuel. *Listen to me, "my Walker"? Get a grip!* Is he truly mine again? I want to believe that he is. We were always perfectly in sync together. It pained me a great deal when I had to deny that irrefutable fact in my goodbye letter. And now he's in my bed. As if we had turned back the hands of time to our past. I wanted to run my fingers through his hair and make love with him again, but I knew I needed to come up for air. His body was a work of art. I always loved to watch him sleep. Rare and precious moments that were forever sealed in my heart.

I gently slid off the bed and padded off into the bathroom. I looked at my reflection in the mirror. Walker had marked my body, clearly showing who I belonged to. The roughness from his cheek stubble was evident all over my neck. I had bite marks and red strawberries along my breast, and more scratches. The only thing missing was "Property of Walker Reed" tattooed on the back of my ass. It's not like I didn't know what Walker was doing. This was his way of owning my body, inside and out. I closed my eyes, remembering every detail of today, committing it to memory. *How could I hide this from Samuel?* I began to shake when I felt Walker's arms encase me.

"Are you okay?"

I nodded and struggled to find my voice. Walker turned me around to face him.

"It's going to be okay, Reese. We will work this out together, but you need to trust me. And this time when I ask you to trust me…please mean it. Baby, do you trust me?"

I wanted to say yes. I wanted to scream it, but it was so hard to actually say the words when he was looking right through me.

"Talk to me. Do…You…Trust…Me?"

I whispered, "Yes."

"Thank you, baby. I'll take it from here. I love you. Say it, Reese."

"I love you, Walker."

Hearing my words reignited the hot flame within him. He kissed me so hard on my lips, plunging his tongue deep inside. I was completely wrapped up into him again. I closed my eyes and allowed Walker to help me forget the fact that I have betrayed Samuel and our marriage. We walked into the shower and we again made love. He lifted me up against the tile wall, with me wrapping my legs around his body.

I never felt this way when making love with Samuel. We were awkward at best with each other. I never shared the same feelings Samuel had for me, and many times I doubted his love and intentions. Now I had betrayed him in the most defying manner. I couldn't sheath my body from him. How would Samuel react to seeing another man's mark on my body? Samuel always had to be in control, and he had a dominating side to him. Samuel proved that to me when I asked him for a divorce. If I told Walker what Samuel did to me, I knew he would go insane.

Walker and I held each other as the hot water began to run cold. We quickly washed each other and stepped out of the now cold shower. Just then I heard the door open to my suite, and to our horror, we heard Jackson and Riley's voices.

Riley was calling out for me. I was frozen in Walker's arms. He calmed me and told me to answer her. I responded and told her that I would be out in a minute.

"Walker, what are we going to do? If our kids find us together, they won't understand." I was nearly hyperventilating. I felt like I'd just been caught with my pants down, but this was way worse. I'm completely naked and in the arms of my former lover!

"Reese, you have to calm down. Tell Riley that you were set to go to the luncheon and you suddenly felt ill and have been here resting."

"What about you? How will you explain to Jackson why you missed today's events?"

"Reese, Jackson thinks I am still out in the Hamptons with his grandmother. I told him not to look for me today, and I would see him tonight."

"Walker, it is tonight." We were both shocked to see the time. The nightstand clock read six o'clock; we spent the entire day together.

"Go out, and calm your daughter. I will remain in here. Reese, if you behave as if nothing is wrong, your daughter will believe you."

I had no time to search for another outfit to put on, so I pulled my hair back and wore the fluffy, white robe the hotel provided. The collar conveniently covered up my neck and the scratches that were still visible.

"Mom, thank god! Are you are alright? I have been calling you for most of the afternoon. What happened to you today? You missed the alumni luncheon. So many people were asking about you, and I didn't know what to tell them about your absence."

"Riley, please calm down and allow me to explain. After reading your note this morning, I was in no hurry to leave. I was about to order breakfast and suddenly came down with a debilitating migraine. I was in no shape to go anywhere and decided to go back to bed. I guess I didn't realize my phone was off." *Liar! I have never lied to my daughter, and now after my day of transgressions, the lies easily slip off my tongue.*

"Now it all makes sense to me. I'm so sorry you were sick today, and I wasn't here for you when you needed me, mom."

"It's perfectly fine, Riley. Please don't feel guilty about it. I took some medicine and feel much better. I apologize, Jackson, if you were worried. I hope my daughter didn't drive you too crazy today."

"It's totally fine, Mrs. Briggs. My dad wasn't there either, but hopefully he will arrive home soon."

"Okay you two, make yourself comfortable. The mini bar is fully stocked. I will just excuse myself and get ready for us to go to dinner."

"Mom, if you don't mind, would it be okay if Jackson and I went out tonight? We have theatre tickets to see *Wicked*. Dinner reservations down in Little Italy, and then we'll be meeting up with friends."

"Riley, you could have asked me before now."

"I did, mom, check your voicemails. Please, say I can go? We spent all day around professors, and our brains are on overload with academics."

"Okay, twist my arm. I do remember what it was like being your age. Go out and have fun, but not too much fun." Riley laughed and hugged me. Jackson thanked me, and they exited the suite hand in hand. Once I knew they were gone, I called out to Walker to come out.

I glanced down at my phone to check my messages. I had several texts from Riley, and one from a friend here in the city. I completely forgot to phone Marsha with Walker's sudden arrival. I prayed I hadn't missed my chance with Freddy. I looked back to my phone, and of course...not one text or voicemail from Samuel. Why didn't that surprise me?

Walker, now dressed, was looking handsome as ever. I couldn't help but stare at him. I was taking a mental photograph of our time spent here together. He wrapped his arms around me and kissed me on my forehead. "I think we broke your vanity mirror while making love. I'm going to have to replace that. I'll have housekeeping take care of that for you."

"Walker, can I ask you a favor?" He replied with more kisses and began to tickle me. "Walker, I'm serious."

"Okay, I'm sorry. What's the favor, Reese?"

"I'm starving. Will you please take me to dinner?"

Walker laughed and turned me back toward the bedroom for me to get dressed. "I will take you anywhere you wish to go. Take your time getting ready, I'll wait out here and make some calls, the first one will be to Jackson."

I quickly kissed him again and ran off into the bedroom to get ready. My room smelled of sex and Walker. It was intoxicating to me. I removed my robe and wrapped my body around the sheets that we had made love in all day. I clutched the pillow to my chest which had the faint smell of his cologne still on it.

I don't know what came over me, but I began to cry and release what I had held in all day long. Our time together was coming to a close and in a few days, we would be apart again. The pain in my chest was crippling me. How could I return to Samuel after being reunited with Walker? I asked Samuel for a divorce before I left. He hadn't called me or given me any sign that he cared.

Why should I return to a home that I am not happy in? I had spent the better part of our marriage alone, and if it weren't for Riley, I would have left Samuel years ago. Walker had made it very clear that he was not willing to let me go and return back to my marriage. I had so many questions for Walker. I had to imagine he wanted to know all about my life as well. We have been apart for nearly eighteen years now. How is it, after all that time, we still have what we had back then? I feel the same connection with Walker as I did the first time we made love. He is as attentive and in tune with every part of my body, just as he always was.

I had to stop all this thinking. Whatever was going to happen, I couldn't worry about it right now. He's here with me now, and that's what matters. Whatever time we had together, I just wanted to hold onto. I ran my fingers across my neck where he had marked me. How could a few love bites make me feel whole again? He put me back together again with his need to stake his claim on what was always his.

CHAPTER SEVEN

Figuring it all out...

AS I WAITED for Reese to join me, my mind was taking me back to the minute she opened the door to me. Her beauty beguiled me, and it made me hard just thinking about her. All of our time apart, and this woman could easily awaken feelings I had concealed deep within my soul. The way we had parted before left us never having any closure, and now we finally did.

Will she see it that way? Had we only reunited to finally say the goodbyes that we didn't say so many years ago? No! I couldn't let that happen. I never wanted to end things with Reese. My father and his manipulations tore us apart, and now that we had been given this second chance, I could not let her walk away.

I knew Reese loved me; she would have never made love to me in the manner she did today if she didn't. I had to calm down and relax. Reese had given me no reason so far that told me she would walk away again. I couldn't pressure her. She needed to be the one that walked away from her marriage, and I could not make that decision for her.

God knows I wanted to lock her up in a room and tie her to my bed. I never wanted her to leave me again. I didn't care about this man she married; Reese was mine first. After what we shared today,

Reese was mine again.

My buzzing phone in my pocket pulled me out of my obsessive over rationalizing moment. I looked down and saw it was my mother calling me. What the hell did she want? I wanted to ignore her, but I took the call anyway. "Hello, mother," I said as my jaw clenched."

"Hello, Walker. I don't mean to bother you, but I wanted to make sure you were alright. The way you left my house today, I fear I may never see you again."

"Mother, I'm sorry if I hurt you today, but what other choice did I have? Father destroyed my life with his incessant need to control me, and I suffered for many years with what he did. To go through my life never knowing why Reese had left me, and then to find out it was because of my father? How the hell do you expect me to be? The old man is lucky he's dead, because I think I probably could kill him now."

My mother began to cry. Dammit! I hurt her when all she wanted to do was comfort me. No matter what he did, Phillip Reed was her husband, and she loved him. Now here I was destroying her with my anger that I had toward him.

"I'm sorry, mother. I didn't mean to say that. Please forgive me? You're the last person I want to hurt, but you need to give me some time to work out these feelings I have."

"I understand, Walker. Believe me, I do. Your father was a complicated man, and he was arrogant and very selfish. I was a fool in love, and I let my feelings cloud my judgment and rational thinking. Your father hated when I would involve myself in the decisions he was making for you. He always reminded me of my place where you were concerned. I should have stood up to him, Walker, and been more assertive when it came to you."

"It's over, mother. We don't need to discuss this ever again. Reading father's letter gave me my answers and the closure I needed. I drove away from your home today with the intent on starting over, and I will get Reese back."

"Walker, please don't do this to yourself. She is married and has chosen her life."

"This is what you don't understand: she had settled for the life she has now, because she thought we would never be together again. It's all changed now, and I will not lose her again. She's mine, mother, and I will never let her go."

"Walker, what have you done?"

"Mother, please stay out of my personal affairs. Learn from father's mistakes and do not ever question me again about my personal life." I ended the call without saying goodbye, she was so infuriating. She felt bad for what my father did to me, but yet she was compelled to defend him as well.

I needed to call Jackson to check in with him. I hadn't talked to him since last night. He picked up right away.

"Hey, dad, how are you?"

"I'm fine, son. Thank you for asking. So how was it today? Did you accomplish everything you wanted to do?"

"Yes, and more. Riley and I went everywhere today. She and I met with all of our professors, they seem pretty cool. I think my favorite class will be Introduction to Film; it's a female professor and she has a bohemian style to her. She has traveled all over the world, and she specializes in documentaries."

"That all sounds wonderful, son. To hear you this excited and happy makes me feel better about you attending school in New York."

"Dad, I promise not to be the absentee son, unlike you and your disappearing act today. I know you had business to take care of, but you really pissed me off. I thought you would have at least shown up at the alumni luncheon. Many people were asking for you, and I didn't know what to say."

"Jackson, if you're angry with me, we can discuss it in person. I am not nor have I ever been an absentee father in your life. Today was unavoidable, and one day I will explain it to you."

"I'm sorry, dad, I shouldn't have said that to you. This trip is exactly how you said it was going to be. I'm spending all my time with Riley, and not with you. What would you say if we extended our trip for a few more days? I would also like to visit with grandmother while I'm here."

"Apology accepted, and I will call my office to rearrange my schedule. As far as visiting your grandmother, you may do so on your own. I have already spent more time than I wanted to with her. Richard will drive you out tomorrow if you wish to go."

"Okay, that sounds fine. Would you object to me bringing Riley? I think grandmother will like her."

"Jackson, I think you should visit your grandmother alone this time. You haven't seen her since the funeral, and you know how clingy she can be."

"Okay, I understand. I'm sure there will be plenty of opportunity for Riley to meet her. I have to go now, dad. Our friends are waiting on me. I'll see you later. And dad…I love you."

"I love you, Jackson." What a convoluted situation I found myself in. How would I explain this all to my son? I couldn't think or obsess about this now. What was taking Reese so long? I needed to be with her…now.

I walked toward her bedroom and slowly turned the knob. Reese was sleeping, her body tangled up around the sheets. Her long, cinnamon hair was spread out over her naked back. She was so incredibly captivating, my heart was racing through my chest at the sight of her. She looked so peaceful and relaxed. I hated to wake her, but she did say she was starving, and come to think of it, I hadn't eaten anything all day. Food that is.

I gently caressed her naked back, hoping she would awaken without being startled. "Reese," I called out her name. She opened her beautiful eyes and smiled back at me. "Hey baby, I thought you were going to get dressed?"

"I planned on it, but then I was distracted by memories of you. You always had the power to distract me."

"You never have to be lost in memories of us again, baby. You have the real thing right here with you."

"Reese? Why are you crying?"

"It's nothing, Walker. I am a silly woman who likes to cry."

"There is nothing silly about you, please tell me what's wrong? I can't bear to see you cry. Have I done something to upset you?"

"No, of course not, Walker. It's not you, it never was you. I guess when I mentioned how you distract me, it triggered a painful memory. Our last night together, I had planned on telling you about the baby, but when I showed up at your apartment, we immediately made love. You were all I was focused on, and I figured I would just tell you the next morning. I never imagined what was going to happen to us. Walker, I need to know that you forgive me for leaving you. If I would have told you about the baby, maybe what happened to us could have been prevented and our lives would have been different."

I cupped Reese's face into my hands, and I kissed her plump lips while wiping her tears away with my thumbs and kissing her in between. "Reese, what happened to us was not your fault. My father and his sick obsessions did this to us. He had devised a detailed and calculated plan to break us up for many months before you left me. Please baby, do not blame yourself for this. We can't regret how our lives turned out after we separated. That would mean we regret our children, and I know you love Riley. Losing you was devastating; it caused me more pain than you can ever imagine, but Jackson was the only thing I did right."

"I love you, Walker." Those were the four words I needed to hear from Reese, and she had now said them to me. I held Reese in my arms, and then my mouth captured hers. I shrugged out of my jacket as Reese craved my touch again. I pulled her on top of me as she straddled my waist. I was giving Reese complete control to do as she pleased with me.

My hard erection was crushing into her, and her body was responding to me, as I hungered for hers. I was on fire as she kept teasing me. "Reese, you need to move, or I am going to explode, and this will be over before we want it to be."

She was such a tease, she winked at me, and I entered her. Reese bucked herself up and down until she got used to me again. This was pure pleasure making love with her. I knew I could never be without her again. Reese was my drug, and I will always crave her.

I took control. I flipped her onto her back and I held her hands above her head. "Stay still baby, and let me love you."

"Walker!" she screamed out my name as I pounded into her and left my mark on her body, and inside of her. We climaxed together, and I never had felt more alive than at that moment with her. I loved her so much, and I wanted to be with her for the rest of my life. Reese Mitchell was mine again, and there was no way in hell, I would ever let her go.

"I love how you say my name when you come. It is the sexiest sound my ears have ever heard. I love you, baby. I can't say that I have been a big believer in the universe, but I know this Reese, we are meant to be together. We were in love first, and now our kids who come from opposite sides of the country are now in love. If that is not fate, I don't know what is. I'm hungry, and this time it really is for food. Let's go before I take you again, and then I may just pass out from starvation."

Reese threw herself at me and held my face to her chest. I breathed her in and was almost dizzy with her scent. Kissing my forehead, she leaped out of my arms to get dressed. I slapped her ass, and she squealed with her sexy laugh.

While Reese was in the shower for real this time, I phoned Stephen to bring me some fresh clothes. He arrived quickly and gave me a meddlesome look. No employee ever questioned me before, but Stephen was more than just an employee. He was the only one that I trusted to always have my back. I still was in charge, but sometimes he couldn't help himself to give an opinion when he felt I needed it.

"Stephen, don't say it. I know what you're thinking, and I do not wish to hear it."

"Sir, I would never interfere in your personal affairs, but... I dare say that you may be crossing into uncharted waters now."

"I know what I'm doing, but thank you for the advice. I need you to take care of something for me, and it can't wait."

"What is it, sir?"

"I need you to phone the house, and have Priscilla retrieve a book for me from my office. I need it couriered over to me right away."

"The book, sir? What's the title?"

"It's called *Redemption...Sins of the Father*. Time is of the essence and will not wait one more day."

"Yes, sir. I will arrange it immediately. Anything else?"

"Please wait for me downstairs. We will join you in a few minutes." I closed the door to him, as Reese entered the room. She was breathtaking. I can stand here all night gazing at her beauty, but she snapped me out of it by kissing me.

"Thank you, Walker."

Now my curiosity is piqued. What is she thanking me for?

She continued, "Before you ask, thank you for today and for forgiving me. I love you so much, and I wanted you to know that. No matter what happens, we will always have today."

"Reese, it's not just today. We have the rest of our lives to be together, and we will be together again. I have so many things to tell you, but we really need to eat first." I took Reese's hand and escorted her down to my waiting car.

Reese wanted burgers of all things, while I wanted to dine on champagne and oysters. What a sight: my lovely chomping on a bacon cheeseburger with loaded cheese fries on the side. We were parked down near the seaport and watched the boats sail by.

"Of all the places that we could have dined tonight, you pick the greasiest spoon in all of New York City."

"Walker, did you forget that I used to be a model? You can't even imagine what it takes to stay in shape. I practically had to starve myself to fit into those tiny outfits. I've been very fortunate to maintain what I worked very hard for, but it's still good to treat yourself once in a while. Not that you understand that. Look at your body! You're in top physical shape, you look better now than when you were twenty two."

"Why thank you, smart ass, but I have to work very hard at staying in shape. I have two personal trainers that help me stay fit."

"Why two trainers? You can't fulfill your needs with just one?"

"Now that sounds dirty, and if you're not careful, you will be eating more than your burger tonight." I winked at her. Reese still had the power to blush, and she was turning red while I couldn't take my eyes off of her. "To answer your question, yes I have two trainers. Usually my business takes me to New York from time to time, so I retain one here in the city, and my primary trainer is in California. Any other questions, my beauty?"

"Why the tattoo? Does it mean something?"

"It does."

"And...? What does it mean?"

I so don't want to go there right now with Reese, but she is not the only one who easily submits. Her eyes alone always wielded a powerful weapon that I was defenseless against. I lifted my shirt to explain the tattoo. "You see here? The sun? That represents Jackson's birth and the light he had brought to my life. The splintered vines with broken roses is death...Elizabeth. The loss I felt when she died. The bottom part where the heart splits, well...that was meant for you. Death and loss, a powerful combination that I never truly recovered from. Anything else you want to know?"

"Yes. I wanted to know what happened today when you were in the Hamptons. It seems pointless now after the tattoo answer."

"Reese, I will tell you anything you want to know." I was about to go on to explain, but her cell phone began to ring.

"Excuse me, it's probably Riley." She looked at her phone, took a deep breath, and stepped away from me, and I knew it was her husband. "Hello Samuel, how are you? ...I'm fine, and Riley is too. How did your surgeries go? ...That's great to hear, I'm sure you're happy with your success. ...When am I coming home? I don't know,

Samuel. Riley wants to stay for a few more days, and I think I want to as well. ...I disagree. We don't have anything to discuss. I told you what I wanted, and you certainly showed me how you felt about it. ...I have to go, Samuel. ...No, I will not come home tomorrow. Please leave me be, and I will see you in a few days." I listened to Reese speak to her husband, and their conversation sounded so cold and distant. Was this truly her life? Was she just merely existing in a loveless marriage?

"Reese, are you okay? Talk to me baby. What did he want?"

"He wants me and Riley to come home tomorrow. You heard me tell him no. I need some time to think and clear my head. I can't go home yet."

"Reese, you don't have to go home at all. You can return to California with me, and you will divorce Samuel."

"Walker, you make it sound so easy. I can't just walk away from my life, and my life with Samuel and Riley. They're all I know, and how will I explain to my daughter that I am now sleeping with her boyfriend's father, while betraying her own?"

"Reese, you said you want to be with me again. Was that not true?"

"It was true, Walker. I meant every word I said to you, but it's complicated."

"Talk to me please, what are you not saying? I could sense it when you were on the phone with him. What happened?"

"I can't tell you, Walker, I'm ashamed and embarrassed."

"Reese, now you have to tell me. What did your husband do to you?"

"Before leaving for New York, I was going through a box that I kept with me all of these years. When I left you, I kept a journal and some mementos that you had given me. Silly things that reminded me of you and us. Along with the photo I had taken from your apartment, I have this one too. I've held onto to it as if it was my lifeline towing me through my pain all of these years we've been apart."

Reese showed me the picture that she was holding in her hand. I remember when she took this picture of me. I was standing against a wall going over some class notes when she called out my name. I looked up and smiled and then Reese captured my picture.

"You remember, don't you, Walker?" I simply nodded at her with my response. "You were so unbelievably sexy. I always loved you wearing that black leather jacket. Anyway, after Riley ransacked my closet looking for clothes, I found your picture. Memories of us flooded my thoughts, you have always been in my heart, Walker. I had been arguing with Samuel for weeks over him not wanting to join us on this trip. He chose his work over his family, and we were about to leave when he unexpectedly came home. For a second, I had thought he was home to pack up and join us, but he only returned to retrieve a file he had forgotten."

She continued, "Riley was crushed and disappointed by her father. I was angry for her and how she was now crying outside probably to Jackson, while her arrogant father blatantly ignored his daughter's feelings. I barged into his office and began telling him off. Samuel didn't appreciate the tone I had taken with him and warned me to stop. I didn't and asked him for a divorce. He then gave me his complete attention and charged at me."

"What did he do, Reese? Did Samuel hurt you?" I was praying that he didn't do what I thought he did.

"Yes, he did Walker. But he hurt my feelings more than anything he could do to me physically. I tried to leave, as he pressed me up against the door and then onto his desk. He held my hands as he had sex with me. All I could do was wait until he was finished. He apologized after he was done and promised that he would make it up to me. I was not going to leave him and no way would a divorce ever be considered. I ran upstairs to change my clothes, and then Riley and I left for the airport."

"Oh my god, Reese. The bastard raped you! I will fucking tear his arms off."

"Walker, he didn't rape me. I let him do that to me. Don't you understand? He is my husband, who was there when you weren't, and now I was asking him for a divorce. Samuel may have been neglectful during our marriage, but he never hurt me until a few days ago when I mentioned divorce."

Hearing what Reese just said to me, I'm out of my mind. Here she is defending her husband and his actions. I don't care what Reese is calling it, she said no, and he took her anyway. How can she expect me not to have a reaction to this?

"Walker, look at me please."

I clasped my hands around my neck, a clear sign I was frustrated and wanted to hit something. She wanted me to look at her, but I couldn't. I was too angry, and I needed to take a breath. Reese went back inside the car, waiting for me to return. I slid inside next to her, and all I could do was pull her into me.

"I'm sorry baby, I didn't mean to lose it back there. I can't stand the thought of you ever returning back to him. Please stay with me."

"Walker, I can't right now. Please understand it won't be easy for me to walk away from Samuel and the life I have in Maryland. I have not only Riley to think about, but I have my work and my friends. No one will understand my reasons on leaving my marriage; if anything, they will think I'm crazy."

"Who cares what people think? The only two people that matter are you and me!"

"Walker! How can you say that? What about Jackson and Riley? I can't just ride off into the sunset with you because that's where my heart is leading me. I'm not free."

I stared into her eyes and said, "Just answer this simple question. Do you want to be free? Free of this loveless marriage you've been just existing in all of these years? You already said you asked him for a divorce. Stand by your decision, and end this marriage before you waste one more day missing out on who you really want. The man that loves you—truly loves you— is right here beside you. It wasn't over for us. I love you Reese, and I will not let you walk away this time without a fight. This is our second chance at forever."

CHAPTER EIGHT

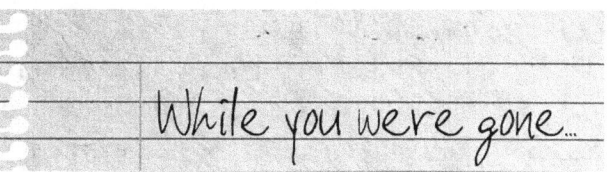

While you were gone...

SITTING HERE WITH her was just maddening. Breathing the same air with her was driving me insane. All my thoughts were sending me almost into a blinding rage. My thoughts were of Reese, and Reese, alone. Burying myself inside of her was all I wanted. Her touch, her scent, her voice, I was already so lost in her. Talk to me dammit! I had to make her see me.

"Reese, look at me." She was staring out the window and ignoring my requests. I wanted her to look at me, but she looked lost in thought right now. I told Stephen to return us to the hotel. She flinched when the car began to move. I sat quietly with my eyes forward. I could play this game just as good as Reese could. Hell, I invented it. Watching her body move the way it did was telling me that she was silently suffering. How could I get through to her without driving her away?

"Walker, you don't understand," she said.

What didn't I understand? I knew she was married, but she didn't want him or her marriage. Reese turned to me and held my hand. "My life with Samuel is complicated. When I met Samuel, I was at the lowest point of my life. I lost our baby and all hopes of ever reuniting with you again. I had nothing to live for but my work, and even that didn't fulfill me. He was there for me. He was the only one I had."

"Dammit, Reese! How could you even say this to me? You had a hell of lot more than just Samuel. What about Freddy? Your grandparents? I would have been with you! All you needed to do was just be honest with me."

"Walker, I told you why I left. Do you think it was easy for me to walk away from you? And believe me when I say that I did try to find you and tell you the truth. Your father was just too powerful for me to go up against. You said it yourself, you were the exception to the rule. I was not, Walker. I remember the day we drove out to your parents' Hamptons estate. You were so apprehensive about me meeting your father. I never understood why, until I met him in person. Your assessment of him was right on, and he scared the hell out of me. He was beyond arrogant, and was intimidating. I had never known anyone like your father. You only told me small parts of your relationship with him. You always gave me the impression that you could handle him, but Walker, could you really? I don't think you really knew who Phillip Reed was at all?"

She continued, "The time I was given with my parents was magical. They were completely different from yours. My parents were always loving, and never a day went by that they didn't tell or show me that love. Your mother may be an exception, but you never had that with your father, and when he did what he did to me, he showed no remorse at all. I'm sorry, Walker, but I was looking at the devil himself. My heart was broken when my mama and daddy died. Thank god I had my grandparents to care for me."

She pressed on, "You want to know why I couldn't tell you about your father. It's because after what my family sacrificed for me, how could I let this man destroy them? I was young and naïve. Yes, I believed everything your father threatened me with. This is why I left. I would have given my life for them, Walker. I did after all, but I had to lose you to save them. When I found out I was pregnant with your child, I had never been happier. I vowed to give our son or daughter a supportive and loving upbringing that you never had. I imagined you holding our baby and being an amazing father. I wanted to tell you that night, and I should have."

Reese continued, "I can't predict what may have happened if you had known. I could have suffered the same fate with the miscarriage, but at least I still would have had you. I am beyond sorry for the choices I made back then. Not for helping my family, but not telling you or them. We could have been a united force against your father, but I succumbed to Phillip and Miles without blinking an eye. You told me over and over again how different you were from your father. I knew you were in line to take over the business, but I also knew you wanted to run it your way with your vision."

She took a breath and went on. "I wasn't afraid of that, and following you to California was never not an option for me. I wanted to go with you Walker, and be with you. The first real test in our relationship, and I failed you. I didn't trust what we had, and for that... I fucked it all up and handed you to another woman, while I suffered in silence. I don't think I will ever be able to truly forgive myself. I just need you to understand the reasons behind my choices. I'm sorry, Walker, I am so incredibly sorry."

I couldn't take it anymore! I was sitting there with her, listening to my broken girl recount the most painful time in her life, and it was all due to my father. God, I fucking hated him and everyone that had a hand in destroying my relationship with Reese. I did what came naturally to me and just pulled her against my body. I needed to feel her heartbeat against my own. I had to heal my woman once and for all and make her forget this nightmare that she had to live with. My father was dead, and he couldn't hurt her anymore. I was there now, and I vowed to make everything that my father destroyed right again, beginning with Reese. I rubbed my hand up and down her back in slow, smooth strokes, and she was slowly starting to calm under my touch.

"Reese, you need to stop this. Dredging up the past is not going to change anything, but bring us more hurt. We can leave that shit where it belongs and begin again. I love you, and I know you love me. Please let's put this behind us. Can you do that, Reese?"

"I don't see how I can, Walker. What about my husband, Samuel? Have you forgotten about him? He was there for me when I had no one. Our baby was gone, and you were gone. I was utterly alone, Walker. I was pretty on the outside because I was a model, but I was ugly inside and feeling empty. Samuel offered me a way out from under the black cloud that was my life. He was about to finish with his fellowship at New York Presbyterian and then onto Johns Hopkins. He asked me to join him in Baltimore and to start over. I thought he was insane with his invitation. I was a stranger to him. I questioned him, and all he said was that he knew me well enough to know that I was worth getting to know better."

She went on, "I promised I would think about it, and then I left for California. My life there was small and unattached. I had a small apartment with minimal things in it that didn't even make it a home. I was just existing and moving through my day to day. I missed you and mourned our child. I would smile pretty for the camera, and then at night, I cried myself to sleep. Samuel and I kept in touch through phone calls, and he even flew out for a weekend."

She looked away from me and continued, "That weekend he flew in to visit me, he had rented a house in Napa. We made love for the first time, and he presented me with a ring. Samuel proposed, and begged me to say yes to him. The whole time I was with him, my mind kept retreating back to you. You Walker, and only you. Here I was with a ring on my finger, a proposal waiting for my answer, and this man making love to me. He was offering me the world, and I only wanted you."

She stammered, and then went on with her story. "The reality was stronger than the fantasy, and I said yes to Samuel. Yes to becoming his wife, yes to having children with him, and yes to having a new life he wanted me to share with him. I guess Samuel and Elizabeth had one thing in common, they both knew that our hearts belonged to another, but loved us anyway."

I had no words to say to Reese. My mind was reeling from her story. She had so much more to say, but I needed a second to compose myself. She was still holding my hands, never breaking our connection.

"Walker, Samuel helped me piece my life back together after losing our baby. He was supportive, and he listened to me cry for endless hours until I had no more tears to shed. Our relationship didn't begin like most do. He was the doctor who treated me in the emergency room. He held my hand while I was sleeping. He was there for me when I had to see you and Elizabeth on Page Six of the paper. He didn't ask anything of me but to take a chance with him to start over."

She held my hand tighter and continued. "Walker, I knew you moved on from me, and were beginning your new life in California. I had a choice to make, and I made it with Samuel. After my weekend with Samuel, he had flown back to New York, and I remained in California to pack up my apartment. I only really had to pack my personal things, most of the furniture was rented along with the apartment. My agent owned a studio apartment in New York, so I forwarded my things to her place and stayed in California until Samuel was ready to leave for Maryland. The day I left, I found myself outside of the great Reed Global Building, and I waited in hopes of seeing even a glimpse of you."

"Did you, Reese? Did you see me before leaving?"

"I did, Walker, and the image of you stepping out of your car and walking into the building is an image I will never forget. You were wearing a dark blue suit, a three piece, I believe. You were carrying a trench coat over your arm and the black briefcase I had bought you for your birthday. That warmed my heart to see you carrying that case."

"I still have it, you know. It's old and tattered, but I can't bear to get rid of it. You had my initials engraved on it. So you saw me and just watched me? Why, Reese? You were so close, but yet you sat back in silence. Why didn't you try to reach out and talk to me?"

"You know why, Walker. I sat there on that stupid bench for hours until you emerged again, but this time you weren't alone. I saw you with your father, and your father saw me, and stared me down with his cold eyes. That was his subtle warning to turn around and go. I did just that and headed to the airport, finally saying good-bye to you. I cried all the way to the airport and for most of the flight. Even after all of those months without you, he still considered me a threat, and I was still afraid."

She removed her hand from mine and crossed her arms as she went on. "The first time I tried to see you Walker, well you know what happened. That Ralston guy grabbed me. Covering my mouth, so I couldn't call out to you. They were the barrier that separated me from you on that day, and shortly after…I had lost our baby. At least this time, he took mercy on me and allowed me to steal one last glimpse of you. I never saw you again, until we met at the restaurant yesterday."

"Reese, don't you see? You don't have to be afraid anymore. You have me, and I will take care of you, and you will take care of me. We are together again like we were always meant to be."

"Walker, you make it sound so simple. I can't walk away from my life with Samuel. I have Riley to think about and how this will affect her. You make it sound easy and effortless. I wish I had your faith. This trip was about a college weekend for me to share with my daughter. I never expected to see you in a million years, and to make love with you again has my mind spinning out of control. How did this happen? How am I even in this car with you? I feel like the fates are still conspiring against us, and this has been all a dream."

"Reese, it's not a dream, and I'm very real. Our love has never faltered, it remains true to both of us, and I know you feel the same way. You can be with me, you just have to trust that I will be here this time, and no one will ever separate us again."

"My life is so different from yours, Walker."

"I know this, Reese. The life you're leading is not the one you want."

124

"You're right, it's not what I want. But it's what I have. I'm exhausted, Walker, and I need some time to think. I have to call Samuel back, hanging up on him wasn't right for me to do."

"Can I see you tomorrow, Reese? Please say yes, and we can talk. I have so much to tell you, please think about it?"

"Walker, I really need to spend some time with Riley. This trip was for her, and I have been with you the entire time."

"I don't think Riley has noticed, all she sees is Jackson. This trip was also supposed to be a father and son trip, but I knew once my boy saw his girl, I would be an afterthought. That's how it works when you're in love, Reese, at least it was for me when I met you."

"Walker, that's one of my problems. It still feels the same. I have never stopped loving you, and yet I still married someone else, had a child with him, and created this facade of my happy domesticated life. The truth is that I always wanted more, and you were my more. I should have had all these things with you, but I ruined us, Walker. This is on me, and you will never convince me otherwise. I don't deserve you. Let this weekend be the goodbye and closure to our story, and we can both return to our lives."

"Reese, are you fucking kidding me? How can you say this to me? If you think I will let you just walk away from me again, then you truly have forgotten who the hell I am. You want to talk about blame? How about me giving up on you? I didn't try hard enough to find you. I had money at my disposal, I could have hired a thousand private detectives to find you, but I didn't. I believed the dead ends were real, and you just didn't want to be found. Even that was premeditated by my father. I chose to drink you away and then when I finally sobered up, I bedded a woman that I didn't want to love, she got pregnant, and I married her. What does that say about me, Reese? We have both been broken, but we can heal together and have the life we always dreamed of. Reese, I will do anything to make this happen. Will you?"

We arrived at Reese's hotel. She turned to open the door, and I pulled her back against my chest. I didn't say a word to her and just inhaled her scent and wrapped my arms around her waist. We had the glass divider encasing us in our private bubble and shutting out the rest of the world.

My hands travelled down her front. My skillful fingers slid down to her waist and slowly slid under her panties. Reese panted with want from my touch. I knew she wanted me and would do anything I asked. Always the vocal lover, her moans of pleasure were crying out for more. I never forgot what we shared in our love making. My desire for her was so strong, I couldn't fight it, nor did I want to.

"Reese, I want you. Turn around baby, and let me see you." I grabbed her by the shoulders and turned her to me. I crashed my lips onto hers and began to make love to her in the back of the limo.

"Walker, oh god I want you. Please take me now."

"Oh I will, baby, I will. Let me love you first. I want you to scream my name as I make you come." Reese didn't disappoint, as she clutched my head and pulled my hair as she screamed out her pleasure. Not that I cared if Stephen heard us, but my divider was also sound proof.

"Reese, open your eyes and look at me. You. Are. Mine! Reese, you're not his. You never belonged to anyone but me. Say the words to me, Reese, say that you're mine."

"I'm yours, Walker. I have never belonged to Samuel, I only belong to you, and I only love you."

That's all I needed to hear to finally explode into Reese. Her body always responded to me, and only me. I would never let her go. I rested my forehead onto hers and tried to get my breathing under control.

"Are you okay, baby?" I asked her. Reese's eyes were glazed over with tears, and I wasn't sure what she was thinking. I only felt her heart beating as fast as mine was. We were connected, didn't she know this?

"Yes, I'm fine, Walker. I haven't felt this way in a very long time, and I still can't believe that you're here with me."

"Believe it, Reese, because I'm not going anywhere. We will work this out together, but you have to give me your word that you will not run again. You can't walk out of this car and out of my life again. I understand what's at stake, Reese, but if you don't take this chance with me now, then you will waste more years in a marriage that you never wanted, and where will that leave you then? Is it fair to Samuel? If he's the man that you say he is, then let him go and give him a chance to find someone that can love him the way he deserves to be loved."

AFTER WE DRESSED and fixed our appearances, Walker just held me as I continued to process what he just told me. *Can I walk away from my marriage and leave it all behind me?* I was brave enough to ask Samuel for a divorce once, but I will have to find the courage to do it again. My cell phone was ringing once again, and it was Riley calling, thank god. I wasn't ready to speak with Samuel.

I let it go to voicemail, and then I played Riley's message.

"Hi Mom, calling to let you know that I'm still with Jackson. Oh my goodness, mom, the play was awesome. I love New York. I will see you soon and tell you all about it. Mom, thank you for this weekend. I have never been happier, mommy. I love you so much, and mom... I love Jackson."

Hearing my daughter sound so happy made my heart sing and ache at the same time. She was in love with Walker's son. How would I ever begin to explain my past with Walker to Riley? The thought of it sickened me, and I was afraid that if I tell her the truth about how I felt about Walker, she would push me away for hurting her father. No matter what I decided, someone would be hurt.

"Reese, who was on the phone? Was it Samuel again?"

Should I have lied and told Walker it was Samuel and that he wanted me to call him back? I had to get out of this car, away from

Walker. I needed to think. Every minute I remained with him was making me just want him more.

"Reese, tell me who was on the phone." He demanded to know.

"It was Riley. She wanted to tell me how much fun she was having with Jackson, and she loves him. Knowing that Riley will have someone with her while she attends school here puts my mind at ease."

"They were friends first, and then it led to what they have now. It sounds like another couple I used to know." He smiled and leaned forward to kiss me. I slowly pulled away from him.

"What are you thinking, Reese?" he softly asked me. I stared at his beautiful face and cherished every single minute that I've spent with him. Fighting to hold back my tears, I whispered the two words that would probably hurt him the most. God knows I didn't want to, but I needed to breathe.

"Goodbye, Walker."

I opened my door and stepped out. He didn't try to stop me this time, so I kept walking until I could no longer feel his presence. When I finally entered my hotel room, I was drained and exhausted. The maid has been here to clean our room, so Walker's scent was no longer on my sheets. I already missed him and it had only been a few minutes since I left him. Was he thinking of me too? I was totally being irrational at this point. I decided to just soak in the tub and clear my head, maybe even get a little drunk, anything to bring me some peace I desperately needed right now. I soaked my sore muscles in the tub, and of course my mind drifted to Walker. I remembered every touch he placed on my body. We made love so many times, I had lost count.

Was Walker right? Could I easily walk away from my marriage and just start over with him? Samuel had been so distant the last few years, all he got excited over was his career. I had just played my role in our story. Once we married he was very clear on the kind of wife he wanted me to be. He hated that I modeled and asked me to walk away from my career. He asked for children right away, so I got pregnant and we had our beautiful daughter.

I suffered another miscarriage two years after having Riley, and that's when I decided I didn't want any more children. To have to go through that loss again was too painful for me to go through again. Samuel was content on only having one, and he wasn't the type of man that needed to continue his family lineage with a son. Samuel offered to get a vasectomy to calm my fears about getting pregnant again. I always respected him for that selfless act.

I felt so much better after my bath, and enjoyed a delicious glass of Barolo. Realizing that I didn't phone Marsha at all today, I immediately dialed her number. She answered on the third ring.

"Well hello, Ms. Thing. For someone who wants to reconnect with her best friend, you sure have a funny way of going about it." Leave it to Marsha for knowing the perfect words to use to make me feel guilty.

"Marsha, I'm so sorry for not calling you today. Something came up that couldn't be helped."

"Couldn't be helped? Who or what had your panties all up in a twist today that couldn't have waited until you met with Freddy?"

Oh my god! I loved her. She and Freddy should have been related. I hoped she was sitting down for what I was about to say next. "Walker."

"What?! Come again? I thought I just heard you say 'Walker.' As in Walker Reed?"

"Yes. The one and only."

"Oy vey! You have to give me a moment here. I think I swallowed my tongue." I waited and silently laughed as she went on and on about her shock. She tended to be a bit melodramatic, but at the same time could be so entertaining. I missed my friend, and I so needed this laugh after the intense day I had with Walker.

"Reese, as much as I want to continue this conversation, I'm kind of in the middle of a party right now. Can we meet tomorrow?"

"Can I call you first before making plans?"

"Sure thing, sweets. You know I love you, and I promise I will not let Freddy out of my sight until you two can talk."

"I know he must be busy with the fashion show, and I don't want to take his focus away from that. As much as I want to reunite with him, he needs to have this moment without my drama."

"He loves you, Reese. His feelings have not changed. Why do you think he used your nickname Peaches in his foundation? He misses you so much. Give him the benefit of the doubt before you decide how he will react to seeing you again."

"Once again, my friend, you're the voice of reason." I hung up with Marsha just in time to hear Riley arrive home.

"Mom! Are you here?" My daughter was finally back from her whirlwind date with Jackson. It was time to catch up with my girl and order some ice cream.

"Hey, sweetie, how was your night with Jackson?"

Riley was glowing, her smile was infectious. "Mom, my night was unbelievable. I'm totally in love with Jackson, and I told him how I feel. He said my words right back to me, and we just held each other. He took me for a horse and carriage ride through Central Park. He is so smart mom, he knows so many things about art, music, history about buildings, and he can describe the littlest details and make it to be so much more than it really is."

"It sounds like you have an amazing boyfriend. Riley, I don't mean to pry, but I feel I need to ask you."

"Mom, you can ask me anything, but I already know what you're going to say. We've had this conversation before, mom, and my answer is still the same. I'm still a virgin, and plan to be until I'm ready for that next step."

"Which will be when, Riley? The way you're talking about Jackson leads me to believe that you have probably at least thought about it."

"Mom, of course I have, but as a couple, we have not. Jackson is so tender and gentle with me, he does not pressure me at all. We kiss and we hug each other, but that's it for now. He hasn't even tried to feel me up under my clothes."

Oh my god, I was so not ready to hear about my daughter's sex life. "Riley! I swear you have no filters when it comes to your mouth. That was too much information for me to hear."

"Aren't you the one that is always telling me to be honest with you? I'm only following your lead, mom. If you don't want to know, then that's fine. I won't continue to tell you intimate details, but don't snap at me. I have always shared things with you that you never had a problem with before."

Dammit! I hurt her feelings, and I could see it all over Riley's face. "I'm sorry, honey, I didn't mean to be insensitive, and of course I want you to share things with me, especially the important stuff. Falling in love for the first time is an amazing feeling, and I really like Jackson. He seems wonderful, and I know he will treat you right."

"Thank you, mom. Jackson is wonderful. I can't believe how much we have in common, his friends are great, and they really welcomed me into their group. Most of the group will be attending NYU, only a few are attending Columbia. I want to say thank you again for allowing me to have this time with Jackson. I know you and I planned on doing some things together, but you were right, mom. I saw Jackson, and my heart just combusted and only wanted to be with him."

"I was once your age, Riley. I get it, and I understand. How about tomorrow we take New York by storm? I actually have a surprise for you."

"A surprise? Oh, mom, please tell me? You know I won't be able to sleep until you do."

"My lips are sealed, Riley, but I will say this. You're going to plotz when you find out where we're going tomorrow."

"Mom…what does plotz mean?" I laugh out loud. Riley is wearing the same expression I wore on my face when Marsha first said that word to me.

"Plotz is a Yiddish word for a feeling of excitement. It was a word that two very special people always used to say to me."

"Sounds like a plan, mom. Jackson is driving out to see his grandmother tomorrow, so you and I will have the whole day to ourselves. Have you called daddy yet? He should know we extended our trip."

"I have, and he's fine with it." I lied. "Speaking of your father, I need to call him, so I'm going to go to bed now."

"Okay, mom, I will see you in the morning. I love you."

I hugged my daughter and whispered "I love you" back to her. My heart was breaking while my daughter's was filled with happiness and newfound love. I had to tell her about Walker. If she found out on her own, she would be heartbroken and not trust me. I would have to call Walker and ask if he planned on telling Jackson.

No missed calls from Samuel, as I looked to dial Walker. His voicemail picked up and I swear listening to Walker's sexy voice over the phone could bring me to my knees. Every word that came out of his mouth was lyrics to a song. Walker was the most passionate man that I had ever known. After tomorrow, I would only have a few more days with him, and then I would return home to begin divorce proceedings. Before leaving for New York, I had already been in contact with my lawyer and had papers drawn up. If Samuel knew of this, he would completely lose it. I just had to keep in mind that no matter what happened, I couldn't allow Walker be the reason for ending my marriage. I wanted this for a long time, and to be fair to Samuel, I had to see it through without the interference from my past. How that would happen was still uncertain.

Walker and I had so much to talk about. He still didn't tell me about his trip out to the Hamptons. I think he wanted to, but Samuel's call interrupted him, and the subject changed. I told him so much tonight, but left out so much more.

If tomorrow goes as planned, I would have reunited with my best friend and then see Walker. I went over the mental list of fences I needed to mend. Freddy, Walker, and then my grandparents. I don't see how reuniting with Walker and not telling them the complete truth would be avoided. I just prayed Nana and Granddaddy would understand why I did what I did. They may be angry at first, but once they see how happy I am again, maybe that will be enough for them.

I never liked keeping secrets from Nana, but again in the name of protecting her, is why I did it. She wouldn't see it that way, but I would try my best. I deserved a good tongue lashing from her. If I had trusted the two people that had always taken care of me, maybe I could have been spared years of pain without Walker in my life. But then I wouldn't have Riley.

I had to believe everything happened for a reason, good and bad. In life we had no absolutes or guarantees. If that was the case, then everyone's life would be perfect, and to believe that is a fairytale. My romance with Walker was like a story in a romance novel. He did everything with perfection, and when we hit our rough patches, the making up part was unbelievably hot and sexy. Walker was my fantasy wrapped up in a perfect package, and when he declared his love for me, he then became my reality. He wanted us again, and as fast as I fled his car tonight, I wanted that too. I was not the same girl that his father chased away all those years ago. I knew I was stronger, but I was human too. I was allowed to be scared and nervous of the unknown, but with Walker beside me this time, I prayed we could finally find our happily ever after.

I realized I was all caught up in the sound of his voice and my thoughts that time had run out, and Walker's phone hung up. I must have left him a voicemail of just silence. I laughed and shut my phone off. I would talk to him tomorrow, but dream of him tonight.

CHAPTER NINE

Deceptions now revealed...

I SHOULD HAVE stopped her, but I knew she needed space. I hated this feeling that had consumed me since leaving Reese at her hotel. I wanted to go back to her and make love to her all night, but I feared I may just push her away. I would see her tomorrow and once again try to convince her that we belonged together. To hell with her marriage and her husband who didn't deserve her.

I walked into my penthouse and eyed Jackson sprawled out on the couch, surrounded by his laptop, iPad and e-reader. *How many devices does my son need all at once?* I laughed and went to greet him. Jackson was out cold and I thought about leaving him where he slept, he looked so content and happy. As I turned away from him, he jolted out of his sleep and greeted me.

"Hey dad, you're home. I tried waiting up for you, but I was beat. My girl and I traipsed all over New York tonight, she has some energy."

"Okay, son. T.M.I."

"Dad, get your mind out of the gutter. It's not like that with Riley. I meant that she is full of life and never slows down to take a breath. She was born and raised in Maryland, never really experiencing a city like New York. She only attended private schools and hasn't really had any independent moments of being on her own until this weekend with me. Her excitement beguiles me. Do you understand what I'm saying to you, dad?"

"More than you know, Jackson." I poured myself a glass of wine, remembering I swore off scotch for the rest of my life.

I took a few sips and then made the decision to come clean to Jackson. I had never lied to him, and I didn't want to start now. He was my whole world, and what he thought of me mattered.

"Jackson, can we talk?"

"Sure, dad. What's on your mind?" I was about to speak when his cell phone went off. Jackson put his finger up to halt me. "Hey baby, I miss you too." I guess I was saved by Riley and her interruption. "Hey dad, would you mind if I said goodnight to Riley, and then we can talk?"

"It's fine, son. Talk to your girl. I will see you at breakfast."

He was more than happy with my answer and took his call to his bedroom. Here I stood in this huge room feeling absolutely alone and missing Reese. I wanted to hear her voice again, so now that I knew Riley was occupied with Jackson, there would be no reason why Reese wouldn't take my call.

I noticed I had one missed call from Reese. I instantly felt relieved and listened to her voicemail, but it was just silence. Dialing her right away, her phone went directly to voicemail. I hung up before her message even ended. She probably shut her phone off and went to bed. Reese was always in the habit of shutting the world out when she needed time to think.

I had to take the edge off somehow; I was so pent up with frustration. We didn't even get to finish our dinner because of her husband calling. Then we jumped head first into a deep conversation. The memory of making love in her hotel room and then again in my car will hopefully satisfy my want for her until we meet again. I changed out of my clothes and went to work-out in my gym, then I called my trainer and requested him to meet me in the morning at six am for a rigorous work-out that I knew my body needed. If I didn't release this tension, at the first sight of Reese I would probably tear her clothes away from her delectable body and take her where she stood.

I had to be out of my mind to think I could take Tyler on with thoughts of Reese racing through my mind.

"Come on, Walker! What the hell is wrong with you today? I have knocked you on your ass twice now, and you make no move to come at me. Are we doing this or what? I don't have all day."

"Tyler, the last time I checked, you work for me, so check the attitude before I fire your ass and then knock you on it."

"I'd like to see you try, Reed. Come on, you big bad corporate mogul, come at me, and show me what you got."

I put my fists up and go to hit Tyler with my right. I missed, he swept my leg, and I'm down again. "Fuck!" I shouted out to him and he extended his hand out to me, but I shoved it away.

"One more time, Tyler, and this time I won't miss." I thought I'd embarrassed myself enough for one morning, so I charged Tyler with all that I had. This time, I took him down and he spit blood as my right leg clipped his mouth.

"It's about time, Walker. Why did it take you sixty two minutes to finally take me down?"

My only defense was Reese, and as much as I needed this work-out, I had needed her more. "I think I've had enough for today, but thank you for kicking my ass, Tyler. How's your mouth. Are you okay?"

"Don't worry about me, old man. Today was just a warm-up. I know you have more inside yourself than you showed me today. To-day you get this hit for free. Next time we spar, you better be all in, because I plan to show you no mercy."

"I'll remember that, Tyler, just send me your bill."

Fucking Tyler McVee, that's what I get for hiring a former UFC fighter to train me. This guy savagely destroyed more opponents in the ring than anyone who had come after him in the last five years since he retired.

After my long, hot shower and then soaking my sore muscles, I got dressed and immediately dialed Reese. It was early, but hopefully I would catch her before I left for the Hamptons with Jackson today. *Shit!* My call went straight to voicemail, *why hadn't she turned her phone on?* Maybe if I asked Jackson to call Riley, I could find out what was going on with her mother, but how could I do that without raising suspicion?

To hell with it, I decided to just call her suite and easily make up a reason to why I was calling. The operator told me that room 425 had a do not disturb on its phone. I was angered when I heard this. Why was Reese making it so difficult for me to talk to her? Now she had left me no choice but to ask Jackson to call Riley.

When I arrived back at the penthouse, Jackson was waiting for me. "Hey Dad, good work-out with Tyler?"

"It was fine, son. How are you? What time did you go to sleep last night?"

"I told you dad, my girl has energy. Riley kept me on the phone until two thirty in the morning. I think I had fallen asleep at one point, but then she laughed about something and the sound of her sweet giggle woke me up."

"Are you ready to go to your grandmother's?"

"Yes, but I thought I was going alone."

"That was the plan, but I changed my mind and will be joining you. I have some loose ends to tie up back at the house, so while you're entertaining your grandmother, I will be working."

I called Miles Jacobson and asked him to meet me up at the house. He hesitated at first but then reluctantly agreed. Having fired Miles over his betrayal, the man didn't owe me anything, but something still stuck in my craw about the story that he fed me the other day.

I read and re-read my father's letter to me, and I still felt like I was missing something. I knew my father was controlling, but he went to extreme measures to make sure Reese was out of my life, and I had a sinking feeling there were more secrets yet to be revealed. My instincts were telling me that they were held by Miles Jacobson, and he was not leaving until he told me what I needed to know. I called Stephen to make sure my book was on its way. I already made the decision to go with Jackson today, so I had Stephen tell the courier service to deliver it at my mother's home.

The drive this time had taken longer than my last trip out here. We were re-routed due to construction, and that delayed our arrival. When we pulled up to the main gate, Jackson screamed into the voice box. He knew my mother was probably waiting for him. For some reason, this always amused her when he called out for her. The gates opened, and we made our way through the rose lined driveway up to the house. As expected, my mother was waiting for her grandson at the front door.

Jackson leaped out from the car and ran right into his grandmother's waiting arms. "Grandmother!" shouted Jackson. I watched as they embraced each other. There was no doubt that my son loved my mother with all of his heart.

"Hello, mother," I greeted her as I walked up to separate the two and place a kiss on her cheek.

"Oh, Walker, do you always have to be so formal? You can hug me and at least pretend you're happy to be here."

"Mother, enjoy your visit with my son, I have other matters that need my attention." I walked away, and instantly regretted my cold attitude toward her when Jackson's eyes widened at me. If Jackson only knew why I was angry. When I left here yesterday and arrived at Reese's door, I had intended to tell Reese everything about what I had learned from Miles. And now I'm back in the one place that I hate. This fucking home held no happy memories for me at all, and I wanted it gone.

"Walker, I'm here as requested." Miles Jacobson walked through my father's study and stood like a soldier in front of me.

"Have a seat, Miles, and get comfortable. We are not leaving this room until I get what I want."

"Walker, I only came here today out of respect for your mother.

I have told you everything I know. When you fired me, which you absolutely had just cause to do, our ties were severed. What are you possibly seeking now?"

I rose from my father's chair and walked around his desk to look in Miles's eyes for answers, but the old man wore his poker face like no other. It would be hard to break him.

"Miles, I'm still trying to wrap my mind around this whole elaborate plan to rid Reese from my life. You must know that I had already planned on joining my father in California and was ready to step up to take over Reed Global. My only request at the time was bringing Reese with me. Why did he really do it, Miles? There has to be something that I'm missing, what is it?"

"I have told you everything, Walker. There is nothing more to say."

He was lying, I could feel it.

"Miles, do you really want to play this game with me? My father is dead, and you owe him nothing. The time where you protected his secrets are over. Now I will ask again: tell me, what am I missing?" A knock at the door interrupted our moment.

"I'm sorry sir for interrupting, but this just arrived for you."

"It's quite alright, Hilda, I was expecting this." I took the package and placed it on my father's desk with Miles eyeing my parcel. Did he know what this contained? He knew everything else, so this would not surprise me. I let him sweat it out for a few minutes before I opened it.

Miles stood up and paced the room. I leaned against the desk and crossed my arms over my chest waiting for his answer. I knew there was more, and now I just had to get him to reveal it.

"Walker, your father was a very complex man, he was the shrewdest business man I have ever known. He always had a card to play and knew when to use it for his advantage. This is where your Reese Mitchell became part of his plan."

"How, Miles? Reese was a simple girl from Pottersville, Georgia. She wasn't rich, she didn't run in the same circles we did. She was a struggling college student who modeled part-time to pay the bills. How could she be a threat to the great Phillip Reed?"

"She wasn't at first, Walker. Your father knew you cared about her and possibly loved her. He always had a plan for you when it came to your future. He never really thought of your love life until he was faced with a crisis involving the company. He made a deal, Walker, to save Reed Global."

"What kind of deal, Miles? And why was Reese a part of it?"

"Reed Global was struggling around the time you were to finish college. Phillip made some poor business decisions and ultimately was facing bankruptcy."

"Get the hell out of here! Our company had never been stronger back then. My father never told me that we were having problems. I was set to take over by September. If the company were in dire straits, then why push me to take over a sinking ship?"

"You don't understand, Walker. By the time you arrived in California, everything had been worked out, and Reed Global paid their debts. With the new projects that were on the table, the company managed to become bigger and stronger."

"This is still so frustrating, I feel like we're talking in circles. Okay, so Reed Global was in a financial crisis and was allegedly facing bankruptcy. Who floated the loan to Reed Global to get us out from our money problems? Miles, if this is the last piece of the puzzle, then I need to know. I can never move on with my life with this shadowing me. Obviously my father wanted me to know, or he wouldn't have left me that letter confessing his sins."

Miles took a deep gulp and said, "TD Incorporated secured the loan that saved Reed Global from financial ruin."

I felt sick to my stomach and fell to my knees. *It can't be true, not Elizabeth. She did this to me?*

"Townsend Development was the company that did this? Elizabeth's father, whom I have always respected, was just as calculating and deceptive like my own father? Miles, you say Elizabeth didn't know about any of this, but how can I believe that now?"

"Walker, she didn't know. I swear on my life she didn't know."

I rose from the floor and held my head in frustration as I listened to how two men single handedly destroyed my life.

"Explain it to me, Miles. How did this happen, and why was Reese and my baby the collateral damage in all of this?"

Miles gestured over to the bar and poured himself a scotch. I knew if I took a drink, I wouldn't be able to stop. At that moment, I believed my world was spinning out of control. My father from the grave was still pulling all the strings, and I had no choice but to go along with it.

"Walker, when Reed Global was beginning to have financial problems, your father and Henry Townsend were friends. You know this. Henry's company was doing remarkably well; they had contracts all over the world for development deals. Your father confided his troubles with Henry, and then struck a deal to save Reed Global. Henry wanted Elizabeth, his only daughter, matched well in marriage, and you were his choice for her. He thought because you grew up together and always remained friends that she would be a suitable match for you. Together, your union would also seal the fate of your father's company."

Miles continued, "No one could predict Elizabeth dying in childbirth. One life was lost when another was born. Jackson was a miracle, and he was all Henry had left of his daughter. When she died, it nearly destroyed him. Henry was broken, and inconsolable after his beloved Elizabeth died. If it wasn't for Jackson, he probably wouldn't have survived her loss. Mourning his daughter, Henry almost slipped and told you the truth, but Phillip stopped him. Then as the years went by, your father's resolve had broken down and he wanted to come clean with you, but then it was Henry who stopped him. He threatened your father that if he told you the truth, he would pull all of his invested money and would destroy the company and your legacy. These two men only agreed on the one thing that kept them from absolution of their conspired sins...your son, Jackson. He was the tie that bound them together."

"How can you sit here and say it was about Jackson? Maybe that was true after the fact, but the beginning of this was all about the money? My father chose to save our company, and sacrifice my happiness with Reese, for a stupid fucking company! How the hell did I not know this? Was I so blinded back then with greed, and the want for power? Miles, I'm no better than my fucking father or Henry. Reese walked out of my life, and I did nothing to find her. I gave up, and then Elizabeth was there when I was at my lowest point in my life. I should have known Reese would have never done this to me on her own, but I was hurt with her leaving that I didn't think beyond my own pain."

I picked the wrong week to quit drinking scotch. I continued, "All of these years I could have been with Reese. We could have had our life the way we had always planned to. My life with Reese was stolen right out from under me, because of a company that was more important to my father than his own son. What the hell, Miles? Elizabeth was a bright and beautiful woman; what was her father thinking? She could have had any guy she wanted. Did he not trust that she could have found someone on her own? For the first time in my life, I'm happy Elizabeth is gone, because if she had to find this out about her father now, it would have devastated her."

I looked over to the box on my father's desk and took a breath before opening it. It's the book my father wanted me to have. I ran my fingers over the hard leather cover as they hovered over the title. *Redemption...Sins of the Father.*

"Phillip Reed did have sins, and many of them. Before he died, he tried to seek absolution from me, but I threw it back in his face. Now, once I know everything, will he finally have his redemption to live peacefully in all of eternity? I don't believe I can be that forgiving. Miles, did you know that on my father's last visit to me in California, he had left this for me?"

"No, Walker, I didn't know. I have no clue to what that book contains."

"I guess there is no time like the present to face another revelation from the deceptive web he had spun for me." I slowly opened the book to find it hollowed out. Inside, I found another letter from my father and a black velvet pouch.

Miles looked over to what my father had left for me. His curiosity was just as piqued as mine. I placed the letter in my jacket pocket and decided to see what the mystery pouch contained. I opened the pouch and let the object slide into the palm of my hand. I felt chills run through me as I was holding the very same locket I had given to Reese on New Year's Eve all those years ago. This was my tangible piece of my heart only meant for her. I rolled it over and read the inscription. ***"You are my forever. Love, Walker."*** How did my father get Reese's locket? The clasp was broken. I opened it up to find the picture I had placed inside of it. It was Reese and me in Georgia. I loved this picture of us. I have its copy in my safe back home in my city apartment. I held out my hand with the locket still in my palm and directly faced Miles.

"Can you explain this? How did my father come to be in possession of Reese's locket? Answer me, Miles!"

He emptied his drink and poured another before answering me. He stammered over his words before revealing more of my father's deceptions.

"Walker, I had completely forgotten about the necklace. I haven't laid eyes on that locket since the day your father took it from Ms. Mitchell."

"So help me, Miles, you better fucking tell me everything before I rip your throat out. My father is dead, so now his sins become yours. You're just as responsible as he is, and Henry. How the hell did my father get this necklace away from Reese? I will not ask you again."

"It was the day she came looking for you in California. She was visibly pregnant and before she had the chance to call out your name, she was stopped by Ralston."

I could feel the bile rising up in my throat, my heart accelerating with rage for my father, and remorse for my broken girl that he nearly destroyed. I waited with the last ounce of patience I had. Miles, the man I had respected and admired while growing up now looked as broken as a fallen bird. His wings had been clipped, and he was struggling to break free. This was what my father had reduced him to.

"Miles, please? Tell me the rest."

"I was already in the building waiting on you and your father to arrive when he phoned me to meet him outside. I had taken the stairs to avoid you coming off the elevator. I met your father outside the atrium, and that's when I saw Ralston holding back your Ms. Mitchell. She was struggling to get out of his hold. He only released her when instructed by your father to do so. She was crying and begging your father to allow her to go to you, but he stopped her…again. She tried to threaten him, but he knew it was all a ruse, and played out his hand to her. He once again threatened her family, and by doing so was able to bring Ms. Mitchell to her knees. She sobbed and sobbed while begging your father to show her mercy. I'm sorry, Walker, but he never did. She showed him her locket and told him that it didn't matter how it appeared in print that you had moved on, she was still the owner of your heart. That's when he did the unthinkable."

"What the hell did he do?"

"He ripped the necklace off of her neck. Ralston was laughing and actually enjoying her visible misery. I was sick over it and wanted to leave, but he ordered me to stay. She begged him to return it, but he said no. We left her there, crying on the ground, Walker. I deserve whatever punishment you want to bestow on me. I will never get her pathetic image out of my head from that day, and her piercing cries haunted my dreams for many months that followed."

Miles took another gulp from his drink and went on. "I'm so very sorry, Walker. No words will ever make up for what we did to that poor girl and what it cost you. I can promise you that I have truly told you everything now. It pained your father for a great many years not telling you the truth, but he made his choice and he had to live with it. Don't let his mistakes and poor judgment define you and take you down the same dark roads as it did for him."

"It pained him? Are you that deluded, Miles? What he did to Reese on that day probably caused her to lose our child. How could she provide a safe environment for our growing baby while she was constantly under surveillance, stress, and then to be physically assaulted by Ralston? Reese may have been tall, but she barely weighed over one hundred twenty pounds. Fuck! She was carrying my child, Miles! How the hell could anyone be so cruel?"

The wheels were spinning in my head. "This just makes perfect sense now. This is what my father was trying to tell me when he visited me in California. I never gave him the chance to tell me the truth. I don't know if it would have made a difference finding out then or now, I still have so much hatred for the man. I can't even see straight. Miles."

"I'm sorry it took me all of these years to finally tell you what you should have known years ago. I truly hope you find what you're looking for and make peace with all of this."

"Is this it? Do I now know everything, Miles, and I do mean everything?"

"Without knowing what his last letter contains, I swear to you I have told you all that I know."

I believed Miles this time. He had nothing to gain by keeping the truth from me. I sat in my father's office for hours after Miles had left. I wanted to go to Reese and hold her. Beg for forgiveness on behalf of my father, and all he had done to her. I placed her locket back into the pouch and placed it in my pocket, vowing to repair it as soon as I returned to the city. I only had one last thing to do: read his letter.

My son,

I promise you that this will be the last letter you ever will read from me. Again, I took the coward's way out by leaving this for you instead of telling you the truth to your face like a man should. I truly intended to tell you the truth on the day I came to your office, but you knew me so well. How could I have done that to you? And on the anniversary of your wife's death and my grandson's birthday. I could see the pain all over your face, but I once again pushed you until you snapped. This was my forte Walker, and although I'm responsible for all of your pain that you have gone through, I still couldn't see past my own righteousness. No amount of apologies will ever make up for what I have done to you. You must know by now that Henry Townsend was my partner in all of this. Ralston and Miles were just players in the game. I expect you will seek out your own brand of justice or revenge for the ones that hurt Ms. Mitchell.

Miles is a good man, and he did try to stop me, but I never listened. What we did haunted him for many years, and I have to presume it still does. Henry has had to also pay for his role in this as well. The night his daughter died, he had said it was God's way of punishing him for what we did to Ms. Mitchell. I didn't believe it then, but maybe in some small way he was right. Not that I'm a religious man, but karma is real, and we have all had our share of it.

If you ever get the chance to be with Ms. Mitchell again, I truly hope this locket finds its way back to her. She was incredibly brave while standing up to me, and I broke her by taking this from her. I hope to one day be reunited with my grandson—your unborn child— and beg him for forgiveness. He should have lived my son, and have you as his father to raise him. You will never know how sorry I am for your loss. Please don't let my sins define you, Walker. I know how much I have hurt you, but you're also your mother's son and have goodness that runs through you. You love more than you hate. Please, my son... let love be your guiding light back to the woman I know you still love. I knew it from the moment you spoke about your life, and who you were missing.

I pray you get your second chance and finally live the life you were meant to have.

In parting...

Your father, Phillip Alexander Reed

Sitting in silence and now staring at my father's portrait, I vowed to take back what was taken from me...starting with Reese. My father was right about one thing. I was very much in love with Reese Mitchell, and she would be mine. Our time together was stolen from us. No letters of apologies can ever make up for that, but our connection was just as strong now as it was all those years ago. I gathered my things from my father's office and took one last look around the room. My eyes found his, and it was my defining moment as Phillip Reed's son.

"You're a coward, father. You hid your treachery from me all of these years simply because you believed you could. You had no right to play God with our lives, and I promise you, father, I will right those wrongs. Death may have freed you of the burdens you carried while alive, but it doesn't mean I will ever forgive you for what you did. I knew you were ruthless, but to do this to your own son is incomprehensible to me, and I hope you carry this with you to the deepest realm of hell." I slammed my way out of his study, and vowed never to return to it again.

Jackson and my mother had now returned. Jackson's arms were filled with shopping bags, as I'm sure my mother had spoiled him with gifts.

"Why, hello there, Walker. We thought you would never emerge from your seclusion. Is all your business concluded for the day?" *Ah my mother, as graceful as she conducts herself, she also has a smart mouth about her as well.*

"Yes, I'm done for today. How about we all have an early dinner before Jackson and I return to the city?"

"Sounds good to me, dad. What do you say Grandmother? Where do you want to go?"

"In honor of hanging out with my amazing grandson all day, let's think out of the box and order...pizza." I rarely remember a time when my mother shocked me, but this took the cake. Olivia Walker Reed wants greasy, cheesy pizza.

"Okay, mother, pizza it is." Jackson smiled and hugged his

grandmother. He loved her so much, and the sight of them made the coldness I felt for my father melt away some in my heart. I will never forget what my father did to me, but I can't keep Jackson away from my mother. A couple of hours ago, I wanted to take gasoline to this house and burn it to the ground. I hated being here, but it's the home she shared with my father, and I would leave it be for her.

We ate our pizza, and Jackson explained in great detail about film school and of course Riley. "Grandmother, as soon as we are settled at school, my first chance I get, you have to meet my girl. Riley is amazing, and I know you will love her. I had a great time today. And thank you for my new camera. I promise you this bad boy will make an award-winning film."

"I love you, Jackson, and of course I look forward on meeting Riley. She sounds lovely, and anyone that can make you this happy is worth getting to know." They hugged one more time, and then Jackson waited in the car for me to say my goodbyes to my mother.

"Mother, if I remember correctly, those were the same words you recited to me when I wanted you to meet Reese. Did you mean it back then?"

"Yes, Walker, I did. Reese was an extraordinary young woman, and she brought you happiness and clearly loved you. I wish I would have known what your father was planning. If I had, you must believe I would have tried to stop him. Remember what we talked about, son. I know you want another chance with Reese, but it's not just about her anymore. She has a husband, and a daughter who is in love with Jackson. This can crumble all around you, and many lives will be affected by the choices you make. Please be careful, my son."

"Mother, I know what I'm doing. None of this had to happen if it wasn't for father manipulating me in the first place. Look, we had a pleasant afternoon. Let's not spoil it now. I will be in touch." I quickly hugged my mother and turned away from her. She wanted more, but every time I felt like she was defending the past or my father, anger burned throughout me.

I glanced down at my phone, no missed calls or texts from Reese. Come to think of it, Jackson didn't speak to Riley at all today. I guess she wanted to give this time to him with his grandmother.

We arrived back in the city by seven. All I wanted to do was see Reese. I was going to quickly shower and change and then go to her hotel. I had so much to tell her and it couldn't wait one more minute.

"Dad!" Jackson screamed for me.

I ran out of my bedroom to find him slamming the phone down onto the counter. "What's wrong, son? Why are you so upset?"

"I just called the hotel, and Riley and her mom have checked out. Riley's phone is going directly to voicemail. What the hell, dad? Why would she leave without telling me?"

My heart just sank deep in my chest. This is why I couldn't get in touch with Reese last night or today. She was running again, and if she told me she planned on going home, she knew I would have stopped her. I tried to calm down and get my words out without alarming Jackson. He was clearly hurt by Riley's sudden departure. So was I, for that matter, but I didn't want him to see.

"Jackson, maybe a family emergency occurred, and they had no time to call." *I was praying my feeble excuse would be enough for Jackson to calm down.*

"This doesn't make sense, dad. Even if Riley had an emergency she would have called me. Did I freak her out last night by telling her that I loved her? How could she leave without telling me?" In a rare moment, Jackson began to cry and sat in pain with all of his unanswered questions about Riley.

"Listen to me, Jackson. I'm sure she has a valid reason why they left. Please calm down, and let's just relax a bit and then call her again. If Riley doesn't pick up, then just leave her a message. I'm sure she will return your call."

Jackson began holding his head. Every time he did this, it scared the hell out of me. This was another reason why I didn't want him on the other side of the country. His mother having a stroke took her life, and since his early teen years, Jackson had suffered with migraines. I had him tested every year with blood work and scans to make sure he's okay.

"Dad, I'm going to take a shower, and then if I don't reach Riley, I'm going to bed. I have a headache, and feel kind of sick."

"Do I need to call a doctor, Jackson? You must tell me if you need one."

"Dad, it's just a headache. I'm going to take some Advil and lie down. You have the look in your eyes again. Don't worry. I swear to you that I'm fine."

"Okay. Get some rest, and I'll check on you in a little while. I love you, son."

"I love you, too. Good night, dad."

Asking me not to worry was like asking me not to breathe. How could I not worry when it came to Jackson's health? How much more could I take today? With all that I found out from Miles and finally learning the truth, my head was pounding. I had to reach Reese and find out why she left without talking to me.

First things first, I had some matters to take care of, and I needed to start with Henry Townsend. That son of a bitch played with my life, and now that I knew the truth, I believed a visit was in order to my father-in-law.

I phoned Stephen and made all the arrangements to leave in the morning, stop in Arizona, then arrive home in California. My next call was to Reese. Her voicemail picked up and this time I left a message.

"Reese, I don't know why you left without saying goodbye. I can't believe I'm actually saying these words again, it's like I'm back there when I discovered you missing the first time. I will find you this time. I promise you that, my love. Reese, I meant every word I said to you last night. I love you, and you're mine forever. You will be seeing me soon. You can count on that."

I hung up and prayed that she didn't delete my message before listening to it. Once I dealt with Henry and got Jackson settled back at home, I could focus on Reese. Before going to bed, I checked on Jackson. He was fast asleep with Riley's picture in his hand. I could tell he was crying from the tear stains on his pillow. *My poor boy, so in love and now missing his girl because she left without as much as a simple goodbye.* I brushed his fallen floppy hair away from his eyes. God! He looked so much like his mother when he slept. I know it's a restless sleep, but I can't help to think of Elizabeth when I get these rare stolen moments with him. I took his phone and placed it on his nightstand and carefully placed Riley's picture along with it.

As I watched over Jackson, he appeared to look more relaxed as he fell deeper into sleep. I turned off his light and made my way to the door, taking one last glance at him.

Believe me, son, I know exactly how you feel. I promise you will see your girl again. This time around, I do not plan on letting Reese walk out of my life to never be heard from again. Her running days are over, and the only running she is going to do is right back into my waiting arms...where she was always meant to be.

CHAPTER TEN

Unexpected visitor...

I REMAINED AS quiet as I could without alerting Samuel that I was actually awake. I squeezed my eyes closed and remembered what I was awakened to.

After leaving Walker, my heart was racing. My head was spinning and my heart was screaming to turn around and run back into the arms of the man that I love. I kept walking and foolishly never looked back. Another mistake I can add to my long list of wrong choices that only brought me the feeling of pain and loss. All these feelings were connecting to my past and now present with Walker. *He must have tried calling me by now?* I thought silently to myself. What about Jackson? He must be upset with Riley as well. She had never missed a call with him, and I'm sure he must be confused about why she is not returning his calls. *I'm back there again, how did this happen?* This was always the question I kept asking myself. I had left Walker again, and not by choice. I was being forced again to leave him, and he had no clue as to why.

My stomach hurt, my head hurt, and I wanted off this plane. Today was supposed to be very different. I had led Riley to believe that we were going to have a spa day, but really we were going to Central Park to see Freddy's show and reunite with my best friend. I had planned this out very carefully with Marsha, and now with the unexpected turn of events, how will she ever understand me not showing up today? Once I had my time with Freddy and Riley, I would reunite with the man that I loved. I had planned on telling Walker that I did intend to move forward with divorcing Samuel, and would join him wherever he wanted me to be. As long as Walker and I were together, I wouldn't care.

Samuel showing up unexpectedly was the game changer in our story. I had awakened to a cold bed, missing Walker, and remembering all of my time with this amazing man who I loved all of my adult life. I touched myself in the places he did when he explored my body. I almost made myself come with the naughty fantasies that were entertaining my mind. I glanced over at the alarm clock, and it was nearing nine am. I showered quickly and got dressed. I glanced at my image in the mirror and what I saw was a different woman. This woman had light in her eyes again, a smile on her face, and renewed hope for her future.

I can't wait to see the look on Riley's face when I tell her what we are really doing today. Then...I will be with Walker tonight. I whispered to myself and walked out of my room to greet Riley.

"Good morning baby, how did you sleep?"

"I slept fantastic, mom, and I can't wait to spend lots of daddy's money today."

"Now, Riley, let's not go crazy. Your father doesn't have you on an unlimited budget."

"I know, mom, but it's fun to say it."

"Riley, I wanted to talk to you about something very important, I'm hoping you will hear me out and let me explain."

"Of course, mom, you know you can tell me anything. I wanted to talk to you too and..." She was interrupted by a knock on the door. "Who can that be? Are you expecting anyone, mom? Is this my surprise?"

"No, that's later on, but we're not going to know who's on the other side of the door unless you answer it."

Riley opened the door, and to our surprise, it's Samuel, standing there with a huge bouquet of flowers. *Oh shit. What the hell is he doing here?* A few days ago, this wouldn't have been my reaction. I had wanted him to be here for Riley, but now everything had changed.

"Daddy!" Riley screeched as she hugged her father with pure happiness on her face. What are you doing here? Oh my god, mom, daddy's here!"

"Oh, sweetheart, I'm so happy to see you. How about you lighten the choke hold you have on me and invite me in?"

"Oh geez, daddy, I'm sorry, please come in. Forgive me, I'm just surprised that you're actually standing in our hotel room in New York City. What about your work? Is someone covering your surgeries? What about your patients? Oh my god, daddy, did something happen?"

"Riley, wow my head is spinning with all that. Take a breath and calm down. Everything is fine, patients are good, and I left my hospital in capable hands. I'm here because I missed my girls, and I'm an ass for not joining you on this trip. Can you forgive me for not having the sense that the good Lord has given me?"

Riley, in tears, again lunged at her father and hugged him and kissed his cheek. One thing I was sure of, my daughter loved her father. *He has made her so happy with his arrival, how can I tell her now that I'm divorcing him?*

"Baby, can you let go of daddy's neck, so I can give a proper hello to your mother. I think she is still stunned that I'm here." Riley laughed and released her father. Samuel put his bag and flowers down, and slowly walked over to me. He's right...stunned would be the appropriate word that would describe this scene, among the other fifty thousand words going through my head right now.

"Hey, baby," Samuel whispered in my ears as he pulled me into a tight hold, caging me in with his vice grip fingers around my arms.

"Hi," I whispered back as he caressed my neck with kisses. I tried not to tense up with his sudden assault on me. Samuel released me and stared into my eyes, as if he secretly knew what I had been up to. I blinked back at him to break the connection.

"What are you doing here, Samuel? I thought you couldn't get away."

"Yes, that's true, but after we ended our call last night, I couldn't stay away from you...not one more minute. I should have never stayed behind and let you come here without me. My place is with my wife and daughter. I was selfish, and for that I'm truly sorry. Riley, please forgive me for not being here from the beginning. I want to hear all about your trip, from the minute you arrived."

"What can I say, daddy? This trip has been amazing, and I can't wait to come back to live and attend school here. I toured the whole campus and met with my professors that I will have for my first and second semesters. I can't even tell you how many friends I made from my last time I was here until now. Jackson has a circle of friends that he has known since childhood. We have spent lots of time with them, a great group of people. Daddy, I can't wait for you to officially meet Jackson. He is so wonderful and smart. He has taken me all around the city, dinner, a night at the theater, and even a horse and carriage ride in Central Park."

"Wow, that sounds great honey, but haven't you spent any alone time with your mother? Wasn't this one of the reasons you gave me when asking my permission to come here?"

"Mom and I had planned on spending today together. We have a spa appointment, lunch, and shopping planned. We were just about to head out when you arrived to surprise us."

I remained quiet until Samuel turned back at me with his happy expression now turning glacial. He can be so mercurial at times.

"Reese, you approved of our daughter roaming the streets at night with her boyfriend, whom you just met? Where were you when this was all happening?" Samuel's tone was now accusatory. I could see from across the room that he was beginning to tense up.

"Samuel, our daughter was not roaming the streets of New York by herself. She was with Jackson, and both were accompanied by his

155

father's driver and security detail. I knew at all times where our daughter was, so why all the questions? She hasn't done anything wrong, but be eighteen and enjoy herself."

"I'm sorry to both of you for my behavior, but Riley, this is New York, and you never really have left home before. Give your father a chance to process all the change that is happening in your life."

"Daddy, why are you so paranoid? Did you forget that I grew up in Baltimore? That's a city too. I was perfectly safe with Jackson's driver. His father made sure we were watched over by him, and we never even got a chance to walk the streets. Richard drove us everywhere."

"I'm happy to hear that. It sounds like Jackson's father is just as protective of his son as I am of you. Reese, how was the luncheon? Did you meet up with some of your old friends from the alumni group?"

"Mom didn't make it, daddy. She missed all of the events." Samuel whipped his head around and shot daggers right at me. *Stay calm Reese, stay calm.*

"Why did you miss the events? Where were you?"

"Samuel, I missed the events because I got sick, and came down with a vicious migraine that incapacitated me for the entire day. I had forgotten my migraine medicine, so I was at the mercy of over-the-counter meds. I rested all day in bed and time got away from me." *Please god let him believe me.*

"Oh, honey, why didn't you phone me right away? I would have had my nurse call in a prescription for you. You went days with a migraine and without the proper medicine."

"Samuel, I'm fine now. I guess I needed the rest, and Riley was having so much fun, why spoil it for her? We met up later that night and caught up." *I was silently praying this would appease Samuel.* "Anyway, I think we have pretty much covered everything, how about we go downstairs for some breakfast, or we can go out somewhere?"

Samuel still eyed me with suspicious eyes, but he finally pried his eyes off of me and turned to Riley. "How about we order some room service, and then I tell you both the other reason why I'm here?"

"Sounds great, daddy. I'll order some food while you talk with mom."

"Reese, can I speak with you privately?" I looked at Samuel, and he mouthed, "Now."

"Of course, let's go into the bedroom where we can talk." I shakily turned the knob and Samuel entered behind me. The door closed rather loudly, and Samuel swung me around and took me in his arms.

"Oh, baby, I have missed you so much. I need you right now. Let me show you how much I love you. I can't begin to tell you how embarrassed I am with my callous behavior when you left. After you left my office, I felt sick to my stomach. You're my wife, and I shouldn't have done that to you. I have never been so rough with you, and I feel ashamed by my actions."

"Samuel, you didn't hurt me, but it did scare me."

"Again, I am so sorry, please let me make it up to you. I love you, Reese. I know we have issues to work out, but please tell me that you didn't mean what you said back at home?"

"We said a lot of things to each other, Samuel. Refresh my memory."

"Don't be prevaricating with me, Reese. You know damn well what I'm asking. Divorce, you asked me for a divorce! Which will never happen by the way. I am not just going to let you end our marriage without a fight."

"Samuel, you can't make me stay in a marriage that I'm no longer happy in. Don't you see how far we have grown apart? We have become more like roommates than husband and wife."

"Reese, how can you say this to me? Were you ever happy with me?"

I was about to answer him when Riley called out to us.

"Samuel, breakfast is here, let's talk about this later."

"No! Dammit, we will talk about it now."

"Samuel, let go of my arm before this gets out of hand again. Our daughter is in the next room and waiting for us to join her for breakfast. We will talk later."

He let go of my arm and his body relaxed instantly with the mention of Riley's name. He would never cause a scene in front of our daughter, but his actions were alarming me.

"This looks wonderful honey, you ordered all of my favorites. So after we enjoy our meal, we are checking out and heading to the airport. I have a jet on stand-by to fly us down to the Caribbean for the next four days."

Riley and I were both rendered speechless.

"Come on, you two, I thought you would love this idea? We haven't had a family vacation for a few years now, and what better way to wrap up spring break than go to a beautiful island?"

"Daddy, that sounds great, but mom and I already extended our stay here. What will I say to Jackson?"

"Well, it sounds like you have already have spent a great amount of time with your boyfriend and no time with your mom, so now you get both your parents on this trip. It's only for four days, and I have cleared my schedule at the hospital, so we're going."

"Daddy, what about clothes and things we will need? I haven't packed for the tropics."

"Riley, you may pick up anything you need when we arrive at our destination. So please, enough with the questions, finish eating, and let's get ready to go."

I sat there in silence and picked at my food. *This is not happening. I can't go away with Samuel for the next four days.* Today was Freddy's fashion show in Central Park, and Marsha had arranged for me to go backstage to see him. I couldn't let her down after all she'd done for me. And what about Walker? He was expecting to see me today, and how do I tell him that Samuel whisked us away to an island to save our marriage? *Oh my god! This is a mind fuck of a situa-*

tion, and I'm completely trapped.

"Will you excuse me for a moment; I have to gather my things in the next room." I clutched my cell phone in my pocket and hurried into the bedroom. I pulled out my phone to text Walker, as Samuel entered the room, causing me to jump.

"What are you doing, Reese? I thought you were going to pack." He startled me, not giving me a moment to breathe.

"Samuel, you showing up here today is a complete surprise, and I'm sure Riley is thrilled, but…"

"You're not? Reese, I've been a fool that has seen the light. Please let me make this up to you. I know I can be a better husband than I've been, but you need to give me that chance to do so."

"I meant what I said back in Maryland. I want a divorce. In time you will see that our marriage has run its course, and now you will have a chance to be truly happy with someone who deserves not just pieces of you, but all of you."

"No! Reese, you're my wife, and you will stay my wife. Now don't push me. Gather your things, and let's go." His voice was laced with anger and dominance. I had to get a message to Walker and to Marsha.

"Samuel, will you sit with me for a few minutes?" He reluctantly did, but was still scowling at me. "Riley believes that we are having a spa day, but the truth is that I am taking her to Central Park to see a fashion show."

"A fashion show? Really, Reese? That time in your life is over. Now let's stop this nonsense and pack."

"Samuel, it was never over for me!" I found my voice. "You made me quit. I enjoyed modeling and I met amazing people while doing it. Do you remember Marsha, my agent? I've been talking to her recently, and I planned on seeing Freddy today."

"You can't be serious, Reese."

"I'm completely serious, Samuel. He was my best friend until I completely crushed him by cutting him out of my life. I miss my friend, and I want to see him. Marsha is waiting on me right now."

"Well, Marsha and Freddy, will have to wait until you return from our trip. Now this conversation is over. Pack your things and be ready in ten minutes." He cupped my face and kissed me on my lips. It was a warning not to argue with him anymore. He turned and left the room while calling out to Riley.

"Riley, get your things together now. We have to leave for the airport."

"Daddy, the trip you've planned sounds wonderful, but I have plans with Jackson, and how can I leave New York without saying goodbye to him?"

"Listen, Riley, you had your fun in New York, and with your boyfriend. We are leaving right now, and when we return home, you can call your boyfriend. Hand me your cell phone right now! We are cutting off the rest of the world, and we're going to spend quality time as a family. We need this time together."

"Daddy, I'm not giving you my cell phone. I need to be in contact with Jackson. I'm calling him right now and letting him know what's going on."

"The hell you are! Now give me your damn phone right now, Riley Taylor Briggs."

"Samuel, please calm down. Riley, please listen to your father, and hand him your phone. Once we get settled at our hotel, you may phone Jackson." My daughter was now in tears. She had never defied her father nor had he ever raised his voice to her in that way before.

Riley gave me her phone and ignored Samuel altogether. She continued to cry and gathered her bags while I was left to face Samuel and his anger. This was my fault; he was mad at me, not Riley. He had come there to work on our marriage, and I wouldn't discuss it with him.

"Reese, I'm sorry. I just wanted to take you away and spend some time with the two of you. This is not how I wanted today to be. Once we board the plane, I will talk to Riley."

"You scared her. I know you're angry, but don't take it out on

160

our daughter."

"I said I was sorry Reese, and I meant it. We will work it all out, but first things first. Get your things."

Samuel checked us out of our hotel, and we made our way to the airport. Samuel had been watching my every move since our argument, and I couldn't check my phone if I wanted to. I was just praying that once I spoke to Walker, he would understand why we had to leave so abruptly. Riley was miserable and giving her father the silent treatment. Samuel gripped my thigh, and I just sat as still as I could throughout the deafening silence.

"You will see, Reese, this trip is going to be wonderful for our family. I have so much planned for us when we arrive. Please put a smile on that beautiful face of yours."

Samuel raised my hand to his lips and kissed me softly. I jerked my hand back from him and he only reached for it again, this time holding it a bit tighter.

"I can be a very patient man, Reese, but you will only try my patience for so long before I have had enough. Please remember that, my love." I nodded my response and closed my eyes.

We arrived at the Parrot Cay Resort and Spa on the Caribbean Island of Turks and Caicos. Samuel had rented a private villa for us away from the tourists. We had our own private beach and pool. A hot tub was on our private deck, and no one surrounded us. He thought of everything to truly conceal us from the outside world.

It was early evening, and Walker must have been out of his mind with worry. I had to reach a phone to contact him, but how was I going to manage that with Samuel watching my every move?

"What do you think? This place is beautiful. This resort came highly recommended by several of my colleagues at the hospital. We can swim, snorkel, and take the sailboat out on the water. Anything we want to do for the next four days is at our disposal."

"Daddy, I need to call Jackson. He's not going to understand why I left without saying goodbye to him. Please let me call him."

"Riley, this discussion is not up for debate. I'm over it already.

Do not bring up your boyfriend again to me. You will just suck it up and enjoy yourself while we're here, do you understand me?"

"Yes, daddy." Grabbing her bag, Riley ran into her bedroom.

"Let me talk to her," I said.

"No, let her be. You've coddled her enough for one day. Let's shower, then dinner will arrive, and after that we can take a walk on the beach."

"You can go first, and I'll unpack our things."

"Reese, when I said shower I had meant the two of us. Now let's go." Samuel pulled me in to the bathroom with him and began to unbutton my blouse. *Please let the marks that Walker left on me be gone.* I was shaking with Samuel's deftly fingers making their way down my chest. He slid my blouse down and let it drop to the floor. He then unzipped my slacks and slowly pulled them down. Samuel's eyes skimmed my body as he licked his lips and pulled me closer to him. "I want you, Reese. I love you, and all I want to do is make us right again. Please allow me to show you how much you mean to me?"

Walker, Walker, Walker, please forgive me for what I'm about to do. I relaxed and closed my eyes as Samuel held me and removed my bra and panties. He quickly removed his clothing and led me into the scalding hot shower. Samuel lifted my leg and wrapped it around his waist. He held me to the shower wall and crushed himself into me. I hated every second of it. I felt like I was betraying Walker by fucking Samuel. I didn't want this, but he was in a volatile mood and I could push him no more. When it was over, I pasted a smile on my face, wincing as he pulled out of me.

Samuel lathered me with body wash and caressed the same areas where Walker had been. I had some faint marks still left, but they went unnoticed by Samuel. He stepped out of the shower while I finished. I held my hand over my mouth as I cried, letting the water wash away my shame and guilt, silently praying that Samuel wouldn't hear my cries.

CHAPTER ELEVEN

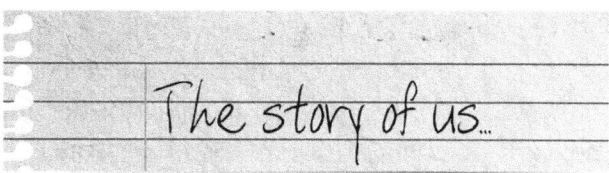

The story of us...

WORKING ON LITTLE sleep after staying up half the night with my distraught son, I finally managed to get some rest of my own. Jackson only managed to sleep for a short while, and then his headache became worse. I phoned our personal physician to come by and examine him. Jackson gave me a hard time at first, but then conceded when I insisted. Dr. O'Larien concluded that it was merely a migraine brought on from stress. He prescribed a stronger medicine and urged Jackson to rest until it passed.

"Walker, you're going to find yourself in an early grave if you don't calm down. Jackson is fine, and his scans always come up clean."

"Liam, I will never waver when it comes to Jackson's health, especially when I have the means to prevent it."

"Walker, will you listen for a minute? You're not God. You can't stop the inevitable from happening. What happened to Elizabeth was extremely rare. Jackson is young and in good health. The headaches he gets are normal, although this one I will admit was stronger than I've seen before. The medicine I prescribed will help, and as long as he relaxes, then all will be fine."

"Liam, Elizabeth was just as healthy and young too. I ignored the signs with her, and she paid the price with her life."

"You need to let that go, Walker, once and for all. We have been over this many times. As of right now, your son does not appear to have CM-AVM. Try not to worry. Sometimes a headache is just a headache."

The sun was just beginning to rise above New York and greet the day. My jet was fueled and ready to go, destination unknown. I paced my office waiting for my phone to ring. Another fifteen minutes later, the call I had been waiting for was patched through.

"Sir, I have located Mrs. Briggs, along with her husband and daughter. They are on the Caribbean island of Turks and Caicos. They are staying in a private villa and the only means of transportation is by boat."

"Excellent work, Stephen. Do you have your men on them now?"

"Yes sir, I do. How do you want me to proceed?"

"Keep on them, I'm on my way. Once I arrive, I will contact you. Any attempts they make on leaving, I must know right away."

I guess the good doctor Samuel Briggs was one step ahead of me, but not for long. Maybe this was just a coincidence that he had swooped in and taken them away, but it seemed all too convenient now. What Reese told me is that he had been an absent figure in their marriage for quite a while now, but as soon as she asked him for a divorce, he's back with a vengeance. This didn't make sense, but I promised Reese that I would never let her go, and I intended to keep my word.

I rushed into Jackson's room, and he was still sleeping. "Jackson, wake up son. You need to get dressed." My son finally stirred and blinked up at me a few times. "Jackson, talk to me. Are you alright? Do you have a headache?" I asked him nervously, hoping that what Liam prescribed had helped him.

"No, dad, my head is fine now. It's my heart that's hurting. Do you know how many times I tried calling Riley? Try thirty two times. Her voicemail box is full, and I lost count with my text messages. I don't understand any of this, dad. What did I do wrong?"

Now it's my heart that's hurting. Listening to my son cry his heart out for his girlfriend brings it all back to when I discovered Reese missing. He's me, seventeen years ago, and I had no choice but to tell him the complete truth about my history with Reese.

He's going to keep beating himself up over this, and I can't bear to see my son in this amount of unnecessary pain. Jackson can't go through what he did last night; his pain level was nearly a ten, and it took forever for him to calm down and get some relief. Every time I see my son get a headache, my memory flashes back to Elizabeth when she grasped her head when she went into labor with Jackson. We never had any idea that she had a ticking time bomb inside of her brain, and the stress of the labor caused the stroke which ultimately took my son's mother from him. Calling our physician to examine him last night was necessary. As much as Liam tried to calm me, I didn't believe I would ever be totally calm about it. I spared no expense when it came to Jackson. His yearly check-ups along with a scan calmed me temporarily. Apprehension was always present until I received the results.

"Jackson, grab a shower and get dressed. Pack only what you need, and then we need to head to the airport."

"Are we going back home today?"

"No, son, we're not. I have located Riley and her mom. We're going to them."

"How dad? Where are they?"

"Jackson, I will explain everything to you on the plane, please just hurry so we can leave."

Without another word, Jackson leaped out of bed and headed off into his bathroom to get ready. I grabbed my bag and briefcase. In a matter of hours, I would see Reese again. Her husband had left me no choice. He took her away, and from what I gathered from Stephen, it was not by her choice. Yes, Samuel is her husband, but she belonged to me, and I'm not going to sit back and let Reese slip through my fingers again.

Within the hour, we boarded my jet and began our destination. I was apprehensive about my talk with Jackson, but I knew if this was going to go any further, I knew I had to come clean with my son.

"Dad, I can't take it! Please talk to me. Where are we going? You promised to tell me and I think I've been pretty patient, but you sitting there staring at me is driving me crazy."

"Jackson, what I have to tell you is a very long and complicated story. It also involves people who you love that have hurt me, and I don't want your feelings and memories of these people to be tarnished because of what I now know. This trip to New York has changed my life in only a matter of a few days, and now it's going to change yours."

"Whatever it is dad, I trust you and will give you the chance to explain. You have always been straight up with me, so let's hear it."

"Jackson, I swear you're wiser beyond your years, you certainly don't take after me. When I was your age, I was reckless and a bit of an ass. You're only eighteen years old and have the intelligence and wisdom of someone in their thirties."

"Dad, you're stalling. Please talk to me."

"Please keep an open mind for what I'm about to tell you. My senior year of college while attending NYU, I had met the most beautiful woman I have ever laid eyes on. Her beauty pulled me in like a magnet. I was drawn to her from the very start, and I knew I had to meet her and ultimately be with her. I dated lots of women back then, and most of them were just conquests and insignificant lovers. I never felt a connection with any of them until I met my beauty sitting in the library one day. She mocked me, and I loved it. No lines worked on her. She was amazing, and after she finally agreed to go out with me, I knew I wanted no one else. Our relationship was solid, and many times when I looked to my future, she was in it."

"I wanted to marry this woman and experience it all with her. The time we spent together was beyond any of my wildest expectations, but also the happiest I have ever been in my entire life. I asked her to marry me many times when we were in bed together. She always thought I was kidding around, but I think deep down she knew I wasn't and that the day was coming for the real proposal. After graduation, I was to go to California and begin working for your grandfather's company. I planned on having her join me once I got settled. She was going to continue with graduate school and work part-time. My last night spent with her was indescribable. We just loved each other with all that we had, and my biggest regret was leaving her in the morning."

"I wanted to surprise her with her favorite breakfast and my proposal. I was called away to handle some unforeseen business at the office, which I now know was orchestrated as a diversion. I didn't know this at the time. My girl looked breathtaking as she slept in her peaceful sleep. All I wanted to do was finish up and return to her. Proposing to her was all I had thought about, but I never got the chance to do so. I returned to my apartment and found it empty. She was gone, and all she left for me was a note telling me goodbye."

"Wow!" Jackson exclaimed, "How could mom have done that to you? Maybe she got cold feet as they say, and needed time to think. Obviously you two worked it out, because you did marry and then had me."

To hear Jackson talk about his mom and think she was *"the girl"* in my story was killing me. This was the part I dreaded the most because he always had this idealistic memory of his mother and the life we had together. I was about to crush his whole image of her. I poured myself a drink and composed myself for what I was to say next to him.

"Jackson, I'm not speaking about Elizabeth. Your mother was my childhood friend, my very best friend. I was a few months from graduating college when everything went to shit in my life. It was your mother who saved me from myself and helped me mend my broken heart. I can never repay her for the kindness she showed me back then. Her generosity was overwhelming. She gave me her heart when I didn't deserve it. I belonged to another, and no matter how much time I spent with Elizabeth, I never loved her the way I should have." I carefully watched Jackson's face, as he struggled to understand where this story was leading to.

"Your mother loved me back with all of my faults, and she always believed that she had enough love in her heart for the both of us. This is how incredibly unselfish your mother was, and in time my feelings did change for her. When we found out she was pregnant with you, I married your mom, and I completely centered my entire world on her and taking care of you. Your mother was so happy to be pregnant with you, and she couldn't wait to hold you in her arms. I begged her to find out what we were having, but she never wanted to know. When you were born, I placed you into her arms, and I whispered into her ears, 'We have a son.' I made promises to your mother that I would be the best father I could be to you. I vowed to always put you first no matter what. Jackson, I pray that I have all these years and haven't broken my promise to Elizabeth."

My son was quiet, and tears are falling down his cheek. I wanted to just take him in my arms and hold him, but I waited for him to tell me or show me what he was feeling. *Please god, don't hate me, Jackson.*

"Jackson, are you alright son?"

"Dad, if it wasn't mom, then who are you talking about? Whatever happened to this woman? Did you ever try to find her and ask her why she left you in the first place? I'm sorry that this happened to you, dad, but if it didn't, I may not be here right now. I guess everything happens for some cosmic reason, at least I try to believe that."

"It does, son, I never believed in theories about what's meant to be, but I do now. Fate has stepped in and has given me a second chance to right a wrong that never should have been. In life we sometimes are not meant to understand everything as it happens. Eventually we may, and we either choose to accept the choices we make and have made, or someone else does it for us. In my story, and unbeknownst to me at the time, outside forces conspired together that separated me from the girl who I was *in love* with. I only re-cently found out who the responsible party was."

"Who is this woman, dad? Was she the big love of your life? The one that got away? Because it sure wasn't my mother!" *It's like Jackson is looking right through me now. Does he know what I'm about to say?* "Dad, what the hell? Who is she?"

"Her name is…Reese."

Jackson was silent.

And then he wasn't so silent. "No fucking way, dad. You mean to tell me it's Riley's mom? Oh my god, I think I'm going to be sick. The way you two acted that night in the restaurant, I knew some-thing felt off about it. Dad, I have never seen you behave that way before; right there I should have called you out on it. I can't believe this is happening, and now it all makes sense to me." *He doesn't know the half of it.*

"Jackson, you need to calm down and let me explain. There is so much more to this story than you can even begin to understand."

"Dad, it seems pretty clear to me. Riley's mom was the bitch that broke your heart and stomped on it all those years ago. You married the consolation prize, my mother, and then she goes and dies on you and straps you with a kid that you probably didn't want."

I grabbed Jackson by the shoulders, and I forced him to look at me. "Jackson, I always wanted you. Don't you ever defile your mother's memory like that again! Do you hear me, son? You're my whole world, my reason for getting up every day and living this life. I will never regret being your father. If you believe anything, you must believe that. I love you, my son."

"I love you too, dad." Jackson wrapped his arms around me and held me in a vice grip of a hug until he cried it all out. My son rarely showed this level of emotion with me. After hearing about his moth-er, he must have needed to get it out.

"Jackson, please calm down. I want you to sit and take a breath. I know this is hard to hear son, but you have to know losing your mother was the hardest thing I have ever had to go through in my life. You, my son, were my lifeline. To be responsible for another human being is the hardest job in the world, and it became my responsibility to care for you and be two parents to you. I never imagined doing this alone, but what happened to your mother was an unforeseen tragedy. You're the one good thing that happened to me after losing her. You have your mother's kind eyes, and I know she is with you. I was lucky to have known her and share my life with her for the short amount of time we were given. Not a day that goes by that I don't remember your mom fondly. How can I not? I see her every day in you. She would be so proud of the man you have become."

"I'm sorry, dad, for your loss and for flipping out. I always thought mom was the one you were meant to be with, and to have that not be true, kind of freaked me out."

"Jackson, you don't have to apologize, your reaction was justified. I never thought I would have to share this with you at all. My life with your mom, and what I shared with Reese, was very personal. I have never talked to anyone about this, but your mom. I wanted to preserve your mother's memory and show you who she was."

"I love you, dad. I couldn't have asked for a better father than you. Can you please continue with your story?"

"As I said, it's very complicated. Please don't think of Reese, Riley's mom, in a bad way. She was a victim in all of this. Reese loved me, Jackson, and her feelings were true. Sadly, she fell prey to someone who manipulated her and convinced her that she wasn't worthy of me and who ultimately pushed her out of my life. I didn't know why she left me, and to have only a note telling me goodbye nearly destroyed me. I searched all over the city for Reese, but every turn I came up empty, and then my anger took over and I gave up."

"Forces around me convinced me that she wasn't worth it, and to move on with my life. As I said, I was self-destructing and not caring about anything until your mom gave me hope. I never expected to turn around and see Reese standing before me that night in the restaurant. My heart was bursting out of my chest, and all I wanted to do was hold her in my arms, but we were both so shocked that we played it off. Sitting so close in her proximity after all of these years, my shock turned to anger and I wanted to just mess with her a bit, so that explains my behavior. I knew you knew me better than that, son. I was waiting for you to confront me, but you never did. I'm thankful for that, because I needed time to compose myself and process it all."

"Dad, does Riley know any of this?"

"No, she doesn't, son. Reese and I both talked about how we were going to tell you both, but we never got the chance to."

"Who was the person that made Reese leave you and kept you two apart?"

"I think you've heard enough for now, Jackson."

"Dad, you said you would tell me everything. You can't stop now."

"Jackson, I don't want to hurt you any more than I already have. Please let's drop this."

"Dad, the only way you will hurt me is by keeping me in the dark. Tell me everything."

I took a deep breath and started. "After you and Riley left the restaurant, I confronted Reese. I forced her to tell me everything as to why she left me all those years ago. We spent hours together talking, fighting, and revealing many things to one another. Reese told me that your grandfather—my father— tried to blackmail her with something from her past. It's not important, and it never was, but at the time it scared Reese. Your grandfather used what he knew to convince her that she wasn't worthy of being with me, and I was only using her to sow my oats until I married the right girl. In a moment of weakness, Reese believed him and left. She left school, her friends, and me all behind, because of a made-up story that she believed to be true."

Jackson looked shocked as I continued, "What I didn't find out until she told me was that she was pregnant with my child when she left. She had planned on telling me about the baby the same morning

I was to propose to her. We both never got the chance."

I took a deep breath and pressed on, "Reese told me that she did try to come back to work things out with me, but fate again stepped in and changed the course of our life. She got sick before reaching out to me and lost our baby. I married your mother, and we left for California."

I went on, "Reese met Riley's father, and began a relationship with him. They married, and the rest is history. I don't know if I was ever meant to find any of this out, but when your grandfather died, he had left instructions with his lawyer to finally reveal the truth to me. This is why I made the trip out to the Hamptons. Reese told me all that she could, but it was my father who held the key to my past and played a role in breaking me and Reese up."

"Why would grandfather do this to you? It doesn't make any sense to me. How can someone do that to another person? I hate him, dad, for what he did to you."

"Jackson, please don't. This is why I never wanted to tell you. You have many good memories of your grandfather, and he loved you very much. I believe he loved me too, but he had a hard time showing it. He had his reasons why he did what he did, but they were his and his alone. I can't continue to try to understand them. When you were born, he changed, and you were his second chance. I allowed him to be a part of your life, and I'm happy you had time with him that I never did. He wanted you to have this watch, which belonged to my grandfather, and now it's yours."

He held the watch as I said, "Please carry it with you as a reminder that time is precious, and life is short. Life is unpredictable and sometimes cruel. We lose the ones that we love, and if we are lucky…we can have a second chance at forever to make it right."

"Is the universe laughing at me now, dad? How did I meet the girl of my dreams who happens to be the daughter of the girl of your dreams?"

"I don't know, son, I'm still trying to wrap my head around that one, but I do know Riley cares for you. When I see you two together,

I see me and Reese all those years ago. It's like I'm watching a movie of my life and waiting to see what happens next."

"What does happen next, dad? She's married to someone else, and how will this affect my relationship with Riley? I love her dad, but she's not going to want to be with me if you break up her parents' marriage."

"Jackson, Reese and I belong together, we always have. I love her, son, and my feelings have never changed for her. She is just existing in a loveless marriage that has never really made her happy. Before coming to New York, Reese asked her husband for a divorce, and then to reunite with me is just fate's way of righting the wrongs that happened to us. Our chance was taken away from us by forces beyond our control. Now is the time to take back what we lost and be together like we always planned to do."

"I get that dad, but at what cost? You love Reese, she loves you, but what about the other people in this story? Riley, her father, and me. It doesn't matter if she asked her husband for a divorce, they still have a life together and have a daughter. Riley is never going to understand this and be accepting to the fact that my father is the reason why her parents are not together anymore. Dad, you really have not given any thought of the damage that you and Reese will leave in the promise of being together. I think at this point, we should just go home and I'll work things out with Riley on my own. But, dad, you need to walk away from her mother."

"I can't do that, Jackson, I won't. I have lost too many years without her in my life, and I can't lose one more day. You always wanted me to be happy and find someone to share my life with; well she's the one I want, Jackson. I can't deny my feelings for her because she is married to someone else. I know our situation is very unique and complex, but you already believe Riley is the one for you, don't you? As I have always known Reese was for me."

"We just need to trust our heart and follow the path that it leads us on. Jackson, I love you, you know this. I would do anything for you son, but this is one request that I have to say no to. I can't let her go and have her slip away from me again. Please understand and give me your support."

"Dad, I want to, believe me I do, but all I see is this ending badly for all of us. I want you to be happy, dad, I really do. You have given me everything and put me before your own happiness. I can't stand here and tell you that you don't deserve some of your own. I will try to do things your way. I want Riley to be my *forever*. I know that we're young, dad, but when I look to my future, I only see her in it. Can you understand that?"

"More than you know, son…more than you know."

"I'm taking a big risk here, dad, but I trust you. I just hope we can separate our two relationships and not destroy what we have."

"Jackson, oh god, thank you." I hugged my son and let out the breath I was holding. We made it through this storm, and now he knows the truth.

"Dad, what happens next? How are we going to explain why we're there? Riley hasn't returned one of my phone calls, and you haven't spoken to Reese. I haven't even met her father yet. How the hell is he going to react to me when I introduce myself to him?"

"Jackson, I must ask you not to reveal anything that I have told you with Riley. I don't know if Reese has told Riley about us. The way they left is leading me to believe that her husband may suspect something, and I have to tread very carefully on how to proceed. I have a contact watching their villa, and once we arrive, I will be brought up to speed."

"I have never seen this side to you before, it's like you have shifted into mega mogul, and you will stop at nothing to get what you want."

"Jackson, I have lived my life at the highest level of control, and I wouldn't be able to run my business without it. When it comes to matters of my heart, it requires a similar level of control and discipline. I know what I want, and who I want, so it's time to get my woman back."

CHAPTER TWELVE

Fighting my way back to you...

WAKING UP IN paradise was not like I expected. As I laid there with Samuel's heavy arm across my chest, I felt as if I was having an out-of-body experience. Samuel was relentless yesterday with his demands of me and Riley. He had forced us on this trip and was controlling every aspect of it. I hadn't had a minute to myself since Samuel showed up in New York yesterday morning.

I carefully removed my body from under Samuel, hoping I didn't wake him. The bathroom would be my safe place to think for a few minutes, I hoped. I took a peek at my phone and of course it was full with text messages from a number that no one would know but me. I quickly read them as they were all in code, just in case my phone ended up in the wrong hands. I did have one voicemail, and it was from Walker. I peeked out from the bathroom and eyed a sleeping Samuel. *Thank god, now I can listen to Walker's voicemail.*

"Reese, I don't know why you left without saying goodbye. I can't believe I'm actually saying these words again, it's like I'm back there when I discovered you missing the first time. I will find you this time. I promise you that, my love. Reese, I meant every word I said to you last night. I love you, and you're mine forever. You will

be seeing me soon. You can count on that."

Oh Walker, I love you too. Please feel my love wherever you are, and know you're in my heart. Please forgive me for leaving you again.

As much as I wanted to save his message, I couldn't take the risk of having it discovered by Samuel, so I deleted it, but not before texting Walker to let him know that I loved him too. I had never texted a message so quickly before in my life. I hope it all made sense to him.

Walker, I love you too! So much that it hurts. Please forgive me for leaving you again. It was not my intention. Sadly, my hands were tied, and I had no choice. Samuel showed up in New York and took Riley and me to the Caribbean. In only a matter of a few days, I fear Samuel has changed into someone I don't recognize. I have to be very careful with him, Walker. Please understand what I may have to do in order to return home to you. You have my heart...always remember that. I love you...Reese.

Once I hit the send button, I deleted my message to Walker. I was going out of my mind here on this island. I had to check on Riley. She cried herself to sleep last night, and Samuel prevented me from checking on her. I tiptoed past the bed and was almost out the door when he called out to me.

"Reese, where are you going?"

Stay calm, Reese. "Good morning, Samuel. I was just going to check on our daughter. I was trying to be quiet so I wouldn't wake you."

"Come here, Reese"

"I'll be right back. Let me just see if Riley is up yet."

"Reese, I won't ask you again, Come here."

Tears were beginning to well up in my eyes, but I managed to hold them back. *I won't betray Walker again by giving Samuel my body.* I slowly walked over to him, and Samuel reached out to me. Instead of forcefully pulling me down, he gently took me into his arms and held me.

"I love you, Reese. I'm sorry I was never the husband you wanted me to be. I made so many mistakes with you, and I can't begin to know how to fix them. I know you're not happy. I would have to be a fool not to know this, but I'm asking you to please try and give me a chance to make our marriage work. Can you try too?"

Here is my chance to tell him no, but I'm afraid. He's being the kind man that I know him to be, but also he is probably praying I say yes to him. I have to follow my heart…Please Samuel, don't hate me.

"Samuel, I can't do this anymore. Hurting you is the last thing I want to do, but I can't remain in a marriage that I'm not happy in. When we get back to Maryland, I want to begin divorce proceedings."

Samuel released me and his face had fallen. He got out of bed and ran his fingers through his hair, a clear sign of his frustration and hurt.

"Reese, how the hell did we get here? You have never given me any indication that you wanted to end our marriage. Why now? What am I missing here? Am I that much of a bastard that you hate me so much to divorce me?"

"Samuel, I could never hate you. You will always hold a special place in my heart. You gave me Riley, our beautiful daughter."

"Yes, our daughter, but what else, Reese? Why can't you give me your whole heart? I have tried over the years to break down the walls that you so meticulously built around your heart. Why do I have to pay the price for the guy that broke you? I have been here for almost eighteen years. I have been here for you and loved you every single day of it. This is how you repay my love, by asking me for a fucking divorce?"

Samuel picked up a vase of flowers and threw it against the wall, smashing it into pieces. I jumped from the sound of it and hoped Riley didn't come running in.

He took a breath and said, "I'm sorry, I didn't mean to scare you. I'm just at a loss here. You want me to just walk away from our life together, and for what, Reese? Where will you go? Do you have a plan? Has this been your intention all along?"

"Samuel, we haven't been happy for a long time now; you know this to be true. You parade me around at all of your hospital functions as if I'm arm candy instead of your wife. I played the role of the good doctor's wife for all of these years now. I made you look good. And when you don't need me to be your trophy wife, you tuck me away and leave me be in our house. It's a game, Samuel, a part that we both play. I'm done with it, and I just want out."

"I can't even begin to understand you, Reese. This is how you see me and our marriage? You were just a pawn in my chess game? You're so wrong, but it's clear to me that you have already made your decision. I can't force you to stay with me, but I have this sinking feeling that there is more that you're not telling me. Did you ever love me at all?"

"Samuel, I never lied to you…not ever. I met you at the lowest point in my life. I had just lost my baby and the man that I loved more than my own life. I never promised you forever, but you still wanted me. Over the years I did grow to love you, but if we are being completely honest here, I'm not in love with you. I never was."

Smack right across my cheek. I fell back onto the bed, and Samuel leaned over me.

"Damn you, woman, and your fucking heart. I love you, and I would have done anything for you. How can you break me down like this? I'm a doctor, I heal people. I would never think of ever hurting anyone, and in the course of a few days, I have become somebody I don't even recognize. You have done this to me, Reese, because you won't stay with me. What makes him so special that no man can hold a candle to him? Tell me, Reese, why after all of these years, you can't let this man go? He abandoned you and left you with nothing but a broken heart. Here you are now, willing to give up everything for a man that you haven't seen in years."

"Get away from me! Don't you ever lay your hands on me again! You're wrong, Samuel, he didn't abandon me…I abandoned him. I told you what his father made me do. I should have been stronger and fight for the man that I loved, but I was weak! I was the one that left him! Please don't make me hate you, Samuel. I am not trying to hurt you, but you never listen to me. I have tried over the years to talk to you and make you see how unhappy I was. You always would convince me that it was all in my head and we would be fine. It's not in my head, and it's certainly not in my heart. I will always be thankful to you for the kindness you showed me when I lost my baby, and the friendship that followed. Having Riley, our beautiful daughter, has been my greatest joy in my life. For that reason alone, I can never repay you, but to stay in a marriage because of that reason, is no way to live."

I rubbed my sore cheek and continued. "You deserve someone who truly loves you, Samuel. Loves you for you, and not because of what you do, or your social standing. This is how we are perceived by the outside world. You're a rock star at Johns Hopkins, and I'm the groupie. Don't you understand what I'm telling you? I love you enough to let you go and be happy with someone that will value your heart. Please, Samuel, give me the same respect, and do the same for me."

I had nothing to lose at this point. After Samuel hit me, I knew we had reached the point of no return. I turned away from him and walked out of the bedroom. I checked on Riley to find her still asleep holding the New York Yankees teddy bear Jackson had given her. Riley, an Oriole's fan, enjoyed teasing Jackson with his Yankees.

When we arrived at our New York hotel a few days ago, a basket of treats and flowers were waiting for us, along with this teddy bear for Riley. Jackson's card was so adorable, it made Riley blush and smile.

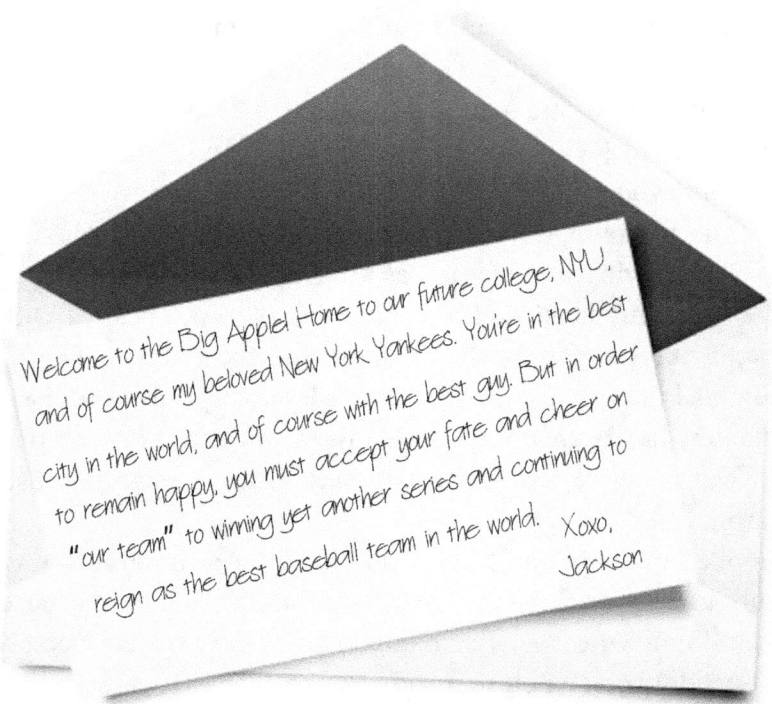

Welcome to the Big Apple! Home to our future college, NYU, and of course my beloved New York Yankees. You're in the best city in the world, and of course with the best guy. But in order to remain happy, you must accept your fate and cheer on "our team" to winning yet another series and continuing to reign as the best baseball team in the world. Xoxo,

Jackson

Riley held the bear to her chest and began jumping up and down. She reminded me so much of the way I was when I was younger and in love with Walker. Now that I knew that Jackson was his son, it's no wonder how Riley had fallen so much in love with him. Jackson was his father's son, dripping with charm and passion. I bent down to kiss my daughter. *Oh baby, you will get your happy ending, I promise you. I will never let you repeat the mistakes that I made. Jackson loves you, and you will see him soon.*

"Mom, is that you?"

"Yes, baby it is. I didn't mean to wake you. Are you okay?"

"I'm fine, mom. I just wish I could understand what is happening? Why has daddy gone off the deep? Oh mom, what happened to your face? Did daddy hit you?"

"Yes, he did, but I'm fine. I will explain everything to you, I just can't right now. Please dry your eyes and don't argue with your father. He's hurting right now, and that's my fault. He loves you Riley, please believe that."

I have maneuvered around one storm, but how will Samuel react when he finds out who Jackson really is?

"Okay, mom I will for you."

"Thank you, baby. Why don't you shower and get dressed? We can talk over breakfast and hopefully make arrangements to leave here today."

The boat arrived at our dock with our ordered breakfast. The wait staff came in to set-up our table. I wished I could enjoy this beautiful place, but without Walker here to share it with, all I wanted to do was leave as soon as possible. Riley came out fresh from her shower. The only evidence of her tough night was her puffy eyes.

"I'm starving, mom. Please tell me you ordered pancakes."

"Yes, all of your favorites are here. I'm going to check on your father and ask him to join us."

I made my way back into the bedroom and found Samuel dressed and packed. I asked, "Where are you going?"

"Are you really going to ask me that, Reese? I never envisioned this trip turning out this way, but you made your decision, so why should I stay? The villa is paid up for the rest of the week, should you choose to stay."

"Samuel, please don't leave this way."

"Leave what way, Reese? You have made it clear that you don't want me or our marriage, so again I ask you, why stay?"

I'm silent. Samuel walked over to me and caressed my cheek that he smacked.

He continued, "You will never know how sorry I am for hitting you. I hope you can forgive me for this and the way I behaved the day you left for New York. No matter what you believe Reese, I truly do love you, and you will always be my wife in my heart. You were never a trophy to me. It's my fault that I never cherished you for the true treasure you are."

"I'm so sorry, Samuel. I hope one day we can be the friends we once were."

"Me too, baby, me too."

We held each other and let go of the hurt that was between us. I had already forgiven Samuel for what he had done. He's a good man and a good father.

My heart always belonged to Walker, but that didn't mean I could just erase Samuel altogether. He had been a part of me for way too long, and we had Riley to always connect us. After we broke apart, Samuel kissed my cheek and then my forehead.

"I need some time with Riley. Reese, how do I even begin to make her understand that we're not going to be a family anymore?"

"Samuel, you don't have to say anything right now. Let's just go have breakfast with her. She's confused as it is, and I can't bear to see her cry again. Please let her be for now, and when the time is right, I will talk with her."

"GOOD MORNING, SWEETHEART," I said to Riley at the table. I walked over to kiss our daughter on her cheek, but she turned away. I guess I deserved the cold reception. "Riley, please don't ignore me. I want to talk to you."

"Hi, daddy."

"Honey, I want to apologize for taking your phone yesterday. I planned on making this trip special for all of us to share and have a good time, but it hasn't exactly turned out to be as I wanted it."

"Daddy, what do you expect? You practically forced us out of New York, and you wouldn't listen when I told you that I made plans with Jackson and how my trip was extended. You wouldn't even let me call him to say goodbye. God knows what he is thinking right now. Daddy, Jackson loves me and I love him, but now that I have run off without a word, I can't imagine what he's thinking of me and my behavior."

"Here's your phone, Riley. Please call Jackson and work things out with him. If I have to, I will get on the phone and personally apologize as well."

"Thank you, daddy."

I gave Riley time to scroll through her messages and listen to her voicemails. I poured myself a cup of coffee. Reese remained silent as I looked at our daughter despondently. The realization had finally hit me. *I lost my family, and it's all due to my selfishness. I took them for granted when I should have always put my family first.* Here is my daughter about to graduate high school and go off to college. She's in love and is beyond happy. All I have left is my work, but who will I talk to when I arrive home after a long surgery? Or help me get over a loss of a patient? I will be left to grieve alone in an empty house that used to be a home.

"Did you get in touch with Jackson?"

"I left him a message, I know he will call me once he gets it."

"Well, we never finished our conversation about your trip. Tell me more about your new school and everything you did."

"Daddy, I pretty much told you everything. I love NYU, Jackson took me all over the city, and I met some great people."

"Tell me about Jackson's family. What are his parents like?"

"Jackson only has his father. His mom died while giving birth to him. She suffered a massive stroke and was put on life support to deliver him by caesarian section. Jackson gets checked out yearly because of his family history."

"That's heartbreaking, honey. Jackson shared that with you?"

"Of course, he told me everything about his family. Sadly, he lost his grandfather last month. He suffered his second heart attack and was rushed to the hospital where he later died."

"Again, that's terrible honey. Your young man has seen his share of loss in his life. How is his relationship with his father? Are they close?"

"Jackson and his father are extremely close. From what Jackson tells me, and what I've seen, they pretty much have a solid bond between them."

"What does his father do?"

"His father is in real estate and development. They build industry, or something like that."

I laughed lightly at Riley. She truly was adorable when telling a story.

She continued, "Jackson and I had an amazing time when his father took us to dinner at Brasserie Les Halles. I just wish mom and Jackson's father had a better time. We were getting whiplash watching them spar with each other."

What the hell does that mean? "I'm sorry, honey, but what do you mean by them sparring with each other? Did Jackson's father say something offensive to your mother?"

"No daddy, nothing like that, it was just tense between them. When I met his father, he kind of stared at me for a minute until Jackson had elbowed him to snap him out of it. His father just said that I reminded him of someone he used to know. Then it really got strange when mom arrived. He stared at her as if he already knew her. Mom behaved the same way, which was really strange. They both attended NYU, but mom explained that she didn't graduate with him."

Please let it not be him. It can't be after all of these years. It just can't be him. "Well, it sounds like a very interesting encounter. Riley, what did you say Jackson's father's name was?"

"I didn't, daddy, but his name is Walker Reed."

I stood silent and motionless, but my mind was spinning out of control. *Oh my god, this is the same Walker Reed who designed and built my hospital wing. Reese never knew who was behind the expansion project. I never told her in fear she would leave me then. Oh my god! Now my precious daughter is dating his son. I can't even begin to understand this. This is the same man that Reese was in love with and still is today. She's leaving me for him.*

"Daddy, are you okay? You look kind of green."

If my daughter only knew half of it. "I'm fine sweetheart, I just need to talk with your mother. Can you do me a favor, and give me some alone time with her?"

"Sure I can, I'll just take a walk on the beach."

I waited and watched Riley walk far enough away from the villa, and then I walked toward the bedroom to talk to my *beloved wife.* I crossed my arms and waited as Reese added her things to her suitcase.

I said to her, "Don't rush on my account, we have all the time in the world to talk."

"Samuel, I thought you were going to head to the airport for home. Isn't that what you told me?"

"Yes, I did. But there has been a change of plans now, so I'm in no hurry to leave, especially when I want to hear all about your time spent in New York."

"I told you everything, Samuel. What more do you want to know?"

"How about you tell me more about Walker Reed, and the fact that he is the father of our daughter's boyfriend? He is the same man that is responsible for my new hospital wing and is the same man that is taking you from me. I'd say we have plenty to talk about, wouldn't you agree, darling? Were you ever going to tell me about this, Reese? Was it a happy reunion for you two? Did you fuck him? Why didn't you tell me, Reese? Now I understand why you want a divorce. But let me tell you something, my darling wife, hell will freeze over before I divorce you and hand you back to him. You're *my* wife! And you damn well are going to stay that way."

"No, I'm not, Samuel. I'm leaving here today, and I'm taking Riley with me. I asked you for a divorce before I even knew about Walker. I was as shocked as he was to see me."

"Did you fuck him, Reese? Was he everything you remembered him to be?"

"I'm not doing this with you, Samuel. It's over, and I meant what I said. I'm leaving"

"The hell you are, Reese. You are mine!"

"No, I'm not! Please let me pass."

"Did you fuck him, Reese? How many times did he make you come? Was it like two souls reuniting again?"

I LISTENED TO Samuel taunt me and try to break me down, but not this time. I am not that broken girl anymore. Not like my mother. This time I will fight.

"Get out of my way."

"Did you fuck him?"

"Yes, I did! And it was amazing! I never came so hard in my life. I loved every bit of him inside of me."

"You fucking whore!" Samuel shouted as he pushed me against the wall and caged me in.

"I didn't want this, Samuel." I cried as he continued to press up against me. "Our marriage is over. Please let me go. It can't end this way. Please don't be that guy."

"What guy is that, Reese? I'm the same man that has loved you all these years. I always loved you more than you loved me. I knew it, and yet I stayed with you. You made your choice to be with me. I didn't hold a gun to your head and force you to marry me. You did that all on your own. You chose to leave your precious Walker all those years ago. No matter what led you to leave him, it was your decision to go."

He looked crazed as he continued his rant. "I have devoted my life to you, and our daughter. How can you possibly think I would so easily let go without a fight? You want me gone, so you can go back to him? I don't think so, my love. You are my wife, and you need a reminder on who you belong to."

"Please don't do this, Samuel. I'm begging you...please don't do this."

"Take off your clothes...now."

I shook my head no, and sunk to the floor. I cringed at the thought of him hate-fucking me to prove he loved me.

"Reese, please don't fight me on this. I love you, and we can

186

make this work. I can't let you leave me. I'll forget about your infidelity, but the one thing I won't do is allow you to walk out on our family."

In my defining moment, I heard my grandmother's voice reach out to me. She told me not to be afraid and to fight. I wrapped her words around me like a protective cloak. I found my courage and tried with all my strength and determination to get away from him. Samuel reached me before I could make my escape. He roughly pulled me back into his arms.

"Let me go!" I screamed and clawed at him.

"Never! So you can go back to him? No fucking way, Reese. I'm done playing this game with you. Take off your clothes...now! Or I'll do it for you."

"Fuck you, Samuel. Fuck you and your threats. Go ahead, take my body. You will never be the man Walker Reed is, and I will not stay in this marriage for one more goddamned day!"

Push...

Smack...

...Darkness

CHAPTER THIRTEEN

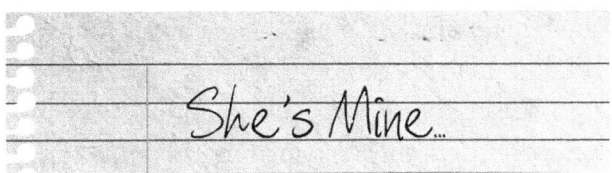

She's Mine...

WHEN OUR PLANE finally touched down, my patience was wearing thin. I had just received a text message from Reese, and I needed off this plane and to find her immediately.

Stephen met us down on the tarmac with his report. "How was your flight sir?"

"It was fine. Where are they?"

"We are about a half hour from the resort, and then we have to travel another ten minutes to their villa. Sir, there is no way to conceal your presence once you arrive at the villa. They have no neighbors on either side of them, and they have their own stretch of beach. The sound of the boat will undoubtedly alert them of our arrival."

"Stephen, I don't care at this point. Reese has texted me, and from what I gather, she is there against her will. All bets are off. I'll have the driver drive as fast as he can to the boat launch. I need to get to her. Jackson is climbing out of his seat and is clearly anxious to see Riley."

"Dad, I finally got a message from Riley. She said that her father took her phone from her yesterday and didn't give it back to her until this morning. Why would he do that? The way Riley describes her father, he is like her idol. Now he just sounds like an asshole."

"Jackson, I fear that Reese may be in danger. I told you that she asked her husband for a divorce back in Maryland; this was before seeing me again. She said her husband didn't react to the news well. If he knows about me, then I don't know what he will do."

"You don't think Mr. Briggs will hurt Riley or her mom? Do you, dad?"

"I'm not sure, Jackson. I only know that Reese didn't want to come here. Being here, isolated from the rest of the resort, she is trapped where she is. You also have to take into account that once Riley's father figures out who you are, your relationship with his daughter may get complicated."

"Why is that, dad? We have nothing to do with what's going on between the both of you. Our relationship is off limits, dad. I'm not going to let anyone come between us."

"Jackson, he is still her father no matter what, and I'm just saying that he may present a problem for you because of who your father is. Listen to me. Try not to worry about this right now. The only thing I want to do now is get to Reese. Are you okay, son? Why are you holding your head?"

"I'm fine, dad. It's just a little headache, nothing like I had yesterday."

"Did you take your medicine?"

"Yes I did, while I was on the plane."

"Jackson, I have told you repeatedly that if you're ever in pain, you must tell me right away. Why don't you understand this simple request?"

"Dad, it's only a headache. Will you relax?"

I looked my son in the eyes and said, "Jackson, I will never relax when it comes to your health. Your mother just had a 'headache,' and then she died. Jackson, I will never forget the pain I went through when I watched your mother slip away from me, and then to almost lose you in the process was the most frightening moment of my life. It was the one and only time that I had zero control. I was left with only my desperate pleas to God to save you, son. The doctors only had a small window to get you delivered. They said the cord was wrapped around your neck, and your oxygen level was low."

I went on, "I have never been so scared in all of my life. When they finally had you in their arms, you let out the loudest piercing cry. It was the best sound I ever heard. I knew then that you would be alright, but the sad reality was that your mother was gone. I had to be the one to be your everything. I will always be grateful for Elizabeth and what she gave me. So please, son, I'm asking you to promise me, if you're ever in pain, you must tell me immediately."

Jackson smiled reassuringly. "Okay, dad, when you explain it that way, I promise. After all these years, you've never talked about mom in that way before. I never knew how scared you really are. I'm sorry that I worry you so much."

"For your benefit, I never wanted you know how badly your mother's death affected me. I wanted to shield you from any sadness or feeling of loss. You need to know, Jackson, I will always worry about you. You're my son, and that's what parents do."

Arriving at the boat launch, we both walked as fast as we could to set out for the villa. *Only ten more minutes Reese. Hold on baby, I'm on my way.* I looked to Stephen, who was clearly packing his service revolver. I hated the fact that he always carried his weapon, but he was my head of security and knew best.

"Stephen, I want you to stand down until we assess the situation. I don't know what is happening there and how her husband will react to my presence."

"Sir, I have everything under control, I have several of my men surrounding the villa."

"I thought you told me that they would know if someone was there?"

"My men are very discreet, sir. They know how to stay hidden and are waiting on my instruction."

"Stephen, this is not a covert mission. As much as I want to make sure Reese and her daughter are safe, I also don't want to scare them."

"Sir, I have the safeguards in place shall the need arise where we need them."

We pulled up to the dock and tied off the boat. Jackson leaped out and began running toward the villa. I tugged him back.

"Jackson, you're to remain here and wait for me, do you understand?"

"Dad, why can't I come with you?"

"I don't know what is waiting for me on the other side of that door, and I don't want you in the crossfire. You stay here. Please wait for me to come for you."

"Please, dad? I can't sit here and do nothing."

"You will wait! Am I clear?"

"Yes, sir."

Stephen and I knocked on the door, but no one answered. We decided to split up and look around the beach for any signs of Reese and Riley. I made my way around the side deck, where I heard Riley crying

"Daddy, why did you hurt mom? She's not waking up. We need to call for help."

"Riley, she slipped and hit her head. You need to calm down and stop crying. I'm a doctor...remember? And I'm telling you she will be fine."

"Mommy, please wake up...Wake up!"

That's all I needed to hear, as I kicked in the door to find Reese lying on the floor unconscious with Riley crying over her.

"What the hell are you doing here?" Samuel shouted as he began to lunge toward me. I struck back, knocking him to the ground. Stephen heard the commotion and came barreling in with his weapon drawn, aimed right at Samuel.

"Oh my god, what's happening?" Riley cried out and protectively hovered over her mom.

"Stephen! Stand down...Now! Riley, everything's okay now. Please don't be scared. This man works for me, and we're going to get you out of here."

"What about my father? What's going to happen to him?"

"Don't worry about your dad. Jackson is waiting for you by the boat. Go to him now, and I will join you both in a minute."

"What about my mom? She's hurt, Mr. Reed. Please help my mom."

"Oh, sweetheart, I will. She's safe now, and so are you." I got down on my knees, hovering over my beautiful Reese. My punch to her husband wasn't nearly hard enough as it should have been. *The bastard hit my angel.* I gently caressed her cheek and softly talked to her. "Reese, can you hear me baby?"

She stirred as her eyes began to slowly open. "Walker, is that you?"

"Yes, baby it is. I'm getting you out of here. How's your head? Are you dizzy or feeling sick?"

"I'm a little dizzy, but not sick."

"Okay, baby, I'm going to pick you up now. Just wrap your arms around my neck and hold on."

I carefully lifted Reese up into my arms, and I carried her to the boat. I saw Riley in Jackson's comforting arms. He was consoling her, as she cried into his chest.

"Where's my dad?" She asked while hiccupping between her sobs.

"Riley, your dad is fine, and he will be brought back on another boat. Right now I want to get your mom to a hospital to be examined."

"Walker, I'm fine. I slipped, and when I did, I hit my head."

"Reese, please don't lie to me. I see the mark on your cheek, and judging from the shape of the mark, it's a man's hand print. You have a sizeable bump on your head. Clearly this was no accident. Please, baby, don't fight me on this, and let me get you examined by a doctor."

"What about Samuel? Where is he?"

"Reese, don't worry about him right now. He's with Stephen

and will be transported and taken to the local police station for assaulting you."

"No, Walker, you can't do that! Please call Stephen right now and tell him not to take Samuel to the police station. He can't be arrested. I told you I slipped and fell."

"Why the hell are you protecting him, Reese? He kidnapped you and took you to this island against your will. He assaulted you, and from what I can see from your torn clothing, he almost succeeded in raping you. After all that, here you sit and try to deny it to me. Your own daughter is a witness to the abuse he has inflicted on you."

Wincing in pain, Reese was holding her head and trying to defend Samuel. The sight of her right now made me want to kill that bastard.

I held her in my arms and said, "You're in pain, baby. Please let me get you to the hospital, and then we will deal with your husband. It's killing me to see you hurt."

"Walker, you don't know everything that has happened. I need to speak with Samuel. I'm begging you to please not have him arrested."

"God, Reese, you're so obstinate at times. Why do you try my patience like this?"

"Walker, he's Riley's father, and I will not press charges and see him in jail. I spent the last seventeen plus years with this man, and he never laid a hand on me until today. You must understand that me leaving him has altered his thinking. When we arrived here, things between us were tense and strained. Samuel knew something was off, but he pretended that we were okay and wanted me to focus on repairing our marriage. Then he made me..."

"What, Reese, what happened next?"

"I CAN'T TALK about it now, Walker, not in front of Riley. Just know that when we talked this morning, he accepted my decision to divorce him. We came to an understanding, and then he just snapped when he found about you."

It was then that I realized I was talking louder than I should have, and my daughter just heard everything that I said.

Riley looked at me and said, "I'm so sorry, mom. I had no idea what I was telling daddy; I still don't. Why did he get so upset and attack you the way he did?"

"Riley, you're making it sound worse than it is. My head is throbbing, and I can't explain it all to you right now. Please be patient with me and give me time. I promise to tell you everything eventually."

Riley just nodded, as Jackson continued to hold her. He was silent. Judging how Jackson was looking at me, then to Walker, he must have known our story. You could see how much Jackson cared for Riley. The sight of them entwined with each other was heartwarming and sad all at the same time. Here was my daughter, so confused right now, and waiting for me to turn her world upside down with my complicated past.

After leaving the hospital, I was cleared to fly. I didn't have a concussion, just a bump on my head that would give me quite the headache. I was given some pain medicine, and we all left for the airport. Stephen had all our luggage already on Walker's plane. Riley and Jackson were settled in one of the back rooms of the plane, and Samuel was in another one. I had to face him, but Walker held me back.

"Reese, my god, if anything would have happened to you, your husband would be dead right now. I love you so much, and I will never let anyone hurt you again."

"Walker, would you please let me talk with him? He is not going to try anything, especially with armed guards on the plane. He's hurt and confused. I never thought he would discover Jackson's true identity especially on the day I was leaving him. Everything happened so fast, he didn't have time to even process it all. At one point he accepted the divorce, and then he came back in clearly angry after finding out about you. He believes that I'm leaving him for you and that we've been planning this all along."

"He's partially right, Reese. You're leaving him and returning back to me."

I smiled up at Walker, and I just let myself breathe him in and feel his warmth radiating all over me. I said, "I missed you, Walker. I hated leaving you the way I did. You must have been out of your mind with worry."

"I was, but I worked it out quickly. I knew after the time we spent together, you would never walk away from me again. We later found out that Samuel had arrived in New York."

"Were you having me watched? How do you know all of this?"

"Reese, I'm a very powerful man, and I have many resources available to me. I wanted to make sure you were okay, but by the time I received my status report, you already left your hotel. I tracked you here. Thank god I reached you in time."

"I'm fine, Walker…Believe me. I need to go speak with Samuel now. I promise everything will be okay."

"I don't like this, Reese. I can't believe how calm you're being right now?"

"That's because I'm in love with a raging bull, and someone has to be calm in this relationship."

"Relationship? Is this what you want, Reese? To be with me and begin again?"

"More than anything in the world, Walker. You're all that I want."

I knew he needed more assurance than just my words, so I did the next best thing. I gently brushed my lips against his, slowly entering his mouth and circling his tongue with my own. Walker began to become aroused with my teasing. I could make love with him right now, but he sensed my hesitation and halted our kiss.

Walker pressed his forehead to mine and asked me again, "Are you sure you want to talk to him now? If he attempts to lay his hands on you again, I will lose all reasoning and beat him within an inch of his life."

"Walker, trust me to know what I'm doing. I owe him this much."

Walker withdrew from me with a horrified expression on his face. He said, "You owe him? Reese, this man assaulted you today, and more than once. Don't sit here and lie to me. Riley told me that he slapped you earlier this morning, but you brushed it off. You don't owe Samuel Briggs anything. The good doctor should be grateful he's not sitting in a jail cell right now with two broken surgical hands."

I kissed Walker quickly on his lips and turned away from him. I could see that I wouldn't be able to change his mind and put him at ease. I knew Samuel better than anyone, so I ignored Walker's wishes and went to talk to him anyway.

When I opened the cabin door, Samuel was sitting in a chair with his head down in his hands. He'd been crying and looked lost. In all my years that I had spent with Samuel, I had only seen him cry once, and that was when Riley was born.

To see him now broke my heart. Walker would never understand why I could so easily forgive Samuel for hitting me. I think if Elizabeth had lived, and he made the choice to leave her, he would know exactly how I was feeling.

Samuel and Elizabeth chose to love us beyond our abilities to love them back. They were extraordinary people who loved us, despite who remained in our hearts. That alone has to count for something, and deep down maybe Walker knew this.

"Samuel, are you okay?" I asked.

Samuel lifted his head and answered me in a tone just higher than a whisper. "How can you ask me that, Reese? When it's I who should be asking you if you're okay."

"Samuel, I'm fine, just a bump on my head. I don't have a concussion, so please don't worry about it."

"Can I take a look at it, please?" I took a step back as he took in a deep sigh at my hesitation. "I just want to see for myself. Did you get scans done?"

"Yes, I did. Samuel, it's not necessary for you to look at my head. I already told you that I'm fine."

"Please, Reese, humor me and allow me to look."

I could see he wouldn't be satisfied until I allowed him to. I knelt down beside him, as he examined the back of my head. Samuel began to cry and professed how sorry he was for hurting me. I cupped his face and cried along with him.

"Oh Samuel, please don't do this. We both made mistakes here that resulted in the situation we are in now. I don't blame you for what happened. I should have been honest with you, but I never really had a chance to process everything that was happening. I swear to you that seeing Walker at the restaurant was the first time I laid eyes on him, since my last night with him all those years ago. He took me by complete surprise, and then to discover that our children were dating each other, you can't imagine how shocked we both were."

"Riley said that dinner was tense, and you both were behaving strangely."

"She's right. It was very tense at first. Walker was angry and confused. He began riddling me with questions about my past, all along knowing already about it. His actions were justified. He only remembers me leaving him...He never knew why."

"Did you finally tell him the truth?"

"Yes I did, and it came in as a close second to the hardest thing I have ever had to do. He forced me to relive my leaving him, my miscarriage, and everything his father did to me. I was exhausted and drained by all that I revealed to him. Then Walker later found out the rest of the story from his family's lawyer. It was just too much for either one of us to bear."

"Did you sleep with him, Reese? I mean really make love to him? I have to know how you feel."

"No, you don't, Samuel. Please don't ask me again."

"Your aversion to my question tells me what I already know. I just wanted to hear the actual words. When I asked you back on the island, I was out of mind with thoughts of another man touching my wife. When you finally screamed it at me, I can't even begin to tell you all the dark places my mind traveled to. It was as if I was standing outside of my body. In under a week, our life has completely changed, and now I'm the one that is broken and shattered."

"Samuel, you're not broken. You're one of the strongest men I know. You perform miracles everyday with your patients, and I see how you care about them. Please don't let what's happening in our personal life affect who you are."

"You make it sound so easy, Reese. Am I just expected to wake up tomorrow and suddenly not love you anymore? Is that how it was for you? The minute you saw the great Walker Reed, I became a mere memory, and the life that we shared didn't hold any value?"

"It wasn't like that at all, Samuel. You're dismissing every part of our time together, and what we did have at one time."

"Forgive me, Reese, but put yourself in my shoes for a damn minute. How would you feel if my ex-lover just appeared out of thin air and staked a claim back on me? How would you feel? You're simply abandoning our marriage and everything we built, so you can run back into his arms. My god, Reese, have you even thought about how this will affect Riley? She is in love with his son. Do you even know how that looks? You were worried how you and I looked in the public eye. How the hell do you think you will be perceived now?"

Samuel's words pierced my heart with the hard reality of the state of affairs my life was in right now. *Is he right?* I knew my stomach was in knots and could no longer continue with this conversation right now.

"Samuel, I have to go, but I want you to know that I will not press charges against you. Once we're home, I will have my things removed from the house."

"Why are you walking away, Reese? Did I touch on a nerve?"

"Samuel, you need to make things right with our daughter. I will send her in to speak with you. As for you and me, I've said all I want to say at the moment."

Entering the main cabin, I walked by Walker, as he rose from his seat to meet me. I ignored him and had to find Riley. The way Walker was looking at me was breaking me down. I had to put Riley first. She needed to understand what happened here today. I just didn't have the strength to deal with Walker's questions and the heavy conversation that would follow.

I knocked on the door and found Jackson and Riley holding each other. I said to her, "Riley, you need to speak with daddy."

"Mom, I don't have anything to say to him right now. After how he hurt you, how can you ask me to do this?"

"Riley, he's your father, and he loves you. There is so much that I need to tell you, but I just can't get into it right now. Please go to your father and hear him out."

"Mom, I already know what you're going to say. Jackson told me about your history with his father."

"I'm sorry, Mrs. Briggs, but I couldn't handle seeing her this upset and being kept in the dark. I already knew, and I figured it would be better coming from me."

"It's okay, Jackson. Thank you. Riley, do you have anything you want to ask me?"

"Are you leaving daddy for Jackson's father?"

"I'm divorcing your father, but not for the reasons you believe. I had already asked your father for a divorce on the morning we left for New York. I had planned on discussing this with you on the plane, but decided against it. Seeing Walker was a complete surprise for me."

"Do you love Mr. Reed?"

"Yes, Riley, I do. I always loved him, but I have so many things to work out before I make any decisions for my future."

Jackson interjected. "My dad said…"

"I know what your father wants, Jackson, but our lives are very different, and I need to take it one day at a time. I promise you, Riley, whatever I decide, I will always be honest with you." My daughter hugged me, and I was thanking God that she wasn't angry with me for leaving her father. She looked relieved and left to speak with Samuel. I stood by the closed door.

"Daddy, may I come in?"

"Oh, sweetheart, of course. I'm so sorry, baby, for hurting you and your mom. I was out of my head. I can't tell you how ashamed and embarrassed I am for my behavior."

"Daddy, you scared the hell out of me; I won't pretend that you didn't. I have never seen you behave that way before. You were un-recognizable, and I'm hurt and angry with how you treated mom."

"There is no excuse for my actions, Riley. I will spend the rest of my life making this up to you if I have to. I swear to you that I'll never let my anger get the best of me again."

"I believe you, daddy. I'm sorry that you've been hurt too in all of this. Mom told me about the divorce. Will you move out of our house?"

"It's up to your mother, Riley. I would prefer to remain in our home, but I will leave it up to your mother. You only have a couple of months left of school and then you graduate. I don't want to see you up and move, especially now. I would like you to stay with me, and then once you graduate, it will solely be up to you where you choose to live."

"I want to stay at home until I graduate. I'm eighteen now and legally an adult. I want to join Jackson wherever he may be."

"Oh my darling girl, you don't have to remind me of your age. I was there when you entered the world. It was the greatest moment of my life. I know I can't stop you. I know I can't stop your mom for wanting what she wants. It's clear to me how much your young man means to you, and you to him. As a father, it doesn't make me happy knowing my daughter is exerting her fierce independence, but I won't stand in your way, especially when it comes to your happi-ness. This is the best time of your life, Riley. Going off to college, meeting new friends, falling in love. I just want you to be happy. I love you so much, and no matter what happens with your mother and me, you're my greatest gift."

"What happens to you now? Are you going to be okay, daddy? What kind of person would I be if I leave you here all alone?"

"Riley, I'm not okay, far from it, but I would be lying if I told you otherwise. Eventually my heart will heal, and I will move on with my life. You're an amazing young woman. Don't worry about me. I will work it out with mom. We've spent too many years together for us not to. Please dry those tears now, and be my happy daughter that I know you are."

"I love you, daddy, always and forever. You will always be my number one in my heart."

"I love you too, sweetheart, and thank you for forgiving me. You will be my light to get me through this."

Jackson knocked on the door and unwittingly interrupted the father-daughter moment. "Riley, are you okay?"

"Yes, Jackson, I am. Please come in. Jackson, this is my father, Dr. Samuel Briggs. Daddy, this is my boyfriend, Jackson Reed."

Samuel took a minute to size up Jackson, who was the painstakingly spitting image of his father. It had to be breaking Samuel's heart knowing that his wife would be reuniting with Jackson's father.

"It's a pleasure to meet you, Jackson. I'm sorry it's not on better circumstances. Riley has been singing your praises for months now. All good, don't worry."

"Thank you, sir, and it's good to finally meet you as well. I'm sorry about my father and how you were treated."

"Thank you, Jackson, but that's not necessary for you to say. Your father was right to hit me. I would have done the same thing. Please don't worry yourselves over our problems. The adults in your life will work things out."

"That's kind of you to say, sir. If you don't mind, can I talk to Riley now?"

"Yes, of course, I will talk to you later once we land," Samuel responded.

"I love you, daddy," Riley said to her father.

"I love you too, sweet girl."

Jackson politely asked, "Sir, can I get you anything? Are you hungry or thirsty?"

"No, but thank you, Jackson. I'm fine. I'll stay back here until we arrive in New York."

"Um...Mr. Briggs, we're not going back to New York. We're en route directly to Maryland."

"Thank you, Jackson, for letting me know."

I watched Samuel as he plastered a weak smile across his face, solely intended for his daughter's benefit. Jackson and Riley left the cabin and happily smiled at one another. I let out the breath I had been holding, and then Walker was now at my side. Then Walker approached Samuel wanting to speak with him, but I tried to lead him away. Walker was adamant about going in for chat with Samuel. I couldn't stand there and listen to what he might have said, so I walked away to find the kids.

"WHAT THE HELL do you want, Reed? Haven't you taken enough from me already? Here to throw salt on my open wounds?"

I said to him, "Don't make this harder than it has to be, Briggs. Once we land in Maryland, you will get to return to your life, and Reese will be coming home with me."

"What about Riley? She has already expressed her wishes to remain at home with me."

"Her place is with her mother, and I've already made living arrangements for them, so don't worry about it. They will remain in Maryland until Riley graduates, and then they're both joining me and my son in California. You see, Samuel, this was how it was supposed to be, and forces beyond our control kept us apart. I know what you did for Reese all those years ago, and for that I'm grateful, but that's over now. And you need to accept that."

"Who the hell do you think you are? You think you can just walk back into her life, destroy what we have, and take my wife while I just sit back and let you?"

"Yes Samuel, that's exactly what is going to happen. Reese was mine first, and I intend to make her mine again. The days of people trying to take her from me are over."

"She's not your fucking property, Reed. She's my wife! Fuck you."

I don't know how he expected me to react to that. I grabbed Samuel by his collar and shook him as if he were a rag doll. He struggled beneath my grasp, trying to break free of my hold. We measured up to be the same height just about, but he didn't match my strength, especially when I was angry.

"No. Samuel. Fuck. You." I enunciated very slowly. "Do yourself a favor, and walk away while you still can. If it were up to me, I would have broken every single one of your surgical fingers, but Reese asked me not to. You can't imagine the level of control and discipline I need to have to respect her wishes with this. I fucking hate that you put your hands on her, not once, not twice, but three times. I know what you did, and only spineless fucks like yourself think that is an acceptable way to handle a woman."

"You don't know anything, Reed. I would die for her."

"Bullshit! If you care for Reese at all, then you would have never raised a hand to her and respected her enough when she said...NO! Walk away, Briggs, because if you ever think of hurting my woman again, then God help you. I will not be so forgiving next time."

I released him, and he fell back to the couch behind him. Trying to get air back into his lungs, he wanted to say something to me, but he hesitated and continued to cough.

"Enjoy the rest of your flight, Dr. Briggs."

I threw down a bottle of water to Samuel and exited the cabin. I stopped to take in a few calming breaths before joining Reese and the kids. I restrained myself for Reese, and only Reese. He's made her feel guilty for her divorcing him and choosing me. Whether I was in the picture or not, their marriage would have seen its ending.

I just thank God that I have been given this precious second chance to be with Reese again. I meant what I said to Samuel, the days of people trying to take her away from me are over. I will never let anyone hurt Reese again.

CHAPTER FOURTEEN

Another door closes...

HOW CAN ONE'S life change in only a matter of five days? I pinched the bridge of my nose trying to obviate my migraine that was slowly making my head hurt. *Where do I go from here?* Walker had all the answers, and he had made it sound so simple: I was supposed to divorce my husband and not give it a second thought.

Walker crashed back into my life like an express train at full velocity. I wanted him. That much was true. My body craved him, and I wanted him burying himself inside of me. *But at what cost?* I had always loved Walker Reed; he was the owner of my heart. I needed time to process all of this change, and I had Riley to consider in all of this.

She was young and in love, and in a few months my daughter would be living away from home to attend college. I would not allow what was happening in my life to concern or affect Riley. My daughter had too many things going for her to stress over her parents' marriage, or what's left of it. Samuel hitting me this morning was a knee jerk reaction to learning about Walker, and add the divorce on top of an already stressful situation, and he snapped. He begged me to forgive him and not divorce him.

Samuel repeatedly questioned me about Walker and if I slept

with him. He pressed and pressed me until I screamed it out. I didn't want to hurt him with that painful truth, but he wouldn't relent on his questions. My answer to him earned me a hard slap. I knew I broke him at that moment. No matter how many promises Walker and I had made to one another, I was still another man's wife. I was the adulterer in this story.

Reliving this was just making me feel sick inside. I never wanted it to turn out this way. My head was beginning to feel worse, probably from my over thinking. Samuel was the one that actually got me into yoga and all of its teachings. Over the years it helped me with my headaches. I was diagnosed with migraines in my first year of college back home in Georgia. I don't believe I ever shared this with Walker. The headache excuse back in New York was just to divert Riley's questions. I knew how his wife died, and that was one of the contributing factors. It scared the hell out of Walker to see me in pain, especially with something that Elizabeth also suffered with. I managed to control my pain with holistic methods, but when they became extremely painful, I had no choice but to seek modern medicine. My migraines increased during my pregnancy with Riley, but I managed to control them over the last few years. I reminded myself to talk to Walker about this. I didn't want him worried about me every time my head hurt.

The plane was quiet. Riley and Jackson were talking, and Samuel was in the next cabin. The only sound heard throughout the plane was the clicking of Walker's keyboard. He was trying to work and give me space, but I caught him looking over at me with his worried eyes.

I swear after all of these years, he still has a secret channel to my inner thoughts. How does he do this? I needed to get up and walk around, thinking maybe that would help with my tension.

I walked past Walker and knocked on Samuel's door asking for entrance. Walker, remaining in his seat, stared at me in shock. I smiled at him. He let out a breath and didn't try to stop me from talking with Samuel. Samuel, not expecting to see me on the other side of the door, looked surprised, but allowed me to enter.

"Samuel, we need to discuss a few things before we arrive home."

"Seriously? We don't have a home anymore. Forgive me for being crass, but the moment you decided to leave me and walk out on our marriage, 'our home' was destroyed. Lines were crossed, and trust was irrevocably broken when my hand—these hands—struck you down. I knew at that moment, I had undoubtedly lost my wife. We have nothing to discuss."

"Samuel, contrary to what you believe, we have to talk, and we need to discuss Riley. She's pretty upset, and doesn't understand what happened. It's been a crazy five days, and her whole world has changed."

"Whose fault is that, Reese? It's not mine. I'm not the one fucking my ex-lover and walking out on the life that we built and shared for all of these years."

"Fine, Samuel. You can call me a whore again if it makes you feel better."

"It doesn't, actually, if you want to know the truth. I hated myself for calling you that disgusting word. You're my wife, mother of my child; you're no whore. You came to me, Reese, please give me a few minutes."

"Okay."

I glanced toward the door, knowing Walker, Stephen, and a team of armed guards were on the other side. Samuel would never dare to hurt me again, but what he was about to say to me would sting just as much as that burning slap he delivered to me earlier.

"I'm sorry, Reese, but let me ask you a question. How do you see this playing out for you? You leave our home with our daughter, and then what? Ride off into the sunset with Walker Reed... A man whom you haven't seen or talked to in nearly two decades? You're my wife, Riley is my daughter, and this means you're my family, not his. Were you really that unhappy with me, Reese? I don't understand you at all, and I'm too exhausted to even try. From the bottom of my heart, you will never know how deeply sorry I am for hurting you, but woman please give me a small window here to sort out what was once my life. What am I going to say to my colleagues at the hospital? Do you even know the position you have placed me in?"

"I'm sorry, Samuel, I truly am, but I have made my decision. Please don't fight me on it. I can only hope that we can come to an amicable understanding where Riley is concerned."

"Please, Reese, don't do this. Give me a chance to make this right. No decisions have to be made today. If I need to, I will move out of the house, and you and Riley will stay. To end our marriage like this without even trying to save it is incomprehensible to me."

"I'm sorry, Samuel."

"Will you stop saying that, Reese? I don't want your apologies, I want you. Why can't you see how much I love you? I don't care if your long lost love has returned; our marriage is worth fighting for, and I'm not giving up on you. What kind of man would easily just give up like that? I am not that man! I will fight for you until I take my last breath, so please give me a chance. Show me that our years together have meant something to you. Please, Reese?"

Hearing Samuel beg me to stay broke my heart. As I stood there I remembered everything about him that made me take that leap of faith and trust him with my heart. I never really gave him a chance to really be in it, since I held back all of these years because of my love for Walker. I walked over to Samuel, and I did the only thing I could think of before completely falling apart.

I wrapped my arms around Samuel's neck and pulled him closer into me. I whispered into his ear, "I will always love you for saving me that night. I will always be thankful for our daughter that we created together. You will always be my friend, Samuel, because that's how we began."

I kissed Samuel with all that I had. He held me as tightly as he could. I struggled to break free of our connection, and he held onto me as if his life depended on it.

"Please, Samuel, let me go."

"I love you, Reese. Please stay with me."

"Goodbye, Samuel."

I left him standing there. He looked beaten down. I turned away from him, and walked out the door. Taking quick strides over to me, Walker scooped me up into his arms and held me. Breathing in each other, my accelerated heartbeat was calming with his gentle strokes on my skin.

"Are you okay, love?" He whispered into my ear, but not before kissing me.

"I'm fine, I just need a minute to compose myself. Please, Walker, can you give me that?"

"Of course. Take all the time you need. I love you, Reese."

"I love you too."

MY PILOT ANNOUNCED that we would be landing in the next fifteen minutes. Jackson and Riley had emerged from their room and took their seats in the main cabin. Samuel joined us and sat by his daughter, never once looking up. Reese was in my private bathroom. I asked her to splash some cold water on her face. She was exhausted, but kept up appearances for Riley. She re-entered the main cabin and took a quick glance around the plane. She instantly reached for my hand, and I guided her down to the seat next to mine—a gesture that of course didn't go unnoticed by the others. I wasn't going to hide my feelings for my woman; I loved her too much for that. This entire trip was quite the mind fuck.

Stephen interrupting my thoughts was a welcomed relief. "Sir, may I have a word?"

I nodded briefly and turned to Reese. "Reese, how are you feeling? You look pale."

"I'm fine, Walker. My headache is gone."

"I have to speak with Stephen for a minute. I won't be long."

I kissed her on her cheek. I was thankful she didn't pull away from me. We haven't really had the opportunity to talk, and god knows what is going through her head right now. Stephen and I went into my office, as I perused the documents that he had given me.

"Is this all of it?" I asked Stephen.

"Yes sir, it is. I had my best team on it."

"Once we land, I want the plane prepped, and ready to leave first thing in the morning, en route to California. We will stop in Arizona so I can take care of this, and then we head for home. Jackson needs to return back to school, and I have a company to run."

"Sir, what about Mrs. Briggs? Will she be joining you?"

"I hope so, but I can't be sure until I have a chance to speak with her. Stephen, she doesn't even know what new information I learned since my second visit to the Hamptons. Now to deal with what has happened with her husband, I'm not sure if she can take much more."

Our flight landed smoothly in Baltimore/Washington International Airport. After I wrapped up my meeting with Stephen, I rejoined Reese for the remainder of the flight. She was so quiet and hard to read. My girl wasn't giving anything away. We landed and prepared to deplane.

Samuel said his goodbyes to his daughter and shook my son's hand. He entered the waiting car and never once looked back at Reese. From the look on Reese's face, I knew she wasn't staying with me tonight. All the light in her had now turned dark. I couldn't allow her to blame herself over this.

"Walker," she breathlessly said my name, "I need to take Riley home and get her settled back into her routine."

I folded her into my arms and closed my eyes, breathing her in and committing every bit about Reese to memory. I will never cross fate again. I am a Forever believer. I have her back, and I will move heaven and earth to keep her with me.

"Reese, please stay with me tonight, we can work everything out tomorrow. Just come back to the hotel with me, and we can talk, sleep, whatever you want. But please just stay with me. I need to be alone with you."

"I can't, Walker. If it was just me, I would go with you in a heartbeat, but it's not. I have to put my daughter first and make sure she's okay."

"She's fine, baby. Just look at her. She's smiling and laughing with Jackson."

"Appearances can be deceiving. Please don't pressure me, Walker. You know I want nothing more than to be with you, but I need some time."

"Are you planning on staying in your house tonight?"

"Yes, I am, and with Riley. Samuel already told me that he will leave the house and not return until I have moved out. Please, Walker, you have to trust me to know what I'm doing."

"Reese, I do trust you. I just don't trust your husband after everything that happened here today. If I can't be with you tonight, then one of Stephen's men will be. You're not returning to that house unprotected."

I lifted her chin, and kissed her softly. "Are we okay?" I asked.

She said nothing. Held back tears finally began to fall as I tightened my hold around her body.

"God! I want to just bury myself inside of you for days, and remain there. I love you so much, Reese. Why do I get the feeling that this is it, and I'm never going to see you again?"

"Oh, Walker, you know that's not true. After everything we've been through today, how can you doubt my feelings for you?"

"Reese, you left me once, and it nearly destroyed me. I just got you back. I don't think I would survive it again."

"Walker, I told you that I'm not going anywhere, and I want to be with you, only you. All that I'm asking for is some time to process all of this and take care of my daughter. Her senior prom and graduation are right around the corner. I can't have her life totally disrupted because of my feelings for you." *Ugh!!! She made perfect sense. I always put my son first. How can I not expect her to do the same with her daughter?*

"Okay, love. Do what you have to do, and then you will join me in California. Reese, I want to marry you and have the life that we always dreamed of having. Please tell me that you want that too?"

"You know I do, Walker. This is our second chance at forever, and I will not give up so easily again. I love you with all of my heart."

"Say it, Reese," I said as I stared into her beautiful eyes and gripped the back of her hair. "Say it, Reese. Say it with all your heart, soul, and love that you have for me. I need to hear it."

"I. Am. Yours.

I. Love. You.

I. Am. Yours. Forever!"

Her words were my undoing. I swept Reese up into my arms and crashed my lips down onto hers. I couldn't hold back any longer. She said what I needed to hear: the same vow that we made to each other all those years ago. *Reese saying them to me now...means so much more. It means that she is here with me now and forever. No amount of time apart has changed our love. Fuck you, father!* I held her beautiful face in my hands and wiped away her tears.

"I love you, Reese. You. Are. My. Forever."

"I love you too, Walker. You. Are. My. Always. We will be to-gether soon. This I promise you."

Jackson and I waved goodbye to the women that held our hearts. Riley was leaning out the window blowing kisses to him. He was catching all of them. It was a beautiful sight to see my son so happy. Reese followed suit and did the same for me. *How did she know that this was exactly what I needed?* I never held back what I felt for her. My feelings for Reese were always intense, but to hear the same in-tensity come from her delectable mouth fed my everlasting desire for her. She knew what I craved. Her hesitation only fueled my desire, but that was her way of teasing me before giving me what I needed. She always knew what I needed. The car drove away and was out of sight.

Leave it to Jackson to lighten the mood. "I don't know about you, dad, but I'm starving."

"I couldn't agree with you more, son. How does a lobster and steak dinner sound to you?"

"Sounds great! Let's go."

Jackson and I dined down at Inner Harbor, and then checked into our hotel for the night. After our long flight and all the drama we went through today, we were both ready for sleep. Jackson went right to bed, while I stayed up to work. I had endless e-mails to answer and reports to go over. I was doing everything in my power to focus, but my mind was completely on Reese. I promised not to call her, but my fingers were rolling over the keys on my phone. I hung up before my call connected. To hear her voice would calm my nerves, but I also feared I would push her away. Stephen had joined me in my suite to go over the papers he had delivered earlier.

After learning about Henry Townsend and his involvement with my father to push Reese out of my life, I was beyond angry. My first thought was to destroy him, starting with his company. I would dismantle it piece by piece and leave him with nothing. He was retired to a degree, but he kept an active role on his board. Reed Global was a privately owned company. Although I had taken over, my father was still actively present in the day to day until he officially retired. He tried to keep his hands in some of the pots, but I kept him on a very short leash. *Not short enough*, I now realize. Now back to Henry. For years I had been blinded by this man and kept in the dark to what he did to me and to Reese.

It would be completely justifiable on my part to seek my revenge on him. He deserved it and he wouldn't give it a second thought if the roles were reversed, but at what cost? I would only be hurting Jackson. He loved Elizabeth's parents very much. Having to explain to Jackson about Phillip already tarnished my father's image and the good memories he had of him.

Henry and Gail were alive and well. I couldn't take Jackson away from them, but Henry needed to know that I finally knew the truth.

"Walker, how do you want to proceed?" Stephen interrupted my train of thought.

I looked up at Stephen and simply answered, "I'm not going to follow through with my original plan."

Stephen's eyes widened as he sat there in shock. I was never a man to change my mind especially when it came to business, but this was personal. To act on my first impulse would hurt many people, and I would never become my father. He wouldn't think twice about crushing his enemies. He treated Reese like one, and because of him, I lost those years with her. Years that could have been spent happily being together, raising our children, and being in love with one another. I have her back now, and I'm not going to waste one precious second.

"What about Ralston? Have you changed direction with him as well?"

"No fucking way. Proceed accordingly per my instructions, and status with me when it's done."

"As you wish, sir."

"Stephen, we will fly to Arizona first thing in the morning and have a talk with Henry. The last thing he's expecting is a visit from me. I haven't told Jackson about our stop yet. I don't want him tipping off his grandfather. I have to tread very carefully tomorrow because of my son. I can't predict on what will happen when I finally come face to face with Henry. I will not allow my hate for Henry to transform me into the one thing I worked so hard to not become: my father...Phillip Reed."

"Walker, you're so much more than the man your father ever was. You must know this. Just look at what you built, and the son you raised. You're not your father."

"Thank you, Stephen, but this I know. I'll cut off my right arm before I ever succumb to be like that bastard."

I dismissed Stephen and finished up with my work. I managed to get through my correspondence and draft what I would need from Jenny upon my return. I managed to sleep for a few hours and then take in a morning work-out. Running always helped me clear my head.

When I returned, Jackson was awake. "Good morning, dad. When are we leaving for home?"

"Good morning. I'll be ready to leave in about thirty minutes. Just to let you know, we are not directly flying home. I need to stop in Arizona to visit with your grandfather first."

"Dad, I need to get home today. Why the sudden trip?"

"Jackson, I have some business with your grandfather that will not wait. While I visit with Henry, you can spend some time with Gail."

"Can I ask what your business is about with Grandpa Henry?"

"No, you may not, Jackson. Please trust me, and don't worry about things you cannot change."

"It's bad, isn't it, dad? Did Grandpa Henry do something to you?"

"Jackson, what did I just say?" I raised my voice a bit louder than I intended to. "I have already told you too much already about my father, and I will not go down this road again with Henry. I just need to speak with him about a few personal matters. Once I do, my business with your grandfather will be finished, and I will put it behind me. Please don't ask me again."

I hated getting angry with Jackson, but the way he was looking at me when he mentioned his grandfather disturbed me. He wore a look of mistrust, a look I was not used to seeing ever from my son. It had taken me his entire life to tell him about my history with Reese, and sadly his mother. The past 48 hours had been difficult for Jackson to come to terms with. I turned his world upside-down. I feel he had to suffer all over again with the loss of his mother. I couldn't imagine how difficult it was to listen to me profess my love for another woman. And I divulged to him how evil my father was. I wasn't going to add any more stress to his already filled mind of worry.

"Dad, I don't want to fight with you."

"Good. Because I don't want to fight with you either."

"Dad..."

"Jackson, what is it? If you have something to say, then just say it."

"Okay, I will. I was only asking because of everything that happened with Grandfather Phillip. Grandpa Henry is all I have left of mom. I know that look on your face, dad. You look like you want to hit something right now. If you don't want to tell me anything more, can you at least please promise me something?"

I sighed in frustration and looked back to my son. "I will if I could...you know that."

"Please don't hurt my grandpa."

His request shattered me.

"I know you've been hurt, dad, but what will it solve seeking revenge on something that happened years ago? You may not think that I pay attention to how you run your business, but I do, dad. I know how intense you can be, and you use your power to get what you want. Please don't use that today with Grandpa Henry.

Please, dad. Whatever he did to you and Riley's mom, please let it go. Let it go for me. Will you promise me, dad?"

I took in a deep breath before answering him, not wanting to believe that this was Jackson, my son, begging me for mercy for his grandfather. *How the hell did I get here?*

"I am not Phillip Reed. Jackson, you have my word that I will not do anything hurtful to Henry. I do need to talk with him and get some answers to my questions. It will be nothing more than a tense conversation. I promise." Once again, I couldn't believe I was there at that moment, having to deal with my son being afraid of me. I had never been out of sync when it came to my son. I didn't know how to shut off my hatred for the two men that were responsible for this situation that I was now left to deal with.

MY SON NODDED and left the table without finishing his breakfast. If I had the time, I would run another ten miles to alleviate my tension, but we needed to go.

We arrived in Arizona, just under four and a half hours. Jackson was quiet and didn't say much to me. I worked on my laptop and talked with Stephen. I had so much to return to in California, and of course most of my thoughts were on Reese. I didn't hear from her as of yet, but again this was me giving her space. *I fucking hate this! She should be with me in my arms, and not miles away from me.* My heart hurt and ached for her so badly.

Our car pulled up in front of the gates to the Townsend property. We were granted access as we descended onto the big house. There he stood, Henry Townsend, smiling at his grandson as we stepped out of our car. Gail had her arms opened as Jackson ran to greet his grandmother. To look at Gail was like looking at an older Elizabeth. For a woman in her sixties, Gail was beautiful. She had kindness that radiated throughout. I walked over to Henry, as he stuck his hand out for me, but I knew what was coming next. Henry always shook hands first and then pulled me into a hug, but I vowed to remain calm and keep my wits today.

"Walker, I can't believe it. Why didn't you phone us and let us know you were coming? We would have been more prepared and had lunch ready. This is a great surprise."

"I'm afraid we can't stay long. We are traveling back from Maryland. I needed to speak with you before heading home."

"Sure, Walker, no problem. Jackson, why don't you visit with your grandma over here, and I will spend some time with your dad."

"Okay, grandpa, I have missed you." Jackson embraced his grandfather and held on tight for a couple of minutes, looking over his shoulder, directly at me. My son was worried for him, and unbeknownst to Henry, Jackson was hurting me with his lack of trust. Even after all we talked about and the promises I made to him. Again, I hated the position that our two fathers had placed me in. If they would have just minded their own business all those years ago…I wouldn't have to be dealing with this now.

"I love you, my boy. You need to stop growing. You're making me feel short. Spend some time with your grandma, but don't eat all of the cookies. She just made a fresh batch."

"I make no promises, Grandpa. See you soon, dad?" Jackson looked over to me with his apprehensive glance.

"I won't be long, son." We both watched Gail and Jackson disappear behind the doors. My plastered smile was now gone.

"So, Walker, what's on your mind, son?"

"Don't ever call me that again! I'm not your son, Henry." Henry's face went ashen and was taken back from the tone that I was using with him. We had always been friendly with one another. Today…that's over.

"Have I done something to anger you, Walker? What's going on?"

"Yes, Henry, you have made me angry. So very angry that I was ready to destroy you yesterday and take away all of your happiness like you did to me. The person you need to thank for my change of heart is your grandson."

"What in the hell are you talking about, Walker?"

"Seriously? You're going to stand here and pretend as if you don't know what I'm talking about. Come on, Henry, you can't be that dense. After all, wasn't it you that orchestrated the great plan to eradicate Reese Mitchell from my life?"

"Walker, I…"

"What, Henry? Cat got your tongue? I should rip your tongue out for all the vile things you did to me, and to Reese. You remember her, don't you? She was my entire world, and you and my father conspired together to force her out of my life. Is it coming back to you now? You and my father destroyed my life. How could you do this to me, Henry? And what about Elizabeth? She deserved a hell of lot better than what she got."

"What do you want me to say? Walker, you must know everything if you're here now confronting me with it."

"I don't know everything, Henry. I know the business side of it, but what I don't know is the personal reasons. Why did you do this,

Henry? Why me? I loved you. I trusted you. Hell, I wished you were my father over Phillip."

"Walker, I knew my Elizabeth always loved you, even when you were teenagers. She would talk to her mother about you and how she dreamed of becoming your wife one day. She was my only daughter. I wanted to make her happy, and when your father was in trouble, I came up with the idea to match our children together."

"Do you hear yourself? Elizabeth was my friend, and friend only. I never returned the feelings that she had for me, and I told her that so many times, even before Reese, came into my life. How could you not know this? Do you even comprehend what you did to me and your daughter that you claim to love above anything else? She was just a second choice, a means to an end. I never loved her, Henry!"

I stopped and took a deep breath. I couldn't stand here and defile Elizabeth's memory. Of course I loved her, but I just wasn't in love with her...not in the way she deserved to be loved.

"You fool of a man did this to her. What do you think she would say had she known this? She would have been destroyed by your manipulations and deceit."

"At the time, Walker, I thought I was doing the right thing. I'm sorry."

"Sorry? That's all you have to say? Sorry doesn't even begin to come close, Henry. What about after Elizabeth died? You still held it over my father's head and forced him not to tell me the truth about Reese."

"Your father was his own man, Walker. Don't you forget that. Yes, I helped him out of a sticky situation that *might have* ruined your company at the time. Your father made his choice, and he was the one that made the decision to keep quiet and not tell you the truth. Your father made some careless decisions that might have cost him everything, including your legacy. He wasn't willing to gamble with his life's work and take anymore unnecessary risks. He came to me and asked me to help him. No favor is free, Walker. You know that. It's business 101, and your father taught you that lesson before you could run."

"What are you telling me, Henry? How much trouble was my father truly in? Are you saying that he could have gotten out all on his own? And without your help?"

"Does it really matter at this point? He asked for my help. I helped him. End of story."

"Like hell it is. You manipulated my father for your own personal gain. You didn't care about helping your friend. All you cared about was getting what you wanted."

"Phillip was my friend, but he also was in need of help. He would have done the same for me. I came up with a solution that benefitted us both. I never wanted my investment back. I was aiming for the bigger prize. All I wanted was to see my girl happy with the man she loved. The road to her happiness was you...you, Walker."

He continued, "You can't stand here and tell me that you didn't love her. I knew in time your feelings would change, and in the end they did. After she died, I already lost my reason for living. My beautiful baby girl now was rotting six feet under. All the money in the world couldn't save my girl. You had a new son to take care of. You didn't need the pains of your past colliding with your present and future."

"Do you hear yourself? Henry, your deceit was not a blessing for me. You played god with people's lives, and clearly you had no faith in Elizabeth. She was strong, independent, and more than capable of finding her own soul mate. It makes me sick that you felt this way about her."

"I loved my daughter! I'm not going to stand here and listen to you spew your hate for me all over her memory. She loved you, Walker. Don't you dishonor her in front of me—Ever!"

"You're the one that is dishonoring her. You and your fucking lies have brought this on here today. That night in the hospital when she died, I knew I heard my name. You and my father were arguing, but when I questioned you about it, my father silenced you. Were you going to tell me then?"

"No, Walker, I wasn't. That was my grief talking. My only child had just died while giving birth to her own. I felt God was punishing me for what I did to Ms. Mitchell. I don't know what I would have said if Phillip hadn't stopped me."

"He did stop you, but what about every day after that? Henry, you should have told me the truth."

"Why, Walker? So you could have run back to her? And have that girl raise Elizabeth's son with you? No way in hell was I ever going to allow that. What do you want me to say? I've been repenting for my sins every day since my beautiful Elizabeth was taken from us. It hurts and cuts so deeply every time I look at Jackson. He carries my daughter in his eyes, and he's so much like her. After she died, Gail and I were left with her greatest legacy—her son, Jackson. He is the good that came out of all of this, don't you see, Walker? I love that boy more than my own life, and I won't lose him. Please don't take him from us. He is our daughter's child."

"He's my son, Henry. My son with Elizabeth. Jackson is not a child anymore. I can't keep him from you, but I promise you this. If you ever try to interfere with my life again, business or personal, I will go ahead with my original plan. I will destroy you, piece by piece. Believe me, old man, I won't lose any sleep over it. I am not a forgiving man and will never forget what you have done to me. Do not believe for one second that this act of clemency is a sign of weakness. Again, this one *Free Pass* that I will grant you is for Jackson, and only him. Don't fuck with me again! If you do…Don't say you weren't warned."

"Walker, I died a thousand deaths the day we lost Elizabeth and was reborn when I held her son in my arms for the very first time. I know pain and loss, Walker. I have lived it with you."

"Henry, the days of pain and loss are over for me. I have found Reese again, and I plan on marrying her as soon as I can. You will not interfere again with my plans. If you want to enjoy your retirement and still have a relationship with your grandson, then you will agree to what I have said here today. You and I are finished. I no longer wish to ever see you again."

"Walker..."

"Save it, Henry! This conversation is over. You and I are over. Cross me again, and even Jackson won't be able to save you. Go say your goodbyes to your grandson. We have a life to get back to."

We walked back to the house in silence. Henry hung his head low and wore a look of shame all over his face. He never saw this coming, but neither did I, when he made the decision to betray me. I didn't want this to fall back on Gail and hurt her. She was as oblivious to her husband's crimes as my mother was to Phillip's. They stood by the men they loved above everything else. Olivia and Gail had fierce loyalty when it came to loving and supporting their husbands. My mother denied emphatically she didn't know and would have tried to stop my father, but would she really? I said my goodbyes to Gail and waited in the car for Jackson to return. I watched as his grandparents hugged him. Gail was a kind woman, and I hated to hurt her.

"Grandma, please don't cry. I'm going to see you next month at graduation."

"Oh, my sweet boy! I love you so much, and I am so very proud of you. Your mother would be too. She is always with you, son. Please believe that."

"Okay, you two, can a grandfather get a word in edgewise?"

"No! I didn't see *you* baking all those cookies this morning?" Gail responded jokingly.

"You got me there, pretty lady, but can you take kindness on an old man and give me a few minutes with our boy here?"

"Less of the old, Henry. You're still the most handsome man I know."

"Oh my goodness, you two. I'm getting a toothache with all of this sweetness."

"Now, Jackson, tease all you want, but one day you will be in love and know exactly what this feels like."

"I'm already there, grandma, but I'll need a rain check on the story until I see you again. Dad's waiting on me."

"Of course, honey. Give me another hug, and then go talk with your grandpa. I love you. Safe travels back home, and I'll talk to you soon." She wiped her fallen tears as she made her way back inside. Jackson had a chance to be with his grandfather for a few more minutes.

"Are you okay grandpa? You don't look so hot right now."

"I'm fine son, just got the wind knocked out of my sails. I love you, Jackson. You know that right?"

"I do."

"I want you to know that you always have a home here with us if you ever needed one. You're my daughter's child, and our door will always be open to you."

"Jackson, we need to leave," I called out from the limo.

"I have to go grandpa. I love you too!"

Watching my son embrace the man I once admired, knowing he was responsible for forcing Reese out of my life, has shattered me. *How could this man look me in the eye all of these years and live with the knowledge that he along with my father was responsible for my pain? Now my son, his only living connection to Elizabeth, is protecting him and vilifying me as the bad guy?*

I saw the fear and mistrust in Jackson's eyes. We drove back to the airstrip in silence. Jackson couldn't look at me. He probably thought I hurt his grandfather and broke my promise. I clearly wanted to talk to my son, but his silence was stopping me. We arrived on the tarmac to our waiting plane to take us back home to California. I handed off my briefcase and jacket to our flight attendant. Once we were in the air, I spoke.

CHAPTER FIFTEEN

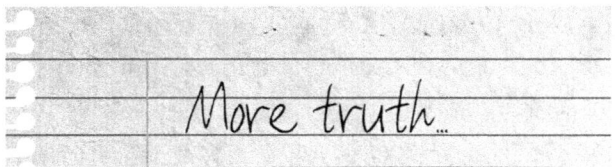

More truth...

"HOW LONG ARE you going to ignore me? This distance between us is killing me."

"It's hurting me too, dad. You lied to me! You hurt Grandpa Henry when I begged you not to. Did you see the look in his eyes when we left? What did you say to him that put that look there?"

Listening to my son accuse me of vile things had me crawling out of my skin with anger. This was what Phillip and Henry managed to do. *Hell no! They will not drive a wedge between me and my son. I will never let anyone ever do that. He wants the truth...the whole truth...okay, he shall have it.*

"Jackson, I didn't do anything to your grandfather but speak with him. Before you try and convict me of crimes you think I have committed, will you listen?" He silently nodded.

I started, "You must understand that this week has completely changed my life, and many secrets to my past were revealed to me. You and I knew two very different sides to Phillip Reed. My father was extremely controlling of me while growing up. Any independent amount of thinking that I managed to do, he was threatened by it. When I legally became an adult—your age as a matter of fact—his dominance increased beyond extreme heights. He wanted to, and most of the time, managed to control every decision I made."

I continued, "Jackson, my entire outlook on life and my future changed the minute I met Reese Mitchell. I came to life when I met her. She gave me light in my life in areas that were dark and unforgiving. I was Phillip Reed's only son, and I knew not cross him within reason. With Reese in my life, I had this level of confidence that I waved in front of my father like a victory flag, never knowing that it also enraged his hatred for her. Foolish in my thinking that I could go up against my father in my younger years, when I took over at Reed Global, that all changed. I was the one that held the power, and the roles were reversed. Little did I know that I was still secretly being deceived and betrayed. To learn that men I trusted and respected like Grandpa Henry hurt me to levels I can't even begin to explain to you."

I went on, "When your grandfather came to visit with me before he died, as you remember it was your birthday, but it was also the anniversary of your mother's passing. It is a bittersweet day for me, as you well know. Even after all of these years, it still pains me that Elizabeth is gone, and you celebrate one more birthday without her. To see my father on this day completely derailed me. He was going on about how sorry he was for not being the father I deserved, asking me many personal questions. I wasn't prepared for this, and I lashed out at him. His visit resurrected many hurt feelings that I kept to myself. For you, Jackson, I never wanted to show you my personal pain, so I buried those feelings along with your mother."

I said, "My father was forcing me to say the words, and when I did, it only proved what I have always known: that my feelings for Reese, have never changed. I had no idea where she was in the world and how she was living her life, but I still loved and yearned to be with her. I felt sick to even be thinking of her on the same day I was still grieving for your mother. I shunned your grandfather and made him leave. He said his goodbyes to me, and I did the same. I never could predict that would be my last time spent with him."

"Did you ever really love my mother?" Jackson asked. His

question was justified, but as it needed to be answered, it still felt like a piercing stab through my heart.

"Yes. I did son."

"You loved Reese more?"

"Jackson, how I can explain it to you when I don't understand it all myself? No matter what I say, you still are going to be looking at me with hurt in your eyes. I can't bear the thought knowing I'm the one that has put it there."

"Just be honest with me, dad! Tell me the truth. Make me understand this."

I took a few breaths and calmed my heavy beating heart. "The love I had for your mother was based on our friendship. All your grandparents were close friends with each other. Our families were connected by our social circle and by your grandfathers' businesses. Elizabeth and I were children when we met. I spent every summer in the Hamptons, and so did Elizabeth. I called her a tag along and teased her relentlessly. She was tough and never gave up. She followed me everywhere, and then she rightfully put me in my place one day, and we were best friends ever since."

I explained further, "As we grew up, somehow her feelings changed for me, and she fell in love with me. She confided her feelings to me one day, and when I tried to kiss her, it didn't feel like fireworks to me. Your mother wanted more, but I never did. We remained friends, and then in my senior year at college, my world changed with the first sight of Reese. I simply fell in love, and wanted to be with her. Your mother knew how much I cared about Reese, and eventually gave me her blessing. Jackson, what I'm about to tell you will be very painful to hear, but if you want the truth then I will continue on."

"Please, dad, I can handle it."

"I thought I had it all figured out. I was going to graduate college, take over Reed Global, marry Reese, and ride off into the sunset. That fantasy never became a reality where Reese was concerned. My father had been threatening her for a while, and she kept me in the dark to his manipulations. When I finally discovered what he was doing, I had confronted and embarrassed him in front of our family and friends. I thought it was over, but I was so wrong. He drove Reese out of my life with lie after lie and continued to threaten to hurt her until she finally submitted to his demands. She was to leave me and never return to me…not ever. What I didn't know at the time is that she was pregnant with my son…my first child, Jackson."

I looked to my boy and tried to assess his reaction to this revelation, but all he did was sit there with a stoic expression on his face. He gestured to me to continue.

"Never giving up to try to reconnect with me, Reese tried to see me several times, but again, my father and his bullies stopped her. The stress was too much for her to bear, and she was completely separated from her friends, family, and me. She tried one more time to see me, but he didn't stop her this time. Reese, overcome with sickness, sadly lost our child. A child that I never knew she was carrying. You see, Jackson? Every single detail I disclose to you will only bring more pain. I can't be the one to do this to you."

"Dad, it's not you. This was grandfather, and if I'm ever to understand anything about this, then I need to know everything."

"Fair enough. The rest you pretty much know already. Your mom saved me. I was drowning in my pain and misery. She kicked my ass back to the land of the living, and she helped me begin again. We became closer friends, then lovers. When Elizabeth told me that she was pregnant with you, something in my world just shifted on its axel. I was working in California, learning how to be the mogul my father wanted me to be, and now I was going to be a father. I was shocked to say the least, but never ever regretful of you Jackson, please believe that. I needed a few days to process the news, but Elizabeth left me, and with the grace of god, fate stepped in and gave me the push I needed to begin my new life with your mother. I never lied to her, Jackson. Elizabeth knew I cared for her, but loved another. Your mother had unconditional love for the both of us and never worried. She believed that in time, our love would grow into something more, and we would have the life she always wanted with me."

I continued, "As I live and breathe, Jackson, we had our happily ever after. I married your mother with the full intention on forever being with her and raising you and any other children we might have had. I couldn't wait to be a father and loved your mother for giving me the greatest gift that I could ever receive. Elizabeth gave me you, and for that...I am forever blessed and thankful."

Jackson and I were both crying now. I had never allowed myself to really feel Elizabeth's loss until now. My son fell into my arms and released his own pain and loss. We stood there for I don't know how long until he gripped my shoulders to look at me.

"I love you, dad. I'm so sorry."

"Jackson, you don't have anything to be sorry for. Why would you say this?"

"I'm sorry for taking Grandpa's side. I judged you before hearing your explanation. I had already made you to be the villain in this story, when clearly you were the victim."

"Jackson, your mother was one of the kindest and generous people I have ever had the pleasure of knowing and loving. I have to believe that she is looking down on us and wants me to be happy. I got my miracle on the day you were saved. Fate stepped in again and gave me another chance with Reese. Jackson, I have to take this chance with her. My father cheated me out of my future with Reese, and now I've been given another chance. Please, my son, allow me to have it."

"I won't stand in your way."

"You will never be in the way, son, I promise you that. You will always be my first priority."

"Can you answer me one more thing, dad?"

"Anything."

"What about Grandpa Henry? Where does he fit in all of this?"

"Jackson, I can't."

"Dad, you promised. Please tell me."

"Jackson, I've already said way too much than I ever wanted to.

My father is gone, and I will never be able to make him pay for what he did to me, and to Reese. As for your Grandpa Henry, he also played a role in this deception. For you, Jackson, and only you, I made the decision to spare him."

I explained, "Phillip left me papers proving that Henry was his partner in all of this mess, the one calling the shots. Henry has been misguided for many years now, and when Elizabeth died, I believe he felt that was his rightful punishment. Discovering all the missing pieces to the puzzle, my first thought was to seek revenge, but then you asked me not to. To see you look at me the way you did, hurt me more than you know. The two men that are responsible are Phillip and Henry. The visit to Arizona was to confront him with all that I knew."

I said, "He came clean Jackson, and his biggest concern is not losing his one link to his daughter, and that is you. My relationship with Henry is over, but you're a man now and can make your own decisions with the people you choose to have in your life. As long as Henry keeps his distance and doesn't interfere with my affairs again, I will forever keep my promise to you."

"He's my grandfather. I can't just cut him out of my life, dad."

"Agreed. He is your grandfather, and he loves you very much. Your relationship with him is yours and yours alone. You just need to understand that whatever will be, I cannot have any part in it. Some things in life cannot be forgiven or forgotten. Henry Townsend is now my enemy, and nothing more."

"Where does that leave me, dad? Am I your enemy now? Because I love him. A few hours ago he was just my grandpa. The same grandfather who I have loved my entire life. Now he's your enemy? What the fuck?"

"Jackson! First of all, you're my son. I love you beyond anything else in my entire life. Don't ever question how I feel about you. For the first time in all the years that I have been your father, you have pierced my heart more than any *enemy* has done before. Why? How can you ever doubt me? I have never given you a reason to ever question me before? I just don't understand it. You wanted the truth, you got the truth. As painful as it is to hear, it's my life he fucked with all those years ago, and I will never forget what he did to me. They not only hurt me, but they hurt Reese and your mother, Jackson. I'm the one that has to carry this now, and live with their sins, or I can choose to cut it the fuck loose. I take choice two. I will not let my father, or Henry, ever have that control over me again."

I went on, "My father got off easy by dying. Your grandfather Henry is getting a pass. Do you want to know why? Because of you! And my love for your mother. I don't ever want to see you look at me like the way you looked at me earlier today. I don't deserve it, son. Now I have told you everything, and my feelings toward Henry are my own. They don't have to interfere with yours. It is up to you on how you want to move forward with all of this new knowledge you now know. Please, Jackson, do not make me feel guilty over that man. He is dead to me, and this is the last time I ever wish to discuss him again. Do I make myself clear?"

"Yes."

I turned away from my son to exhale the much needed breath that I had been holding since embarking on this fucked up conversation. Dammit! Dammit! I hated this, and I hated them for causing this rift between Jackson and me. The plane was silent, and I turned back to once again see my son in tears. I didn't think my heart could be shattered anymore than to witness my son hurting. I took him in my arms to comfort him.

Jackson said, "I'm so sorry. Dad, please forgive me. I don't even know what ever drove me to say what I said. I'm so fucking sorry."

"Jackson, look at me." I held his face in my hands and begged him to open his eyes and look at me. He did, but clearly he's full of regret.

"You. Are. My. Son. And I love you with all of my heart. You never have to ask for forgiveness from me. I will love you unconditionally until I take my last breath." He wrapped his arms around me and hugged me tightly until he had no more tears to shed. I gestured to him to drink some water and sit with me. Our conversation was far from being over.

"I promise you, Jackson, everything will be alright."

"I don't see how, dad. What about Riley? And how she feels about my dad being with her mom? This is all like an *E: True Hollywood Story*, if you ask me. You can't make this shit up."

"Well my son, it is very real, and it happened to me. Let's get home and return back to our lives. In a matter of weeks, you have a prom and a graduation to look forward to. I'm sure you want to have Riley be your escort."

"Yes, that was the plan, but I don't see how that's even possible now."

"Have faith, Jackson. A wise woman many years ago told me never to give up on faith and love. I didn't believe her then, but I sure as hell do now."

"Who was the woman?"

"Lila Mitchell. Riley's great grandmother. She is an amazing woman with the kindest heart. She had given me a family ring to present to Reese whenever I was ready to propose to her. After Reese left me, I tried and tried to return the ring back to Lila, but she always refused. She always told me that true love will find her way back to me, and never give up. I still have that ring to this day."

Jackson looked at me and said, "I guess she was right. You finally have your second chance with Reese. You two can have the future you always wanted to have. I hope I can have the same chance with Riley."

CHAPTER SIXTEEN

New day...New life

LEAVING WALKER AGAIN was incredibly hard to do, but I knew I needed some time to think. He was always the master of his universe. The Walker Reed I knew then, and the one I knew now were one and the same. He still was the master of his universe and the owner of my heart. If this was someone else's story, I don't think I would quite believe it. My life had completely changed over the course of a week, and I feared my decisions would hurt my daughter in the end. I knew Samuel was devastated by me asking him for a divorce. Whether Walker was in my life or not, I wanted out for a long time now.

It was too late for regrets. In life, you make decisions, and you have to be responsible for the choices you make. My marriage to Samuel produced my greatest accomplishment...my daughter Riley. Riley would always be the thing that sealed my bond with Samuel, but a long time ago, I had given my heart to someone else and never got it back. It felt like I'd been living someone else's life all these years, and now I had a chance to get my old one back. Was this just a fantasy I was trying to convince myself to believe?

Our connection was still as strong as ever. The sex between us was unbelievably amazing. Walker had told me that once I submitted my heart over to him, I was his. *You are mine* took on a whole new meaning once we reunited. He promised me that I would never have to return back to Samuel, and I was home where I belonged. He didn't know that I had already broken the new promise of commitment I pledged to him. I had sex with Samuel. I tried with all my effort not to, but Samuel was determined to bed me again, and I had no choice. I kept reciting over and over again "It's just my body, and Walker is the one who has my heart." Samuel was in complete denial. He thought that making love to me would make me realize how much we belonged together, and that the idea of divorcing was unfathomable.

I blamed myself for what happened after. Samuel would have never hit me if I didn't push him to the brink. He kept pushing me to be honest with him, but as much as I didn't want to hurt him, that's exactly what I did with my revelation. I practically screamed it at him, throwing Walker in his face. Last night after leaving Walker and Jackson, we returned home to this house.

Riley immediately ran upstairs to her room, and I heard her cry herself to sleep. She refused to speak with me. Samuel was packing another bag for himself to take to the hotel. The sight of him packing hurt my heart. Samuel looked defeated and sad. With Walker's insistence, I had a guard posted outside to watch my home, safeguarding Riley and me. The thought of Samuel hurting us was abhorrent to me. What happened in the Caribbean was already forgotten and forgiven. I could only speak for me, but I held no ill will toward Samuel. Once again, his actions were on me. I made the decision a long time ago to leave my marriage, and now it was time to face my choices head on…beginning with my daughter.

It was just about six a.m. I went downstairs to make some coffee. No use going back to sleep now. Samuel and I agreed on meeting today to talk. I would meet him over at the hospital after his morning surgeries. I also had to phone Marsha and explain all to her. Riley broke me out of my deep thought as she entered the kitchen.

"Good morning, baby. Are you leaving?" I asked.

She sighed, and wiped a tear from her cheek. "I'm meeting daddy for breakfast at his hotel before I go to school."

I shouldn't have been surprised by this. Riley and Samuel were very close, but I feared sides would be taken.

"Did he ask you to do that?"

"Yes, he did mom. He's my father, and I wasn't going to say no to him."

"Riley, that's not what I was implying. I just want to know if you're okay."

"Are you serious, mom? How can you ask me that after all that's happened? To be honest, mom, I really don't know how I feel. A week ago we were sitting in your walk in closet surrounded by clothes, and we were laughing. I was so excited to get to New York, visit my school, and be with Jackson. Now a week later, my mother is divorcing my father, leaving him for my boyfriend's father—her long lost love—and you want to know if I'm okay? Um…No! I'm not."

"Riley, my past with Walker is complicated, and up to a week ago, it was very private. I never shared my past about Walker with anyone but your father. You can't even imagine how I felt when I saw him again in that restaurant. I never in my wildest dreams ever thought I would lay eyes on him again."

"That's just it, mom. You did, and now you're leaving my father for him. Did you ever really love daddy? What happens to him now? I'm all for the happily ever after's mom, but you're leaving a trail of pain a mile long to get what you always wanted, and I can't help but feel incredibly sorry for my father. He loves you, and no matter what happened while we were away, that can be forgiven. He was out of his mind when I told him who Jackson's father was. In a way I feel like this is my fault. If I hadn't been going on about him, maybe he would have found out in another way that he could better handle it."

"Riley, nothing that has happened is your fault. Do you remember how I was crying the day we left for New York, and you asked me what was wrong. I gave you a half truth when you questioned me. I had just gotten off the phone with Grandma Lila, and it wasn't an easy conversation."

I continued, "I was remembering my time with Walker and what happened to make me leave him. Circumstances led me to your father, but Riley, I can't sit here and tell you that it was true love for your father and me. This, my daughter, would be a lie, and I have had enough of that to last me a lifetime, maybe more. I will always love your father for being my friend. He helped me through the toughest time in my life, and he gave me a chance to start over."

I went on, "Riley, I tried to love him, really love your father in the way he deserved, but I was never really able to give him my whole heart. I'm so sorry if this hurts you, but you need to know the truth. My life with Walker was stolen from me. His father brutally forced me out of his life. I lost my baby…my baby with Walker. I was alone and completely isolated from my friends and family. I wanted to die, Riley, but your father saved me and gave me hope. His friendship helped me heal, but I never ever lied to him. He believed that true love would come in time for us, and he would be there waiting when it did. Once I agreed to marry him and we moved to Maryland, the Samuel I knew began to change. He was ambitious in his career. He wanted the brass ring, and his hard work has paid off, Riley, but it has also cost him a great deal as well."

"Oh my god, mom, this story just gets worse and worse. I don't think I have the stomach to hear anymore. I know Jackson filled me in on some of it, but I had no idea about any of this. I have to go, mom."

"Riley, please don't hate me. I'm so sorry that I'm hurting you right now."

She wiped her eyes and turned away from me. I wanted to make her stay, but I knew I'd given her much to think about.

"I don't hate you mom, I'm just trying to understand you. Daddy is waiting on me."

Shit! This was so not how I wanted to handle today. What the hell was wrong with me? I should have just kept my mouth shut and let Riley talk, but no, I had to run off about my past with Walker and revealed so much to her already fragile state. *She's eighteen years old, for god sakes. This is the best time of her life right now. She's about to graduate high school and go off to college, but instead she is knee deep with my drama.* My cell has gone off again for the third time this morning, no doubt Walker calling me. Four missed calls all from Walker, and one voicemail.

"I guess I'll settle for hearing your voice on your voicemail than not to hear it at all. Baby, I know you're hiding right now, but you don't have to. Please, all that I ask is for you to have faith, and please Reese, don't run again. New York, and what happened in the Caribbean, was a complete mind fuck. I know this, but it also led me back to you. I love you, Reese, and I meant what I said...I am never going to let you go again. Please call me."

I saved his message, but I didn't call him. I wanted to more than anything, but I couldn't have Walker completely consume me. I quickly got showered and dressed. Not only was Walker on my voicemail, but one angry text was also waiting for me and it was from Marsha. She said that she would be flying out to Maryland and would be seeing me today. Her no-nonsense attitude was screaming at me through her text message. I knew she was angry at me for bailing on Freddy, but hopefully once she hears why I didn't make it, she will understand.

Two hours after receiving her message, here she was barreling through my door with her hands flailing in the air.

"Do you want to tell me why the fuck you didn't show up in Central Park to see Freddy? What the hell is wrong with you, Peaches?" She said my nickname mockingly, and her voice was so laced with anger.

"Marsha, I know you're angry, but don't think I'm just going to allow you to come into my home and spout out obscenities at me, especially when you don't even know the story."

236

"Okay, Reese, I'm sorry for the potty mouth, but don't act all innocent. It's not like you haven't heard it before. The last time we talked, you mentioned your hot guy, Walker. Now, I'm sure the re-union was sheet clenching great, but oy vey, Reese, what about Freddy? You said you wanted to see his show and talk with him."

"Marsha, I had every intention on meeting up with you. I was so excited to finally see Freddy again. I had told Riley that a spa day was all arranged for us, but the truth was so much better. I was going to surprise her with the fashion show, and then I would speak with Freddy, but someone stopped me from doing that."

"Who, Reese? Walker?"

"It wasn't Walker. My husband showed up in New York and forced me to go with him to the Caribbean. He thought if he took us away on a family vacation that all our problems would magically disappear. You know I had asked Samuel for a divorce, and needless to say he didn't take it very well. He wouldn't take no for an answer. He forced us to check out of our hotel in New York. He took Riley's phone, and within an hour, he had us on a private plane. I had no choice but to go with him. Riley knew nothing of Walker and me. It wasn't like I could just tell Samuel about my former lover."

"Oy vey, Reese! What the hell happened next?"

"I'll give you the short version. The truth came out about Walk-er and me. Samuel was devastated. We argued verbally, and then physically, and then Walker showed up and rescued me. My mar-riage to Samuel is over, and Walker is back home in California, waiting on me to return to him."

"Is it too early for a bourbon? Because after that, I sure could use one. I'm sorry, honey, for flying off the handle. I should have trusted you better than that. I just wanted you and Freddy to recon-nect so badly."

"I know, I'm sorry too. How is he? And how did the show go?"

"The show was a success. The foundation raised over a hundred thousand dollars, and you know Freddy, he's an attention whore. He strutted his bad self all over that runway, but he was incredibly proud that all of his hard work has led him here."

"What's next for him?"

"He's still in New York, if that's what you're asking. He told me he has no plans of returning home to Milan at this time. He has everything running smoothly over there under the watchful eyes of his partner, Fabrizio. Fabs is the C.O.O. and keeps everything in top form while the boss is away."

"Wow, Freddy has certainly come a long way. His father always predicted success for him, and now he is the C.E.O. and lead designer of his own fashion house. He lives in Milan?"

"Primarily, yes, but he splits his time in New York, as well. He tried Los Angeles many years ago, but he never enjoyed the west coast."

"I guess Freddy is very fortunate to have a trusted employee to help him with the business."

"Read between the lines, country girl. Fabrizio is not only his business partner, but he is Freddy's life partner. They've been together for more than ten years now."

Pangs of guilt once again riddled through my heart. I should have known this. I knew absolutely nothing about my best friend's life anymore.

"Hey, Peaches, where did you just go?"

I smiled back at Marsha, while trying to fight back the tears. "Oh Marsha, he's never going to forgive me for leaving him the way I did. I wouldn't forgive me. I've missed so much in his life. We were supposed to be friends forever and live in each other's lives. This is what I tried to explain to Walker, that not only did I leave him, but Freddy too! I was fooling myself if I thought for a minute that Freddy would just act as if the last years didn't happen. I think him seeing me would have just caused him pain, and that would be the last thing I would want to do. I'm happy for Freddy and will continue to do so from a distance."

"You can't be serious, Reese! Do you not know Freddy, at all? That man loves you and has never forgotten you for all the Peaches in the entire state of Georgia. He named his foundation after you! What will it take for you to realize that your friendship with Freddy can be salvaged if you would just stop feeling sorry for yourself and go see him? You said you wanted to reclaim what you lost, well start with repairing your friendship with Freddy. He loves you, and I promise he won't turn you away. If I'm wrong, then sue me, but I don't think so. Life is too short to be carrying around all this bullshit. You're the only one that can change your life, Reese, but it needs to start by putting one foot in front of the other. It's up to you, my friend."

"Marsha."

"Yes, Peaches."

"What's his address in New York?"

I said a tearful goodbye to Marsha, with the promise of seeing her soon along with Freddy. I was thinking of my daughter. Riley was so upset when she left here this morning. She hadn't returned any of my text messages, but she was in school, so I hoped to speak with her when she got home. Before leaving for Johns Hopkins to meet with Samuel, I phoned Walker. He answered on the second ring.

"Reese, are you alright?" His voice was laced with anxiety.

"Hi," I said, barely above a whisper. "I'm okay, Walker. I'm sorry I didn't call you back sooner." I heard him sigh on the line, probably counting to ten. *Oh, my mercurial man.*

"Reese, I've been worried, to say the least, and then you released your guard? What were you thinking?"

"Walker, knowing you I'm sure your watchdog is nearby. You don't have to worry about me. Samuel is not going to hurt me."

"Well, that remains to be seen, Reese. He already has more than once, and I'm here in California, where I can't protect you. I need to know that you're safe."

"I am, Walker. Please believe me. I will call you later this evening once I return from meeting with Samuel."

"What! Why are you meeting with Samuel? You don't owe him

anything, Reese. Let the lawyers handle this. He's already been served with papers."

"What? How? I didn't even have a chance to phone my attorney yet."

"Reese, I had my lawyer contact yours, and it's a joint effort."

"Walker, how could you do that without talking with me first? He was meeting with Riley this morning for breakfast. If she was present while he was served divorce papers, it's no wonder why she's ignoring my texts right now."

"Reese, did you really think I was just going to sit back and do nothing? You know me better than that. I only expedited what you already had in motion. Please don't be angry with me. I've been going crazy wondering how you're doing, and you not keeping in touch with me like you promised you would is driving me to the brink of insanity."

"I'm sorry, Walker."

"Reese, I don't want your apologies. I just want you. Please tell me that you're coming to California?"

"Walker, you know I can't do that right now. Riley is still in school, and it will be weeks before I go anywhere. I also have to make another trip to New York, then down to Georgia."

"I'll come with you, Reese."

"Walker, I need to do this on my own. You and I still have so much to talk about, but before I do that, I need to make things right with Freddy and Nana."

"How long will you be gone for?"

"I haven't booked anything yet. I still need to speak with Samuel, and then work things out with Riley. I won't go anywhere without calling you first. I promise you that I am not running."

"Okay. I trust you baby, and I'll be here waiting for you."

Our call ended, but somehow I knew I would be seeing my Walker sooner rather than later.

CHAPTER SEVENTEEN

Don't hate me...

"GOOD AFTERNOON, MRS. BRIGGS."

"Hello, Gretchen. Is he in?"

"He is, and he's waiting for you."

I'm sure he is, I muttered under my breath. Taking in a few deep breaths before entering Samuel's vast office, he looked up from behind his desk with sad eyes staring back at me.

"Come in, Reese, and please close the door behind you."

"Gretchen, please hold all my calls until I say otherwise."

"Yes sir."

"Please, Reese, have a seat. I won't bite. As if seeing our daughter this morning wasn't hard enough to take, I return here to my office only to be served with divorce papers. Divorce papers. Really, Reese? My side of the bed is probably still warm, and you serve me with this crap!"

"Samuel, you should have never been served with those papers today. It was a mistake on my lawyer's office."

"Don't fucking lie to me, Reese. I know this was him. So is this is how your new life is going to be? He's going to control you and make decisions for you? This is not about him, Reese. This is our marriage, our life together. How could you allow this to happen? It's bad enough that I had to be totally decimated to my very core by flying home with the happy lovers, but now he goes and does this? Did you fuck him in our bed the minute I left?"

"No, Samuel, I didn't. He's in California, and yes, he was the one that had these papers served to you. But I was the one that had them drawn up weeks ago."

"Why, Reese? Why are you doing this to us?"

"Samuel, I'm saving us, before it gets so bad that we will have nothing left. I decided on this long before Walker ever re-entered my life. I know you don't want to believe that, but it's the truth. Our marriage is simply over, and it's been over for quite a while now. You just won't come to terms with it. I tried talking with you, but you never listen."

"I'm listening now."

"Samuel, please let me go."

"How do I do that, Reese? How do I do that? You've been my entire world since the day I treated you in the hospital. I loved you then, and I still love you now. I will go to counseling. I'll take a leave of absence from the hospital. I will do anything to save our marriage. Please Reese, give me that much." Getting up from behind the desk, Samuel kneeled before me, taking my hands in his own. "Please Reese, don't leave me. I love you."

"I love you too, Samuel, but I'm in love with Walker. He never left my heart. I can't walk away from him this time."

"You love him more? Has it always been this way, Reese? Have I been blind all of these years? What makes you think you can make a marriage with him work, while ours didn't? I have devoted my entire life to you and our daughter. If you can so easily just erase me from your life, then get the hell out! You're right, baby. You don't deserve me."

"Sam…"

"What, Reese? What can you possibly say to me? Clearly you don't love me, you don't want our marriage, or our family. Why the hell are you still here?"

"I'm so sorry, Samuel. I was just hoping that we could remain friends for Riley's sake."

"Oh you're concerned for Riley now? Where was your concern when she had to witness me being served with these papers? She cried practically the entire time we were together. She may have given you the impression that she's okay with all of this, but she's not. You have irrevocably destroyed her faith in you. Believe me, Reese, I'm no better. She is not going to soon forget me assaulting you. I have repeatedly apologized to our daughter, but I broke something in us when I did that to you, and now with you ending our marriage, you finished it off."

"Samuel, I will speak with Riley when I get home. She is not lost to us. I swear to you that will never happen."

"It already has, Reese, but you do whatever you have to do. God knows I'm done trying to change your mind. I have my pride, woman, and if you want out so bad, then take it. I hope you find what you're looking for."

"Samuel," I called out.

He didn't answer me. His back was turned away from me. I got up from where I'd been sitting, and I wrapped my arms around his back, willing him to turn around. He struggled against his pain, a pain I caused him. He turned and held me in his arms. I whispered into his chest, "Please don't hate me, Samuel." His arms tightened around me, as he kissed the top of my head. He was breathing heavy, as his chest rose up and down.

"I'm mad as hell at you, but I can never hate you, Reese. I'll always love you. I hate the fact that he will be holding you instead of me. I hate him for being the man that has your heart when I so desperately tried. I guess I never stood a chance to make you happy."

"Samuel, that's not true. Please don't belittle what we have shared. I don't know what will happen once I walk out of that door, but I have to try. I will never forget what you have meant to me in my life, and no matter what you think, you will forever be my friend." I gave him a chaste kiss on his lips and slowly made my way to the door.

"Goodbye, Samuel."

"Goodbye, Reese."

I cried the entire way home. I had never wanted to run away more than I did right then, but that would be the coward's way out, and god knows I'd already done that. I needed to get to Riley and beg her for forgiveness. I never wanted her hurt in any of this. I'm just praying she would give me the chance to really talk with her.

Her car was in the garage, that's a good sign she's home. I quietly walked around and searched for her, and saw light coming from under Samuel's office door. I slowly entered the dimly lit room and found Riley curled up on her father's couch near the fireplace. Riley was surrounded by crumpled up Kleenex and her homework. Although I knew she had been crying, she looked peaceful at the same time. I pushed her hair away from her face, as she slowly stirred and woke up. She took one look at me and began to cry again. My instincts kicked in and immediately went to hold her.

"Oh, baby, I'm so sorry. Please don't cry."

"I can't help how I feel, mom. Daddy's heart is broken, and our family is no more."

"Now, Riley, you listen to me, and listen very carefully. Our family may be changing, but it is not broken beyond repair. I know you're young, and you believe in the happily ever after. I still do, but sadly it's not with your father. I will always love and care about him. My heart has always belonged to someone else, and I'm done denying it."

I continued, "You, Miss Riley Taylor Briggs, are our daughter, and we love you with all our hearts. Your father and I never want to cause you one day of unhappiness, but I can't always shield you from life's tough times that may hurt once in a while. It sounds like a cliché, but it's true, honey. On a good day, life can be complicated."

Riley dried her eyes and gathered up all of her tissues. She looked at me with the same sad eyes as Samuel did. They were each other's match, but at least she's here at home where she belonged.

244

"I saw your father today. I know about the divorce papers being served to him, and I know you had to witness it. Again, I'm sorry."

"Why mother? Couldn't you have waited a few days? A week perhaps. All daddy and I wanted to do was enjoy a nice moment together to talk. The processor guy was a jerk; he looked like he enjoyed his job a bit too much."

"I have a phone call in to my lawyer's office to figure out how and why they were served without my knowledge." I lied to Riley, knowing full well who was responsible for this. I didn't even know if I was angry, since he gave me the push that I needed. "Riley, I don't expect you to understand right now, but in time I hope you can come to terms with the decisions I made."

"I don't know how I can do that, mom. You did this all on your own without ever considering how I felt about it."

"That's not true, Riley. You have been the driving force behind every single decision I have ever made. I have without a doubt always put your needs above my own. This is what parents do. You're eighteen years old and about to go off to college to begin what will be probably be the most exciting time of your life. Look what already happened in New York for the few days we were there. Riley, you didn't even blink twice. That city lit a fire within you, and you took off right from the starting gate. I felt the exact same way when I arrived in New York for the first time."

I held her hand as I continued, "We are not so different, my daughter. You're in love, I was in love. You're beginning a new chapter in your life, I did the same thing when I left Georgia. You always have a choice, Riley. The difference between our stories is that my choice was taken away from me. I suffered unmeasurable amount of pain that I hope and pray you will never experience in your life."

"Why didn't you fight mom? You just rolled over for Jackson's grandfather like an obedient dog. I just don't get it."

"When I figure it out, I'll let you know. After all of these years, I still don't understand why Phillip Reed hated me so much, but he's gone now and can't hurt me anymore. In the end, I won, Riley, because after all that he did to Walker and me, I now have a second chance with the man I have loved all my adult life. And if it's truly meant to be, then we will make it this time."

"Only my father loses, right mom?" Riley said, letting go of my hand. *Ouch.*

I decided at that moment that my daughter had put up her protective stance and was clearly not ready to hear all the details of my past. I simply tabled this already tense conversation and let her know I'd be there when she was ready. I decided to change the subject.

"Riley, I have to go out of town tomorrow."

"To see *him*?" Her facial expression darkened, making me wince. This is not the same girl that was blindly happy last week.

"Not to California, but back to New York. Do you remember when you asked me about Freddy?" She nodded. "Well, when I told you that I had arranged a spa day, it was not exactly the truth." Her eyes now brightened, and I had my daughter's full attention. "I've been in contact with my friend, Marsha Malin, who was my agent back when I modeled. She's also very close to Freddy. Marsha had arranged for me to see him while we were in New York during your college trip. His foundation was putting on a charity event in Central Park, and of course he was front and center. I was planning on surprising you with a meet and greet of your own, had things gone well between Freddy and I, but I missed out on my chance."

"Because of daddy showing up?"

"Yes. I still wanted to see Freddy and take you with me, but you know what happened next, and we had no choice but to go with your father. I'm sorry."

"It's not daddy's fault for wanting to be with his family. I behaved badly when I should have been happy that daddy was trying. He's sorry for everything. You know that, right?"

"I do, Riley. I understand why he behaved in the manner he did, and I have forgiven him for it. You need to do the same. Your father is one of the best men I will ever know in this life. He loves you, so please love him back. He is still the same man that you adore."

"But…"

I put my hands up to Riley. I was not going to keep talking in circles every time I said something positive about her father, only to have to defend myself again.

"Mom, how long will you be gone for?" Clearly the fight seemed to be out of her system.

"I'm leaving in the morning. I'm hoping my friend will give me the time I need to reconnect with him."

"If he doesn't, then will you come home?"

"No, I won't, Riley. From New York, I have to make another trip to Georgia to visit with your great grandparents. If you think the talk we just had was hard, then sit back and get ready for the fireworks display. I owe Nana Lila a long overdue explanation, and it's time."

"Can I go with you, mom?"

"I'm sorry, baby, but no you can't. You have school, and it's nearly over. You will be busy with prom preparations and graduating festivities. I'll be home as soon as I can."

"Mom, can't you go and return from New York, and then this weekend we can fly to Georgia together?"

"Well, I know your Nana would love to see you. Okay, I'll make the arrangements, and we will leave on Friday, after your morning classes."

"Yay! I'm so excited. I can't wait to see Nana." She hadn't smiled like that since we said goodbye to Walker and Jackson at the airport. *This* was my Riley, smiling and happy.

"Your father only has morning surgeries scheduled tomorrow, so he will be here waiting for you when you return from school. I'm leaving before dawn, so hug me now, and I'll call you from New York." She didn't hesitate, and walked toward my waiting arms.

"I love you, Riley. I promise we will work this out."

"I love you too! Have a safe trip."

I watched my daughter climb the long staircase up to her room, never looking back at me. I felt as if I had a thousand pound boulder sitting on my chest. This was not something I was familiar with when it came to my relationship with my daughter. We never had this distance between us.

My phone had been going off the entire day. I avoided every single call and text from Walker. He must have been going out of his mind wondering what was going on with me, but I was sure his man outside was keeping him updated.

I packed for my trip, and before going to bed, I looked at his picture, and got lost in his beautiful eyes staring back at me. Even through a picture he had this magical power to pull me in and make me submit to him. I grabbed my phone from off the side table to call him.

I quickly dialed his number before I chickened out, and I hung up. I wanted to hear his voice. I wanted to touch him. I missed him so much, but I needed to take care of me before I could be with him. His voicemail picked up after the fourth ring. I simply left him a message.

"Hi. Please don't be angry with me for not returning your calls sooner. This day has been taxing, to say the least, and I'm happy it's over. I'm leaving in the morning for New York. We talked about righting the wrongs in our past; well Freddy is one of my wrongs. I need to make things right with him, and I truly have no idea if he will even see or talk to me, but I have to try. Walker, I have so much to tell you, but I can't right now on this message. If you believe any-thing...please believe that there is not a second in my day that I'm not thinking of you. I love you, and I promise I'm not running. I promise to call you soon. I love you."

Before I could say another word, his phone cut off. I wasn't go-ing to call him back. I was exhausted after my emotional day with Samuel and then Riley. I took one last look at his picture before I turned the lights off. *I love you, Walker.*

The next day at JFK Airport in New York, Marsha greeted me with her usual effervescence. Marsha was always on. She was both a morning person and a night owl. I couldn't imagine how much coffee was running through her veins.

"Well, look at you! All bright and shiny. It has to be a crime to look this good, and so early in the freaking morning."

"Good morning, Marsha. Thank you for picking me up."

"What? You think I drove? That's what limos are for, doll. Come on, Freddy is waiting for you."

"What? He knows I'm here?" I started to feel completely nervous.

"No, that's not what I meant. Reese, he's been waiting for this day since you left all those years ago. He loves and misses you more than you know."

"What if he refuses to see me?"

"Not a chance."

I took a breath, and we exited the airport. Marsha fired out instructions to her assistant, while I sat there tapping my knee. I don't know why I was so nervous. This was Freddy we're talking about. He didn't have a mean bone in his body.

"We're here, baby girl. Go get him." Tears began to fall down my cheeks with anxiety coursing through my body.

"Hey now, come on, sweets. Today is a good day, and I promise you he is going to plotz when he sees you. Now dry your eyes, and get your ass in that studio." She pointed her long finger at me.

"I love you, Marsha."

"I love you more. Now get the hell out of my car."

That did it, and all my anxiety was gone. Time to see Freddy. I left my bag with Marsha, knowing I would see her later. His studio was beautiful. Freddy's success was lining the walls of his entryway. This was what he always wanted to do. His designs had changed the face of fashion, and his foundation was changing lives. I prayed our reunion today would change mine.

"Reese Mitchell?"

I turned around and saw a familiar face.

"Hi. I don't know if you remember me, I'm Trina Blair. I met you in Milan when you did your first Cosmo cover."

"Of course I remember you, but you had blazing red hair back then."

"Yes I did, but thank you to the color gods. How the hell are you? I can't believe you're standing here in our office."

"Our?"

"Let me re-phrase. I'm Freddy's assistant. I run his New York office."

"You don't model anymore?"

"No. I gave that up a long time ago. I'm married with twin boys and have lived in New York for the past twelve years. My husband is a photographer and travels with Freddy on the European locations. It all makes sense to me now. Marsha had phoned me after the Central Park show, and asked me to clear his entire schedule for this week. I knew I couldn't do that without raising any red flags, but she said it was life or death, so I guess she meant you?"

"Marsha does have a unique way of being melodramatic, but I guess yes, she meant me. I've lost touch with Freddy, and I'm hoping he'll see me today."

"Well, you won't know until you walk through that door." She gestured down the long hallway to the last door on the left. It was Freddy's private office where he designed. Trina gave me a hug for good luck, and I made my way to his office.

I slowly walked inside, and no Freddy. This place was huge. I walked around and took in the beautiful view from his window.

"Peaches... is that you?" So much for being strong. The sound of Freddy's surprised voice brought on my falling tears. I quickly wiped them away and turned around to face my friend.

"Hi, Freddy."

He just stood there staring at me, as if I was a ghost or something.

"How are you standing in front of me now?"

"It seems I've been getting that reaction a lot lately. I'm here for you, Freddy. I needed to see and talk with you."

"Go home, Reese, back to wherever you came from."

"What?" My legs felt like jelly. This was what I feared from my best friend…rejection.

"Go home. I have nothing to say to you."

"Freddy, please?"

"No! I do have something to say. You took away our friendship without ever discussing it with me. That friendship was more important to me than anything. I trusted it, I believed in it, and now it's gone. Did you know how much I needed you? Did you know my career was in the toilet? You never answered one of my calls or letters. If you would have answered one damn call, but no you never did, and now you're here? For what, Reese? What the hell do you want from me?"

I'm looking at my best friend—my Freddy—and all I want to do is laugh out loud and run into his arms.

"Did you just quote the reunion scene from *Beaches*?"

He finally breaks and laughs along with me.

"Really, Freddy? *Beaches*? I guess Bette Midler is still your favorite."

"Well, I had to say something, and I just watched that movie over the weekend. It was Cry Me a River Weekend on cable television." He opened up his arms for me. Oh, thank god! Three strides and Freddy was holding me. He kissed the top of my hair and tightened his arms around me. My cheek was nestled on his chest…I was home.

"I missed you so much, Peaches. I can't believe I'm looking at you right now."

"Freddy, can you ever forgive me for leaving you? I'm so sorry for any pain I caused you. I can't live one more day without you in my life. Please, Freddy? I need you to forgive me."

"Are you staying this time?"

"Yes."

"Well, then you're forgiven. Don't you ever leave me again." We just continued to hug and cry until we had no more tears to shed.

"Talk to me, and tell me everything," Freddy said.

"Oh, Freddy, that would take way too long. How about the short version? And we will table the long story for another time?"

"Fair enough, I always did better with the short version anyway."

"Freddy, I never wanted to leave you. After I lost my son…Walker's child, I was lost. The life I knew in New York was over, and I was truly alone."

"Bullshit! Reese, you had me. I would have been there for you, but you left me without ever asking how I felt about it. You never called me back, and you disappeared."

"You're right. I did those things and so much more, but Freddy, losing Walker and then my baby was my breaking point. Walker's soulless father stopped every single attempt I made to see him. After I lost our child, I had nothing left of him. I don't expect you to ever understand my reasons for what I did, but at the time I truly felt I was doing the right thing. I needed to protect my Nana and Granddaddy, and I wasn't going to let Phillip Reed destroy what they had built and worked so hard for. He could hurt me all he wanted, but my family was off limits."

"Reese, don't you know that we would have fought him with you? Walker would have never left you. He would have chosen you before his bastard of a father, you know this. He told you time and time again how he felt about you and also how he felt about his father. Why do you have this self-deprecating side to you? If you would have just trusted the ones that loved you, all of this could have been avoided."

"You don't know that, Freddy. It's on me, all of it. I take responsibility for the part I played in literally breaking apart my life, but it was my choice."

"All I know is that I hated to leave you in the hospital, but you asked me to go. I thought we would be seeing each other soon, not nearly two decades later."

"Freddy, it's so much more complicated than you know. After you left, I had suffered a breakdown. I woke up days later bound to my hospital bed. The hospital staff said I tried to hurt myself. I wasn't Freddy, believe me. The thought of suicide is abhorrent to me, you know that. I was just in pain and suffering the many losses in my life."

I started tearing up when I continued and said, "First my parents, then Walker, then my child...All gone. I felt I had hit rock bottom and had nothing left. I just wanted to run as far as I could, but I didn't get too far. Once I was calm and returned back to the living, my doctor who had treated me from the first night was there again by my side. Dr. Samuel Briggs was holding my hand and smiling at me as I opened my eyes."

I pressed forward with my story. "Freddy, I wasn't ready to face Nana and Granddaddy. I couldn't bear to tell them the truth and have them see my shame. You were back in Europe, and it seemed everyone else was going about and living their lives. Walker had already moved on with Elizabeth, so when Samuel offered me a way out, I took it and simply never looked back."

I continued, "He asked me to take a chance and move forward with him. At the time I had thought he was insane, but he wasn't. Samuel was on the verge of becoming a rising star in his chosen field. He was on the fast track, beginning his career as head Neurologist over at Johns Hopkins. We dated for several months, and then we married. He never gave up on his pursuit of me. I never lied about my feelings for Walker, and although Samuel wanted more, he took what I could offer him. We were friends, then lovers, but I was never truly in love with him. My heart had always belonged to another."

"Poor sap. That's tough when you're trying to fill shoes like Walker's. So are you still married to this guy? Do you have kids?"

"I'm divorcing Samuel. Our one and only daughter, Riley, is about to go off to college in a few months, and I felt this was my chance to leave. I stayed way longer than I should have, but he always convinced me to stay and try."

"He wasn't abusive, was he?"

"No, Freddy, nothing like that. Samuel is a good man, just neglectful, and married to his work more than he ever was to me. I want him to be happy with a woman who will truly love him the way he deserves, not a half of a person like I was."

"Daughter? She must be beautiful like you."

"Riley is amazing, Freddy. She does look like me, but she has her father's eyes. She is so smart and very sweet. She is fearless, Freddy. Sometimes I'm in awe of my own child. She exudes confidence and grace."

"Come on, Peaches, like mother like daughter. She sounds wonderful. I would love to meet her someday."

"You would have last week at your fashion show, but my attempts to see you were stopped by my husband. But now thanks to Marsha, I'm here."

"Are you the reason why my calendar is clear this week?"

"Guilty as charged!"

"So are we going to address the elephant in the room who is aptly named Walker?"

"How do you do that? It's like you and Walker have a direct line to my thoughts."

"It's a gift. Now tell me everything, Peaches."

"Freddy, I got the shock of my life last week when I was here in New York. Riley and I were here for a college tour and also to see you, a surprise for my daughter. She's a huge fan by the way, your clothes line both our closets. Anyway, she has a boyfriend. His name is Jackson. They met at Johns Hopkins, where a building was being dedicated in his late mother's name. They kept in touch, and after finding out that they are both attending NYU this fall, majoring in the same field, well that's the universe's way of making a perfect match, right?"

"Wow. That is something."

"Oh, it gets better my friend. Our first night in the city, we had dinner plans to meet Jackson and his father."

"Nice! Is his dad hot? Single? Did you hit it off?"

"Hot?" I had to pause and reminisce about my Walker. "Oh, he looked so good. He aged like a fine wine, better after seventeen years..."

"Oh, hell no, Reese. You don't mean to tell me that this kid's dad is Wa..."

"Yes, Freddy, that's exactly what I'm saying. Jackson is the son of Walker and Elizabeth, and he's now in love with my daughter, Riley."

"Holy shit! I need a drink."

"I almost fell over when I saw Walker again. He was visibly shaken and completely surprised. Needless to say, that reunion wasn't as easy as this one, but eventually I told him the truth about everything. And that's one of the reasons that led me back to you, Freddy. I had been planning on seeing you anyway, but now with Walker back in my life, I so desperately needed to fix things with you. You know you were really my first love at NYU." We hugged.

"So how is the hot man these days? Can he still do the wall thing?"

"Oh my goodness, Freddy! How long will you keep reminding me of that? You haven't changed a bit."

"Never, Peaches. It was the best sex of my life, even if I had to hear it from the next room."

"Stop it. You're terrible, but I love you, Freddy. I missed you so much."

"I've missed you too, baby girl. Don't ever leave me again! Or I swear I will hand in my sketch pad and never design another piece of clothing again. You will ruin me."

"What movie is that line from?"

"No movie. It comes from my heart, and I wasn't kidding. To lose you again would hurt so much more than the first time you left. Reese, you have to come to terms with the past once and for all, and figure out what the hell you want. Stop being afraid, and live the life you've always wanted to have."

"I am, Freddy. I promise you, no more running. I have my second chance with Walker, and now you."

Freddy and I spent hours locked away in his office catching up on everything we could think of telling one another. His assistant, Trina, ordered us lunch and dinner. Freddy told me about his parents. They were alive and well, enjoying their retirement in Florida. His uncle and aunts finally sold off their businesses they owned in New York and joined the rest of his family. I heard about Fabrizio. I couldn't wait to meet the man that captured my guy's heart.

Freddy lit up while talking about him. Freddy had never forgotten about me and told his husband all about me. Freddy called Fabrizio on Skype, where we talked and laughed some more. He had a heavy Italian accent and was devilishly handsome. Freddy told me all about his foundation and his vision to help the children all around the world. His bookshelves were lined with humanitarian awards and of course awards for his work in the fashion industry. I was so proud of my best friend, and I was so happy that he had found his Forever.

I couldn't have asked for a better day with Freddy. He had forgiven me, and I had my best friend back. He couldn't wait to meet Riley. She was going to go major fangirl when she met him. I'm sure Freddy will teach her a few words that she will need to survive the big city. God knows he put me through New York 101 when I first arrived. Marsha had sent over my favorite wine and some treats for Freddy and I to enjoy. I said a tearful goodbye to him, but we promised we would see each other soon.

I finally checked in to my hotel room later that night. I only briefly talked to Riley, and I sent Walker a text. He never returned my phone call, but I wasn't worried. I asked for space, and I knew this was him giving it to me. I knew he hated it. I didn't want to be the cause of anymore hurt for the man I loved, but I had one more thing to do.

If I was ever going to be happy with Walker, I knew I would

have to come clean with Nana. I just couldn't show up on her door-step hand in hand with Walker and expect all to go back to how it was. The last time I spoke to Nana, I was still very much married to Samuel, and now we were divorcing. She never came out and said how she really felt about my marriage to Samuel, that wouldn't be the Christian way, but I had always known. Nana always respected my choices and feelings.

In the comfort of my hotel room, soaking in my jasmine filled bath, my body was completely relaxed, and all thoughts went to Walker. I dreamed of him touching me, loving me with his body, and then me feeling the intense pleasure of his sensual assaults. I found my hand slowly lowering over my clit and picturing Walker's mouth hovering over it. Just then my cell was ringing, bringing me out of my sexually infused thoughts.

How the hell does he know he was on my mind? It's Walker!

"Hello," I barely spoke above a whisper.

"Reese," his voice was smooth as velvet gliding along my skin. "I miss you, baby. I almost shattered my phone today when I real-ized I had missed your call. What are you doing? Or do I even have to ask?"

"I miss you too, Walker. I'm taking a bath."

"Don't touch yourself! I want all your pleasure, and I will soon be giving it to you. This separation is slowly killing me, Reese. You should know by now, I am not a patient man."

"I wish you were in this tub with me right now. What was I thinking of ever asking for time, when you know you own my body and soul."

"You don't know how much I've been wanting and needing to hear those words come from your delectable mouth, but you were right to ask for space. I can't just expect you to drop everything in your life and join me out here in California. I asked you once to do that, and I lost you. I will stray away from anything that will put me in that position again."

"Walker, please don't do that. You did nothing wrong, and I

willingly accepted everything you ever asked of me. I wanted our life together, but I ran. I'm done hiding and not trusting in what we have. Do you believe me?"

"How can I not? Of course I do, baby. I just need you so much, and I have Jackson here and my work."

"It's the same for me. It's been a rough few days with Riley. She is so confused with everything that has happened. She loves her father and never wants to choose between the two of us.

"She doesn't have to, Reese. She knows how much her parents love her and will always be there for her. It wasn't easy for Jackson to hear, but I think he understands it all now. I'm giving him the time he needs to process it all."

"You haven't told me about your trip out to the Hamptons."

"No, I haven't. I'm still reeling from all of it, but I promise I will tell you when we have the time. I won't ever keep anything from you."

Now that Walker had opened up the door for my next question, I needed to know. "Walker, can I ask you something?"

"You know you can."

"I know I can, but I wanted to ask anyway. I need an honest answer no matter how much it angers you."

"Reese, don't play with my emotions when I'm thousands of miles away from you. Ask me."

"The divorce papers, Walker! My divorce papers intended for Samuel. How did you manage to have them served to him without my knowledge?"

He sighed deeply on the line before answering me. "Reese, I'm a very powerful man. I didn't get where I am today without knowledge and influence. I had my lawyer contact yours and simply take over the proceedings. Once your husband signs the papers and they are filed, we can begin making plans for our wedding and making me your husband. Please don't be angry with me. You do want this right, Reese?"

"Of course I do, Walker, but you didn't see the hurt on Samuel's face when he showed me the papers. He was beyond devastated. I just want this to be done as amicably as possible."

"Reese, it will be. As long as this divorce is uncontested, and it will be, you have nothing to worry about. All you need to do is walk out that door, and go straight through mine. I love you so much, and I need you with me."

I said to him, "Just for the record, I'm not angry with you. You took something that was hard for me to do, and you handled it for me. I love you too. My skin has now pruned, and the bath water has turned cold. I need to get some rest before flying back to Maryland in the morning."

"Jackson spoke to Riley, and she mentioned that you're going to Georgia on Friday."

"That's the plan. I was going to go on my own, but Riley wants to see Nana and Granddaddy."

"Can I join you in Georgia? I would love to see Lila and Thomas again. I was afraid to even ask you about them, and you couldn't imagine my relief when you told me that they're alive and well."

"You really want to fly down to Georgia?" I asked.

"More than anything in the world, so please say yes, Reese"

"Yes. I can't wait to see you again."

We exchanged our "I love you's" and struggled to hang up the phone. How this man affects me even miles away is beyond all logical thinking. For the first time in days, I slept so soundly. Of course all my night's dreams were of Walker. I dreamed of our son for the first time in years. This time around, though, it wasn't scary and sad. He was beautiful and happy in heaven. He was surrounded by light and warmth. He looked just like Walker. He was being held by a woman, I recognized her to be Elizabeth. She was rocking him to sleep. I could hear the lullaby she was singing to him. Elizabeth never had the chance to be a mother to Jackson, and I never had the chance to be a mother to our son. I felt happy believing that Elizabeth was watching over mine and Walker's child.

He was safe where no one could hurt him. In the past, anytime I would remember my son, I would feel cold and alone. I wanted him so much and was devastated when he didn't survive. I had never felt peace in my dreams until tonight. Seeing Elizabeth with him erased all the loss I ever felt. I couldn't explain it, this feeling was something that was new and unexplored. I just knew I was okay. I didn't know if I should mention this to Walker, would he understand? He never knew about our son, but he may have needed this closure as well. He loved Elizabeth, and she loved him. Knowing that the two losses in our lives brought us together again should hopefully bring him the peace and closure he needed.

CHAPTER EIGHTEEN

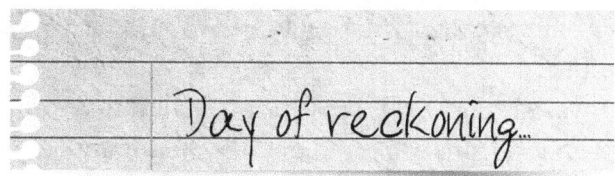

Day of reckoning...

DAYS OF WORRYING about the unknown ceased last night after speaking to Reese. She wasn't angry with me about my calculated intrusion with the divorce papers. I hadn't heard from her in a few days, and I was going out of my mind here in California. In a few days, she would be back in my arms where she belonged. She had to know that I would do everything in my power to keep her safe and happy.

Before leaving New York a few days ago, I examined the contents of my safe once more. It contained tangible and precious memories of Reese from our life together all those years ago. *The life I said goodbye to. The life I intended to have with Reese.*

The ring box was there right where I placed it years ago. I opened the box to see this exquisite ring shining back at me, Reese's ring that would soon be gracing her hand and remain there forever. It was the ring that her grandmother had given to me. This is the same ring that I had redesigned for my true love, and the same ring that I couldn't bear to look at once I knew she was never coming back. Her grandmother never allowed me to return it.

Nana always told me to believe in true love, and eventually this ring would find its rightful owner. And now it had: Reese, the woman who held my heart, was wrapped around my soul, and was the only one that truly could hurt me. To lose Reese now would destroy me beyond any hopes of survival. I was now a believer in love, fate, and the universe with all of its signs. I would never doubt it again and the possibilities of a happy future with Reese.

It had been days since I returned to my office. Today was the day I righted a wrong that should never had happened. The smug bastard would not see me coming, and I would enjoy every minute of his misfortune.

Jackson was sitting at the breakfast bar with his headphones on. I waved my hand in front of him to get his attention.

"Hey, dad, I thought you would be gone already."

"Good morning, son. Normally, I would be, but I caught up on some sleep last night and will be going in a little later this morning. I also wanted to have a chat with you before you leave for school."

"I have time, dad. My first class is not until ten. What's on your mind?"

"Jackson, above anything else in my life, you know you're my number one priority, right?"

"Yes, I know, dad."

"You and I have been quite the team all of these years, and I know the past week delivered you many changes that will now affect your life, as well as my own."

"Dad, I'm fine. I've had a lot of time to process it all, and I'm secure enough to know my place in your life. You don't need to worry about me."

"Jackson, I will never stop worrying about you. That's my job, but thank you for letting me know. How are things with Riley, if you don't mind me asking?"

"Lack of a better word? Emotional. We've been talking every day, but she's not the same. She's hurting over her parents' breakup, and I'm just afraid she's going to resent me for it."

"I hope that doesn't happen, son. The dissolution of their marriage has nothing to do with you, or even with her, for that matter. I know how much you care for her, and I've seen Riley return your affections."

"Dad, when we were on the plane, and you were telling me all about Reese, I told you that I hope your relationship with Reese doesn't spill over into mine with Riley. Well, its already happened, dad. I love and care about her. I think she is amazing and worth waiting for, but I also can't sit back and have her crush my heart because of something that was beyond our control. It's like her feelings for me have changed, and no matter what I say, it leads to an argument where she's crying and I'm apologizing."

"Jackson, I'm sorry. I never want to cause you one day of unhappiness. I hope everything works out for you and Riley, but be patient, son. Riley clearly needs time to work it out, and once she does, I'm sure you two will be okay."

"If we're not, then what happens? You and Reese will ride off into the sunset, and Riley and I will be over? I won't let that happen, dad!"

"Okay, okay, calm down Jackson. You will see her on Friday in Georgia, and then the two of you can go off somewhere to talk. Pottersville has a way of bringing people together, and wait until you meet her great grandmother, Lila. She is so sweet, but a spitfire who says it how it is. No man is left standing when her feathers are riled up. I can't wait to see her again. It's been too many years."

"You're actually smiling, dad."

"That I am, son. For the first time since I lost your mother, today I just feel at peace, which brings me to the next thing I have to tell you. Reese has filed for divorce from her husband. The divorce will not be challenged, and I have been able to lift the customary waiting period to a shorter time. Once that is all complete, I plan on marrying Reese and finally making her my wife."

I watched Jackson's expression fall, and he looked down to his hands. I lifted his chin to see him crying. "Jackson, this is not the reaction I wanted to see. Talk to me, son. Why are you upset?"

"I'm not upset, dad. I just wish my mother had lived. I almost feel disloyal to her memory for supporting you and your relationship to Reese. Does that sound crazy?"

"No, it doesn't, Jackson. It makes perfect sense, because I've been where you are. But I have to believe Elizabeth would want me to be happy. Jackson, I've never been able to give my heart to another in all of these years after losing Reese, and then your mother. I did love her, son. Please know that. Jackson, I have never asked anything of you until today. I want your blessing and support for my marriage to Reese. It's just not okay for me to be alone anymore, and now that I have her back, I don't plan on waiting one more day."

My son appeared to be struggling with his reply. I was just about to say something to him when Stephen interrupted us.

"Sir, excuse me for the intrusion, but you don't want to be late for your appointment."

I groaned rather loudly, but he was right. I had to leave for the office. "Jackson, we will finish this conversation tonight."

Not one word, he just quietly nodded. *Fuck!* This is not how I envisioned our talk would go.

In record time, we arrived at Reed Global. I'm greeted by Jenny, who has returned from her vacation.

"Good morning, sir, and welcome back," she says warmly and nods at Stephen.

"Good morning, Jenny." I say to her, as I move past her and right into my office. It's just as I left it, maybe a bit tidy. Clearly, Jenny has been in here. Catherine knows not to enter without my permission. "Oh, you put flowers in my office?"

"You look oddly happy this morning." Her comment is not lost on me, as she entered with my coffee.

"Why odd?" I look over myself, and then back over to Jenny, who is shyly smiling at me.

"It's not odd at all, you just look…different, and whatever has made you this way, I hope it continues. I put flowers in your office every week, and you've never noticed them before."

"Thank you Jenny, but that conversation will have to be for another time. Has Donovan checked in yet?"

"He has, but has been delayed by traffic. He should be here soon."

"Send him in as soon as he arrives, and we are expecting Jake Ralston momentarily."

"Yes sir. The papers you requested are on your desk, and the other files you asked for as well."

"Excellent. Thank you, and Jenny…"

"Yes, Mr. Reed."

"If Jackson calls anytime during that meeting, please patch him through without hesitation."

"Always, sir."

Stephen took his place while I began to look over the documents I had Jenny put together for me. That file contained everything I needed to single handedly take down all of my enemies who played a part in my separation from Reese: Miles, Ralston, and Henry. I'm still shocked about Henry's role in all of this. Of all people, I never imagined he could or would ever hurt me. My father was the only one that got off easy…or did he? His life was cut short by a heart attack, and my mother was mourning his loss each day. My heart hurt for her, but not for him. He left me with his letters of apology and the information I needed to close this chapter of my life, but I was conflicted.

I wanted my pound of flesh. I wanted the men who hurt me to suffer and pay for what they had done to me and to Reese. I kept hearing Jackson's words replay in the back of my mind, "At what cost?" I think I doubted my decisions because of how I left things with Jackson this morning. We were at a crossroads, and I needed to have us be on the same page. I needed his support more like my next breath. My son was everything to me, and the uncertainty of the unknown was killing me.

"Sir," Jenny called over the intercom. "Mr. Tate has arrived."

"Send him in, Jenny, and please hold my calls."

"Welcome home, Walker. I'm sorry I'm late, traffic was horrendous with a five car pile-up."

I raised my hands to silence him. Hearing his excuses to why he was late was irrelevant to me. "Donovan, take a seat, we have much to discuss."

He looked over nervously to Stephen, who remained focused on what he was reading. "Is this about the Reinhart plans? The plans have been delivered, and all is right with them. They are currently looking the plans over, and we will meet again next month in Germany."

I cut him off. "Donovan, this has nothing to do with the Reinhart building. Yes, I want to talk about that, but not today. I have other matters that we need ironed out. Now, don't interrupt me again." He quietly nodded, and I continued, "While I was in New York last week, I traveled to my family's estate and discovered some unsettling revelations that need to be addressed, and they will be today. Do you remember Reese Mitchell?"

"Of course I do. Why do you ask?"

"I'm asking because her husband happens to be Samuel Briggs, the same Samuel Briggs that is a neurosurgeon over at Johns Hopkins Hospital in Maryland. He's the very same doctor whom Reed Global designed and built a building for."

"Yes on all counts. Walker, I'm not following."

"Let me bring you up to speed, Donovan." I opened the file and showed Donovan the contents of it. His eyes widened when he found the picture of him, Dr. Briggs, three men from the board of directors, and a beautiful woman in the background. My Reese.

"Well?" I asked him.

"Well, what?"

"Donovan, are you really going to play this game with me? You will lose, and lose a great deal if you don't tell me the truth, and right fucking now! Do you see the woman in this picture?" I point to her. "Did you or did you not know that this same woman was Reese Mitchell? The same Reese Mitchell who I was madly in love with? The same woman who I planned to marry until she disappeared out of my fucking apartment? The very same woman who hasn't been in my life for the better part of eighteen years?"

"Not at first, but then once I heard her speak and talk to her more I did place her as one and the same."

I slammed the folder down and grabbed Donovan by the throat. Not knowing what I would do next, Stephen rose out of his seat and looked over to me. I ignored him and proceeded with Donovan.

"Why didn't you tell me this?"

"Would it have mattered? She brought you nothing but hurt and misery, Walker. I was there for you when she left, and then by your side when Elizabeth died. I hadn't seen Reese since New Year's 1997. I had no idea who she was at the time, and when I finally did remember, I kept it to myself. She clearly didn't remember me, and if she did, she never said anything."

He continued, "All the times I was there in Maryland, this was the only time our paths crossed. This picture was taken the day the papers were signed to finalize the project. It was after you met with the board the first time. Walker, you never returned to Maryland after that, and I felt it was best not to say anything to you. I never saw her again after that day."

Trying to get myself in check, I let go of Donovan and watched him slump down in to his chair. "It would have mattered to me, Donovan. Everything matters, and she was my life."

"I'm sorry, Walker. I thought I was protecting you. I've been your friend since college, and I have always had your back in business and your personal life. I just didn't want you to get hurt again."

"It wasn't your call to make, Donovan. I lost more precious time when we could have been together, but it's all changed now."

"What's changed?"

"I have her back, and we will be marrying very soon in the near future. When you lift your jaw from off the floor, you can say something."

"Wow, Walker. I'm stunned to say the least. How did this happen?"

"Donovan, you know I'm not one to share intimate details of my personal life to anyone, not even you, but I will give you the short version. Our children met during the dedication celebrating the new building. They formed a friendship, and now are seeing one another, never knowing that their parents also shared a connection many years ago. While I was in New York for Jackson's college trip, I had the opportunity to meet his girlfriend, and to say I was shocked was an understatement. Riley, hands down, resembles her mother. I sucked in a breath with the sight of this young beauty standing before me. I nearly died when Reese walked in. I was out of my mind. All the feelings I had for Reese came flooding back like a tsunami. I knew this was fate giving us a second chance."

"What about her husband? She's married, Walker."

"That's the perfect part, Donovan. Before she left for New York, she asked her husband for a divorce. Now if you want to challenge fate after that, then I'm going to fire your ass."

"I never took you for believing in the universe and all that sentimental shit, but I'm happy for you. I truly hope it works out this time for the both of you."

"I have no doubt in my mind about ending up with Reese Mitchell. She will be mine very soon, as I always planned on her to be. Donovan, everything I do in my life matters, personally and professionally. You may have thought you were protecting me, but don't ever take my choice away from me again. I've been down that road, and I won't travel it again, especially with you and the history we share. I will sever our ties and have your office cleaned out so fast, your head will fucking spin off. Do I make myself clear?"

"Crystal."

"Good. Now let's get down to business. We need to discuss the Reinhart Project, but that will have to wait. These matters of importance take precedence over everything right now. Here in these files contain the last three projects my father had a hand in. I want you to gather as much intel as you possibly can on each deal and report back to me. Also here is a file on Townsend Development. Henry assisted my father with getting out of some unfortunate situations."

I flipped through the file with Donovan and said, "In these papers, you will find that three migrant workers died on the project Phillip handled in Argentina. I want everything on their families. No amount of money will bring back their loved ones, but I at least want to give them some sort of settlement. Knowing where the money came from will do no good for any of us, so this is to remain on the highest level of discretion. Again, Donovan, am I making myself clear?"

"Yes, sir."

"Now onto Jake Ralston. He is due here in an hour and is in for the shock of his life. I've acquired his company, Ralston Security Firm. That smug son of a bitch is not going to see this coming."

"A hostile take-over? When did this happen? How did I not know about this?" Donovan looked over to Stephen.

"I'm informing you now, and I want you to peruse the file and know it front and back within the next thirty minutes. Come back with your balls out, because I'm about to hand Ralston his in the same manner he treated Reese. That fucker is responsible for hurting the woman I love, and even with as many years that have gone by, no sin is ever forgotten."

"Today is Ralston's day of reckoning. Ralston made a choice in helping my father, and he chose wrong. You don't hurt the woman I loved all my adult life and not expect to feel my wrath."

I dismissed Stephen to make a private call to my woman. I was in complete search and destroy mode, but Reese kept invading my every thought. I dialed her cell, and she picked up immediately.

"Hi, baby," I am pleased to no end to have her on the phone.

"Hello, Walker." Could she be any sexier? Her southern accent simply rolled off her tongue like silk. I was already hard with only the two words she had spoken.

"I'm just about to board my flight. Oh, Walker, I had the most amazing time with Freddy. He forgives me, and we spent hours together catching up. I miss you baby, more than you know. Once I get settled back in Maryland, I will call you. Do I expect security to be there when I arrive home?"

Oh, she knows me so well and is laughing at me. I'm afraid Reese still viewed the outside world with rose-colored glasses, and did not realize that there were dangers that could harm her. I replied, "Yes to the security. A car will be waiting for you to drive you home. While we are apart, Reese, this is the only way I know to keep you safe. I don't know how Samuel will react from day to day, and I'm not willing to take any chances. Please don't fight me on this, okay?"

"Okay."

"Good girl. I can't wait to see you on Friday and bury myself deep inside you."

"Enjoy your fantasy, Walker, but how do you intend to do that with my grandparents and our kids around?"

"Oh, I have my ways, Reese. Don't you worry about that. I love you so much. I have to go, baby, call me when you land."

"I will. And Walker…"

"Yes, baby?"

"I love you…Forever."

"Forever, Reese. I will take nothing less." We stayed on the line to listen to the other breathe, until she giggled, leaving me with the sweet sounds of her beautiful voice. I called Stephen back in to my office.

"Stephen, is everything set-up in the gym?"

"It is, sir, but do you think this is the best strategy when it comes to Ralston?"

"Absolutely."

"I have his company no matter what, and now I want his ass beat down by my own hands. Knowing the smug bastard he is; he won't back down, and probably will believe that he actually has a chance against me."

Stephen said to me, "Well, we're about to find out because secu-

270

rity has just alerted me that he is in the building."

"Perfect."

Donovan returned and took his seat next to Stephen, while Jenny announced Ralston's arrival over my intercom.

"Thank you, Jenny, and please hold all my calls."

Ralston walked in making eye contact with Stephen and Donovan before approaching me at my desk.

"Walker, for what do I owe the pleasure of being summoned here today? It's been a long time."

"It has, Ralston, if you don't count my father's funeral."

"I figured not to bring up any sad memories for you."

"No need to care about my feelings now, Ralston. It's not like you had my back all those years ago when it would have mattered."

"Come again?"

"Reese Mitchell, does that name ring a bell?" I had his attention, and his expression went from smug to apprehensive. "Well? Do you remember Ms. Mitchell?"

"Yes, I do," he answered curtly.

"Good. This saves me the trouble of making you remember the girl that you agreed to help my father destroy."

"Now, Walker..."

"Shut-up!" I walked around from behind my desk and shoved him down into the chair. Clearly he wasn't expecting me to strike at him. "Did you honestly think that what you did to Reese was simply going to be forgotten? And never avenged for? This is not how the game works, Ralston. You of all people should know that. I would think working for my father would have taught you a lesson or two, but it makes perfect sense to me that the old man didn't keep you around for your intelligence. If you were a smart man, then you would have known that as of nine o'clock this morning, your company now belongs to me."

"What the fuck are you playing at, Reed? You just can't take my company right out from under me."

"Yes I can, and I most certainly did. Losing a company is nothing compared to what you've taken from me and Reese. Your brutal actions caused the woman I love to lose our child…my child, you son of a bitch! Reese never stood a chance against my father and you. Your company is nothing to me, but my baby was everything. Correction: *would have been* everything. Children can never be replaced, and this is why you're here today. I wanted to look into the eyes of the bastard who killed my child."

"Walker, you have to believe me, I never meant to hurt Ms. Mitchell. I was only trying to prevent her from seeing you. I was under instructions by your father to stop her. I had no idea that she was pregnant."

"Are you fucking kidding me? You're a liar, fucker. You stalked and tracked her every move for three months, and when she was so close to finally reaching me, you put your hands on her again! The stress alone contributed to Reese losing our baby."

"My father paid you, and paid you well, to be his enforcer. It was your job to intimidate his enemies. Yes, Ralston, he saw my woman as his enemy, someone that needed to be taken care of. Isn't that where your skills always came in handy? It was your brother who put Reese on the plane that day when she was forced to flee New York. Yes, I know about him too. I know everything, and today is Judgment Day for you. I don't care about your company. I will sell it off, piece by piece. I will simply forget about it, like you did when it came to my woman. After today, I will forget about you, but not before I get something else from you."

"What? I have nothing else," he shouted back at me.

"Wrong again, Ralston. I'm feeling generous today. You want your company so bad, I'll make you a deal. I want my pound of flesh, and it is long overdue. If you manage to take me down, and keep me down, then you may have your company back."

"You can't be serious. You have never been able to get past me, Reed. You may have taken my business, but there is no way you can win a fight against me."

"Try me."

He got up and walked over to Stephen.

"Come on, man, tell your boy over here that he's crazy to think he can actually fight and beat me down."

"On the contrary, Ralston, I believe Mr. Reed has the ability to break your spineless back if he so desired. If you're so confident that he will lose, then off to the gym we go." Stephen was almost laughing at him and waited for Ralston to take the bait.

"Fine, Reed. I'll fight you for my company." Ralston said, "Don't say I didn't warn you."

Stephen led Ralston out of my office and down to my private gym. I changed and was ready to go in no time. I dismissed everyone upstairs on my executive floor except for Jenny, who was now doting on me like a small child.

"Sir, please don't do this. That overgrown ape is not worth it. What if you get hurt? What will I tell your son?"

"Jenny, I'll be fine, and I will be right back."

"Foolish man," I heard her say as I stepped onto the elevator.

I was far from foolish, and this was one lesson I would enjoy giving. My father laid it all out for me in his papers. It was as if he were willing me from the grave to seek my vengeance on the ones that had hurt me and Reese. Phillip Reed may have led the pack, but he got off easy by dying. I told myself as I entered the ring: *I am not my father, but what kind of man would I be if I just let this go? Ralston deserved this beating, and I would be happy to give it to him in the name of my lost child.*

The smug bastard was actually smiling and bouncing around the ring like he's Rocky or something. I'd been trained very well by professional fighter Tyler McVee, a detail I forgot to mention to Ralston.

Stephen gave us the signal, and Ralston charged right for me with his fists up in the air. I saw it coming, immediately ducked, and did a leg sweep which toppled him over. Ralston bounced back up and went to swing, but I was too fast and ducked again. I hit him directly in his ribs, and when he was caught off balance, I threw an uppercut to his chin. Every punch I landed on Ralston was igniting my thirst for revenge to return all the pain he caused us. Ralston gathered his wits and landed a right hook above my eye, causing it to split open. I had blood slowly trickling down the side of my cheek.

"That will be your one and only hit," I said as he tried to hit me again. I dodged and delivered a roundhouse kick to the side of his head, and then I repeated the same move with my left leg. He went down on the mat, and my last punch was to his jaw, where I heard the shattering of bones. Stephen was now pulling me off of him as I kept swinging.

"Mr. Reed! Walker! He's out cold, that's enough!"

Stephen's men now came into the ring and picked up Ralston's broken body off the floor. He slowly came to, and I walked over to him where he was being held up by two men. "Now listen to me very carefully," I said to him, "If you ever come near me or anyone I care about, then the next time we meet I. Will. Kill. You. Now get the fuck out of my building!"

When I returned to my office, Donovan was waiting for me with a nervous Jenny. She gasped when she took notice of my swollen eyebrow. I waved my hand up at her, showing her that I was fine and to leave Donovan and me to discuss our business.

"Was that Jake Ralston that I saw get carried out of the building?" Donovan nervously asked.

"It was. Have you looked over the files?"

"Yes, I have."

"Good. Dump the company, and sell it off."

Donovan was shocked. "You never meant to hold on to it?"

"No. It was only a quick means to an end. Are you clear on the other matter?"

"Yes, it all seems in order. I leave in the morning for Buenos Aires."

"Perfect. I've already briefed Tom, and he will accompany you to Argentina. I expect a report on my desk and a resolution to this matter within the next week. I will be out of town as of Friday. All status reports will go through Jenny, and she will forward them to me. Are we clear?"

"Yes sir."

After dismissing Donovan, I slowly got myself back in check. I showered and changed back into my suit, already forgetting the morning events.

"He's a good man, sir, and has been nothing but a loyal employee and friend." Stephen said to me.

"This I know, Stephen, but thank you for the reminder. Although in some small way I understand Donovan's reasons for keeping quiet about Reese, another part of me is just so incredibly angry with him. He's been like a brother to me, and that bond should have easily guided him to do the right thing." Stephen began to say something more, but I raised my hand up to silence him. "This discussion is over."

I needed this time to focus on other matters, and sending Donovan away would help me calm my heated emotions toward him. I knew that once I saw Reese on Friday, most of my pent up rage would be sated. I was 24/7 hard for her. All I wanted was to be buried inside of her for days and shut the rest of the world out.

"Stephen, please send Jenny in."

"Yes sir."

Jenny walked in with her iPad and took a seat. She looked at me with her concerned baby blues, but I assured her that I was fine.

"How was your trip sir?" Her question alone made me smile.

"I took your advice and got myself a life, or should I say...I got my life back while I was in New York." I told Jenny about Reese and how we reunited. I left out the parts that she didn't need to hear, but after my explanation, Jenny was very happy for me and her eyes were filled with tears.

"I'm so happy for you, Mr. Reed. I can't wait to meet her."

"You will soon, Jenny, once she arrives in California. I plan on marrying Ms. Mitchell as soon as possible."

I finished up with Jenny and completed all the pressing matters on my desk. Beginning Friday, my main focus would be Reese. My heart was feeling lost every second she was not with me. I headed back home.

"Jackson, are you home?" I called out for my son. I was greeted by Priscilla, my housekeeper, who took my things and told me that Jackson was in the media room with some friends from school. I entered the darkened room and found Jackson and two of his friends, Brandon and Clay, editing their project for film class.

"Hey, dad, sorry we didn't hear you come in." The other boys greeted me with pleasantries, and I took a seat to watch what they have done so far. Jackson powered down the video and turned the overhead lights back on.

"Sorry dad, but it's not finished." He enjoyed himself with the look I just gave him. His friends eventually left, and I asked Jackson about his day. Of course my bruised eye did not go unnoticed by him, and he questioned me about it.

"You should see the other guy," I said to lighten the mood.

"What happened? Are you okay?"

"I'm fine, son, nothing to worry about. I took care of some unfinished business today. Now, how are you?"

"Seriously, dad? That's all I get? You're not going to tell me anything else?"

"Jackson, I'm fine. You don't need to worry about me. I would rather hear about your day, and especially this film you're working on."

"I'm fine too, dad. The film is for my class project, and it will go toward my final semester grade. I think it's a win. Brandon and Clay shot most of the location, and I wrote up the documentary part of it. The film is kind of a tribute to Max Azarian, who died last year from a brain tumor."

"I'm sorry, son, I didn't know."

"He was only at our school for a year, if you want to even say that. He was in and out of hospitals for most of the term, but when he was in school, kids just seemed to flock around him. Kids like

Max could have been helped by doctors like Riley's dad."

"I'm sure Max's doctors did everything they could for him." I tried to ignore my son mentioning the good doctor. He was the last person I wished to talk to my son about. I quickly changed the subject.

"Are you excited for Friday?"

"Clearly not as happy as you seem to be, but I'm looking forward to it."

"Is it that obvious?"

"It's written all over your face, dad. I'm happy for you."

"What about you? Are you okay?"

"I'm fine. I've been keeping the conversations with Riley to a minimum until we can be together and really talk it out. I guess I should be happy that she hasn't completely cut me off."

"Give her time, like I said. I promise you that she will come around."

"I wish I had your confidence, dad, but for you, I will try."

"That's all I ask."

After dinner, we talked about Jackson's upcoming prom and graduation. He had all intent and purpose on asking Riley to be his date for the function. They were not graduating at the same time. Jackson's prom and graduation were weeks ahead of Riley's, so he wanted to fly back to Maryland to escort Riley to her prom and stay for the graduation that would be one week later. Things always had a way of working out; my relationship with Reese was living proof.

CHAPTER NINETEEN

Heart of the matter...

YOU ARE MY Forever. Love, Walker.

My fingers glided over the inscription I had engraved on Reese's locket. I repaired the broken chain and had the heart polished to look brand new.

As I went through my father's papers, I not only found the watch he wanted Jackson to have, but also this necklace, the locket I had given to Reese on New Year's Eve. I remembered word for word what I said to her that night and how this heart would symbolize our love as one. I should have proposed to her right there but I wanted it to be perfect, and when she said yes to my proposal, we would make love for days to celebrate our union. We lost so much time with one another, but I couldn't worry about what I couldn't change. I had her back, and that was all that mattered.

My iPad alerted me of an incoming video chat. I put away the gift box and opened up the window to see my beautiful angel smiling back at me.

"You were supposed to call me when you landed in Maryland," I said. I tried to keep the agitation out of my voice, but looking at her beautiful face had me softening to her.

"Well, I'm sure your security team informed you of my arrival and let you know that I was safe. I wanted to contact you in a different way, if you allow me to show you."

"What did you have in mind?" I leaned back in my chair.

"Are you on your own?" she asked.

"I am."

"Good. Because I want to show you something."

"Have we played this game before?" I teasingly asked her.

"Oh, we've played this game before, but as much as this is visual, it is also a trivia game."

"So if I win at this game, what will my prize be?"

"Anything you want," she said seductively.

Her cheeks were fiery red, and I could almost see her pulse throbbing from her succulent neck, which I just wanted to stroke my tongue over.

"I like this game, Reese, and I do intend to win. Please carry on with your little show and tell."

"I will, but I need you to close your eyes first."

The second my eyes closed, my dick stood at full mast.

"Open your eyes, sexy" she whispered.

My eyes quickly found hers, and then they travelled up her body, and I knew exactly what she wanted me to remember. My beautiful Georgia Peach was laid out on her king-sized bed, displaying her beauty before me and wearing the same lingerie she wore on the night we made love for the first time.

"You're a tease. Haven't I warned you about playing with my emotions, especially when we are miles apart from one another? I can have my plane ready in an hour." She giggled and enjoyed my obvious discomfort. I showed her my erection, and her giggling increased to a laugh out loud roar. She held her stomach and wiped her tears from her eyes. I couldn't help but to laugh as well. It felt good to laugh and finally feel something more than hate, loneliness, and despair.

"Well, Walker? What am I wearing?" She knew I would remember, and my angel definitely wanted to lose this wager, oh I loved her so much. She wanted me as much as I wanted her.

"You, my love, are wearing the same corset that I peeled off of you with my teeth on the night we made love for the first time. However, I do remember tearing your panties."

"These are new, but everything else is the same, down to the shoes." She showed me her feet.

"I hadn't known that you kept it all."

"I did, baby. I only wore this on our first night, and then after we parted, I tucked it away along with the rest of my brokenness. To see it was too painful, but I knew I couldn't part with it. I found it tonight in my closet and wanted to show you how much I missed and loved you even when we were not together."

God! She wounds me with her honesty and beauty. I closed my eyes and counted to ten before I opened them up to her again. Thinking of the pain of our past was the last thing I wanted to revisit, but I knew that if we were ever to move forward, she would need to know everything.

"I love you Reese, more than you will ever know. Thank you for my surprise, and I will look forward to my reward."

She smiled back. "I look forward to giving it to you."

"One more comment like that, Reese, and I will call my pilot. Friday seems too far away, and I'm barely hanging on as it is. Can you put a robe on, and then we can talk?"

She smiled and bounced off of her bed, but not before giving me a twirl and blowing me a kiss. When she returned back on the screen she was wearing a silky, black sleeveless top and matching short shorts. I couldn't decide if my heart or dick was throbbing more at the sight of her.

"Reese, I asked you to put a robe on, not change into another provocative outfit."

"I did, Walker. I'm completely covered up."

"Have it your way, love, and enjoy your version of pajamas, because when I get my hands on you, they will be the only things on your body."

"I'm sorry to tease you."

"No, you're not sorry, but you're forgiven anyway." She smiled and began to blush again.

"Are you all set for Georgia?" I asked.

"Yes, I am. I have my luggage and Riley is already packed. She's excited to see Nana and Granddaddy. I am too. I've stayed away longer than I should have, but Samuel could never take the time to get away, and yet he minded when I went without him."

So Samuel kept her from Lila and Thomas? That bastard!

"You don't ever have to worry about missing or seeing them again. We will all be reunited soon enough." Her face fell as she struggled to say her next words to me.

"What is it, Reese? Why are you upset?"

"Walker, I want to talk to you about our trip. I need to see my grandparents alone, before I tell them about us." My heart plummeted in my chest.

"No, no Reese, we agreed that we would face them together. Why are you now changing your mind?"

"Walker, please try to understand that I'm not trying to hurt you, I just need some time with my grandparents before I announce my divorce to Samuel and my reunion with you. My feelings have not changed, believe me. Every single day and year that passed while we were apart, I kept my reasons to myself. I never told anyone the real truth behind me leaving you. Only Samuel knew, and I have had to carry it all with me all of these years. I know they will be happy for me, but I have to believe they will have questions and may even be angry with me for not going to them when I should have."

Everything she said to me made sense, but at the same time, it felt like rejection. I tried to gain control over this conversation, but it appeared that Reese had made up her mind.

"Okay, Reese, when can I arrive?"

"Saturday morning, first thing."

CHAPTER TWENTY

Nana's truth...

I COULDN'T REMEMBER a longer week than this one, but we made it to Friday, and Riley and I were meeting with Samuel before heading to the airport. I kept my conversations with Samuel to a minimum, and when we spoke, we only discussed Riley. I didn't wish to remind Samuel of my relationship with Walker and the fact that our divorce was moving along to its finality. He kept himself busy with work, and while we were going to Georgia, he had to go to London to attend a medical conference. It was to take place later in the year, and while I was in New York the first time, it had gotten re-scheduled. Samuel stopped by the house before leaving for the air-port to say goodbye to his daughter.

I gave them their privacy, and when they emerged from his of-fice, surprisingly Riley appeared to be in good spirits. I watched them embrace once more, and then Riley took her place in the limo and waited for me to join her. Reaching for Samuel's hands, maybe on instinct, I wanted to know that he was okay, or at least trying to be. I held his hands in mine and looked up to his sad eyes.

"I'm so sorry, Samuel. I never meant to put that look there. I on-ly hope that one day we can be friends again for the sake of our daughter."

"We were always friends, Reese. I guess that was one of our problems. If I would have treated you more like a lover, then maybe we would have made it. Don't feel sorry for me. That is the last thing I need or could ever want from you. You made your choice, Reese. Now go live your life, and I will do the same."

Our hands disconnected, but not before Samuel leaned in and kissed my cheek. "I will always love you, Reese, but I would rather have you as a friend than nothing at all." I just nodded and watched him leave into the other waiting car.

I composed myself before stepping into the limo. Riley looked at me with her hopeful eyes, but I quickly dismissed her question.

"I'm fine, baby. Now let's go see Nana and Granddaddy." She held my hand and leaned her head on my shoulder. I wouldn't tell her how much I missed this from her. I just took in the warm affection she showed me. This was my girl, and this was her first step to finding her way through the mess my past had created for her.

While we waited for our flight to be called, I gave her some privacy to phone Jackson, while I called Walker. My call was brief. As much as he wanted to talk to me, I had caught him walking into a meeting. He wanted to wrap up everything on his desk before flying out tonight to join us. I was already regretting my decision to have him and Jackson wait back, but I had no idea how Nana would react to my news, and I didn't want to put Walker through any unnecessary pain. He handled my change of plans quite well, and if he didn't, he covered it up very discreetly.

I watched Riley. She was smiling and laughing. The sight of her made me smile. It gave me the extra dose of courage I would need to face Nana with.

"Hey, you look all sparkly," I teased her.

"I'm trying, mom. I miss Jackson so much, and I haven't been very nice to him lately. I think he was guarded and preparing for another mood swing of mine, but I told him a joke and the obvious tension faded away."

"Riley, everything happens for a reason, and what you share

with Jackson is a wonder to witness. You're so carefree. When I was your age, I was very shy. When I met Freddy, he brought me to life, and then falling in love with Walker completely changed me. Yes, I may have started out as the shy southern girl from Georgia, but I felt alive in New York. I was on my own, really on my own, and I was in love."

I continued, "I see the way Jackson looks at you, he loves you Riley girl, and if he is anything like his father, he will love you hard and will always protect you. I never gave Walker the chance to do that for me, but I will now. I vow never to second guess anything ever again."

"You still care about Daddy?"

"Of course I do. I will always love your father. Riley, how can I not when he gave me you?"

"He's going to be okay, right mom?"

"We all are, Riley. We are exactly where we are supposed to be, and that, my daughter, is not something you want to argue with the universe about."

"Oh my goodness, Mom, you and your sonnets of fate and ever-lasting love! You should have been an astrologer." I laughed, and we hugged each other.

"Oh baby, I should have been many things, but an astrologer is not one of them. I do believe in fate. I gave up on it for a good many years until Nana reminded me to believe and take control over my life and focus on what I want. Now, she never knew that piece of advice would lead me back to Walker but it has, and who am I to argue with the universe or Nana?" We both laughed.

Our flight was on time and landed us in Georgia just before noon. I knew Nana and Granddaddy took Fridays off from the shop. Granddaddy usually went fishing, and Nana baked during the week-ends. As we left the airport and traveled in the direction that would lead us to Pottersville, I began to feel a bit nervous. My stomach had been off lately, but I chalked it up to nerves. *This is Nana we're talking about? What's wrong with me? I have no reason to be this nerv-*

ous about talking with her!

As we entered the town limits of Pottersville, I watched Riley's eyes light up. She rolled down the window to take in the honeysuckle smells and remember all of her favorite places she liked to visit. She begged me to stop at Nana's shop. Of course, I said yes. She leaped out of the car and ran into the shop.

Riley came out a few minutes later with a bag of goodies and two coffees. I was nervous enough that coffee would only increase my anxiety, but I took it anyway. Nana's chocolate chip croissant melted on my tongue. Oh my goodness, my Nana could bake, and something fierce. I was in awe of her energy, and her passion for moving forward every day. My fingers were crossed that she could help me do the same.

"Oh mom, the house looks great! I can't wait to see Nana and Granddaddy." Once again not waiting for the driver to open her door, Riley made a beeline for the house and straight to Nana. We heard barking, and from the sounds of it, there was more than one dog. *When did they get a new dog?* I had thought after Bubba died, Granddaddy would never get another pet.

Sure enough, the screen door flew open, and two beagles came charging at Riley. She dropped to her knees, and they jumped on her, showing much affection. I never saw my daughter happier. Samuel never allowed her to have a pet in our house. He had too many precious things and never wanted to find a chewed piece of furniture or heaven forbid one of his shoes ruined.

"Oh my goodness, Mom, look how cute they are." Looking at Riley now, how foolish I was to allow that rule. Children needed pets especially growing up.

I think Granddaddy was a bit surprised about our grand entrance as he slowly began walking toward us. My last talk with Nana, she had asked me to visit, but I never said when. This trip was a surprise. I met Granddaddy halfway and walked right into his welcoming arms.

"What a surprise, darling! Why didn't you let us know that you were coming down to see us?" he asked.

"Oh I missed you, Granddaddy, but if I had told you, then it wouldn't have been a surprise. Where's Nana?"

"She's down at the Harper's farm. She is determined to show that Clara how to properly make sweet potato pie, but I don't think Clara has the knack for baking, or even cooking for that matter."

"You're terrible, Granddaddy! Nana would skin you alive if she heard you talking this way."

"I only speak the truth. I'm telling you honey, the last thing Clara baked, I ended up with food poisoning for two days." Now I knew he was joking, because he was blushing and laughing out loud.

The driver brought our luggage in, and we made ourselves comfortable in their living room. It had been too long since I was last there, and yet everything was as it should be. Nana had photos all around the room and traveling up the stairs. Riley's and my pictures covered the mantle along with photos of my parents. I only noticed two of Samuel: one taken on our wedding day and the other a family portrait from a few years ago.

Nana always showed respect toward Samuel, but nothing compared to how she felt about Walker. He won her over from the minute I brought him home to meet them. While Riley was still occupied with the new puppies, I glanced around the room to look for the familiar picture. The same one that I took from Walker's apartment when I left him. Sure enough, Nana had kept it. The picture was inside her curio cabinet with some knick knacks she had been collecting for years. Tears began to pool in my eyes as I looked at the photo. *She kept it after all these years, even though I was with Samuel.*

Before I could wipe my falling tears, the door opened and closed, and there stood my precious grandmother looking beautiful as ever. Her hair was pulled back into a braided bun, her skin was lined, but flawless at the same time. Nana had a natural beauty about her, and she always said good living will keep you young. I guess she was right. You would never know she was in her late seventies. She dropped her bags, opened up her arms, and invited me in. Oh, I needed this hug, and somehow she knew. I cried onto her shoulder, and she stroked her hands up and down my back to soothe me, slowly releasing the tension I felt.

"Oh, my sweet girl, I kind of suspected I would be seeing you soon."

Drying my eyes and looking into her eyes, I asked her, "How?"

"I keep track of Riley, and her...what do you call it? Tweets, yes, that's what that is." Riley just laughed and hugged Nana.

"How you even know about Twitter and the other social media sites are beyond me, Nana, but you never cease to amaze me."

"Reese, you have to stay in the game nowadays, especially if you want to keep up with the youngsters. My lovely great granddaughter here showed me the ropes the last time she was here to visit. We now Skype with each other all the time. The kids at the shop showed me that pinning stuff. Now, that board is fun."

"You mean Pinterest?"

"Yup, that's the one. I put one of my croissant recipes on it, and last time I checked, I think I have over five thousand likes. It warms my soul to know my recipes are now in the cyber world."

She smiled and laughed while hugging Riley. My head was spinning with Nana's revelations. She knew social media and conducted video chats with my daughter, who never once mentioned this to me.

"So, girls, what do you think of our new additions to the family?" Nana asked.

"I love them! What are their names?" Riley asked. Granddaddy picked up one of the pups, and Nana picked the other.

"This is Socks," Granddaddy answered.

"This is Pockets," Nana replied.

"How did you come up with those names? I would have thought you would have picked a name like close to Bubba's?" Riley asked Granddaddy.

"Well, Riley girl, Bubba was one of a kind, and no dog would ever replace him. But you know I like to hunt, and I figured it was time to have some companions with me. These two are brothers, and you never separate a family, so they both joined us."

I smiled. "Granddaddy, why Socks and Pockets? Who came up with those names?" I asked again.

"I did," Nana answered. "You see, Reese, these two little devils like to chew up your Granddaddy's socks and roll around in his shirts, tearing at least one or two pockets a week. I do more mending to his shirts than ever before. I figured they were the perfect names for these two."

"Well, they are fitting. I'm so happy for you, and Riley sure loves them."

I immediately felt better, and Granddaddy took our bags upstairs to my old bedroom. Nana once again never changed it, leaving it how I remembered. I took in the fresh flowers sitting on my side table, and the rollaway bed was in place. *How did she know to bring out the rollaway bed?* I turned to my Nana, and she simply replied "Twitter." Apparently Nana had known all along that we were visiting today, but she played it cool as always. Once we were settled in, Riley and Granddaddy took a walk by our pond, while I stayed behind for my talk with Nana.

She had prepared tea and scones for our talk. She poured me a cup on her fine china and one for herself. She handed me a scone and placed one for herself. She gestured for me to take a bite, but my stomach was in knots already. Nana knew me like no other, and simply nodded with understanding and waited for me to start.

"Nana, I don't even know how to begin this conversation with you. I'm at a loss for words."

She placed her tea down and wiped her mouth with her linen napkin. She reached for my hands and folded them in with hers.

"Reese, in every story you have a beginning, a middle, and an ending. How about you start from the beginning, and we take it from there?" Tapping my hands, she sat back and gestured for me to begin.

"I have filed for divorce from Samuel." I practically spit out, as

I struggled with those seven words. Nana was silent, but encouraged me to go on. "Nana, I already came to the decision to leave my marriage, but after talking with you, I had completely accepted my decision. I promised myself not to waver or let Samuel change my mind. He stopped me before, and this time I was leaving for good. I truly did my best throughout the years, but I wasn't happy, just existing, and I wanted more than he was willing to give. He's a good man, Nana, but he will be better for someone who truly can love him the way he deserves."

"I couldn't agree with you more, Reese. You and your doctor husband were never a good match."

"Really? That's how you felt all this time? Nana, why didn't you ever say anything?"

"Why would I do that, Reese? You seemed to have made up your mind about him, and I wasn't going to stand in your way of something you truly wanted."

"I didn't want Samuel, Nana! I wanted Walker!"

"I know that too. Now why don't you tell me the real reason why you left Walker, and don't even try to tell me any foolish stories. I want the truth, Reese. I see the burdens that you have carried on your shoulders all of these years. You have spent so many years hiding what you feel from me. I never could understand why you couldn't bring yourself to confide in me. Haven't I always given you the impression that you can tell me anything? Do you even know how much that hurt me; to know that I couldn't help you, because you shut me out and simply didn't trust me?"

"Not trust you? Oh, Nana, that was never the reason. Nana, please forgive me? I never meant to ever hurt you. I did this to protect you and Granddaddy, never to hurt you."

"I know that too, but why, honey? Granddaddy and I come from strong Irish stock. We are tough, through and through. As long as we are together, no one can ever hurt us. That fact was lost on you, Reese. You stopped believing in our family's strength and allowed Walker's father to run you off like a scared rabbit, never to be heard from again. Am I wrong, honey?"

Nana had never been more on the mark than she was right now. How could she have known the truth about me leaving Walker, and not tell me all of these years? She was just as guilty of keeping secrets like I was.

"Yes, it's true. Walker's father, Phillip Reed, forced me out of his life. How did you know this, Nana?"

"I suspected, honey, but never knew until you just confirmed it. I had a few conversations with Walker, and he told me about his father and how his father would stop at nothing to control his son's life. When Walker showed up here after you left New York, that poor boy was left devastated and lost. He was desperate to find you, and it broke my heart that I couldn't help him. Had I known where you were, I would have told him, Reese. I suspect that's why you didn't tell me your location."

"I couldn't, Nana. It was too dangerous, and I was being watched at all times. Please just let me give you the short version. I don't think I could take this for much longer."

"You tell me what you can, and we will deal with the rest later."

"Nana, I loved Walker with all my heart. We were planning a life together, and the plan that Phillip designed for his only son did not include the country girl from Georgia. No matter how I tried to reason with him, or ignore him completely, he just hated me on sight and plotted against me. Walker and I actually confronted him once, and Walker thought he had a put an end to his father's machinations, but it only angered Phillip more."

I went on, "My last night spent with Walker was magical. We made love and committed ourselves to the promises made that night. I knew a marriage proposal was coming, but he never got the chance to ask me. The morning I woke, Walker had left to run some errands, and an emergency at the office detained him from returning home to me. Another strategic move planned by his father. To my surprise, Phillip and his lawyer, Miles, showed up and barged right in to Walker's apartment. I had no choice but to listen to what they had to say."

I took a break, and sipped my tea to calm my nerves. The next piece of my story would certainly anger my Nana. "Phillip's lawyer handed me two envelopes, one contained the naked modeling photos of me, and he threatened to use the pictures to hurt me. The second envelope contained documents on this home, property, and your business. Phillip told me that if I didn't leave his son, then he would own everything you and Granddaddy had and destroy our family."

I began to sob to Nana as I said, "I begged and begged him not to hurt you, but he said this was my fault for not listening to him, and now it would be me destroying my family, not him. I couldn't let him hurt you, Nana! So I did what he told me to do. He thought of everything. All I had to do was get on a plane and never bother his son again."

"Oh, my sweet girl, how could you go through this and not tell me? That man didn't have the power to just buy our home and land without us knowing. He tricked you, honey, and fed off your fear. He knew your Achilles heel and played it perfectly against you. Don't you know we would have fought that bastard with all that we had? I know you believe you were doing the right thing by us, but all this proved was your unhappiness in the end, and the love of your life living day after day without you."

"There's more, Nana. I was pregnant with Walker's child." I watched Nana close her eyes and lean her head back onto her chair. "Nana, I wanted his child more than anything, but I never got the chance to tell him about the baby. For the next three months, I tried to talk and see him, but every time I tried, my efforts were stopped by his father or bodyguards. Walker was untouchable, and then I got sick. I was so sick that I miscarried and lost my last piece of Walker."

Nana got up from her chair and walked into the kitchen to splash water on her face. I tried to comfort her, but she put her hands up to me. She asked for a minute to process all I had told her. I walked out of the kitchen and back to my seat in the living room. *I hurt her, I know I did. What seemed like hours was really only ten minutes?* Nana had returned and sat down beside me. She wrapped me up into her arms and let me cry out my lost years with Walker and the pain it had caused me.

"I'm so sorry, Nana. Please say you forgive me?"

"Oh, my precious girl, don't you know there is nothing to forgive? You could never do anything that would ever make me not love you and hold you in my arms like I am right now. You're our most precious gift God has ever given us. We thought we were blessed with our son, but then he had you and it was the best day of our lives."

"You can't change the past, Reese. It is what it is. You need to let it go if you're ever going to be happy in your future." She kissed the top of my head and poured some fresh tea.

"Nana," I say just barely above a whisper, "I wasn't finished with my story."

"Before you begin, do I need to drink something stronger than tea?"

I laughed, and so did Nana.

CHAPTER TWENTY-ONE

I always believed...

NANA AND I were both calmer and, thank goodness, got through the tough part of my story. I was still treading lightly on what I was to tell her next, but she had this gleam in her eye that told me that she knew what was coming.

"Do you remember my trip to New York with Riley?" I asked her. She nodded, and I continued. "That trip changed my life. Riley's boyfriend turned out to be Walker's son from his marriage to his friend Elizabeth. Our children met over a year ago, became friends, now a couple, and they will be attending the same college in New York. I never knew this until I walked into the restaurant and met his father…My Walker. We were completely shocked and taken aback with each other. Not knowing what to do, we just pretended to not know one another until we found an appropriate time to talk."

I added, "Our actions confused our kids, and when they finally went their separate ways, Walker demanded the truth from me as to why I left him. I was in no shape to discuss this with him so I ran from him, but he had other ideas. Walker manhandled me on the city street and placed me in his limo. We drove around the city, talking for hours, until I was completely exhausted. My truth destroyed him, Nana. I just wanted to climb inside his arms and be with him again."

I went on, "Our feelings hit us like a freight train and blindsided us both. He never stopped loving me, and I told him the same. He raised Jackson by himself after his wife passed away during childbirth. He's been on his own all of these years. I explained my life with Samuel and how he helped me after I lost our baby. Walker vowed he would reclaim us again, and after I told him my plans of divorcing Samuel, our fates were once again sealed with one another."

I continued, "For the better part of the trip, I had spent every waking minute wrapped up in Walker, until Samuel surprisingly showed up. Samuel whisked me and Riley away to the Caribbean to fix our marriage. He wouldn't listen to me and denied the divorce. I felt like I was cheating on Walker with my own husband. Not taking the news well, Samuel and I fought, and he slapped me and then shoved me. I ended up falling and hitting my head."

"Oh, dear lord! I will skin his ass alive. How dare that man put his hands on my granddaughter?"

"Nana, please don't get upset. You don't understand what happened down there. I provoked him and pushed him to his limits. He hit me out of panic, and once he realized what he did, he was sorry."

"Oh please, Reese! Wake up and smell the chicory coffee. No man, and I mean no man, should ever lay their hands on a woman. I feel like breaking those surgical fingers of his."

Throughout this exhausting talk with Nana, I finally was able to smile and laugh. Nana had just said the exact same words Walker had said to Samuel. *Oh my goodness, they are so much alike, it's kind of scary and funny.*

"Nana, please calm down. Samuel was devastated after he hit me, and knowing that I planned on reuniting with Walker just sent him over the edge. We talked it out, and I don't hold it against him. For me, this is over, and I just want to move on. He is Riley's father, and he will always have a place in our life."

"Reese, if that man ever thinks of hurting you again, I swear as long as I draw breath, he will regret it." I hugged her with all I could,

294

and then tried to finish up and tell her the good part of my story.

"Nana, my divorce to Samuel will be finalized very soon, and once that happens, Walker and I plan to marry right away."

"As it should have been all those years ago. Oh my sweet girl, you and Walker now have your second chance at forever. You must take each other's hands and stay together this time. Fight for it this time, and never ever let anyone stop you from being happy and in love with one another. You promise me this."

"I promise, Nana, that this time with Walker will be forever and I promise that my days of running are over. He knows everything and still wants me. Our kids are working it out, and we can only hope they remain happy. But they're young, so who knows?"

"I know. I knew from the moment I met your Walker. That man loved you with all he had, and I should have pushed you harder, Reese. I always sensed something was holding you back, but it was your life, and I knew I couldn't make up your mind for you. I'm so sorry that we were the reason you lost your love."

"Nana, isn't it you who always told me that everything happens for a reason, and we're not meant to understand what God challenges us with? Well, I'm done trying to figure it out. Walker and I have both have had our share of loss, pain, and times of despair. That is over now, and through some magical force in the universe, we found our way back to one another. We have the rest of our lives to be in love and happy. I'm so much stronger now, and I truly believe in love and what I feel for Walker. I completely trust him to guide us down the path that will lead to our happily ever after."

A man's voice sounded from behind me. "Well, that's good to know, baby, because I plan on making you happy every day for the rest of your life."

I turned around to see Walker standing there in my Nana's living room, armed with two bouquets of flowers.

"Walker!" I broke away from Nana, and ran right into my man's arms, forcing him to drop the flowers. "I am so happy to see you!"

I took his gorgeous, chiseled face into my hands and crashed my lips onto his mouth. I had no shame in kissing him like that in front of Nana. This was the reunion she had always hoped for, so why be bashful now? We slowed our breaths and he held me secured to his chest.

"I'm home," I whispered for only him to hear. He kissed me behind my ear and whispered, "Forever."

After our extreme PDA moment, Walker introduced his son to Nana. She immediately hugged Jackson and welcomed him in to her home. Riley was very forthcoming with information about Jackson. I was still in shock about how much Nana kept in touch with Riley. They had their own special relationship, as I always had with Nana.

Walker and Nana embraced and hugged for a few minutes. He looked so happy to be reunited with her, and she wore the same expression on her face. It looked like an expression of knowing that after all of these years, she was relieved that her prediction came true. I had found my true love when I left home all those years ago, and although circumstances separated us, that love had found its way back to us.

"You look amazing, Lila. I have missed you and thought of you often throughout these last years. How's Thomas? Is he here?"

"He is, but he's out with Riley now."

I guessed that answered Jackson's unspoken question. He appeared to be nervous standing there in our home. I walked over to him and gave him a hug.

"Jackson, are you okay? You look a little pale. Can I get you anything? Water, perhaps?"

"I'm fine, Mrs. Briggs."

Although he was well mannered, his greeting earned him a look from Walker. I think just the mention of my marital status didn't sit well with Walker, but that would change soon enough. I looked back over to Walker and gave him a wink. His expression calmed, and he continued talking to my grandmother.

CHAPTER TWENTY-TWO

Working it out...

SHORTLY AFTER WALKER and Jackson arrived, Riley and Granddaddy returned from their excursion. Granddaddy was carrying a bucket full of freshly caught fish.

"Oh sweet lord, Thomas, you've been fishing this entire time?" asked Nana.

"Well, woman, what did you expect? My lucky charm is here, and she always brings good luck when she visits her Granddaddy. The fish must smell that fancy perfume she wears, because I have enough fish here to feed an army."

I interrupted their friendly banter and tried not to shock my grandfather into a heart attack at the sight of Walker. He was so excited to announce his catch that he was totally oblivious to others in the room. I was about to say something when Walker beat me to it.

"I guess I picked the right day to visit. Got any trout in there?" Walker asked my grandfather.

Granddaddy turned around and nearly dropped his bucket of fish, but Riley was quick to grab it from his hands. I thanked her as she took it into the kitchen. Jackson remained by Walker until introductions were made and the shock wore off.

"Walker Reed. How the heck are you son? And how are you

standing in my living room?"

"A very long story, sir, but nonetheless, I'm happy to be here and to see you again." Walker extended his hand, and Granddaddy shoved it away.

"Come on now, son, you're in a man's home that you've already been welcomed in. Handshake will not do. Get over here, and give me a hug."

I watched the two men in my life embrace, and I couldn't help but stop my tears from falling. It was like I was back to the very first day Walker had met my grandparents. He instantly loved them, and they mutually cared for him. They never treated Samuel this way, and he was the man I married.

Riley returned from the kitchen and was apprehensive around Jackson, until Jackson slowly walked up to her and asked if they could take a walk. My girl smiled and took his hand in hers. They excused themselves after Jackson was introduced to Granddaddy and also given a round of hugs to.

Riley AND Jackson...

"MY FATHER TELLS me that this path leads to a meadow filled with flowers and it ends by a huge oak tree," Jackson says to me.

"Your father has quite the memory for only being here twice in his life."

"It's no wonder why he hasn't forgotten. This place is beautiful, and the feeling of love and family hits you like a runaway train the minute you cross over the threshold of your grandparents' home. My dad told me all about his time spent here and how much he cared about your great grandparents. I'm so happy to be here too."

"Are you, Jackson? Or are you just here to support your father and his romance with my mom?"

"You know that's not true. How can you say that to me after all that we shared with each other?"

We reached the tree, and the swing under it caught his attention. On my Nana's seventy-fifth birthday, Granddaddy had a swing built under the tree with an inscription engraved on it:

"For my best friend and love of my life.
From Thomas, who will forever sit beside you
in this life and the next one we will share."

Jackson sat down on the swing and gestured to me to sit beside him. He turned me to look at him, and I was on the verge of tears. I knew I was being unfair to him, but I was so unsure of myself lately and questioning every decision I made. My mom tirelessly kept talking with me, helping me understand her reasons for divorcing my father. Deep down, I did understand but I felt my loyalties were being challenged, and I knew one of my parent's would be hurt with my choice.

Jackson gently lifted my chin so I could look into his beautiful green eyes. "Riley, please talk to me. Every time, I think we are close to being back where we were, you seem to pull away from me again. You're breaking my heart, baby, and I don't understand why. Don't you love me anymore?"

That did it, and my tears began to fall. I couldn't hold back any longer, and I fell into Jackson's arms. He let out a breath and held me for as long as I needed. Taking my face into his hands, he took his thumbs and wiped away my tears.

"I love you so much Riley, but you need to talk to me and we are not leaving this spot until you do. Now answer my question. Do you still love me?"

"Yes, Jackson, of course I do."

"That's a start. Now talk to me. I can't help you if I don't know what is hurting you."

"If I tell you, Jackson, then you will hate me, and then not want to be with me anymore."

"Not a chance, baby. Why don't you give me the benefit of the doubt before you try and convict me." Jackson once told me that those were the words his father had said to him. He also told me that if his father had taught him anything, it was to always be fair, show kindness, and try to find understanding. I needed all of that from him at that moment.

"I'm spinning out of control because of your father and my mother. It's like the past eighteen years have just been a layover to the next stop of their romance. How can my mother so easily just walk away and divorce my father? How can your father just reunite with my mom and forget how much she had hurt him? I just don't understand it at all. Maybe I don't understand relationships at all anymore. Maybe I never did." He placed my head gently on his lap, and I took a few breaths.

"Riley, we've been over this already, but hopefully I can find the words to make you understand how the two people that we love have come together. My father has been alone since the day my mother died. He never connected with any other woman in all of these years that passed. He privately mourned the loss of the two women that mattered most in his life. His feelings were divided and compartmentalized. He tried to be loyal to both loves without desecrating the other's memory. Can you understand that?"

I silently nodded.

He continued, "I'm the dreamer of my family, the idealist. For so long my father believed in black and white, no colors in between. Your mom is his kaleidoscope of colors, and she has given him a new sense of purpose. He now has hope and believes that fate has given them a second chance at love. It's a miracle to find love once in a lifetime, but twice? I think they need a new word for miracle. Riley, my dad and your mom are meant to be, and they deserve this chance to find out what the future holds for them. I love my father, and he has never asked anything of me until now. I can't turn my back on him and not support him."

I lifted my head. "What about my father, Jackson? Does he get a say in all of this? He's the one that's getting kicked to the curb, and I'm just supposed to be okay with it? I don't know how I can do that."

"Yes, you do, Riley. You just don't want to say the words out loud because if you do, then you feel you would be taking sides and being disloyal to the other. Your parents had their problems long before my father ever reentered the picture. You told me countless times how unhappy your mom was and how you feared leaving for college would leave her completely alone."

Jackson continued, "You don't have to choose sides, Riley. Just support both your parents. You can love them both and still be happy with me. My dad and your mom were cheated out of something that was always meant to be. Second chances don't easily come around, and the two of them had to wait nearly two decades for this one. Do you even know what a gift that is? Their relationship doesn't have to reflect on us. I told my father how I feared his choices would endanger my relationship with you, but he told me that we would be fine if we believed in what we have."

He held my hand and asked, "So, Riley, are we fine? Do you love and believe in us? Because if you don't, then you need to tell me right now. I'm preparing to close one door and walk through another in a few months, but one question remains."

"What's the question?" I asked him through my fallen tears.

"Will you take my hand, and walk through with me?"

Oh my god! How can I resist him? My heart was beating at a rapid rate. Jackson had never been calmer and was giving me an ultimatum. Of course, I loved and trusted him, but how would I convince him that my feelings were real for him? I'd been so confused over my parents' divorce. My mood swings had nothing to do with him, but yet he'd been the bearer of my anger.

I could only do what seemed fitting at that moment. I sat up and pulled him to me. I kissed him with all I had to give and prayed it was enough for him to feel how much I loved and wanted him. After a lingering pause, he pulled me closer and held me tighter. He let me hear his desire for me with soft moans. My body was easily responding to him. I began to pull up his t-shirt from the hem, when he stopped me.

"No, baby, not like this."

"I want you, Jackson. Please make love to me." *Did I really just ask him that?*

"Not here. Not now. I love you…so much, but I want our first time to be special and belong to us. This is not that time, but please believe that I'm not rejecting you. I want you more than anything else in the world right now."

I threw my hands around his neck and held him as close as I could. He was amazing, and I closed my eyes to silently say thank you to the universe for giving me Jackson. The Mitchell and Reed love story had finally rubbed off on me. I believed, and I believed in Jackson and his love for me. Finally he knew my readiness and intentions of wanting to make love with him. He hadn't pressured me about sex, so I never really knew how he felt about it until just then. Was Pottersville magical? I was beginning to believe in that tale as well.

"I love you, Jackson. I am so sorry for hurting you and being a royal pain in your ass. I can't always be sparkly."

Holding me, Jackson laughed out loud and cradled me onto his lap.

"Oh, baby, that's my girl. I love you too. Are we okay now? I need to know before anything else is said here today."

"A part of me will always worry about my dad, but I promise not to let my parents' problems become my own. Yes, Jackson, we're okay."

I HELD MY girl for a little while longer until it was time to head back to the house. I took a huge chance today by pushing her and having her admit her feelings. It was a rough few weeks questioning the unknowns and having to deal with my headaches that I have kept from my father. They tended to hit me hard when I was under stress. My father had to witness the one I had in New York when I thought Riley had broken up with me. It was a bad one, but I lied to him and said it wasn't. I was so tired of him worrying about me, even though he had no reason to. I kept telling myself that, because if I believed it, then he would too. Dr. O'Larien gave me a list of ways to calm myself if I felt a headache was on the rise. Most of the exercises worked, and I didn't need to take my medicine.

With Reese back with my father, he hadn't argued with me about attending NYU in the fall. His mind had been pre-occupied with Reese and my grandfathers, which gave me hope that he was coming to terms with my decision. In a few weeks, Riley and I would be graduating and beginning what I hoped to be the summer of our lives. She hadn't mentioned it since New York, but I hoped she still wanted to join me out in California. We talked about many things today, and I didn't want to push my luck with her. She was very sensitive and required patience and understanding. I vowed to always be those things with my girl, and so much more, as long as she didn't shut down again. We took our time walking back, stopping to pick flowers along the way for her grandmother and mom.

This place was beautiful and quiet. I would have loved to have my camera with me to take a few scenery shots of the meadow. We were out here for hours with no interruption. My girl smiled as she looked up at me.

"I love you, Jackson."

"I love you too, Riley."

My mind flashed forward with visions of Riley looking beautiful and breathtaking under the Georgia sunshine in her wedding dress. I saw us marrying under the oak tree, surrounded by our family and friends. I couldn't help but think of her that way. I saw her by my side in all things. I just smiled and remembered my father telling me the same wish about Reese. This girl took my breath away with her smile, and I couldn't help but feel complete happiness.

I believed I may have loved at first sight and when she held my hand the first day we met, staring at my mother's portrait and mourning her loss. I only knew her through stories, photos, and home movies. It didn't change the fact that it still hurt not to have her with me, but Riley, simply being kind, reached out to hold my hand that day. It made me feel better. I was happy to know that the universe could know us better than we do ourselves. After all, our love story was unique and filled with all the trappings of the Happily Ever Afters.

Riley was the one who held my heart. Walking hand in hand now, she was innocently oblivious to my thoughts. The light returned to her beautiful smile, and to know that my love had put it there made me smile too. I told my father that I wanted him to get his Happily Ever After with Reese. They deserved it and waited long enough to have it. I also wanted mine with Riley. I hoped today was our new beginning of Our Forever Promise. The house was in sight now, and my girl had walked enough. I bent down, and I scooped her onto my back for a piggyback ride.

"Jackson!" she shrieked but laughed, as she wrapped her legs around my waist.

"What are you doing?" she whispered in my ears and then began kissing me.

"Giving my girl a lift and enjoying some lovin from her."

We laughed the rest of the way. I placed her down onto the porch, and she instantly wrapped her arms around my waist, giving me a tight hug.

She said, "We're okay, baby…I promise. I love you."

Hearing her words once more bonded our love together and gave me hope for our future. Riley Taylor Briggs, was my Forever, and I, Jackson Walker Reed, was hers.

CHAPTER TWENTY-THREE

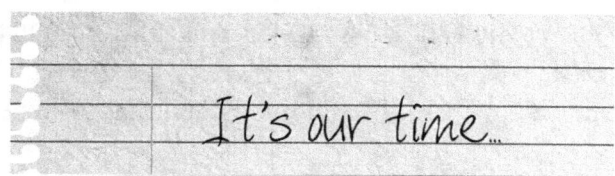

It's our time...

"YOU WERE RIGHT," I said to Lila, as we talked in her sitting room. We were surrounded by picture after picture of her love story with Thomas, as well as Reese's childhood. Not one empty space was to be found on these walls. This was my favorite room in this house, and I couldn't help feeling that dull ache remembering the last time I sat here with her. It was the day I had come to beg Lila to tell me where Reese had run off to. She didn't know, and I believed her. My heart was shattered, and I felt completely betrayed by the woman I planned on marrying. Now all of that hurt and feelings of loss had been replaced with new purpose and promise for our second chance at getting it right.

"You were right."

"Walker, you've said that, now twice. How do those three little words taste coming out of your mouth?" She mocked me with that twinkle in her eye.

"A few months ago, I probably would have said it tasted like castor oil, but now it feels like heaven to be wrong. You never gave up on us, Lila. How did you keep on believing in us after all of these years?"

"Walker, I may be an old woman, but I am not foolish nor blind.

I knew from the minute I set my eyes on you that you were the man for my baby girl. She loves you something fierce, and it was that love that drove her to make the decisions she made. I always felt something was wrong about how you two broke up, but I left it up to her to tell me when she was ready. I'm just happy I'm still here to witness your reunion. Now, my son, where's the ring?"

God, she knows me too well. I pulled the tattered box out of my pocket and showed her the engagement ring that I planned on presenting to Reese.

"It's beautiful, Walker. The additions you made are perfect, and she will love it."

"I hope so, Lila. This ring has quite the story to tell. I never thought I would see the day. I'm so sorry for giving up."

"Hush now. You didn't give up, and neither did she. You and Reese were dealt a bad hand that lasted way longer than it should have, but now that's in the past and what you have is now. You have today, tomorrow, and the rest of your lives to be happy with one another. Don't waste one more second on what might have been; that part of your story is over. Start a new chapter by asking my granddaughter to marry you, and put that ring on her finger where it belongs and will stay, now and forever. Do you get what I'm saying to you?"

"Yes, ma'am, loud and clear," I firmly replied.

She got up from her chair and took me lovingly into her arms. I gently hugged her back and whispered "Thank you" in her ear.

Reese popped her head into the room. "Hey, you two, there you are. Dinner's ready, and I have a table full of fried fish, broiled fish, and sautéed fish. We have lots of fish, and a table full of hungry people. Coming?"

"We are," I replied as Nana and I hugged. I walked over to my girl and scooped her up into my arms. She squealed with happiness, not even embarrassed by our display of affections in front of Lila. Her grandmother gave us a minute, and when we were really alone, I kissed her with all the love I had, sealing my commitment to Reese.

"You look so happy, Walker."

"I'm happy because I have you back, Reese. In my arms is where you belong, and I vow never to let you go again."

"I'm not going anywhere, Walker, I will never leave you again."

"Good, as if I would let you."

"Watch it, caveman. I'm still a very independent woman and will remain to be."

"Oh, you can be independent all you want, but always depend on me."

She looked at me with one brow raised.

"Does that even make sense, baby?" she asked.

"Of course it does. It means I don't ever want you to change who you are, but I want to be the one—your only one—who you depend on above anyone else. I want to be your husband, your lover. I want to be everything to you, and that's what it means."

"You are, Walker. Always."

We kissed and made our way into the kitchen. What a sight to take in. Lila and Thomas were here. The love of my life was here, and our kids who were happy in their own love story were here. I looked around to all of them, and all I felt was love for each of them. Plates of delicious smelling food were being passed around, and I took my plate from Reese, as she smiled at me. I took a quiet minute to look over to my son, who was laughing at Thomas's stories. I silently thanked God for this moment. We had our guardian angel always shining down on us, and all I felt was peace. Closing my eyes, I saw her smiling back at me...*Elizabeth, thank you, my friend.*

We all enjoyed the delicious feast which Reese had prepared for us. She gave her grandmother time to explain all to Granddaddy...the short version, and then I had my own catch up talk with Thomas. Dessert was served in the form of Lila's award winning apple pie. She even made homemade vanilla ice cream to put over it. Jackson was in heaven and helped himself to two servings. Thank goodness Lila made more than one pie.

Our happy reunion soon came to a close. The grandparents said their good nights, and the four of us were left on our own. Riley gave Jackson a tour of our sleeping space. Thomas had converted one of the barns to look like a mini bed and breakfast. It held the old world charm of a country inn. It was equipped with a huge en suite, a living room, and two bedrooms. I was hoping I wouldn't need to book a hotel room anywhere and was thankful to Lila for extending an invitation to stay.

Before turning in to sleep, she gave me a hug and told me "No funny stuff tonight, buddy." I laughed and hugged her again. She reminded me that she wasn't too old to hit me upside my head with her ladle if I broke the rules while under her roof. Her warning was also extended to Jackson and Riley. As much as I teased Reese about fooling around while here, I would never do anything to upset Lila and Thomas.

They knew we were together, but in the eyes of the law, Reese was still a very married woman. She didn't want her grandparents to judge her, even though deep down, we knew they wouldn't. All they ever wanted for Reese was to be happy, and now she was.

The kids were in bed, and I finally had a quiet moment with Reese. I held her in my arms under the Georgia sky. Thousands of stars were out tonight. I was hoping to see a falling star to make a wish on, but all I ever hoped for had come true already.

"I want to take you somewhere tomorrow." I said, as I kissed her along her neck.

"I'll go anywhere with you, Walker."

"I'm counting on that."

"Walker."

"Yes, my love."

"Thank you for not listening to me and arriving a day early. I don't think I could have waited until tomorrow to see you."

"As if you could keep me away. I love you, Peaches." Even under the moonlight, I could still see my girl blush. I watched as my beautiful angel walked into the house, and I joined Jackson out in the barn.

I knocked on his door and hoped he was still up. This would be my first chance to really catch up with my son since we arrived.

"Hey, son. So what do you think of Pottersville?"

"It's everything you said, and more. I can see why you love it here."

"Everything okay with Riley? You two appeared to have worked it out."

"We're okay, dad, let's leave it that. So tomorrow is your big day with Reese?"

I smiled at his question. "It is, Jackson. Let's leave it that."

SLEEPING IN MY childhood room and smelling the sweet scent of freshly picked flowers on my nightstand, I felt happy to be home. I couldn't remember when I had a more blissful sleep. Yesterday was a whirlwind of revelations. I had finally come clean to Nana, and then to see Walker back here in this home felt like a dream coming true. He was taking me somewhere, but where? This town was too small to have any hidden spots I wasn't aware of. It didn't matter, as long as we were together. I quickly showered and dressed for the day. It would be a hot one, so I put on a light sundress and wore my hair pulled back. I left a few curly tendrils hanging along my cheek. Walker loved to wrap my hair around his fingers while kissing me. I had to keep in mind to keep my hands in check when Nana was around.

Coffee was already on, and the house smelled of fresh bacon and cinnamon rolls. Granddaddy greeted me with a floor lifting hug.

"Granddaddy, put me down before you hurt your back."

"Nah, don't worry about me, honey. You're light as a feather." He laughed and went back to reading his morning paper.

"Where's Nana?" I asked my grandfather.

"Your Nana is already out and about with the youngsters. They went into town to do some sightseeing, and then are going to the book depot. Your spunky daughter wants to show Jackson all around

309

town and then have lunch with Nana at the shop."

"That sounds lovely, but I hope they don't wear Nana out."

"Don't go worrying about your grandmother; she's the one that will wear them out first. We Mitchells come from strong stock, baby girl. Don't you know that by now?" He winked.

"I believe I've heard that once or twice, Granddaddy." I gave him a hug and kissed the top of his head. I poured two traveling mugs of coffee and wrapped up some cinnamon rolls for Walker and me to enjoy. The car was outside, ready to take us on our mystery trip.

"Bye, Granddaddy. Be good today."

"I should be saying that to you, my darling girl. Have fun." Oh, he was wiser than I ever gave him credit for, him and Nana.

"Good morning, baby. Are you ready?" Walker said while slowly walking over to me, as if I were his morning breakfast. He was licking his lips as he reached me, taking one of the coffees out of my hand.

"I am, but where are we going?" I replied.

"All in good time, all in good time," he said with a smirk.

He kissed me and held the door for me as I entered the car. We enjoyed our coffee and light breakfast while we talked about the kids and how happy they seemed to be. In just a few weeks, they would both be graduating high school and beginning their summer vacation. They had a good month head start before summer actually began. I wanted to take that time to pack up my house and vacate it, so Samuel could move back in. That Baltimore home was always his more than it was ever mine, and it would please Walker to no end if I could join him in California.

We drove out of town, up to a look-out spot where you could take in the mountain scenery. I knew this spot all too well. I shared many happy times here with my parents and grandparents. We were at Clover Lake. Luscious greenery surrounded the lake with wild flowers and of course clovers. This was my father's favorite place to bring me when I was a child.

I remember spending hours with him looking for four leaf clovers. Nana had a picture of us canoeing taken the year before he died. I turned to Walker, who was nervously smiling up at me, not sure if he had picked the right place to bring me to today. I smiled back, showing him that it was perfect.

Walker had a picnic basket packed for us and brought a blanket for us to sit on. We walked down to the lake and picked a spot for lunch. The sun was shining, but it was a few degrees cooler up here. He wrapped my sweater around my shoulders and pulled me to his chest.

"Are you okay that we're here?" he asked me.

"It's a beautiful spot, Walker. Thank you for coordinating with Nana." We both laughed. He wouldn't have known what meaning this place held for me if Nana hadn't told him. He held me in his arms, and I could feel his mood changing. Something was weighing on his mind, and we both had enough secrets to last us a lifetime, so I simply asked him what was wrong.

"Are you okay, Walker? Do you want to tell me something?"

"You know me so well, but what I have to tell you will hurt you. And I can't bear to ever do that to you. You have been through so much already, baby. I love you so much."

"We're together now, and no one or anything can ever hurt me again."

"Let's hope that's true, baby," I replied.

He took my hands in his and let out a few deep breaths.

"REESE, FROM THE minute I saw you walk into that New York restaurant and back into my life, it has been a non-stop ride of revelations. Secrets that have been kept from me for all of these years were finally revealed. I not only heard from you, but literally from beyond the grave—my father's grave. He must have known his time was coming. In the end, my father was very sick. When he came out to California to talk with me, I guess he was trying to make amends and say his goodbyes. He left me a box of personal items in it and a dossier of the crimes he committed against you and me."

"I was out of my mind when I discovered it all. It was one thing to hear it from you, but then to read it from his own hands completely decimated me. I confronted Miles Jacobson, his lawyer, to tell me the truth. I could have killed Miles, if it weren't for my mother interrupting us. He took his beating like a man, and then told me everything. The story didn't end with my father; it was only beginning. The true master of this grand illusion was Henry Townsend."

"Elizabeth's father?" Reese questioned.

"Yes, the one and only. You see, he had the deluded notion that if he removed you from my life, then it would pave the way for Elizabeth and me to be together."

Reese shifted out of my arms and stood up to look out to the lake.

"He succeeded, Walker. They both did. You married and had a child with Elizabeth." I watched my girl cover her eyes to hide the falling tears that were now drenching her beautiful face.

"Reese, I'm so sorry. Please, baby, look at me."

"You're sorry? Why would you say that to me, Walker? You have nothing to be sorry for. You thought I had left you for good with no hope of ever returning. How could I expect you to wait for me when I did the same thing with Samuel? It may have appeared to the outside world that I moved on, but here is where it counted. I never strayed from our love." She held her hands over her heart as she once again cried out her feelings for me.

"I feel the same way, Reese. Yes, my feelings for Elizabeth were real, but never in the same way as how I felt for you. And you said it yourself that we can never regret our children."

"Of course not! I will always be grateful to Samuel for giving me the chance to become a mother, but Walker, you were the man that made that dream happen for me first...with our son. Why didn't he make it? I wanted him so much, and I couldn't wait to tell you that you were going to be a father."

She cried, holding her face, and then fell slowly to the ground. She was mourning our son, *my son*. Damn, this hurt. It felt like a thousand knives piercing my heart. God, I hated this! It was breaking my heart to go through this with her, again and again. I could never bear to see her cry, and I would do everything in my power to prevent her from ever shedding a sad tear again.

"Reese, look at me, please?" She dried her eyes, and did what I asked. "Reese, I know how hard you fought to protect him, but some babies are not meant for this world. And, sadly, our son was called home before we had a chance to be his parents. I will never blame you for losing him. Please believe that."

"I dreamed of him the other night, but he wasn't alone. I wasn't sure if I was going to tell you, but for the first time since losing him, I actually felt peace and a sense of closure."

"Our son? You said he wasn't alone? Who was with him?"

"Elizabeth. She was holding him and rocking him to sleep. She looked beautiful. Our baby was healthy and looked like you. You said that Elizabeth would want you to be happy and move on with your life. Did you mean that, Walker? Was she this saint that could do no wrong and die a martyr? I'm sorry. I shouldn't have said that about her."

"Reese, you didn't say or do anything wrong. Elizabeth was simply a kind soul. She loved fiercely with her heart, and I think she would laugh at the saint reference. If I can be certain of anything, I know Elizabeth would want me to be happy again. For so long, I've been alone just raising my son and working. My assistant told me to get a life when I left for New York. Little did she know that my life has never been the same without you in it, beautiful girl."

"We have been given a second chance, and I will never doubt fate again. I'm done living in the shadows of being half of a man who is so closed up and unwilling to let someone in. You're in, Reese. God, you never left. I want you, and I know you want me. Please believe in what we have now, because we're starting over. We cannot change our pasts and how we lived our lives. We have today, tomorrow, and the rest of our lives to be happy."

I took her into my arms and held her closely to my chest, so I could feel her heartbeat against mine.

"Reese, it was too late for my father to make amends to us for what he did. He left me several letters with words of regret and apologies. I don't know if I will ever truly be able to forgive him, but I can promise you that his machinations will never be able to hurt us again. As for Henry Townsend, he is only still breathing because of his grandson. I can't hurt him, Reese, not only for Jackson, but for Elizabeth. She would not want me hurting her father, no matter what he has done."

"For the sake of her memory, and my son, Henry gets to continue on with his life and live out his retirement out in Arizona. As for continuing a relationship with me, well that's over. He is dead to me. Jackson knows the truth, but is still hurt and confused by the actions of his grandfather, who he loves. While we're on the subject, I also took care of Ralston."

I felt my girl shake with the mention of that bastard's name. "Yes baby, he will never be able to hurt you again. I gave him a beating he won't soon forget."

"Oh my goodness, Walker. What if he comes after you? What will you do then?"

"He can't hurt me, and he certainly can't hurt you, not anymore. He may have thought he was only doing his job, but his actions cost us our son."

"You don't know that, Walker. I was sick, and it was a tough pregnancy from the beginning."

"Reese, I know enough, and he got what he deserved. If anything, I was easy on him. Listen, enough about my father, Henry Townsend, and Ralston. They do not matter to us, and you don't ever have to think about them again."

"Walker, before we go any further here today, I now need to tell you something. Something that will hurt you, and once again I will be the bearer behind that hurt."

"Reese, you can only hurt me by leaving me again, and I think you know I will find you this time. So please, baby, no more tears."

"Not until I tell you this. Please, you have to know."

I felt it deep inside my core that it was about Samuel, who I didn't want to hear about, but until I allowed her to say the words, I was just going to continue to fight against my internal struggle.

"Okay Reese, you have my attention. I promise you that whatever you're going to tell me is not going to change how I feel about you."

"You may want to hold off on that until you hear it, baby."

Looking at Reese's beautiful caramel eyes drew me in like a moth to a flame. She was breathtaking, and if I could, I would climb inside of her and stay there for the rest of my life.

"No one was more surprised than I when Riley opened our hotel room door to find Samuel standing on the other side of it. He looked hopeful and happy to see his daughter. Then he rushed over to me like he was seeing me for the first time. Samuel was in complete denial of what was taking place in our marriage. I asked him for a divorce, and of course he told me that would never happen."

"He fucked me across his desk and then apologized like he just spilled coffee on the rug. He never got it, and still doesn't. I didn't want to leave with him, Walker, but he gave me little choice. And I was back to a place of being scared and letting another person force me to do something I never wanted to do. Thoughts of your father's bossiness flashed in my mind at that very moment, but I was ordered to pack my things and leave for this magical family trip he had planned for us."

"Reese, why are we discussing this at all? Baby, I know all of this already. Remember, I was the one who rescued you." I wiped away more of her falling tears.

"Please, Walker, let me finish. If I'm ever to truly move forward with you, then I have to be completely open and honest with you and tell you everything."

I held her hand reassuringly. "Okay. Go on."

"Riley was crying and did not understand what was happening. Samuel took her phone and wouldn't allow her to call Jackson. I barely had time to think or react. I'm so sorry, Walker, but I cheated on you. I wasn't strong enough to say no, and he reminded me that he was my husband and that my body belonged to him, so I had sex with him. And I have regretted it ever since."

"Samuel must have known something, but never said anything. We fought on the island, and I begged him to let me go. He did, Walker. He finally accepted my wanting a divorce. The minute he made the connection to who Jackson really was, it didn't take him long to figure the rest out. He made Riley leave the house and came after me. He smashed things around the room and confronted me about you. He said we wouldn't be divorcing, and he would never let me go."

"I decided that I had enough and screamed back. He asked me coldly if I had 'fucked you' and I screamed back, 'Yes.' Samuel's words were ugly and sounded so cold. I wasn't ashamed, and I was done hiding the truth. God! For years, I was living my life in hiding, and I was so done with it all. I repeatedly told Samuel that I loved you, and yes...I did fuck you, and it was the best sex of my life. Well, he hit me after that, and the room went dark for the second time that day. Then you came crashing through the door. Yes my love, you rescued me."

"Please, Walker, say something."

I sat there, just silent, and the color slowly drained from my face upon hearing her harrowing plight with that horrible man. I paused for a few more seconds and began to smile. "Best sex of your life, huh? I guess I haven't lost my touch."

Reese lunged herself at me, holding on as tightly as she could.

"God! I love you, you amazing man."

"I love you too. Reese, you didn't cheat on me, and everything you just said to me does not change anything. I told you this, and I need you to believe it. No one can understand having control better than me, Reese. I crave control. I couldn't have run my business, and be the man that I am, without it, but I would never use that type of power over you."

"I want you to completely submit your mind, body, and soul over to me because you want to, not because I demand it. I will give you all of me, if you'll have me. Reese, it's all I want. You're all I will ever want or need. Now dry your eyes, baby, because I want to give you something. And any tears I see from here on out will be happy ones, I promise."

I walked her over to where our blanket was laid out onto the ground. We were surrounded by flowers, and a warm breeze bounced off the lake water. I poured us both a glass of crisp Prosecco and topped it off with fresh strawberries. Reese's smile widened with the memory of this simple act. We shared this delectable white wine many years ago, countless nights of making love in front of my fireplace. I fed her a few berries and kissed the sweetness off of her lips. I would make it my life's mission to make her smile every day.

I dreaded to tell her anything about what I learned about my father's role in separating us, but it was a part of our story. We needed to find closure to move on from it once and for all. She also needed to bear her soul to me, and by god she did it today. I think we both had been cleansed and re-born.

"Reese, close your eyes baby." I said to her.

"Walker, what are you up to?" She closed her eyes but began stroking my chest up and down, until I let out a desirable moan for her.

"Behave yourself, or you don't get your surprise."

"I'll run the risk. I want you, Walker. I'm desperate for you to be inside of me. Please, Walker, let's make love."

Well that did it. I captured her mouth with mine, and I sucked on her tongue. She tasted delicious with the mix of wine and berries. We were alone out there, and I could easily strip her bare and make love to her, but first things first. I needed to show Reese just how much I loved her, and I wasn't going to wait one more second.

"Reese, please allow me to give you your gifts, and then I promise to fulfill all of your desires."

"Gifts? I thought I was only getting one gift?"

"I never said just one, you need to pay closer attention. Now close your eyes, baby." I placed another burning kiss on her sweet lips, and she did what I asked. I held her platinum locket in the palm of my hand. I meant every word I had engraved on it all those years ago, but my bastard of a father forcefully removed this from her neck, taking what she had left of me. Along with the ring that will soon grace her finger, my heart locket will once again return to its rightful place.

"Come on, babe, I can't wait. What is it?" She still had her eyes closed.

"Reese, I will never forget the night I gave you this, and what it meant for me to see it on you. I loved you then, and I love you even more now. You will always be my forever, and my heart is yours...always."

Her hair was already up, making it easy for me to place the necklace around her neck. I secured the clasp and allowed her to open her eyes. She gasped in surprise as her fingers touched it at the base of her neck.

"My locket? Oh my god, Walker, I thought this was lost to me! How did you ever find it?"

"My father. I never gave him the chance to hear him out when he visited me in California before his death. With a letter addressed to me, he left your locket in my study back at the house. When I went through his papers back in New York, he told me about it and where to find it. Reese, I nearly fell to the floor when I held this necklace in my hands. I hate him for hurting you, baby. I hate him for taking this from you. He caused you an unmeasurable amount of pain, and to be here with you right now just proves that our love can sustain anything, even Phillip Reed."

"You are my heart, now and forever. I love you, Reese, and you will always belong to me, as I belong to you. We were always meant to be together, I knew that from the very first day I saw you gnawing on your pencil in the library."

She laughed, and her soft giggle was the best sound my ears could hear right then. That, and an eventual "Yes."

I took a deep breath in and began. "I should have given you this a long time ago, but today is my second chance to right that wrong." I pulled out a ring box from my pocket. Reese gasped, because she knew this was our moment that was stolen from us all those years ago. She looked like she was fighting to hold back her tears. I took her hands into mine and slowly opened the ring box.

"Marry me, Reese. Let me be your husband and love you for the rest of my life."

My beautiful girl was crying, smiling, shaking, and nodding her head all at the same time. I waited so long for this day, and finally I was looking into her caramel eyes, waiting to hear that one little affirmation from her.

"Ask me again," she said. I smiled.

She wiped away her tears, but more fell as she leaned in to kiss me. Her kisses were sweet and mixed with her salty tears.

"Reese Mitchell, make me the happiest man in the world, and marry me."

"Yes. I will marry you, Walker Reed."

I slid the ring onto her finger, and I placed a kiss on it.

"This was my mother's ring." Reese recognized it immediately. "She never took it off, and I remember when I was little watching my father kissing her hand. He never stopped showing his love for her."

"Neither will I, baby. I can't wait to marry you and make you mine. We are where we're supposed to be, and these arms will never stop holding you. Come on, baby. No more tears."

"I can't help it, Walker. I made so many mistakes, and leaving you was the biggest regret of my life. I should have trusted you to help me fight your father. I should have told my family and Freddy, but I was a coward who ran. You begged me to believe in us, and although I told you that I did, in the end, I ran. I don't believe I will ever truly forgive myself for hurting you like that."

"Reese, can you say with your whole heart that you believe in us now? Do you trust me completely? Do you love me?"

"With every breath I have in my body, yes, Walker. You own me, body and soul."

No more words needed to be said between us. Reese was here with me, and said yes to become my wife. I craved her, and I needed to be inside of her, marking every inch of her delectable body. Reese needed to be worshipped like the princess she was. I held her in my arms and slowly began to separate her from her clothing, piece by piece. My body covered hers, and I made slow sweet love to my future wife, savoring every inch of her. She urged me to move faster as she clawed her nails up my back, her markings I would proudly wear as a badge of honor.

"Walker, please move faster. I won't break," she called out to me.

"I know what you desire, but right now, I need to take it slow," I whispered back.

I could feel her body tensing up as she was close to her release. We matched thrust for thrust and came together with Reese biting down onto my shoulder.

"I love you, Reese. Today marks the beginning of our Happily Ever After, our fresh start."

We cleaned ourselves up and packed to head back to Pottersville.

"Will you tell my grandparents about the proposal?" she asked me.

"I think once Lila sees our faces, she will know. Your grandmother has been waiting a long time for this day. I don't think she will be surprised by it."

"Walker, if you wouldn't mind, I would like to keep today between us until my divorce is finalized. As put together as Riley appears to be, she is still hurting, and I don't want to flaunt our engagement in front of her right now. Are you okay with that?"

"Truth?"

"Yes, that would be nice."

"No, I'm not okay, but I will do it for you. I want to scream it to the world that you're finally mine and we're getting married. As soon as the ink is dry on your divorce papers, I will have my PR department issue a press release. Agreed?"

"Agreed."

WE ARRIVED BACK at my grandparents' home and found Nana and Granddaddy sitting on their porch. They were enjoying some sweet tea, while under the guise of waiting for us to return. Nana must have had her alerts on, because her eyes went right to my hand as I got closer to her. She pulled Walker and me into a hug and whispered low enough for only us to hear.

"I don't want to be the one to say it, but I will. I told you so, Walker. Never give up on love." We all laughed, and I watched Walker hug Nana and give her a quick lift off the ground.

"Thank you, Lila, for your blessing. I promise I will love and protect her for the rest of my life. Not a day will go by that I won't make her smile."

"I don't doubt that, son. I never did."

Granddaddy interrupted their moment and gave Walker a slap on the back and then a hug. He never mentioned Samuel. I guess that was his discreet way of minding his own business. Nana must have told him, but Granddaddy, the man I knew him to be, didn't need the play by play of our very long and complicated story. He only ever wished for me to be happy and to follow my dreams. The day I left his home here in Georgia for my new home in New York City, he wished me well. I was nervous but not afraid. I was excited for what was next to come, and who knew that New York would bring me Walker?

I would never understand all that happened to us, but Walker was right, along with Nana and Freddy. The past was the past, and that's where it belonged. I couldn't change our story, but I could promise the man I love my heart—my whole heart—that would belong only to him.

Taking in the scene unfolding in front of me was beautiful. Everyone that I loved was here with me, and I had never been happier. I looked up at the twinkling stars above and thought of my parents. I carried their love with me each day. The love they shared and time spent together was short, but they lived each day to the fullest. As a child, I never understood how mama could give up so easily, but it all made sense to me now. She could not live one day without her beloved by her side.

I left Walker then, and it nearly destroyed the both of us. Our lives were always intersected with the yearning desire to be together, but that part of our story was over. We had a new story to write as husband and wife. I loved him with all of my heart, and I completely, undoubtedly trusted him with it.

Pottersville was indeed a magical place. This home was extraordinary and not one day went by when I didn't feel love in it. With my eyes still focused on the night sky and completely tuning out the conversations around me, a shooting star flashed above me. Two tears fell at that moment, one on each cheek. One for mama, one for daddy. My angels in heaven.

I blinked and looked over to Granddaddy who smiled at me. He watched me the entire time my head was deep in thought, and then he gave me a wink. I loved his signature gesture that signified all was right with the world.

His world.

Our family.

EPILOGUE

Full circle...

THE FOLLOWING WEEKS after Pottersville were non-stop happy events after another. We watched our children become high school graduates. Their prom pictures were now lining the walls of Nana's home, as well as Walker's home and office. Riley looked amazing in her Freddy Mac Original, designed by the man himself. I could hear the shrieking sounds of my very excited daughter resonating all throughout the house as she opened the door to see Freddy behind it. He was carrying her dreams wrapped up in one large, beautifully wrapped box. I watched my daughter bounce up and down in excitement, and when I finally reached her, I encouraged her to let him in.

My best friend was smiling, trying to hold back his laughter. Introductions were made, and he handed her his gift. Ever so gently, she opened up the box, as if it was in slow motion, and she gasped when she lifted the tissue paper that was holding her dress. At that moment, Riley lunged at Freddy and gave him the biggest hug I had ever seen her give. They laughed together, and I laughed along with them and may have shed a few happy tears too!

Freddy and I had easily picked up where our friendship left off. I loved him so much, and I was forever thankful to him for bringing a smile to my daughter's face. She was not the same girl I left with when we went to New York. Her head was not in the clouds and holding on to the fantasy of her father and me reuniting. Divorce is never easy on children, and I hated that my daughter was hurt by my choices. But hopefully one day my choices would make her stronger for the ones she decided for her own future.

All the time I spent worrying about Samuel, and his feelings were finally put to rest the day I came home to see the "For Sale" sign on my front lawn. He put our home up for sale without even discussing it with Riley or me. I was so angry with him, not for me, but for Riley. He once again was punishing me and not caring about who he would hurt. I thought we reached a turning point after he returned from his London trip. He seemed different, more at peace. I was not under any false illusions that Samuel and I would ever truly be able to be friends again, even for the sake of our daughter. He was stubborn through and through, and I silently prayed that he would change and move on with his life.

With graduations and proms behind them, Jackson and Riley began their new adventure in California for the summer. The first stop on their trip was Big Sur. Jackson was the adventurist enthusiast, and Riley not so much, but she promised she would try. Jackson texted his father a picture of a tree he marked in the deep forest of Big Sur. He carved a heart with both of their names inside of it. I cried when I saw it. Jackson was so much like Walker, and no matter how young they were, their love was real.

We were easily blending our lives together as one. I couldn't wait to marry Walker and become his wife. He was forever surprising me with flowers, gifts of his devotion, and whispering sweet words in my ear as we endlessly made love.

Soon I found myself standing in my big, empty house in Maryland for the very last time, but Walker was with me. I had to pick up the last of my things and say goodbye to my old life. I couldn't deny the happy moments I shared here with Samuel and Riley. My beautiful daughter was born and raised in this house. We measured her growing height against the wall in her nursery. I glided my hand over the bannister where I nearly had a heart attack when I saw her slide down it. Multiple birthday and sleepover parties were held here. Yes, that home did hold good memories for me. It was a good house and would give its new family the chance to make new memories there too.

"Are you okay, baby?" Walker asked. He put his strong arms around my shoulders and breathed me in.

"I am, honey, more than okay. I'm completely happy and so in love with you."

Crashing his lips down onto mine, I melted as his tongue entwined with mine.

"I have to make some calls, baby. Can I use that room to do so?"

"Well, that used to be Samuel's office, but it appears to be empty now, so yes, you may use it. I'll just go upstairs and take one final check before we leave."

He smirked. "I won't be long, baby."

"I'm not going anywhere, Walker. Never again."

OH, HOW I love that woman. I walked over to Samuel's former office and called my assistant, Jenny. I noticed some boxes in the corner and realized that Reese must have forgotten about these.

The day her divorce became final, Reese and I turned our phones off and locked our doors. I proposed to her again in front of my fireplace back in my New York penthouse. I took her to the library at NYU and I proposed to her there, and then I did the same thing at her old apartment building in Tribeca. She laughed and cried every time I asked her, but she indulged me, and I loved her even more for it.

"No, Jenny, I can't make that meeting. That one will have to be handed off to Donovan. What's next on my calendar?"

"What the fuck are you doing here?" I spun around to see a very angry Samuel standing before me.

"Jenny, I'll have to call you from the plane...Oh, and Jenny, Reese can't wait to meet you." I ended my call to look into the eyes of my girl's ex-husband.

"What the hell are you doing here in my house, Reed?"

"I'm here with Reese. She's upstairs, and I was here using this room to make a call. Sorry."

"Sorry? You're unbelievable! Well, since you helped yourself to my wife and my daughter, I guess using my office is small compared to what you have already taken from me. You made my wife into a whore who cheated on her husband! Oh, make way for The Great Walker Reed and his adulteress!"

I slowly walked up to meet his angry eyes.

"Reese is no whore, and she is not an adulteress. You think by calling her names it makes you a big man? How dare you, Briggs? Reese has been nothing but considerate when it comes to your feelings. Do you think I don't know what you're saying behind her back? For some hot shot, respected doctor, you sure act like an ass. I didn't take anything from you, Briggs. You lost her all on your own. You never treasured her like she needed to be. You loved your job more and took her for granted, and never truly appreciated the gift you had. The only one true thing you did for her was take care of her when she lost our son. For that, I will always be grateful to you for getting her through those tough months that followed, but if I ever hear you spew ugly invectives about Reese again...I will rip out your filthy tongue."

"She was mine! And you took her from me."

"No! Samuel, she was never yours. Reese was always mine, and no matter how many years we spent apart, we always belonged to each other. My father lost, and you will too. No one will ever break us again. You have a daughter who loves you, and whose heart was broken when you didn't show up to see her off. Why, man? Because of me? Well, don't worry Samuel, because after my son dried her tears, Riley smiled again and left happily with him. If you want to shut her out because of your wounded pride, be my guest. But you will be the one who ends up alone."

"I'm already there, you bastard. The life that I had here with Reese and Riley does not exist anymore because of you, and only you. Your privileged upbringing should have taught you not to covet another man's wife."

"Yes, and your upbringing should have taught you to listen when a woman says the word 'No.' Yes, I know about that too, Samuel."

"I had every right, Reed. She was my wife!"

"Well, she is not anymore and will never be again. You need to accept that once and for all."

"I hope you and your whore are very happy together."

Motherfucker! My eyes closed tightly, and I inhaled a deep breath before my fist made contact with his face. I knelt down and hit him again.

"Stay down, Briggs, because if you say one more word, I will fulfill my promise of ripping out your tongue. I have exercised every bit of control for Reese and Riley. You have proven here today that you do not deserve it."

My back stiffened, and I felt her presence behind me. I slowly turned to see Reese standing in the doorway to the office.

"Walker, I'm ready to go."

She walked over to me and reached for my hand. Samuel got up from the floor and wiped his bleeding mouth with his engraved handkerchief. As we held our hands, Reese turned to look at Samuel.

"I love *him*, Samuel. I never meant my love for him to hurt you."

He stood in the empty room in silence as we walked out of his home and closed the door to another chapter in our story.

"ARE YOU FREAKING kidding me with this news? It has got to be the wall sex," Freddy nearly shouted. I swatted his arm. "I am so happy for you, Peaches. Your man is going to plotz when you tell him."

"You and your Yiddish words, Freddy. You know I love them, but I'm hoping for a less than freak out moment from Walker."

"When is he expected home?" Freddy asked and looked at his watch.

"Any minute, my friend, so you have to leave. But I promise to call you tomorrow. I love you so much, and thank you for spending today with me. It feels like I have come full circle with my life with Walker, and I'm back here experiencing the same moment from so many years ago. Thank you for sharing this with me."

"It's my honor, baby girl. Give your hot man my love, and I'm holding you to your word."

"You have my promise, best friend. You're the one." As we hugged each other, Walker arrived home.

"How many times do I need to tell you, Mac? Keep your hands off my woman!" He playfully said to Freddy. I leaped into Walker's arms and soundly kissed him. Blowing me a kiss, Freddy slipped out the door.

"I am so happy you're home, Walker!" I excitedly said.

"Yes, I can see that. So what were you two plotting? How did the dress fitting go? I can't wait to see you in it, or take it off of you with my teeth. You look amazing, Reese. Let's go to bed and make love until we pass out."

"You read my mind, but can I tell you something first?"

"Anything." He whispered and trailed more kisses down my neck. "You started a fire? And set up a picnic in front of the fire-place? Oh, baby, I love how you think."

He shrugged off his jacket and loosened his tie. I wanted to rip his clothes off of him, but it would have to wait until he heard my news. He placed me on top of him and ran his fingers up my spine. He never took his eyes off of me and whispered how much he loved me. I closed my eyes and let his words wrap around me. The boy that nervously walked up to me in the library has become the man who I love more than anything in this world.

"Walker, these past few months have been amazing, and I have never been happier in all of my life. Your love—our love—has made me feel invincible and free. I don't believe I will ever have the right words to express how I feel about you, but I can show you in about six months."

He continued to kiss me, and then when my words finally registered, he stopped and held my face. "I don't understand, Reese. Our wedding is in a few weeks, what is happening in six months?" he nervously asked. I quickly wanted to calm him, so I smiled and kissed him.

"Something wonderful, Walker. Not only will we be ringing in the New Year as newlyweds, but we will also be celebrating the upcoming arrival of our new baby! I'm pregnant, Walker, and you will soon be a father to our little girl!" Tears were now streaming down his face as he gently kissed me on my lips.

"A baby? Oh my god, Reese, we're having a baby?"

"Yes, we are. I wanted to make sure everything was okay with the pregnancy before telling you."

"Is everything okay?" He nervously questioned.

"It is. Our daughter is growing as she should be, and we are both healthy."

"I love you so much, Reese. Thank you for making me a father again." Walker, now ever so gently placing me down, hovered over me. He unbuttoned my blouse and placed kisses on my stomach.

"Hey there, little one. I'm your daddy. I love you, princess." He wrapped himself around me and never stopped kissing me. We made love in front of the fireplace and recited new promises for our growing family.

Loving Walker Reed was effortless. All he ever asked of me was to trust him, and he would do the rest. I did completely, and I would for the rest of my life. Everything we went through has led us here to this moment. We truly had become two hearts, one love, and now that same love had blessed us with a daughter. I couldn't be certain when our daughter was conceived, but Freddy's ideas made me laugh out loud.

Joking aside, I believe it could have happened at Clover Lake. The old fashioned ones like my Nana say: If you wish upon a four leaf clover and then see a falling star on the same night, your wishes will come true.

I learned my lesson a long time ago not to doubt Nana and her predictions. After making love in our meadow, Walker and I did witness a falling star, and we both laughed. Nana always believed that my connection with Walker was stronger than anything in the world. Our love would see us through the hard times and make us stronger in the end.

As always, she was right, and I never minded telling her so. Her beliefs easily rubbed off on my man. Walker had once said to me that Pottersville was a magical place and would always hold a special meaning for the two of us.

Nana was the one that made me believe in unconditional love.

Walker made me believe in everlasting love.

He was my Happily Ever After.

I believed in our love.

I believed in him.

I believed in our **Second Chance at Forever.**

THE END...FOR NOW

WALKER AND REESE'S LOVE STORY CONCLUDES IN
BOOK THREE OF THE FOREVER SERIES:
OUR FOREVER PROMISE

ACKNOWLEDGMENTS

WHEN I FIRST began writing the *Forever* series, Book One was actually supposed to be *Second Chance at Forever*. I practically wrote the stories in reverse, not knowing where it was leading and second guessing myself into thinking whether I could really write it into a trilogy. I was so happy that I had many cheerleaders in my corner that never gave up on me or the story of Walker and Reese.

I have been blessed with the support of friends and fellow authors in the writing community who help me in so many ways. They offer up their friendships with unconditional love and support. You don't have to know a person or people for a lifetime to call them Family. I have been accepted into The Sisterhood. They are a group of many talented women from all over the country who I have come to know, respect, and admire. You will always hold a special place in my heart. **Wendy Ferraro, Alice Tribue, Tracey Manning, and Mindy Guerreiros:** I love you gals. The universe got it right when it brought us all together.

I have the best fans that follow me and support my work. I have a few stand outs that make me smile every day. Not one post gets missed by you ladies, and I am so very thankful for your support. **Thank you to Angela Seattle, Emine Fougner, Nancy Gennes Metsch, and Donna Lottmann.** Your comments make me laugh out loud. Thank you, friends, for making me smile.

I can't forget Ella Frank, another sister author who I love and respect so much. I almost fell over when she bought my books. I think I recall telling her that even if it takes 5 years for you to read them, just knowing you have them is pretty cool. I've had the pleasure to spend some time with Ella and laugh with her over a Cosmo. I love her street team. **Jen Gerschick, MJ Fryer, and Candace Wood,** you all are fabulous. Thank you for your friendships.

Thank you to Mindy Guerreiros for our daily chats. You are an amazing beta reader, and yes, I do listen. Your feedback was invaluable to my story. You also helped me bring my vision of "Walker" to life. You found the perfect picture to grace my cover. Speaking of which... **Thank you, Renee Ericson,** for designing my book cover. It's epic. You're a rock star. I love it, and it's exactly how I envisioned it to be.

To Julie Titus of JT Formatting, your talent astounds me. Once I hand over my work to you, I leave it in your very creative hands. You know exactly what I want and make my book look beautiful. Thank you, my friend.

My thank you's would not be complete without mentioning my favorite bloggers. You ladies are great at what you do. You take time out of your busy lives to read and do so much for authors. I am very grateful for all the help and support you have lent me:

Natalie Catalano of Love Between the Sheets, thank you for organizing my cover reveals and blog tours. They are so much fun, and I love that I have gotten to know so many of you in the blogging world:

Abby & Lisa – Abby & Lisa's Book Blog
Amber – Lady Ambers Reviews
Cris – The Book Avenue Review
Debra & Tami – The Book Enthusiast
Evette – Sassy Girl Book Reviews
Mindy – Talkbooks Blog
Ren – A Little Bit of R&R
Sheraka – Crazy, Chaotic Book Babes
Tanya – The Book Obsessed Momma
Tara – Halos and Horns Book Blog
Tiffany – Once Upon A Twilight Blog
Verna – Verna Loves Books

You ladies all rock! From the bottom of my heart, I thank each and every one of you. Your support means so much. I hope you love what I have written for Walker and Reese. If I get a message saying, "Damn you, Mary Wasowski!" then I know I did my job.

Xoxo

Saving the Best for Last...

A WRITER CAN create this imaginary story about the perfect book couple. Throughout the pages the story can take you many places. You can experience many emotions while reading what is played out in front of you, but it takes the talent of an editor to perfect it. Oh, how I love bamboozling the two people in my life that help me make my book what it is.

Joe Marron: Thank you for all of your time and energy spent on making *Second Chance at Forever* perfect. You have such a talent at wielding words. I loved our editing sessions where we laughed the entire time. You made this arduous task seem effortless and constantly made me smile. You were there for me on the tougher days when I just wanted to give up. Your humor and words of encouragement got me through it, and for that, my friend, I am forever thankful.

Kathleen Vaughan Candelario: You are so much more to me than an editor. You are my friend and sister. No matter what you have going on in your life, you take time out to lend a helping hand to others. You've been with me from the beginning of Walker and Reese's love story. Your ideas and feedback have helped me make their story better.

I am so grateful to know you both. You each bring your individual talents to fuel my creativity and in turn help me write an amazing story for my book couple. I love you both with all of my heart.

Xoxo

ABOUT THE AUTHOR

I AM A dreamer. I've always been a dreamer. Some may not have worked out the way I hoped they would, but I also believe that everything happens for a reason.

Writing has changed my entire life. It brings happiness and fulfillment to areas in my life that I didn't even know I was missing. It's also one of the hardest jobs I've ever done. It takes me away from my family, friends, and the little day-to-day tasks that once upon a time seemed normal. Sometimes I like to revisit my portfolio of old short stories, poems, and the inspirational quotes I have kept for many years. Reading through it all shows how far I've come and that the journey I am on now is exactly what I dreamed of many years ago. This makes me smile.

A long time ago, I used to write short stories and poems in journals and kept them privately to myself. It took quite some time and many sacrifices, but now I have three published books and have my very own writing cave. *What the heck is that?* Well, it's my second home where I laugh, dream, imagine, and write my heart out to hopefully produce something that will make other people smile.

Never one to dwell on what I don't have, I value what I do have. I couldn't do what I do without the love and support from my husband, Henry Wasowski. We have been happily married for twenty two years and still have the passion from when we were first dating. Our love story created the family we have today, our three sons: Zachary, Christopher, and Cameron.

Family is everything to me. When I take a much needed timeout, I love to be with them, have friends over for wine night, and just talk and laugh for hours. Summer days in NJ are spent down the shore, and nights are spent at home around the fire pit toasting s'mores.

One of my most valued lessons that I've learned in this life was from my beloved mother-in-law, Julia Wasowski. She was an amazing woman, and I miss her every day. A role model for many, including myself, I don't believe there was anything she couldn't do. She taught me to never take one day God has given you for granted, because you never know what tomorrow will bring.

She had many words of wisdom that I carry with me and have passed along to my kids and friends, and now to you, dear readers. They come in handy on the hard days when life treats you harshly and you just want to give up:

Life is an incredible journey.

We are all an open book. Every day is a new chapter to write in our story. Lessons are to be learned and shared.

Keep moving forward.

Never give up on your dreams.

Smile, and make others smile.

Believe me…Your spirit will thank you for it.

Xoxo

I would love to hear from you. Please feel free to reach out to me:

Email:
AuthorMaryAWasowski@gmail.com

Facebook:
https://www.facebook.com/pages/Author-Mary-A-Wasowski

Twitter:
https://twitter.com/wasow6

www.ingramcontent.com/pod-product-compliance
Lightning Source LLC
Chambersburg PA
CBHW071247250626
47163CB00002B/361